BETWEEN NEVER AND FOREVER

THE HOMETOWN HEARTLESS

BRIT BENSON

Between Never and Forever

BRIT BENSON

Cover Design: Kate Decided to Design

Editing: Rebecca at Fairest Reviews Editing Services

Proofing: Shauna Casey, The Author Agency

PLAYLIST

cardigan – Taylor Swift
Your Name Hurts – Hailee Steinfeld
Matilda – Harry Styles
hope ur ok – Olivia Rodrigo
Feelings – Lauv
Miss You a Little – Bryce Vine, lovelytheband
Live Forever – Bazzi
Girl Almighty – One Direction
Ain't It Fun – Paramore
Help I'm Alive – Metric
No One Compares to You – Jack & Jill
Gasoline – Halsey
Blame Me – The Pretty Reckless
Wish I Never Met You – Loote
Serial Heartbreaker – FLETCHER
If I Died Last Night – Jessie Murph
Beggin for Thread – BANKS
Name – The Goo Goo Dolls
feel something – Bea Miller
Another Life – Surf Mesa, Josh Golden, FLETCHER
All I Wanted – Paramore

Back of My Mind – Two Feet
Healing – FLETCHER
Goddess – BANKS
Criminal – Fiona Apple
Dazed & Confused – Ruel
Cardiac Arrest – Bad Suns
the 1 – Taylor Swift
Backseat (Kiss Me) – Jutes
Sex on Fire – Kings of Leon
Bright – Echosmith
cardigan – Taylor Swift

For the extended playlist, please visit my website, authorbritbenson.com

CONTENT WARNING

Please be aware, *Between Never and Forever* contains some difficult topics that could be upsetting for some readers.

Topics that take place on page are: vulgar language, sexually explicit content, physical and verbal abuse of a child*, violence, drug use and addiction, sexual assault*, unprotected sex, unplanned pregnancy, near-death experience*, traumatic religious experiences*

Topics that are referenced but do not take place on page are: rape, overdose, addiction relapse, loss of a loved one to terminal illness.

*If you require a content-specific chapter guide for these topics, you can find one **one my website.**

This one is for the brats.
Go off.

PROLOGUE

A HIGH-PITCHED SCREAM WAKES ME, and I shoot upright in my bed.

My heart is in my throat and my breath is straining my lungs when I hear it again. Another high-pitched scream. *Brynn*. My feet hit the floor just as a chanted stream of *oh my god* begins, and I sprint down the hall toward her room.

I have never known fear like this.

For these few seconds, terror turns my blood to ice, and the need to protect overpowers everything else. Logic, reason, self-preservation—they all disappear in the seconds it takes me to cross the house. Only the primal instinct to protect, to defend, remains.

I shove through the bedroom door at the end of the hall with my fists raised, ready to fight. Ready to kill, if necessary. When I find Brynn sitting cross-legged on her bed, alone, my eyes immediately dart around the room to find the threat.

The closet door is open, displaying clothes on hangers. The second-floor window is closed tight. Everything seems as it was hours earlier when I hugged her goodnight.

"What's wrong?" I ask, my voice urgent. I glance back at her and find her staring at her tablet with her hand covering her mouth. She doesn't answer.

"Brynn?" I ask again, rushing to her bed and dropping to my

knees, reaching for her shoulders while scanning her body for injury.

She jumps with a gasp as her eyes shoot to mine.

"Dad," she shouts. "Oh my gosh!" Her hand splays over her chest. "What the heck? You scared the crap out of me!" She takes off her headphones and lets out a laugh, her eyes wide. "Oh my gosh, Dad, you look like a ghost. What's wrong? Are you okay?"

My jaw drops, and I suck in a breath. Possibly the first one since being jarred awake.

"You screamed," I say. "I thought something was wrong! I thought you were...that something..."

I can't stop my eyes from scanning her features, my sleep-fogged brain still not grasping that fact that Brynn is fine. She is not hurt. She's not in danger. I don't need to beat the life out of an intruder. She's safe in her room.

I consciously unclench my fists.

"Oh," she says sheepishly. "I'm sorry I scared you."

"Brynn," I breathe out, dropping my head to her mattress and trying to get my heart to calm down. "Jesus Christ, Brynnlee."

"Sorry, Daddy."

We sit in silence for a minute, and when my chest no longer aches with panic, I bring my eyes to hers and raise a stern brow.

"Why the hell are you screaming in the middle of the night? You know you're supposed to be asleep, and you're not allowed to be on your tablet after 7 p.m."

"I know," she says, a smile stretching over her face. "I was asleep, I swear, but then Cameron messaged me and—"

"Cameron messaged you at—" I check my watch "—three in the morning?"

"Yes, because—"

"Why were you screaming?"

"*Ohmigod*, Dad, I'm trying to tell you," she says with a roll of her eyes. "Cameron messaged me because Sav Loveless is coming here!"

My shoulders tense again, but Brynn doesn't notice. Her voice rises in pitch with each word as she bounces on the bed, speaking quickly.

"She's coming here, Dad! Here! Here to our dumb, boring town. Nothing good ever happens here, and she's coming, like, right here. Maybe I can meet her? Maybe I can actually get her autograph? Can you take me to meet her? And get a photo or a hug or—"

"I thought that band broke up," I say calmly, trying to ignore the pain in my hands as my fingers curl back into fists.

I *know* that band broke up.

Brynn has been sobbing about it for two weeks, and I've felt terrible. I'd planned to let her go to one of their shows on the next tour, but now she won't get the chance. They announced that their current tour will be their last, and there are only three shows left, all at the Garden in NYC. They're sold out, and of course, now with the news, scalped prices have skyrocketed.

Brynn's only just stopped tearing up every time one of their songs comes on the radio, and their songs come on the radio constantly.

"Actually, Dad, they didn't *break up*," Brynn corrects, a slight edge to her voice. "The Hometown Heartless is *on a hiatus*, and now I know why."

Brynn shoves her tablet into my hand, tapping the screen to show me the news headline.

"Sav's going to be in a movie," she squeals. "The movie that's filming *here* next month! Oh my *god*, Dad, I can't even believe it. This is prodigious. This is...this is...immaculate!"

Brynn continues to chatter excitedly, but her voice fades into the background as I focus on the tablet screen. The headline confirms what Brynn said.

Sav Loveless, frontwoman for rock band The Hometown Heartless, has been cast as the lead actress in a new movie. I don't scroll to read the rest of the article. I can't. Instead, my attention is held frozen by the photograph of the woman staring back at me.

It's the same woman whose face taunts me daily from the posters plastered on Brynn's bedroom walls. The same face I avoid in every grocery store checkout, smirking or scowling from the covers of magazines boasting tell-alls about her various rehab stints, numerous Hollywood hookups, and scandalous on-again-off-again relationship with her bassist.

It's the same face I've seen in my dreams. In my nightmares.

Sav Loveless is a lesson in contrasts.

Every detail about her directly contradicts another. Silver hair and soft, pale skin, with swirling, storm gray, depthless eyes. A heart-shaped face. A delicate jaw. Cupid's bow lips. Her angelic features suggest innocence and kindness, but the stories that precede her prove the exact opposite. She projects this façade of fearlessness, as if nothing can hurt her, while her lyrics rage with pain. Her tongue slices as sharp as a jagged piece of glass, but I know from experience how plush the lips are that contain that tongue, and I know how gentle it can be when coaxed.

She's ethereal and untouchable, yet she was so soft under my palms...

I close my eyes quickly, severing the invisible line of tension between myself and the woman in the photograph.

I'll never forget the way I felt the first time I saw her photo in a tabloid. I almost crashed my car the first time I heard her voice on the radio. My gut still twists at the memory.

After years of nothing, she was everywhere overnight. Then, as if her global popularity wasn't enough, my own daughter had to go and become a diehard fan.

It's been a poetic sort of torture. Perhaps deserved.

Most people get to move on from their first love. Heal from their first heartbreak. Learn from their first big mistake.

But me? I can't seem to escape mine.

I take Brynn's tablet and tell her she needs to go back to sleep. She's got school in the morning, and even though there's only two weeks left until summer break, she still needs to be awake for class.

In theory, anyway.

I think Brynn might be a bit more advanced than the average seven-year-old. I had to download a dictionary app on my phone just to look up the words she uses on a regular basis, and the other day she spent an hour lecturing me on ways to make my business more environmentally friendly.

I'm proud of her intelligence, but it makes me nervous for the years to come. I can barely keep up with her now.

Once Brynn's light is off and her room is quiet, I make my way out onto the back deck. The rhythmic sound of the water flowing from the ocean and the briny scent of the air, usually so relaxing, do little to calm my nerves. I have an early job in the morning, but I'll never get back to sleep. I might as well make some coffee and enjoy the sunrise in a few hours.

I brace my hands on the deck railing, the cool band on my left ring finger glinting in the moonlight and drop my chin to my chest. I close my eyes, focus on the sounds of the water, and take a deep breath, letting reality settle over my skin.

It prickles uncomfortably, and I grit my teeth.

Savannah is coming here. Back into my life.

She's occupied a space in my head for years. A space that I've tried like hell to avoid. To forget. But here, in my town, avoiding her will be impossible. I have to prepare myself for that.

Savannah may be coming here, but I can't let her back into my heart.

And I can't let her upend my life again.

THEN

PART ONE

Streetlamp silhouette,
wore my shoes out on that pavement.

1

15 years old

"HEY." Savannah steps in front of me and kicks dirt onto my clean tennis shoes. "Lemme see your math homework."

I flick my eyes across the street toward my house. My mother's face is peeking through the gray curtains of our front window, watching the bus stop like she's started doing ever since my bike got stolen and I had to stop riding it to school. I glance back at Savannah, but I don't speak. Her eyebrows scrunch before she looks toward my house and sighs.

"You're such a weenie, Cooper," she grumbles loudly, making the other kids at the bus stop laugh. My ears heat, but I still don't talk to her.

Savannah rolls her eyes and takes a dramatic step away from me before crossing her arms over her chest and setting her attention on my house. She doesn't break her stare with my mother until the school bus pulls up in front of us.

I step onto the bus and make my way down the aisle until I reach the seventh seat from the front, then I sit on the hard bench. Savannah drops down next to me, shoving my shoulder with hers and slinging her backpack to the floor between her feet.

I hate the bus. The seats are uncomfortable, and it always smells like feet. The only okay thing about taking the bus is Savannah.

"Gimme your math homework, Weenie," she taunts with a smirk. I roll my eyes and pretend to be annoyed, but I open my backpack anyway.

"You really should stop copying my work, Savannah. You'll never learn how to do it on your own," I tell her flatly as I hand her the sheet of paper.

Savannah snorts. "Why would I wanna learn how to do this crap?"

She scribbles the equations from my worksheet onto hers, changing the answers to a few so she doesn't get them all correct. She does this every time. She's been doing it since fifth grade. I asked her once why she didn't just copy my work exactly as it is to get the better grade, and she said it would be too suspicious if she suddenly started getting As.

I'm a C student, Weenie. Gotta stay a C student.

I didn't bother pointing out that the math she had to do to make sure she would always get a C was proof that she could be an A student if she wanted to be. She'd have just slugged me, anyway.

I wait quietly as she finishes copying the work, then she hands it back to me and I put it back into my backpack. She doesn't say thank you. She never does.

"You goin' to The Pit tonight?" I feel my cheeks warm as I shake my head no. "Oh, right," she says wryly. "I forgot."

She didn't forget. She just likes to give me crap about it.

"I wouldn't go there even if I didn't have youth group, Savannah. That place is lame." I try to sound confident even though I'm not.

"You're lame."

She's such a brat. I shake my head.

The Pit is a place out of town where kids race their cars and bet on fights and drink beer. It's mostly juniors and seniors, some college kids who come back to visit and some who never left, but Savannah started going last year when we were in eighth grade.

She's always sneaking out of her house. One of these days, she's going to get herself into some real trouble. Or, at least, that's what my mother says. It makes me nervous for her.

I glance quickly at her before swinging my eyes back in front of me, then forcing myself to sit up a little taller.

"You can always come with me, you know. To youth group, I mean. You might like it."

Savannah barks out a laugh.

"Oh, I bet your momma would love that one." She screws her face up in disgust and changes her voice to imitate my mother. "That girl is *trouble*, Leviticus! *Trouble*, I tell you. She'll corrupt you with the drugs and the curses and her demon woman breasts!"

My lips twitch, and a laugh catches in my throat. I try to hide it, but Savannah sees, and her smile stretches wide over her face. When she continues, her voice is higher pitched, and her southern accent is thicker.

"You stay far away from that devil girl, Leviticus! Oh, my poor heart! I cannot handle the thought of that girl sullying you! She is dirty, and you are my sweet, sweet angel boy. I mean it, Leviticus Matthew Mark Luke John Cooper! You keep your distance from that evil Savannah Shaw!"

I bump Savannah with my shoulder and shake my head with a laugh.

"That's not my name."

"Close enough." She grins and bumps me back.

I don't acknowledge the other things she said. No point in denying it. My mother doesn't hide how she feels about Savannah. No one does, really.

"It's so weird you have two first names, you know?" Savannah says, changing the subject. "Your parents should have mixed it up and gave you a last name as a first name for balance. Havin' two first names is probably why you're such a weenie."

"Cooper isn't a first name," I grumble.

"Is too."

She's such a brat.

"Yeah, well, at least my first name and last name start with different letters," I say back with a roll of my eyes. "Name alliteration is so lame."

Savannah huffs a laugh and bumps me again, then rests her head back on the bus seat and closes her eyes. Her black lashes cast shadows over the light purple circles under them. She probably didn't sleep last night. She doesn't sleep most nights. She says she can't relax in her house, and that's why she's always out roaming around. It's why my mother thinks she's bad news. Sav hates being home.

I still wish she wouldn't go to The Pit, though.

Savannah slaps her math book onto the lunch table with a thud, then drops down on the seat across from me.

She doesn't say anything as she reaches over and takes half my sandwich, but she moves slowly, like she's giving me a chance to snatch it back. I don't. She's the reason I cut it in half to begin with.

She takes a bite and chews, staring silently out the window of the cafeteria. Her messy brown hair is falling into her face, but I can still tell her eyebrows are scrunched up. She does this a lot. Gets quiet and kinda sad looking. On instinct I scan her arms, but she's wearing long sleeves, and my stomach drops. It's almost 90 degrees today. I don't like what that means.

I give her shoe a nudge under the table.

"What did you get on the math homework?" I ask her, trying to draw her attention to me. It works, and her mouth tips into a proud half-smile.

"C minus."

I roll my eyes. Savannah and her Cs.

"I got an A."

Savannah scoffs and puts her half-eaten half of my sandwich back on my napkin.

"Did you do the history study guide?"

My shoulders tighten. I screw up my lips before I can school my face into something less ashamed. She catches it immediately.

"What? What's wrong?"

"Yeah, I did it." I shrug. "But I don't have it."

"Why not?"

I shrug again, but my eyes flick to a table across the cafeteria. Savannah's gaze follows, and when she sees who I'm looking at, her brow furrows.

"Connor Lawson is a douche. He messin' with you again?" I shrug a third time. "He took your study guide?"

I bring my eyes to my lunch and don't answer.

"Jesus, Levi." Savannah growls. "You gotta stand up to him. He's never gonna leave you alone if you keep bein' such a weenie."

I scowl at her.

"*You* take my homework all the time."

She rolls her eyes as she stands up and tucks her math book under her arm.

"That's different."

"How?"

"Cause we're friends, idiot."

Friends? She thinks we're *friends*? I mean, I think of her as one, kind of, but I never thought she'd think of me as one. It makes me feel weird. Warm and tingly and weird. Before I can say anything else, Savannah is halfway across the cafeteria heading straight for Connor Lawson.

Oh no.

I stand quickly and rush to catch up with her just as she stops in front of his table.

"What do you want, crack baby?" Connor says as Savannah stands in front of him.

She crosses her arms over her chest, with her math book cradled between them, and cocks her head to the side, looking down her nose at him.

Savannah is small, but somehow, she can make herself look like a giant. Like she's fearless and unbreakable, even though I know she's neither.

"I want Levi's study guide. Give it back to him."

She says it clearly, fearlessly, and Connor barks out a sarcastic laugh. I try to reach for her arm, to pull her away, but she shrugs me off. Connor leans back in his chair and crosses his arms over his chest.

"Yeah, I'm not gonna take orders from the daughter of a whore."

I wince as his friends all laugh, but when I look at Savannah, she's smirking.

"Should probably be nicer to me, Connor," Savannah taunts. "Your daddy comes over to my house all the time, you know? We might end up bein' siblings, and then you'll be callin' that whore your step momma."

Everyone at Connor's table shuts up, and his face turns murderous. I grab at Savannah's arm again, but she elbows me away, still smirking.

"Shut your slut mouth," Connor threatens, and Savannah lets out an airy laugh before lowering her voice and taking another step forward.

"Give me the study guide and leave Levi alone, and maybe I won't tell the whole school about how your daddy is bangin' the town crack whore." Savannah's voice is taunting and steady. She's downright scary. "You think your momma knows?"

I don't know how she does it. Connor is staring at her like he wants to rip her head off, but she's so calm. I've always wondered if Savannah has a death wish. She's always doing stupid stuff. She's unbothered, and I can hear my blood whooshing in my ears.

Connor sits up in his seat and leans toward her, talking through his teeth.

"I'm warning you, Shaw. Shut your lying mouth or I'll shut it for you."

"Gimme the study guide and leave Levi alone, and I will."

The next part happens so fast, I only have a chance to gasp. Connor acts like he's reaching toward his backpack, but then he shouts something that sounds like "she's dead" and lunges across the table at Savannah.

His arms are outstretched, hands wide open like he's trying to grab for her neck. To do what, I don't know. Strangle her? Nothing good. He doesn't reach her, though. Before Connor's fingers have a chance to wrap around any part of Savannah, she swings the thick math textbook at his head, catching him right across the face, and he flies to the side and hits the table with a bang.

Everyone starts shouting. Calling Savannah all sorts of names, yelling for a teacher or the principal. Connor is bleeding from his mouth and pushing himself to stand while glaring at Savannah. Some of his friends are trying to hold him back, so I try to pull Savannah away again.

"Come *on*, Sav. You're gonna get yourself killed."

I yank on her arm, but she kicks back at me and takes a step forward with the book held up like a baseball bat, ready to swing again.

"Can I call your dad *Daddy*?" she croons, everyone in the cafeteria *ooooh*s, and my stomach falls to my feet.

She's dead. Savannah is going to be murdered right here in the high school for everyone to see.

"You're done, bitch," Connor shouts, then lunges for her again, but his friends are in the way and his head injury makes his movements slow. Savannah acts faster, kicking a chair at his feet, and when he trips and falls, she hurls the math book at his face.

Everyone starts screaming. Connor lets out a high-pitched shriek that sounds like an animal dying, and blood gushes from his nose. The sight of blood makes me want to puke. I wrap my arms around Savannah's middle and pick her up, swinging her around in an attempt to get her out of there, but a loud whistle blows, and I stop in my tracks when I see the principal flanked by two school resource officers.

Immediately, kids start pointing at me and Savannah. Two teachers rush to Connor, and the principal and one of the officers step up to us.

"Put her down, Mr. Cooper," the principal says, but I hesitate.

I hold her tighter and flick my eyes toward the door. I wonder if I could make it without getting tazed or tackled.

"Put her down," he repeats.

When I bring my eyes back to him, he's staring at me sternly. When I look at the officer, he's glaring at Sav. I still don't move to put her down until she grunts and wiggles free, kicking my shin lightly then shooting me a narrowed-eyed glare before squaring up to the officer.

"Come with me, Miss Shaw."

Savannah tightens her jaw and moves to walk toward him, but I grab her wrist and pull her to a stop.

"It was self-defense," I say quickly, and the officer raises an eyebrow.

"It was!" I look at Savannah. "Tell them, Savannah."

She stays quiet, so I turn back to the officer.

"It was self-defense, sir. Connor jumped at her. He was going to hurt her. He looked like he was going to strangle her or something."

The officer looks at Savannah for confirmation, but she keeps her mouth shut, and my jaw drops.

"Sav, tell him," I insist, frustrated.

Usually she never shuts up, and she chooses *now* to be silent?

"It was self-defense. Connor said 'you're dead' and then tried to attack her. That's the truth, sir. Ask anyone. Watch the security cameras."

The officer just sighs and jerks his head in the direction of the office. He turns and Savannah follows, back straight and head held high.

I don't see her for the rest of the day, but I'm brought into the office and questioned before school lets out. I tell the principal the same thing I told the officer. Savannah acted in self-defense. If she hadn't swung the math book, Connor definitely would have hurt her.

I don't tell them that Savannah provoked him into it.

I definitely don't tell them that I think Savannah might have *wanted* him to hurt her.

I try my best not to think about that possibility at all, but it still bothers me the rest of the day. I'd send her a text, but my mother checks my phone. She'll flip if she sees me messaging Savannah. Sav's phone is probably off anyway. She has one of those prepaids and gets in trouble when she uses up all her minutes.

The bus ride home is boring, but too short. Walking up the sidewalk to my house feels like a death march.

"Levi," my mother calls from the kitchen when I step through the door.

Even though I expected it, my shoulders tense. She sounds angry, and I know why. I take off my shoes slowly, then put my backpack on the bench by the door.

"Coming."

When I step into the kitchen, Mom is already sitting at the table, and she hits me with a cold stare. I stand tall and jut my chin out when I see the thick, leather-bound book next to her.

"I got a call from the principal today."

"Yes, ma'am."

"I told you to stay away from that girl."

She says the words calmly, but her face is tight. I can already tell she's going to lose it. My mother is kind of terrifying in that way. The angrier she is, the calmer she acts, until she strikes silently, like a copperhead. She's just as venomous, too.

"I was trying to help, ma'am. Connor Lawson tried to attack Sava—"

"I do not care about Savannah Shaw or the trouble she causes. You shouldn't have involved yourself."

"But he was saying bad things about her mom—"

"And I'm sure they were true."

I close my eyes and try again.

"I was just telling the truth. Isn't that what we're supposed to do? Stand up for what's right? Savannah was only talking to Connor to try and get my study guide back for me—"

"And how did Savanah know that Connor had your study guide?"

My shoulders fall, and my breath whooshes from my lungs. Now *I'm* dead.

"She was sitting with me at lunch."

My mother doesn't say anything for a long time. She just stares at me with narrowed eyes and pursed lips until she stands. She pushes the Bible toward me, along with a stack of paper and a pencil.

"Matthew 15:4," she says, even though I already know.

"How many?"

Her nostrils flare, angry that I asked.

"Until your father comes home."

When she leaves the kitchen, I glance at the clock on the stove. It's four. My dad won't be home until eight. I close my eyes and stifle a groan. If she hears me complain, she'll make me go longer, or worse.

Maybe God will be merciful, and my dad will come home early.

I pick up my pencil, and I write the verse from memory.

2

SAVANNAH'S not at school for over a week.

I heard she got suspended. That's not a surprise, but it's bothering me that I haven't seen her. I've kept my curtains open and my window unlocked since the day of the fight, but nothing.

Sav disappears often. Usually, I just wait around until she decides to return. She's kind of like a stray cat. Unpredictable and wild. She comes and goes as she pleases, but I always feel a little lost when she's gone.

I don't even know how it happened. Sav's always been around. The girl my parents warn me about. The one everyone sneers at and whispers about. I used to watch her out of the corner of my eye. I'd study how straight her back was, how high she held her head, even when everyone was talking about her. I'd watch her, but never outright, until one day she pushed me off the swing without any explanation. I didn't tattle. I just watched her skip off from my place in the dirt. Then, the next day, she sat down beside me at lunch. That's where she's been sitting ever since.

I don't have any other friends, but I don't really have an interest in other people.

Just Sav.

My mother is cheery as ever. She's all smiles every morning I have to wait at the bus stop alone. The bus sucks, but the only time I really miss my bike is when Sav is absent.

Connor comes back after a week with greenish bruises under both eyes and his lip still swollen and purple. I heard someone in the hall say Sav broke his nose with the math book, and one of his teeth cut through his lip.

I smile a little at that. I shouldn't, but I do.

Sav is like five foot nothing, and Connor plays varsity baseball. She beat him up without even breaking a sweat. Not for the first time, my fear for Sav mixes with my awe of her, creating something that makes me feel a little confused. I shouldn't like her attitude so much—it's wicked and sinful—but that doesn't stop me from wishing I could be a little more like her.

If I had her nerve, I'd stand up to my mother and father.

If I was brave like Savannah, I wouldn't be pushed around so much at school.

Sometimes, I want to be a little more reckless, even just a tiny bit like her.

My stomach twists with guilt while my brain scolds me for being ungrateful, for being blasphemous and immoral. I shove my books in my backpack, slam my locker shut, and walk slowly to the bus. I don't need to rush. I'll be riding it alone.

The storm outside gets louder as my window is pushed open slowly, and it startles me awake.

The rain splatters on my floor, making rapid tapping noises, and I sit up quickly. My heart beats fast, but my shoulders relax for the first time in almost two weeks.

I look at the clock. Two in the morning. This is late for her, but I don't say anything as Savannah crawls through my window, then pulls it closed before slipping her shoes off and scooting them up against the wall.

I kick my comforter off and go to my dresser, pulling out a pair of pajama pants and a t-shirt. Without a word, I walk them to where she waits, soaked with rain and creating a puddle on my floor. A jolt of lightning flashes through the night sky, making her glow, and I hold the bundle of clothes out to her. She takes them, sets them on my desk, and I turn around as she wriggles out of her wet clothes and into my dry ones.

Her clothing plops onto the floor, one by one, and when I hear her moving toward my bed, I turn and follow.

Just like all the other times before, she crawls in first and scoots over just enough so I can get in behind her. My bed is a full, so there's room, but I pull her against my chest, ignoring the way her cold, wet hair seeps through my shirt, and rest my chin on her head anyway.

The first few times she showed up here, I laid stiff as a board the entire night. Afraid to move. Afraid to touch her. I'd stare at the ceiling, reciting Bible verses in my head and listening closely as she'd fall into a deep sleep, and I'd pretend to be asleep when she'd sneak out at sunrise.

Then, one night, she showed up crying.

I've never seen anyone cry the way she does. She cries without making a sound. No whimpering, no sniffling. Just constant tears streaming down a blank face. That night, I pulled her close to me and held her. Not because it felt like what I was *supposed* to do, but it felt like what I *needed* to do. She didn't push me away, and since then, that's how we sleep. Wrapped up and silent.

I do the same tonight. I listen to her breathing for a sign that I can let myself drift off, but it doesn't come. Instead, her quiet, flat voice cuts through the silence.

"Do you think bad things happen for a reason?"

I consider it for a minute. My mother says bad things are God's will to punish the wicked. I don't say that to Savannah.

"I don't know."

She's quiet for so long that I think she might be falling asleep. Then she speaks again. This time, her voice is angry.

"I don't think bad things happen for a reason. I think sometimes life is just shitty, and sometimes it's shittier for some people than it is for others. And I don't think there's any reason behind it besides where you just happen to be born. And you and me just happened to be born in different shit piles."

I think over her words. They jumble up inside my head, my mother's voice fighting them with her acid tongue.

"What about God?"

Sav doesn't even hesitate.

"If God is real, then I hate him."

I don't say anything else. I just pull her tighter against me, and we fall back into silence. Soon, her breathing goes slow and steady, so I close my own eyes and let myself fall asleep, too.

A couple hours later, a noise wakes me for the second time. I crack my eyes open and see Savannah near the window, struggling to get back into her wet clothes. I start to roll over, so she has some privacy, but my attention is grabbed by a large mark on her side.

My skin prickles and I stare, hoping it's a shadow or a trick of light, but the longer I look, the more I want to throw up.

Savannah has bruises often. On her arms and legs, usually. A few times on her cheeks or a busted lip. She always says they're from falling off her skateboard or fighting at The Pit. I believed her at first, but I don't anymore. I haven't for a while now. I keep my mouth shut because anytime I try to talk about it, she slugs me and tells me to shut up or calls me a weenie.

But this bruise is different. It's ugly, so deep purple in places that it looks black, and it covers most of her side. Stretches from the bottom of her bra to the top of her underwear. Maybe even farther, but she pulls her jeans up before I can be sure. She's moving so carefully, and now I know it's not just because she wants to be quiet. It's because she's in pain.

"What the heck happened, Sav?"

My voice breaks the silence and Savannah freezes.

She stays still, facing the window, for three whole breaths before looking over her shoulder at me with a scowl.

"Nothin'."

She pulls her damp shirt over her head, grunting a bit when her arms have to rise higher than her shoulders. I swing my legs out of the bed and stand.

"That's not nothing, Savannah," I whisper. "You look like you were kicked in the side with a steel-toed boot."

The way her shoulders jerk tells me I'm probably right.

"Who did it?"

"Shut it, *Leviticus*," she spits, then starts to open my window like she's going to leave.

I step up and place a hand on her shoulder, turning her back to face me.

"Savannah, who gave you this bruise?"

My whisper is louder, my eyebrows scrunched. She looks into my eyes, then clamps hers shut.

"Just forget it, Levi."

I reach down slowly and grab the hem of her shirt. When she doesn't bat me away, I carefully lift it until I can see her entire side. My breath catches, and I swallow hard.

"*Savannah...*"

I can't say anything else. My tongue is numb.

The bruise looks even worse up close. Purples, blues, and blacks swirl together. There are areas of raised swollen flesh. I squint at it, and I think I can almost make out a boot tread mark, but it might be my imagination. I use my other hand to trail my fingers lightly over her skin, and Savannah sucks in a harsh breath, stepping away quickly. My hands drop to my sides.

"Savannah, that's...this is bad. This is worse than before."

"Just leave it alone. Please."

"You can't stay there anymore."

I don't know what else to say. I don't know what I can possibly do. How can something like this happen? How can God let something like this happen to Savannah?

"You have to leave," I stress, and she laughs.

It's hollow and eerie. When she speaks, she sounds defeated.

"And go where?"

"You have to tell someo—"

"No." Savannah's eyes go wild, and she shoves my shoulder. "You can't tell anyone, Levi. You can't. You have to swear."

"Savannah, someone kicked you so hard half your body is black. You have to tell someone."

"You know what happens if I tell someone, Levi? I get sent somewhere worse." She closes her eyes and tilts her head to the ceiling. "At least I know what to expect with him."

I shake my head. How can she think that? He's unpredictable.

"He's going to kill you, Sav. You know that, right? He'll kill you. You could have internal bleeding or something."

"This happened days ago," she says with a sad smirk. "If I was bleedin' internally, I'd be dead already."

"Dang it, Sav, how can you be so *okay* with all of this? How come you're not trying to get some place safe? You need to protect yourself."

"Why do you think I'm *here*?" she snaps. "Why do you think I come here? You think it's just 'cause I wanna be closer to the Lord?"

I bite my tongue. I want to tell her that if she told my dad, he could help. That's what he does. He helps people. It's his job as pastor. He could help her, but apparently, she'd rather let her mom's boyfriend beat her to death.

"If you don't want me to come here anymore, fine," she says, turning back around and walking back to the window. "I don't need you, ya know. I can j—"

"Shut up, Savannah. You know that's not it. Stop being a brat."

"Did you just call me a brat?"

She laughs, then tries to hide the wince that follows.

"You gonna kick me after I've already been kicked?"

My mouth drops open. I'm horrified. I feel terrible. I start to apologize, but she rolls her eyes.

"I'm just kiddin', *Leviticus*." She slides the window back open. "Stop bein' such a weenie."

Now I roll my eyes.

"That's not my name."

She smirks.

"Close enough."

We don't say anything else. Savannah thinks the subject is settled, and I let her. I stand and watch as she inches out my window, and I don't lie back down until she disappears into the semi-darkness. I stare at the ceiling until my alarm goes off, and then I make up my mind.

"Mom," I say when I step into the kitchen. "Where's Dad?"

3

I SLIP out of Levi's house as the sun starts to come up. Quietly, so I don't wake up his kraken of a mother.

She's such a jerk. She thinks I'm going to corrupt Levi or something.

My lips twitch and I laugh softly. I mean, she's not wrong, I guess. I did just climb out of his bedroom window after sleeping over. I'm back in my soaked jeans and t-shirt, but just a few minutes ago I was wearing Levi's pjs, too.

But still. What's she think I'm gonna do? Have sex with him? Use him as a human sacrifice? Brainwash him into joining a satanic cult?

No, thank you. None of that interests me.

I kick a rock on the sidewalk. I hate that she hates me. But I hate it even more because she's probably right to hate me. I just wish it didn't make it so hard to be friends with the only person I can tolerate in this stupid freaking town.

I kick another rock and try to ignore the way my shoes squish with each step, and how I can feel blisters forming on my heels. I shouldn't have been out in the storm last night, but I really didn't have much choice.

Screw up my only pair of shoes or stay at the house for worse.

No shoes are worth it.

I cross town in silence, moving from smooth pavement, sidewalks, and streetlights to dirty grass, cracks, and darkness. It's crazy the difference a mile can make. The houses get smaller, the weeds taller, until I reach my block of single-wides. I step off the road and cut through a few of the neighbors' yards. It's getting lighter as the sun rises, and I don't want to be seen.

Not that I will be. They're probably passed out. If I was a lucky person, which I'm not, they'd both be dead.

I slow my steps to a crawl as I enter the yard of the house next to mine, tiptoeing carefully so I don't scrunch the grass. I check the front of the house and note that there are no extra cars at the curb, which means Terry hasn't brought any of his *friends* over. I hold my breath to listen, and when I'm met with silence, I pick up my pace until I'm at my window. Slowly, I push it open until I can fit my body through. Lifting myself over the ledge hurts more than usual, my side throbbing with heat and pain, but I don't stop until I'm crouching on the floor of my bedroom. I pause again to listen, waiting to see if anyone heard me come in.

Still silence.

I move quickly, stripping out of my wet clothes and changing into dry ones. My heel is bleeding, so I put on two pairs of socks, and I stifle a groan as I slip my feet back into my wet shoes. Then my stomach rumbles. I try to remember the last time I ate. Definitely not yesterday.

I tiptoe to my door and put my ear against it. It still sounds quiet, so I turn the knob and push it open just far enough to peek through the crack.

The scent of cigarettes, stale beer, and something chemical hits me immediately. The smell always seems stronger after I've stayed the night at Levi's or The Pit, and it takes me a minute to adjust. The curtains are pulled shut over the windows and there isn't a single light on in the house, but I can hear snoring coming from the living room.

The living room I'd have to walk through to get to the kitchen.

I pull the door shut again and rest my forehead against the wood. I can't risk it. I'm screwed if he wakes up because I can't run fast with my side all beat to hell the way it is. My stomach rumbles again, the hunger ache mixing with the pain from my side, and I blow a harsh breath through my nose.

Three more years.

I just have to make it three more years.

Then I'll be eighteen with a high school diploma, and I can tell my mom and her skeezy, asshole boyfriend to fuck off. I'll never have to see either of them again.

I can do this for three more years.

I stalk toward my bed, pull my backpack out from underneath it, and crawl back out my window into the early morning. The bus won't be at Levi's stop for a couple hours, but I don't want to be in my house. At least it's not raining anymore.

I consider walking the few blocks to the river but decide against it.

Instead, I cross the street and walk to the small neighborhood park that's about halfway between my place and Levi's. I sit on one of the rickety swings, and my wet shoes squish as I push off the ground. My hands grip tightly at the chains and my legs pump hard until I'm soaring high. I close my eyes, feeling the wind whooshing over my skin and through my clothes.

I get high enough that when I reach the farthest point, my butt comes off the seat just a little before the swing arcs back toward the ground. My stomach does a flip, and I can almost forget about the hunger pains. I can almost ignore the constant ache from where Terry kicked me. I can almost make myself believe I'm free.

I wonder what would happen if I let go.

If I just kept my eyes shut until I reached the highest point and then released my grip on the chains.

I'm not stupid. I know I wouldn't fly. I wouldn't continue up, up, up like a sparrow. I'd plummet to the ground like a damn frozen turkey. But would I break my neck? Would I die? How long would it take? Would it be instant? Would it hurt much?

No.

I'd probably bust my leg and then be stuck on crutches. I'd end up weak and defenseless. If I'm going to die, I don't want it to be at the hands of my mom's stupid fucking boyfriend. If I'm going to die, I want to have some say in it.

I sit down at the cafeteria table across from Levi, and he silently pushes a sandwich toward me.

He hasn't spoken to me all morning. He gave me a granola bar and then ignored me the whole bus ride, and it's really ticking me off.

I take a bite out of the sandwich he handed me, then speak to him with my mouth full because I know he hates it.

"What the hell did I do this time?"

His forehead scrunches but he doesn't answer me, so I reach across the table and punch him in the shoulder.

"Ouch!" He swipes back at me but misses. "Why the heck did you hit me?"

"Why the *heck* are you ignorin' me?" I slap my half-eaten sandwich on the table. "You been a jerk all day."

"I haven't been a jerk."

"Yeah, you have."

"I gave you food," he argues, and I scowl.

"I don't want your charity if it comes with your attitude, *Leviticus*."

"Stop freaking calling me that!"

"Stop bein' such an asshole!"

"I'm not being an asshole!"

"Yes, you are. You're bein' an asshole, and you know it."

We stare at each other. His teeth are gritted, and his nostrils are flaring, and I can tell his heart must be beating wildly. The way his jaw is clenched makes the dimple in his chin look deeper. Levi is never angry. Irritated, yes. Almost always irritated with me. But angry? Never. My stomach clenches, and when I speak, it comes out quieter than I want.

"What did I do?"

I wince because I sound like a wimp, so I straighten my shoulders and try to school my face into something less bothered.

"Just freakin' tell me."

"You need to go talk to someone," he says firmly, repeating what he told me this morning.

I glance around to make sure no one is listening.

"Shut up," I whisper, but he shakes his head.

"Savannah, I'm serious. This is too much this time. This is worse. You need to tell someone, and if you don't, I will."

Fear sparks through me, like spiders on my skin, and my eyes narrow with a threat.

"I swear to god, Levi, if you tell anyone, I will never forgive you. Ever. I will never, ever speak to you again. I swear it."

The silence between us stretches, and our eyes stay locked. When he finally opens his mouth, his voice is a sad whisper.

"I'd rather you never talk to me again because you're angry than you never talk to me again because you're dead."

I want to argue, but I can't. He stands up and leaves me sitting at the table before I can even get a word out.

I spend the rest of the school day hiding out in the bathroom, then I walk home instead of taking the bus, because I don't want to see Levi right now.

He's wrong. Talking to someone about Terry won't fix anything. It will make it worse. I can't get sent to some messed-up foster family, or one of those shitty group homes. I've heard stories about how nasty they are. I'm better off just laying low until graduation.

The kick was my fault, anyway.

I got in his way when I knew he was messed up and looking for a fight. I should have just stayed in my room. I should have climbed out the window and peed in the yard. I should never have been in the same room with him, and when he started in on Mom, I should have kept my mouth shut.

My side aches with each step, and I breathe through the pain. At least it's dulling by the day. It will be healed soon.

It won't happen again. I'll keep my head down next time. Levi's wrong. Terry isn't going to kill me. He won't even touch me again.

I swallow back the impulse to throw up.

It's only a few more years.

There are no extra cars on the street, so I creep up to the corner of my house. I hold my breath and listen for a few seconds. When I don't hear anything, I walk up the cracked sidewalk, grab the rusted knob, and let myself into the dark, dirty house.

I'm halfway down the short hallway when the door to my mom's room swings open, and Terry steps out, halting me in my tracks. He's wearing just a pair of boxer shorts, and he has a beer can in one hand and a lit cigarette hanging from his lips. The pain in my side intensifies as every muscle in my body tightens.

I should have waited a little longer before coming in. I should have climbed through my window. I should have crept around the side of the house and listened outside Mom's bedroom window first.

"You're late," Terry sneers, the scent of alcohol on his breath. "You got chores."

"Leave her alone," my mom calls from somewhere inside the bedroom.

I don't look toward my mom. I don't take my eyes off Terry. You don't let your guard down around a coiled pit viper. If I act scared, he'll strike. If I act cocky, he'll strike. I try to gauge his mood based on his tells, but he just looks angry.

"I didn't take the bus," I say clearly, making sure my voice doesn't shake. "I'll do 'em now."

He takes a step toward me, and I grit my teeth, but I don't flinch, and I can tell immediately that I messed up. My lack of reaction pisses him off.

I should have flinched. I should have cowered.

Before I can fix it and act terrified to feed his ego, Terry swings on me, cracking my cheek with the back of his hand. It hurts like a bitch, but it's nothing compared to what I know he's capable of, so I play it up. I cup my face with my hand and whimper, staggering backward a step as my mom yells from the bedroom.

"Don't start in on her again," my mom slurs. "Come back to bed, baby."

When I glance in her direction, I notice a second body in the dark room with her, and my fear spikes. I didn't see any extra cars out front. Did I miss something? Was I too distracted to notice? I try to avoid the house at all costs when Terry brings his friends over.

What he lets them do to my mom...What he makes my mom do...

It makes me want to vomit, and there's always that terrifying reality that it could be me next. Would she let Terry's friends pay for me? Terry would do it. No doubt. But would Mom allow it?

I always put myself between her and Terry when he's beating on her, but she never does the same for me. Usually, she's already passed out or otherwise occupied. She's never stepped in to try and protect me before. Why would she start now?

I hate her. I hate her more than I hate him, even. It takes all my strength not to scowl in her direction. She's such a shit mom. This is all her fault.

I hope they all die.

"Your daughter's lookin' real pretty, Sharon," the man in the bedroom with my mom says. I don't recognize his voice, but it's hard to hear much with my heart pounding in my ears.

"I'll do the chores now," I repeat quickly.

I'm so busy panicking inside my own head, keeping one eye on the bedroom, that I miss Terry taking another step toward me until he is gripping my hair by the root and shoving my body into the wall.

"Don't talk back to me, you ungrateful little shit."

He yanks my hair again, and I suck in a sharp breath. I know he wants me to cry out, but now I refuse. I shrunk back when he hit me. I whimpered like it hurt. It didn't make a difference. He wants my tears? He's not going to get them.

Instead, I grit my teeth and I stare right into his bloodshot, dead looking eyes. Milky blue and sickly, with yellow tinged around his irises. I looked it up once. The yellow means there's something wrong with his liver. I used to hope it would kill him but now I think he'll never die.

My nostrils flare with the thought, and his eyebrows narrow at my defiance.

Levi thinks I have a death wish. Maybe I do. Or maybe I just refuse to bow down to the devil.

"You got somethin' to say, girl?"

The way his breath slithers over my skin makes me want to vomit. The place where his hand is fisted at my scalp burns like a thousand ant bites. My stomach churns with the absolute hatred I feel for this man. For my mom. For this house.

I should kill him in his sleep. I should wait until he's passed out with a needle in his arm and then set the whole damn house on fire. It would be doing the world a favor.

There are so many things I want to say to him, but instead of responding, I bring my knee up hard into his balls. He grunts and doubles over while his fingers stay clenched around my hair, and he yanks hard enough that I can feel some strands get ripped from my scalp.

I hear my mom screech from somewhere behind Terry's hunched over, growling form as I use my elbow to jab upward into his face. It hurts like hell, a shock of pain shooting from my elbow up through my shoulder, but I manage to get him good. He screams *fuck,* and releases my hair, falling backward a step before lunging at me.

"Fuckin' cunt," he shouts, and I scramble backward. "I'll fuckin' kill you, you little bitch. You little fuckin' cunt."

My hip slams into the small table next to our couch. Glasses and cans clank together, some crash to the floor, and I reach behind myself blindly and wrap my hand around the thick neck of a liquor bottle, just as Terry closes the distance between us.

I don't think. I just swing.

The sound of my mom's yelling blends with the strange thudding sound of the bottle connecting with Terry's head. The way the impact ricochets from the bottle, up my arm, and down my legs is something I know I'll never forget. The way his blood feels as it spatters my face is something I hope to god I do.

To my horror and disappointment, Terry doesn't drop immediately to the ground. He staggers and sways. Brings his hand to his head and covers the ugly gash. Blood gushes through his fingers and flows quickly down his face. When he sneers in my direction, it paints his teeth and lips red.

I don't wait to see what happens next. I just turn and run out the front door and down the block. I ignore the shooting pain in my side and the throbbing at my scalp, and I don't stop running until I'm hurling myself into one of the bathroom stalls at the park and shoving my body between the toilet and the wall.

Then I start to cry uncontrollably.

I can't stop, and when I realize I can't stop, I start to laugh. It's maniacal and terrifying, a sound that makes me burst into goosebumps and cry harder. My fingers are cold and shaking. When I wipe tears off my cheeks, my hands come back stained with blood, and I turn my body just in time to vomit my pathetic lunch into the toilet. I heave until nothing comes up but bile, until my throat burns the same way my scalp does and the pounding in my head doubles.

I hate this.

I hate this life. I hate Terry and my mom. I hate Levi's mom. I hate this pile of shit I was born in. It's not fair. I'm not bad. I'm not evil. None of this is my fault. I hate that everyone treats me like it is. I hate that I'm starting to think I deserve it.

I hate everything.

Will I survive three more years? Is Levi right? Will Terry kill me?

Do I even care?

I pull myself onto the toilet seat and drop my spinning head between my knees. I try to slow my breathing. Try to stop my chaotic, strangled sobs. I don't know how long it takes before I finally calm down, but I don't move from the position until my body is no longer shaking, and then I sit up slowly.

I run my clammy hands up and down my thighs, bringing feeling back into my fingers, and then I stand. I let myself out of the bathroom stall and step in front of the grimy mirror. My eyes well back up with tears when I see Terry's blood smeared on my face, but I don't let them fall. Instead, I focus my attention on the nasty bruise that's forming on my cheek and the way the swelling makes my eye squint. Without looking away from the bruise, I pull a wad of paper towels out of the dispenser, wet them with water, and scrub my face clean.

4

"AREN'T YOU HUNGRY, HONEY?" Mom asks from across the dining table. "Pork chops are your favorite."

I shrug, but I don't answer. She's kissing up to me because she knows I'm mad at her, but I don't care.

"Levi," my dad says on an irritated exhale, "you're acting like a child. Show your mother some respect."

I sit up straight and look from him to my mom and back.

"Helping Savannah would be the right thing to do," I say, and my mom's pleading face switches to something more menacing.

I know bringing it up again will make her angry. She threatened to whoop me this morning when I wouldn't let up, but I don't care. I don't care how many verses she makes me copy or how many whacks I get with the belt. Savannah needs to get out of that house. She needs to get someplace safe. I won't stop until she does.

"Would you cool it about that girl?" Mom snaps. "What happens in that house is none of our business—"

"He is hitting her!"

"Do not raise your voice at me," she yells, then stands quickly and starts clearing dishes from the table. I take a breath and try again without shouting.

"He hits her, and he hits her mom, too."

"Well, that's what happens when you choose that kind of lifestyle," Mom says dismissively.

It's the same thing she told me this morning. Along with a bunch of crap about God's Will and how Savannah should learn to pray.

"*Savannah* didn't choose that lifestyle, Mom. It's not her fault." I look toward my father. He's cutting into his pork chop with his eyes fixed on his plate.

"*Dad*," I plead, "isn't it our job to look out for each other? Isn't it *your* job?"

"It is not our place to meddle in the affairs of others," my dad says slowly. He brings a forkful to his mouth, chews, and swallows. "Proverbs 26:17. *A person who is passing by and meddles in a quarrel that's not his is like one who grabs a dog by the ears.*"

He never once looks up from his dinner, and I clench my fists at my sides.

"This isn't meddling in a random quarrel," I argue. "It's doing what's right. It's protecting Savannah. He's going to kill—"

My mom slams a plate onto the table, cutting me off.

"That. Is. Enough."

Her words are clipped and angry, and her neck and face have turned a bright red.

"That is the last I will hear you speak of Savannah Shaw, Levi. Your father and I are doing our best to raise you to be a godly man, and I will not let that girl ruin it. She's rotten and wicked. That whole family is no good, and if I so much as hear you whisper her name, there will be consequences. Do you understand me, Levi? You will be punished."

There are a thousand things I want to say to my mother in this moment, but I bite my tongue. I swallow every single one of my protests. My throat literally burns with frustration, but Matthew 15:4 starts on a loop in my mind, and it renders me speechless. My defense of Savannah chokes me, and all I can do is jerk out a reluctant nod.

I hate myself for that nod.

Satisfied with my response, my mom smiles then reaches up and cups my cheek.

"You're a good boy, Levi. Your heart is in the right place, but some people aren't worth the trouble."

She pats my face softly, then walks into the kitchen.

All of this is bull.

I look at my dad, but he's still focused on his plate, eating slowly. None of this aligns with what I was taught in Sunday school, or the things we talk about in youth group. *Some people aren't worth the trouble*? How can she even say that? Aren't we all made in God's image? Aren't we all worthy of love and kindness? Yet my father, the pastor of our little church, says nothing. He sits back and eats his dinner like everything is fine, while my mom says hateful, hateful things.

I scowl at him. For the first time ever, I feel angry with him. I feel betrayed.

For the first time ever, I question my parents' judgment. They're wrong, and if they won't help me save Savannah, then tomorrow I'll go to someone who will.

It's a little past midnight when my window opens and Sav crawls through it.

"Are you okay?" I ask, but she doesn't answer.

I climb out of bed to get her some pajamas, and when I hand them to her, my stomach sinks. Her face is blank. Her cheek is bruised, and her eye is swollen. She looks haunted. She's not crying, but my fear spikes.

"Savannah, what's happened?"

"I hit him with a liquor bottle," she says flatly. "Gashed his head up pretty bad. Lot of blood."

My jaw drops. "Is he dead?"

She shrugs. "Don't think so. He was still standin' when I ran out."

"Did he hurt you again?"

She doesn't answer, so without thinking, I reach out and run my hands over her, searching. I brush her hair out of her face and inspect the fresh bruise on her cheek. I sweep my fingers down her shoulders and arms, feeling a few new scratches that weren't there earlier. I want to lift her shirt and inspect her stomach, but I stop myself.

"When did this happen?"

"After school."

"That was hours ago," I say, panicked. "Where the heck have you been?"

"The park. In the bathroom."

I don't ask anything else, even though I want to know everything. What was she doing in the park bathroom for eight hours? Is she scared? Sad? I can't tell what she's feeling, and it worries me more than anything. I almost wish she was crying, instead.

I put my clothes in her hands and turn around while she changes. After a few minutes, she taps my shoulder. When I turn back to her, she hands me her shirt.

"Can you throw this away? It has his blood on it."

My face pales and my eyes go wide, but I nod silently and tiptoe to the kitchen without looking at it. As quietly as I can, I dig to the bottom of the trash can and shove the shirt under balled up paper towels and the food scraps from dinner. Then I scrub my hands with scalding hot water and dish soap in the kitchen sink.

When I get back to my room, Savannah is already curled up in my bed, so I climb in behind her.

"Tomorrow, we can go talk to the someone. The police," I whisper as I tuck her into my chest. I expect her to agree, but instead, she shakes her head violently.

"No. No, he just needs to cool down. I'll stay out of the house for a few days. It'll be fine."

"Savannah, you bashed him over the head with a liquor bottle. Half your face is swollen. You can't go back there."

"Drop it, Levi," she says. It's the first time I've ever heard her voice crack, and my heart cracks with it. "I'll be fine. It'll be fine in a few days."

I don't say anything else. I don't argue because it's obvious she will never agree. Sav needs sleep, so I stay quiet until her breathing evens out. I'll let her rest, let her mind settle, but tomorrow, I'm getting help.

This isn't happening again.

When I wake up, Sav is gone. I never even heard her leave.

I get dressed quickly and head into the kitchen, but I stop short when I see my mom, my dad, and Officer Denton from church sitting at the kitchen table. He's not in uniform, but the hairs on my arms still stand and my neck still prickles with unease.

"What's going on?" I ask, and my stomach falls to my feet when Officer Denton sets Savannah's shirt on the table. The one I threw away last night. The one covered in her mom's boyfriend's blood.

"You tell us."

5

I DON'T SEE Savannah all weekend, and she isn't at school on Monday.

She doesn't come over. She doesn't text, not that I expect her to. She's probably pissed at me, and I don't know if I blame her. But this time feels different. I'm worried for her. I keep thinking of the boot print. The blood on her shirt. The fear.

Turns out, my mom heard me in the kitchen Friday night. Then one of the neighbors from across the street saw Sav leaving through my window early Saturday morning. The neighbor called my mother, and my mother flipped out.

I don't know what led to her digging through the trash to find the shirt. I don't know why she didn't just come wake me up. All I know is she called Officer Denton first thing, and we had a "talk" as soon as I woke up.

I told him everything. How Sav's mom's boyfriend drinks or does drugs and then gets mean. How Sav's always covered in bruises, and how sometimes she'll go days without eating. Sometimes she sleeps at the park or at The Pit. Sometimes she'll disappear for days before turning up at my window late at night.

My mother hated that last part more than anything else. Even more than when I talked about the horrible bruise on Savannah's side from where her mom's boyfriend kicked her, or how Savannah had to hit him with a liquor bottle to protect herself. All my mom cares about is that Savannah slept in my room, in my bed, and that it's been happening for at least a year.

Talking to Officer Denton and my parents about everything made me feel slimy, like I was betraying Sav, even though I know it's the right thing to do. Officer Denton said Savannah wouldn't get in trouble for hitting her mom's boyfriend, and he said he was going to get her someplace safe. I made him promise, and he gave me his word.

That was Saturday morning. It's now Tuesday, and Sav is still missing at the bus stop.

I go through the whole first half of the day with my head down and slide silently into my usual place in the cafeteria at lunch. I eat half my sandwich while scowling at the untouched other half. Savannah's half. I kick the table leg. What the heck is going on with her? My parents said she'd still be at school. Officer Denton promised she'd be back.

Unless...

Did Sav run away?

I get a sinking feeling in my stomach. She would do it. I know she would. Now that she's been taken out of her house with her mom, I could definitely see her running away.

Crap. Did I mess up?

I thought I was helping. No, I was helping. I *am* helping. Savannah can't stay in that house anymore, but she is so stubborn. She wouldn't see that this is what's best for her. If she ran away...

I stand abruptly, my sandwich dropping to the table as I step away from my chair and start walking quickly toward the office. I have to tell them that I think Sav is going to run. I have to tell the principal what I did or call my parents and get ahold of Officer Denton. Maybe she hasn't gotten far, and they can still find her.

I'm twenty feet from the door when it swings open and Officer

Denton steps out, then, before I can fully register what's happening, Savannah follows behind him. My breath rushes from my lungs, and my shoulders sag with relief.

"Sav!" I move toward her but stop in my tracks when she hits me with a glare.

She's mad. I knew she'd probably be mad, but she looks like she wants to kill me. I grit my teeth, ready to face off with her, and take another step, but she shakes her head.

"Stay away from me, *Leviticus*," she says loudly, "unless you want me to break your nose the way I broke Connor's."

I jerk my head back, and my eyes go wide.

"Miss Shaw," Officer Denton scolds, grabbing her by the upper arm. "You've been warned to be on your best behavior. Go to class."

Savannah doesn't even acknowledge him. She just narrows her eyes once more at me, then drags them away and stalks off down the hall.

"Get to class, Levi," I hear Officer Denton say. He puts one of his big, meaty hands on my shoulder and gives me a pat. "Don't you concern yourself with her."

I nod absently, but I don't speak. I can't take my eyes off Savannah's rapidly retreating back. I didn't notice it at first because I was so excited to see her, but Sav's hair has been cut. It used to be really long, touching just above her waist, and now it's at her shoulders. It's brushed and pulled back in some sort of shiny clip thing. Sav's hair is never brushed. It's always wild and tangled and falling into her face.

When my attention moves to her outfit, my jaw literally drops.

She's wearing a dress.

Sav never wears dresses. She always wears ratty t-shirts and the same pair of ratty jeans. I turn to Officer Denton.

"Where did you put her? Where is she staying? Why is she dressed like that?"

My voice is thick with confusion, and when he looks down at me, his smile makes me want to grimace.

"She's staying with Mr. and Mrs. Oglesby."

My head jerks back. I know them from church. They're older than my mom and dad but they don't have kids. They're not very friendly toward me, but they always make sure to talk to my parents after Sunday service.

I can't see Savannah living with them. No way she likes it there. I mean, they put her in a dress and brushed her hair. She's got to be miserable.

"Why them?"

"They're going to be her foster parents," he tells me absently, then pats my shoulder again. "This is only temporary. Go to class, and don't concern yourself with Savannah Shaw."

I nod and tell him thank you, then go back to my lunch table and gather my things. My brain is in a fog, and all I want to do is talk to Sav. All I want are some answers.

Why is it only temporary? Why did she have to cut her hair and wear a dress? Since when are the Oglesbys foster parents? They've never had a foster kid. And what about Sav's mom? What about her mom's boyfriend? What about how Sav bashed him over the head with the liquor bottle? Does this mean they aren't pressing charges? Does this mean her mom doesn't want her anymore?

I'm not sure what I thought would happen, but it sure wasn't a haircut and a dress and the Oglesbys.

I throw my trash away and then walk quickly to my next class.

I have to talk to her. I need to make sure she's okay.

Sav ignores me.

She won't speak to me except to tell me to leave her alone or to threaten my life. I stopped trying to approach her after the first week because I didn't want to get my nose broken, but I've been watching her.

She looks sadder than usual. She keeps wearing dresses, and putting her hair in shiny clips, and she doesn't talk to anyone. She doesn't ride the bus anymore, either. I saw Mr. Oglesby dropping her off one morning, even though their house is on our bus route. I wait another whole week for her to cool down, but when she still refuses to glance in my direction, I've had enough.

I'm in band practice when she's in gym, and through the window, I can see her outside running the track with her class. That's what does me in, the sight of Savannah actually dressed and participating in gym. Hair clips and dresses and now gym?

It's all just too weird.

I shoot my hand up.

"Mr. Parker, can I go to the bathroom, please?"

He gives me a nod from his place behind the piano. "Take the pass."

I stand, drop my trumpet on my chair, and book it out of the room, down the hall, and out the double doors that lead to the track.

The moment I see her, I run to meet her and keep pace at her side.

"Go away, Levi," she pants without looking at me.

"No," I say back, my voice less wobbly than hers because I haven't been running for most of the class period. "I want to know why you're ignoring me, Savannah. This is stupid."

She doesn't answer.

"Savannah."

Still nothing.

So, I make a dumb decision. I grab her by the forearm and jerk her to a stop. We both stumble back a bit from the force of it, and then she whirls on me, shoving my chest hard enough that I topple back on my butt.

"I don't want to talk to you," she seethes, and I pop back up on my feet quickly.

"Why the heck not? You said we were friends—"

"Friends don't tattle, *Leviti*—"

"I didn't tattle," I shout. "You were going to die! I did what I had to do to keep you safe."

"Oh, that's great." She laughs, but it's mean. "Yeah, because Barbara and Ted are so much better."

"Bet they don't get drunk and kick you in the stomach," I spit out.

She shakes her head, then forces her voice to a low, angry whisper.

"You know I gotta ask permission to use the bathroom? They keep it locked up, and when they let me go, one of 'em stands right by the door. I'm not even allowed to shut it, you know that? Same with when I shower. No privacy at all."

The news shocks me, but before I can say anything, she steps closer and gives my shoulder a shove.

"Same with food and drinks. Everything is under lock and key at that damn place. Like they think I'm gonna steal it or something. They trashed all my things—all of 'em, everything—and only let me wear these damned ugly dresses. They practically tied me up so they could cut my damn hair. And they lock me in my bedroom from 7:30 p.m. to 6 a.m."

She shoves me again, harder this time.

"I'm fuckin' *locked* in there. I can't come out for anything. Not for *anything*, Levi. Not even to pee."

Her eyes are wild as they scan my face, her teeth are gritted tight. I don't understand. Why would Mr. and Mrs. Oglesby have such weird, strict rules? They watch her go to the bathroom? They watch her shower...?

No way.

No.

But it has to be better than before. Right?

"But you're not in danger anymore," I force out. "No one's beating on you or anything. I got you out. You're safer now."

"Levi," she says, closing her eyes tight, "I just traded one hell for another. That's it. It's just another hell, but now I don't know my way around this one. I'm blind, ya know? You didn't save me, you *blinded* me."

"I'll tell my dad." She shoves me again.

"No! God, Levi, just freakin' stop. I'm not even supposed to be talkin' to you anyways. Just stay out of my life right now, okay?"

"What do you mean you're not supposed to be talking to me?"

She drags her palm down her face and sighs.

"Your wonderful, Jesus-lovin' momma said that if I don't leave you alone, she'll have Denton arrest me for assaultin' Terry. Said I could be charged with attempted murder or assault with a weapon or some bullshit."

My jaw drops.

"She wouldn't do that." I say it even though I know it's not true. My mom would do it. I'm not surprised at all.

"It's whatever," Savannah says with a roll of her eyes. "I got a plan, anyways."

My skin prickles with unease, and I cock my head to the side.

"What's your plan?"

She snorts and gives me a side-eyed glance.

"Like I'd tell you. You'd just go an' tattle on me again like a little weenie."

"I wouldn't."

"You *would*," she stresses, then starts running again, so I run beside her. "Go back to band, Levi."

She's going to run away. I know she is. Fear rackets inside my chest.

"The Oglesbys aren't *that* bad, right?" I try again. "It's better than any alternative. I could start bringing extra food to school for you, if you want. You can keep it in your room."

"They *are* that bad. And it's not just all that, either. It's the way Ted looks at me. It's creepy. I don't like it at all."

I glance at her to find her lip curled and her eyebrows scrunched.

"Don't run away, Sav."

I just come right out and say it. I don't even try to hide the plea in my voice. I brace myself for a shove, or a fist to the shoulder, but instead, Sav just sighs.

"Go back to band, *Leviticus*."

Then she takes off on a sprint, and I stop running. I watch her run the track until it curves around the opposite end, and then I turn and walk back to band class. Sav's going to do what she wants. She always does. There's nothing I can do about it.

6

Two weeks of silence later, there's a tap on my window in the middle of the night.

I glance at the clock, then shoot upright and hurry over to it.

Savannah hasn't even looked at me since that day on the track, and I haven't tried to talk to her again. I've watched her like crazy, though. I don't know what I was expecting to see when I pushed open the window, but Sav standing with her backpack jammed full at her feet doesn't surprise me.

I stare at her for a minute, but she doesn't make a move to climb into my room.

"Are you coming in?" I whisper, hopeful.

When she shakes her head with a small smile, my chest aches.

"You come out."

I look over my shoulder at my door. It's closed. The house is quiet. If I tell her no, she'll just call me a weenie. Besides, something in my gut is telling me I shouldn't tell her no. So, I climb out. It's awkward, and I basically fall on my face in the dirt, making Sav cover her mouth with her hand to silence a laugh.

"Nice," she says between giggles.

"Shut it."

I stand up and brush off my pajama pants. I don't know how she does this all the time. I didn't realize it was so hard.

"Well," Savannah says, dropping her hands to her sides. "I wanted to come say goodbye."

I stand up straight and shake my head.

"What do you mean goodbye? You said you wouldn't run."

"Never said that."

She kicks some dirt on my bare feet. When she speaks again, her voice is softer, and I know this is real.

"I can't stay here anymore, Levi. I'm—I'm gonna *lose it* if I don't get out. I'd stay if I could. I swear. But I can't. I can't, Levi. So, I just wanted to say bye...and...and thank you for, ya know, bein' my friend and stuff."

"Savannah..."

Her name leaves my mouth and trails off. There's no use trying to talk her out of it. She's so stubborn. She won't listen to me.

And anyway, she's probably right.

"Where are you going to go?" I ask instead, and she shrugs.

"I got a few ideas." She chews on her lip for a second. "I can't tell you. I don't want you to tell your momma."

I just jerk a nod, and she kicks more dirt on my feet.

"Don't forget about me," she whispers, and my eyes sting.

"I could never."

I mean it. I could never forget about her.

I look her over as she stares at the ground. Her hair is loose and wild like usual, blowing in her face with even the slightest breeze, and she's wearing a pair of jeans and a shirt that are a little too big. They look like boy's clothes.

At first, I wonder where she got them, and then...

"Are those my clothes?" I blurt out, and she meets my eyes with a smirk.

"I'd say I was borrowin' 'em but you probably won't get 'em back."

"How'd you—" I shake my head. "Never mind. I don't want to know."

She laughs, and then crouches down quickly and starts digging around inside the front pouch of her backpack.

"I almost forgot."

She stands back up and holds something out to me. When I don't reach for it, she rolls her eyes and grabs my hand, pressing something cold and rigid into my palm. When I turn my hand over to inspect it, my jaw drops and my eyes go wide.

It's the key to my bike lock.

The bike that was stolen from my house in the middle of the night.

I look up at her and cock my head in question. She bites her lip and lowers her eyes, almost looking shy, and my throat burns.

"It's behind the shed at The Pit," she says to the ground.

"You found my bike?"

She scrunches her nose and kicks more dirt.

"I'm sorta the one who stole it."

"What? Why?"

She shrugs.

"The bus was boring, and your momma wouldn't let you ride it unless you didn't have your bike."

My lips twitch into a grin.

"You stole my bike so I could ride the bus with you?"

My heart races a bit, and my stomach flips when she rolls her eyes, and her cheeks turn pink with a blush.

"Shut it, *Leviticus*."

I swallow a laugh, but I can't tame my smile. When she sees it, she smiles too, and our eyes lock. The moment stretches in the darkness, our faces lit up by the moon and stars and the neighbor's outside porch light.

And then it really hits me.

I'll never see her again.

This is the last time I will ever see Savannah, and suddenly, I want to cry.

"You could come with me," she says quickly, her voice cracking.

For a few seconds, I consider it. I *want* it. I want it more than I've ever wanted anything. But then the questions flood my brain, the reality of it all, and I shake my head no. She jerks a nod.

"Okay. Well..."

She lifts her hand to wave, her mouth in a forced, tight smile, and my body moves on impulse. I take two steps to close the distance, place my hands on her shoulders, tilt my head downward, and put my lips on hers.

They're soft and warm, and my skin erupts in tiny goosebumps. I feel her breathe out through her nose, tickling my upper lip, and I realize that I'm kissing Savannah Shaw. And she's kissing me back.

For a split second, anyway.

Until she shoves me backward and slugs me in the shoulder.

"Ouch," I say with a grunt, gripping my shoulder and rubbing at the sting.

"What the hell was that?" Her hand is pressed to her mouth and her eyes are wider than I've ever seen them. "You just kissed me?"

I open my mouth to say something, and then close it. I shake my head a bit to clear the fuzz. I just kissed Savannah.

"Yeah," is all I say.

"What the hell for?"

I shrug and decide to go with honesty.

"You're leaving. I'll never see you again. I wanted to know what it felt like. I...Well, I guess I wanted you to be my first one."

She stares at me for a minute, eyebrows slanted, and my cheeks heat under her scrutiny. I start to feel bad. I start to regret it, even though I don't want to, and then she smiles.

"Oh," she says. "Don't you know you're supposed to ask first?"

I shake my head slowly. I didn't know that.

"Well, go ahead." She takes a step toward me. "Try again."

I narrow my eyes with suspicion.

"Try *what* again?"

She huffs and puts her hands on her hips.

"The kiss, *Leviticus*. Do it the right way. If we're gonna be each other's firsts, we might as well do it right."

"That's not my name," I mumble on instinct, but I'm already

taking the last step toward her, so we're just a few inches apart. I take a deep breath and square my shoulders.

"Close enough," she whispers.

At first, I think she means our bodies, but then I realize she meant my name. I shake my head just a tiny bit, give her a small, exasperated smile, and then I do it.

"Savannah. Can I kiss you?"

She cocks her head to the side and lifts her eyes to the sky, tapping her chin with her index finger like she's considering my question. I raise an eyebrow at her, making her laugh. Then she gives me a curt nod that makes my excitement spike.

"Yeah. You can kiss me, Levi."

Slowly, with my stomach full of butterflies, I lean in and kiss her for a second time. For a moment, we just stand there, lips pressed together, and I bring my hands to her shoulders again. Her wild hair tickles my nose, but I don't pull away. Then, I feel her mouth open the smallest bit, so I do the same.

My whole chest is on fire. My heart is racing, and I have to remind myself to breathe.

Nothing has ever felt like this.

Her breath is hot when it mixes with mine, so different from the cool night air I was just breathing, and when her tongue touches mine, my body quakes with a shiver. She glides her tongue over mine, and I feel her move closer, erasing all the space between us that was there before.

I grow bolder, moving my tongue a little more, mimicking her movements. It's weird, warm and wet, but nice.

My fingers tighten on her shoulders. I want to keep her here. I don't want her to leave. Not now that I know how this feels. Savannah is usually so prickly, so hard. I didn't know she could feel so *soft*.

Too soon, she ends the kiss, closing her mouth and pressing her lips to mine one last time before taking a giant step back. My hands fall from her shoulders, and we stare at each other. Her chest is heaving, just like mine, and I can tell from the heat on my face that I have a matching blush, too.

"Well..." she says quietly.

"Well?"

I watch as she reaches up and brushes her lips with her fingertips, a small smile lifting her cheeks.

"Well, I guess that didn't suck."

"You're such a brat, Shaw," I joke with a scoff, and she narrows her eyes playfully.

"Better a brat than a weenie, Cooper."

I puff out my chest and lose the smile, taking a step in her direction.

"Would a weenie have kissed you breathless?"

The sharp edge in my voice surprises even me, and when Savannah's eyes flare and her mouth parts in shock, it stirs something deep in my stomach. She pulls her lower lip between her teeth and shrugs.

"Dunno," she whispers. "Never been kissed before."

My mouth twitches in a smile, triumph surging in my chest. Knowing I was her first kiss fills me with something I don't understand. Pride or possessiveness, maybe. I'll always be her first kiss. No one and nothing will ever change that. Doesn't matter where she goes after this.

That kiss, her first kiss, will always belong to me.

"Savannah, I—"

"No," she says quickly, stepping backward just as I step forward. "Don't say anything else, okay? I gotta go. I *need* to go, Levi. Please."

It's the please that does it.

My shoulders drop and I plant my feet firmly on the ground. I nod once and suck in a breath.

"Okay."

She smiles and takes a few steps backward, adding more distance between us.

"I'll see ya around, Levi Cooper."

"Will you?"

"I think so." She purses her lips to hide her troublemaking smile. "I don't think the universe is done with us yet."

Her statement gives me hope. Makes me feel a little less like I'm losing something and more like I'm just loaning it out for a while.

"Wait," I say quickly, reaching into my pocket and pulling the bike lock key back out.

I hold it up in front of me and mime an underhand toss twice before actually letting it go. Sav catches it with one hand. She looks from the key in her palm then back at me, brow raised in question.

"You can give it back when I see you next," I say with a shrug. "Don't forget."

I watch her slide the key into the back pocket of my jeans—her jeans now, I guess—and her smile is bigger than I've ever seen it. She takes a few more steps backward.

"I could never," she says softly, and then she turns around and disappears into the darkness.

I wait until I don't hear her footsteps on the pavement anymore. I resist the urge to walk to the front of my house and see if I can see her down the road. Instead, I turn back to my window and attempt to climb back inside.

Once I'm finally over the window ledge, the weight in the room feels heavy. My skin prickles and I swallow around a lump in my throat. When I turn around, I find my mom staring back at me. She doesn't even try to mask her fury, so I don't bother to explain myself. When she reaches up and flips the light switch, dread coils in my gut.

The Bible is already lying open on my bed, and Dad's belt is in her hand.

I grit my teeth. It's been a while since she's used the belt. Years. But despite the time, I know what she expects from me. I haven't forgotten.

"Now," she hisses.

Slowly, I walk toward her, but instead of cowering, I keep my eyes locked on hers. This time, I don't look away until the last minute, when I have to turn around and face the Bible on the bed.

"Pants," my mom seethes, and I obey, tugging my pajama pants down until they pool at my feet. My movements are jerky, but with anger, not fear. Then I brace my hands on the bed and set my eyes on the Bible.

It's open to Matthew 15:4 like I knew it would be. I breathe through my nose slowly.

"Read."

I keep my mouth shut and I don't move. I used to think I deserved these punishments, but I can't for the life of me understand why helping someone like Savannah should warrant this. My mother is wrong. She and my father are both wrong. I grit my teeth and say nothing.

I will not read Matthew 15:4. I won't read it ever again.

"Read!" my mother shrieks.

When I still don't speak, I hear her raise her arm seconds before the belt cracks on my backside. A muffled cry escapes me as I bite my tongue. I taste blood in my mouth, and my eyes sting, but I still don't read the verse like she wants.

I stay quiet. I refuse to speak.

It doesn't matter.

She's going to use the belt either way.

THEN

PART TWO

*Thought you were my safe place,
baby, but look how wrong I've been.*

7

18 years old

"FIVE MINUTES, VIXEN!"

Bobby, one of the bouncers, shouts the warning into the dressing room just as I finish the last buckle on my stiletto. These shoes are super uncomfortable, but they make my legs look long as fuck.

"I'm ready," I call back.

I stand and look in the mirror, using my hands to fluff my already curled and sprayed hair. I run a finger down the side of my mouth, cleaning up the lipstick there, and then I do a little spin.

This is my favorite outfit in my rotation. Black leather and lace. It makes me feel like a badass. An avenging angel. The shorty shorts show just enough of my ass cheeks to be sexy, and the matching vested top makes it look like I have more boobs than I do. I cup my hands under each breast and give them a lift, adjusting my illusion of cleavage, just as Bella leans on the vanity table next to me and holds out a shot.

"Want? We're packed with Spring Breakers, so you'll probably need it."

"Hell yeah."

I swipe the shot glass from her and throw back the cheap tequila, wincing as it goes down.

"Are they assholes?" I rasp out, clearing my throat to ease the burn.

She scrunches her nose and gives me a shrug.

"Nah. Young, dumb, and full of cum."

We both laugh as she pours me another shot.

"As long as they have deep pockets and are generous with Mommy and Daddy's cash, I don't care what they're full of."

"I'll cheers to that."

We clink our shot glasses together and then toss back the liquor. This is going to be a long night.

"Two minutes, Vix!" Bobby shouts again.

"Coming!"

I check my ass one more time, then turn to head to the stage, but Bella grabs my hand and turns me back around.

"You got time for a line."

She waggles her brows, gesturing to the small mirror covered with white residue on her vanity table. Bells is always getting into trouble, but I don't mind. It's why we get along so well. I grin at her.

"Mack's gonna be pissed if she finds that shit in here."

I saunter to her vanity and use the acrylic nail on my pinkie to scoop a bit of the powder.

"Hurry up, then, and I'll hide it," Bells says, and I roll my eyes as I bring my nail to my nose and inhale. "Ooof."

It burns like I knew it would, the smell reminding me of the house where I grew up, but it only lasts for a few seconds. I shake my head and rub at my nose, then bend down to check my face in Bella's vanity mirror.

"Okay, now put it away before you get us both fired."

Bella laughs at me, but she does what I asked, and not a breath later, the dressing room door flies open, and Bobby pops his head back inside. He hits me with a no-nonsense glare.

"Would you move your ass, girl?"

I roll my eyes and prance past him, making sure to jab his big body with my shoulder. He chuckles and I stick out my tongue. I couldn't hurt Bobby even if I wanted to. He's three hundred pounds of solid muscle. You'd never know from looking at him that he's a big marshmallow teddy bear.

"Thanks, Bob-O," I say sweetly, shooting to my tiptoes quickly so I can pat his shiny bald head before darting away from him and up the stage stairs.

I can hear the chatter in the audience, but with the house lights low, everyone just looks like black blobs. I know from experience that I appear the same to them.

Once in place at the center of the stage, I glance to Kenny, the DJ, and give him a nod. He flashes me a thumbs up, then my music starts to drift through the speakers.

"We've got a real treat for you all next," Kenny croons into the mic. "Our next dancer is a crowd favorite, but don't let her sweet smile fool you. Forget sugar and spice and everything nice. Vixen Viper is all tequila, sass, and a fucking great ass."

I stifle a snort at his cheesy announcement. He changes it up all the time, and I never know what bullshit is going to come through the speakers. From the way the crowd cheers, though, I'd say this one hit the target.

Young, dumb, and full of cum indeed.

"Y'all treat Miss Viper *real good*, now," Kenny says, "and I promise she'll give you a show you won't forget."

With that, he cranks my music and flips on the stage lights.

When I first started dancing here, the quick change from dark to bright would mess with my head and make me feel a little disoriented, but I got used to it quickly. Now, a few months into this job, I can adapt like a pro, and I move seamlessly into my routine.

I slide my hands down my body and sway with the music, gripping the pole and launching into a wrist seat spin. Once I hit the bottom of the spin, I make sure to spread my legs wide and drag my palms up my inner thighs before popping back up to standing and going straight into a post spin.

This club doesn't do full nudity. With the exception of my ass cheeks flashing out the bottom of my leather booty shorts, everything important from navel to tiptoes is covered, but I like to tease them anyway. It's crazy the tips a caress on the inner thigh or a finger brush over the crotch of my costume bottoms can produce.

These men are damn horny bastards, so I use it to my advantage.

More whistles hit my ears as I hook my leg on the pole and seat myself, arching my back and letting my hair cascade behind me. I use one hand to undo the zipper on my black leather vest. The audience goes nuts, shouting encouragements at me, and I smirk. I let the vest fall open as I complete my spin, then slide it down my arms and fling it to the side of the stage once my feet are on the ground.

My red lace bra is completely see-through except for at my nipples, where there are black leather hearts sewn into the material. I don't flash full tit until the floor portion of my set. Gotta build up to it.

I climb the pole on autopilot, going through the motions of my routine and letting the music guide my movements. It's not hard to tune out the crowd, and if I'm not careful, I'll disassociate entirely. Tips are better when I interact with the patrons. Like Kenny said, they want a show. If they were interested in just dancing, they'd have gone to the ballet.

No, they want the illusion of seduction, so that's what I give them.

I bite my lip. Pretend to giggle. Make lingering eye contact with a few of the guys who look particularly hard-up for some action. The stage floor is littered with cash before I even finish the pole portion of my routine.

I haven't even taken off the bra.

Just as I loop into my last spin—one where I'm suspended upside down with my legs spread wide—a face at the edge of the stage snags my attention. It catches me off guard, and I almost fall on my head. I do a double take.

No way.

It can't be.

I'm so stunned that when my spin slows and my first song fades out, I don't get down right away. I just stare. It's only a half second or so, but it feels like longer, and it's not until my second track starts that I remember I'm in the middle of my routine. I should be starting floor now, but instead, I do one last slow spin on the pole so I can sneak another peek at the patron sitting off to the side of the stage.

Levi Cooper.

I'm not imagining it.

If his sandy blond hair and stern eyebrows didn't give him away, the stiff and uncomfortable way he's sitting sure does. I have to stifle a laugh. Levi Cooper in a strip club. That was definitely not on my spring break bingo card.

I strut to the far side of the stage to start the floor portion of my set, but as I go through the motions, I sneak glances back toward Levi. It's obvious he hasn't recognized me. I'm not sure he's even paid the show any attention, judging by the way his eyes are glued to his phone.

The group of guys he's sitting with are another story, though. I have them rapt as they sip watery mixed drinks and rib one another anytime I do something even remotely sexy. They're all whistles and cheers and lewd comments, and Levi's the only one who looks like a fish out of water. It fits perfectly with the memory I've kept of him.

Buttoned-up and clean cut. Respectful to a fault. Serious and stern.

A Grade-A Weenie.

I dance my way around the stage, making sure everyone in the audience gets a show, but when it's time to face Levi's table, I switch it up. Instead of crawling over there like I've choreographed, I sashay back to the stairs and head into the crowd.

I flick my eyes to Bobby and give him a little head shake. He's tense and ready to snap.

Don't come for me, Bob-O. I got this.

I'm not supposed to move into the audience until later. Mack, the owner of the club, takes the safety of her dancers seriously. We don't step foot into the crowd without an assigned bouncer. That way, if anyone gets handsy, the matter is taken care of immediately. Mack was a dancer before she bought the club, so she knows exactly what could go wrong and the best ways to avoid it.

She's going to be so pissed at me. I can tell Bobby already is by the way he's snapping into his walkie. I flare my eyes and flash him a sweet smile as I make my way to Levi's table.

Get back up there, he mouths, nodding toward the stage.

I blow him a kiss and give him my ass instead.

I'm going to catch so much shit for this, but I push that thought out of my mind and zero my attention in on the side of Levi's head. It's still bowed, and his face is lit up by the phone screen. I'm actually offended that I'm so easy to ignore. Is the ruckus of the crowd not telling enough that I'm worth watching?

I dance as I weave my way through the tables, stopping here and there to let someone shove some cash in my shorts or garter. I play it up as best I can and try to hide the fact that all of my focus is on the blond square in the corner, but by the time I'm standing next to his table, my attention is obvious.

Well, obvious to everyone but him.

That damn phone.

I plant myself in front of him, snatch the phone from his hands, and shove it in the waistband of my shorts. His eyes fly to mine, and I have to bite my lip to keep from laughing at just how irritated he looks. I remember that look. I used to know it well.

The myriad of emotions that pass over his face is so entertaining.

First, he's angry. He's mid-reach to take back his phone when his jaw drops and he scans my face, shocked. I purse my lips in an attempt to hide my smile and cock my head to the side, daring him. I put my hands on my hips and push my pelvis out just a little. An offering. You can have the phone back if you take it yourself.

He doesn't make another grab for it, though. Instead, his lips curl into a boyish smile and he shakes his head slowly.

"Savannah?"

I can barely hear him over the music and the whooping of the crowd, but I wink and close the distance between us, stepping between his widespread legs and placing my hands on his shoulders. I lean forward and invade his space, taking pride in the way he sucks in a surprised breath, before bringing my lips to the shell of his ear and whispering.

"Hey, Weenie."

He laughs, his breath skirting over my collarbone. I pull back just enough to flash him a taunting smile before putting my palms on his chest and pushing him back forcefully in his chair. His eyes flare wide, and his mouth opens on a gasp. I drag my hands roughly down his chest and up his arms, then I arch an eyebrow.

"You been working out, Cooper?"

I shout the question over the music and give his biceps a squeeze. His mouth lifts back up into that lopsided grin, and it makes my stomach flip over on itself, so I do what I need to regain the upper hand. I bite my lip, run my palms over his muscular thighs, and croon into his ear, "How 'bout a dance, big boy?"

Levi looks terrified as I turn my back to him, and it takes all my self-control not to laugh out loud. I glance up to look for Bobby and find that he's followed me. He's now standing just two tables over with his arms crossed and an intimidating look on his face. He's such a good bouncer. I give him a small smile, then focus back on Levi.

I don't usually do lap dances. Getting this close to patrons skeeves me out, and Mack is awesome enough to let me be a bottle girl when everyone else is working the crowd. But the moment I lower my ass over Levi's lap, and he growls my name in warning, I'm glad I'm making an exception for him.

"*Savannah.*"

His tenor is low and threatening, completely at odds with the voice of the boy in my memories, but the scolding way he says my name fills me with nostalgic glee.

I'm downright giddy to be irritating Levi Cooper again.

"Yes, Levi?" I sing as I rub up on him.

I flex my fingertips into the space just above his knees where I've braced my hands, and I feel his muscles tense. It makes my smile grow, and I roll my hips, so my ass just barely grazes the crotch of his pants. It's more of a tease than anything else—the only place we're actually touching is where I've planted my hands on his legs for stability—but something about the proximity has my heart racing.

He doesn't say anything else. Just sits stiff as a board as I move over him, and I glance down to see his hand clenched into a tight fist at his side, almost as if it's taking all his strength not to shove me off of him. I can't tell if that amuses me or upsets me, but I stand and turn to face him anyway.

His jaw is tight, eyes locked on mine, and his nostrils flare as I straddle him. Levi's friends are hooting and hollering like a bunch of chimps at the zoo, but we never look away from each other. I grab his hands and place them on my waist, then wait a few breaths, giving him ample time to remove them. I arch a brow in challenge, and when he presses his fingers into me, I smirk.

I throw a quick glance at Bobby to let him know I'm still good, then lace my fingers behind my head and start to roll my hips, lowering myself down Levi's body then back up again. I practically shove my boobs in his face, but he never breaks eye contact. Never once takes a peek at my chest. I bite my lower lip, lick them seductively, grab my breasts and give them a little bounce. The only reaction I get from him is a heated stare and a faint twitch at the corners of his mouth.

It's a bit of an ego kill, if I'm honest.

My thighs burn from suspending myself just above his, and I can tell from the chorus playing through the speakers that my last track is almost over, so I drop down into Levi's lap for the final verse. His chest rumbles in a way that makes my skin prickle with awareness. Emboldened, I start to roll my hips again, but stop abruptly when I feel him beneath me.

Now it's Levi's turn to smirk.

Because he's hard. *Big* and hard, from the feel of him.

I can only imagine how ridiculous I must look, stripper frozen mid-lap dance because of a boner, and I only snap out of it when Levi raises a brow in challenge. That eyebrow—the absolute deviousness of it—does more in way of turning me on than any man ever has before.

I tighten my lips to keep from laughing, and my eyes scan his face as I start to move on him again, this time making sure to keep full contact. I roll my hips over him, grinding down on his erection, and his throat contracts with a hard swallow. The way his Adam's apple bobs makes me breathe faster, but other than that tiny reaction, he gives me nothing else. His pupils are blown wide, and the pulse point in his neck is thrumming so rapidly that I can see it moving, but his hands stay firmly where I placed them, and his body is as immobile as a statue.

In a last-ditch effort to win whatever seemingly one-sided game I've gotten myself into, I take my hands off his shoulders and bring them to the straps of my bra. I hook my index fingers around the straps and slide them up and down, making it obvious what I'm intending to do, and the guys around us go nuts. Whistles and cheers and lewd comments are thrown everywhere as I ready to take my top off.

"Savannah." Levi growls in warning.

I bite my lip and slide the first strap down my arm.

Someone in the crowd shouts something about my tits, and Levi's eyes leave me for the first time since I started this "dance." He glares in the direction of the voice, expression threatening and lethal, and when he looks back at me, his jaw is tight for an entirely new reason. He shakes his head once. It's a jerky, almost violent movement.

"Don't you dare," he commands, and a thrill skates down my spine.

I slide the other strap down my arm, and he tightens his fingers at my waist, halting the roll of my hips. His eyes dart from me to my chest, to the people around us, and back. He's protective and possessive, and it's really fucking sexy.

I never, ever thought I'd be calling Levi Cooper sexy, but here we are.

I bring my hands to the clasp at the back of my bra.

"Sav," he snarls, and it's downright feral.

I unhook the clasp and move to let the bra drop just as Levi wraps his arms around me and slams my body into his chest, shielding me from the crowd.

And then all hell breaks loose.

Someone puts Levi in a headlock—Bobby—and I'm hauled out of his arms by another bouncer. I can tell from the tatted hands that it's Red.

"Bobby, no!" I shout, squirming out of Red's hold. "Put me *down*, Red. Right now!"

Red sets me back on my feet and Bobby loosens his hold on Levi, cocking his head in my direction, and for a minute, I think all's well, but then Levi has to go and be a dumbass and throws a punch over his shoulder, clocking Bobby right on the cheek.

"Goddamnit, Levi!" I yell as Bobby grabs Levi by the neck and slams him onto the table.

Levi is kicking and bucking like an idiot. Bobby is huge. Why would anyone try to go up against him? Even Levi's friends have taken giant steps backward away from the scuffle. Some friends they are, letting their buddy get roughed up like this, but I don't blame them. I wouldn't want to take on Bobby. Seems Levi didn't get the memo.

"Just stop fuckin' fightin' him!" I stamp my foot in a weak attempt to get his attention. "You wanna get yourself killed?"

"Put your damn top back on," Levi yells, and it's a little garbled because of the way his face is smooshed to the tabletop.

I glance down. Looks like I ended up losing my bra after all, and now I'm standing in just a pair of little flower pasties. I plant my hands on my hips and glare at Levi.

"I don't take orders from you, Levi Cooper."

"Stop being a brat, Savannah. Put on your fucking top."

I grin a little at hearing a swear word leave Levi's mouth. He was always such a pure little square before. I'd swear just to make him uncomfortable, but he just spit *fucking* like it was nothing. Bobby shoves Levi a little harder into the table, and Levi lets out a grunt.

"Your word, Vix," Bobby says, leaving it up to me what we do with the squirming idiot under his palms. I sigh and roll my eyes.

"Put him in the Pen," I say with a shake of the head. "I'll be right there."

Then I turn and march my half-naked ass back to the dressing room.

8

FIFTEEN MINUTES LATER, I leave the dressing room wearing sweats and a tank with my face scrubbed clean, and I run smack into Mack.

"Boyfriends aren't allowed if they can't behave themselves," she says. "You know the rules."

"He's not my boyfriend. He's just an idiot."

She smiles. "He know that?"

"That he's not my boyfriend, or that he's an idiot?" I give her a sly grin. "He probably knows both."

Mack shakes her head with a sigh, lifting her eyes to the ceiling.

"You girls are turning me gray."

I snort a laugh. Mack is only in her early thirties, and there's not a gray hair on her head. She looks back at me with an arched brow.

"You're off until Monday."

I open my mouth to argue, but she holds up a palm.

"It's not a punishment. Red told me about your shows. I don't want you to worry about pulling doubles. You can make the hours up next week."

"Really?" My smile must cover my entire face because her lips curve slightly in return. "Thank you."

She nods, then turns to leave.

"Remember us when you're famous," she calls over her shoulder before heading around the corner and back into her office.

There's a bounce to my step as I walk to the Pen. It's a storage room that we use to hold drunk assholes before the cops come cart them off. It cracks me up that Levi ended up in there. First the strip club, then the lap dance, and now the Perv Pen.

What a day for good old Levi Cooper.

I wipe my face of any expression before I swing the door open, and it's difficult as hell not to bust out laughing when I see Levi slouched in a metal folding chair, holding an ice pack on his face. His eyes jump to me immediately, but I settle mine on Red.

"I got it from here, Red."

He nods without saying anything. Then he pushes himself away from the wall where he was leaning, gives me a wink, and walks out the door. It's not until the door clicks shut behind me that I let my attention drift to Levi.

He's glaring daggers at me, and my head jerks back on instinct.

"What?" I spit out.

"Vixen Viper?"

"We have to have a stage pseudonym." I shrug. "It's better than Candi or Cookie or Cupcake. At least a viper isn't easily consumed."

He doesn't nod. Doesn't say anything else about my name. He just cocks his head slightly to the side and keeps his eyes narrowed on me. I put my hands on my hips and glare back until he decides to speak again.

"You're a stripper."

And *there* is the patronizing tone I didn't miss.

"*Dancer*," I correct, and he scoffs.

"Half-naked dancer."

"It's my job."

"This isn't a *job*. It's a *joke*."

"Well, *you* paid the fifty-dollar cover charge to get into this *joke*, and I didn't see you complainin' a half hour ago."

I have to bite my cheeks to keep from smiling while we stare off. He can't even argue. He knows I'm right. To further prove my point,

I lower my eyes to his crotch, pucker my lips and let out a long, slow whistle.

"Alright, alright," he says quickly, turning his body to the side, as if trying to hide from me.

"Never would have guessed you'd have such a big dick, Cooper."

"Jesus Christ, Sav."

His ears turn pink, and I smirk, waltzing up to him slowly.

"Oh, the Lord's name in vain, too? Well hung and a sinner to boot. Just my type."

I lean my hip on the table next to him and look down through my lashes. He meets my gaze, then scans my face with his big brown eyes. His nostrils flare, and I can tell he's trying not to smile.

"Still a brat," he says finally, and I let my grin slip.

"Still a weenie."

His lips twitch into a smirk that makes my pulse speed up.

"A sizable one, at that," he adds in a low cocky voice that has my mouth dropping open with a laugh.

Now *my* ears are turning pink, I can tell from how much they're burning, and all I can do is shake my head. Un-freaking-believable. I stick out my foot and nudge his shoe with mine.

"Whatcha doin' here, anyway?"

He stretches his legs out wide, bracketing me between them, and slides his body lower in the metal folding chair so he's peering up at me. He sets the ice pack on the table, letting me get a good view of the bruise that's formed on his cheek, and my fingers itch to reach out and touch it. To smooth away the hurt. His face is farther away from mine now than it was moments before, but something about this position feels *closer*.

"It's my first spring break. Miami won the coin toss. Luck."

Luck? Hmm.

"Where are you going to school?"

"UNC."

There's no hiding the pride in his voice, and though I'm impressed, I'm not surprised. Well, not surprised that he got into

UNC, anyway. He was a straight A student. Did all the extra credit, too. A little surprised he didn't end up at one of the Christian colleges, though. I squint at him playfully.

"Southern Baptist Ministry? Biblical Studies?"

He rolls his eyes. "Architectural engineering."

That makes sense, too. He always did like building things. I used to make fun of him for his Lego sets and the doodles of buildings in his notebooks. I trace my finger along the edge of the table and let my eyes follow it.

"What are you doing later?"

I try to keep my voice neutral, act nonchalant, but I know he hears my excitement. I can tell from the way he tilts his head at me like a curious little puppy.

"We were going to hit up the beach." I curl my lip in disgust and he laughs. "You live in Miami. You can't tell me you don't like the beach."

"Too much sand. Too many critters." I shudder. "The beach would be better if it was a pool."

He laughs again, then tilts his outstretched leg so his knee bumps my calf.

"You got something better in mind?"

I meet his eyes and give him a troublemaking grin. The same one I'd toss him when we were kids. I shrug.

"I might."

Then I turn and walk out the door, working to tame my giddiness when I hear Levi stand and follow.

"This is a closet."

Levi leans on the door frame to the room I rent from another dancer at the club as I dig through my "dresser" to find the outfit I want to wear tonight. It's actually a plastic bin that I got from the resale shop, but it works as my dresser and nightstand. Even a desk, in a pinch.

I stop my digging and glance around the room, trying to see it how he's seeing it. The paint is dull. The ceiling light flickers. The window AC box barely works. And yeah, it's super tiny.

But it's *mine*.

I go back to shuffling through my clothes as I respond.

"I can come and go as I please. I don't have to be locked in from sundown to sunup. I can close the door when I use the bathroom. I can walk through the front door without listening for danger first. I don't have to tiptoe around for fear of getting the shit kicked out of me."

I pull out the outfit I was searching for and toss it on my mattress, then put the plastic lid back on the bin.

"Maybe it's not big or luxurious, but I don't need much space, and it works just fine for me. It's mine. I like it."

I push myself to standing and meet his eyes. His brow is furrowed with contrition, probably seconds away from apologizing. I wave him off.

"Forget it." I give him an honest smile. "Only forward from here."

He purses his lips and nods, but he doesn't take his eyes off me. It's unsettling, and I don't like feeling unsettled.

"Turn around so I can change, perv."

"Why?" he asks as he obeys. "I already saw your tits."

I bark out a laugh, stripping out of my tank and sweats.

"Since when do you say tits?"

His chuckle rumbles through the room, and I have to fight off a shiver. I'm thankful his back is turned because now my nipples are hard and my face is hot, and I'm not ready to deal with whatever that means.

"I'm eighteen, Sav. I say a lot of things I didn't used to."

I flick my eyes to his back, taking note of the way the fabric of his t-shirt stretches over it. His shoulders are broad, his arms larger than I remember. He's not fifteen, anymore. That's for sure.

"Is this the obligatory sheltered church boy rebellion? You gonna join a frat or date a goth girl, next?"

He laughs but doesn't answer, which means I'm right. A Levi Cooper rebellion. How fun. I think I'd like to see how this plays out.

I finish dressing, then I toss my discarded clothes into my small hamper in the corner.

"Alright, I'm good."

Levi turns around smiling, but the minute his eyes land on me, his smile disappears. His gaze slides from my face to my lips, then down my body slowly, sticking on certain places that make my nipples pebble again under the tight fabric of my push up bra. I bite my lip and squirm a little under his heated attention, but then his eyes turn angry, and my defenses shoot up.

"What the hell are you wearing?"

I gape, and then I'm pissed.

"Just what exactly is wrong with what I'm wearing, *Leviticus*?"

His nostrils flare at the old nickname, but then he drags his hand down his face.

"Don't you have anything that doesn't make you look like a stripper? Put the damn sweats back on."

I clench my teeth at his tone, then put my hands on my hips and glare at him.

My outfit is sexy as fuck, but it's not something I'd wear at the club. Hell, you see more skin just walking down Ocean Drive. Sure, the men's dress shirt is hanging off one shoulder with only two buttons fastened in the middle, and it's exposing my electric purple push up bra and my navel, but my black leather short shorts and fishnets cover almost my entire ass. My arms are covered, my back is covered, and the combat boots I plan to wear come to mid-calf.

If anything, I'm *over*dressed for Miami.

"If you've got a problem with the way I'm dressed, then you can go back to your little frat bros and hit up the beach. Maybe you'll get lucky and the sand you get up your ass will turn into a pearl."

I say the last sentence with a sweet smile, batting my eyelashes at him, and he tips his head back. He doesn't say anything, and the longer he breathes in and out at the ceiling without acknowledging me, the angrier I get.

What the hell is he so frustrated about? He's got no right to police how I dress.

I snatch the pillow off my mattress on the floor and swing it at him, hitting him square in the gut. He grunts and doubles over, hugging the pillow to his body and turning quickly so it rips from my hands. Then, quick as ever, he swings it back and it smacks me right in the face.

The tension is gone before the whoosh of breath leaves my body, and we start to laugh at the same time. When our gazes lock, my excitement for his presence sparks once more.

I can't fucking believe he's here in my little rented bedroom in Miami, Florida. Here after showing up at the club while I was performing.

God, it feels like it's been so much longer than three years.

I fight the urge to shut my eyes against some of the memories that assault me.

I wonder if he's experienced as much as I have. I wonder how much these past three years have changed him. He looks so different than he did the last time I saw him. Still boyish, but less so. He's taller. His cheeks aren't as plump. There's a smattering of scruff on his jaw and product in his hair. But I still knew who he was the second my eyes landed on him.

He's still Levi.

When our laughter slows, I drop my pillow back on my mattress and pick up my combat boots. I shoulder check him when I walk past, smirking when he huffs out an *ouch,* then glance at him over my shoulder.

"C'mon, Weenie. We're going to be late."

9

I TRY my best not to grimace as I glance around the seedy bar, but I'm pretty sure I fail.

"Why are we here?"

Savannah glances over her bare shoulder at me and laughs.

"Why do you look like you just smelled something nasty?"

I widen my eyes. "Because this place smells like something nasty."

She laughs again, louder this time, and I shake my head. She's delighted that I'm uncomfortable, and I can't help but smile. It feels like before she left. Sav always did like making me squirm, and no matter how much I tried to pretend, she could tell it bothered me less than I let on.

I trail her through the bar, keeping my eyes firmly on her shoulders despite the pull to let them fall lower. It's going to take a lobotomy for me to forget the sight of her topless with just some little plastic flowers on her nipples. I don't need to add anymore NSFW content to the Savannah folder.

Because the feel of her in my lap...

I grit my teeth and give my head a little shake.

When the guys tricked me into tagging along to that strip club, I was furious. I've grown a bit since my days of Bible camp and purity lectures, but the idea of sitting in the audience watching some women get naked on stage still triggered my fight or flight response.

Involuntarily, verses about lust and modesty started cycling through my mind and it gave me an instant headache. I had just started distracting myself with architectural digest articles on my phone when this blast from my past yanked it from my hold and bowled me right over.

I was shocked at first. I couldn't believe what I was seeing. Savannah Shaw, alive and well, and smirking at me. The look in her eyes—the one she always used to get when she was purposely trying to irritate me—sparked instant excitement. I wanted to jump up and grab her. I wanted to hug her and hold her and laugh out loud. I don't think I've ever been that happy.

The last time I saw Savannah, I kissed her because I believed I'd never see her again. I spent the entire next year after she'd left dreaming about her. Worrying about her. I would spend my whole study period in the library, just so I could scour the internet for news stories about runaways. I dedicated every mealtime prayer to Savannah, begging God that the next breaking headline wouldn't be about her. Wishing her safe. Needing her happy. Telling myself that no news was good news.

To see her standing over me with that smirk removed three years of bricks off my chest, and it felt amazing to finally breathe her in. For all of two seconds.

Until I felt a whole slew of new things that made my head spin.

Her hands on my body, squeezing my biceps, her lips on my ear.

Damn.

I spent a whole year with her in my bed, sleeping most nights with her tucked close to my chest, yet none of it compared to those first few seconds of contact in that club. I felt like my body was on fire. I thought I would die just from that.

But because she's Savannah, she had to go and take it further.

How 'bout a dance, big boy?

I'm going to be playing that memory over and over for years to come.

A chorus of greetings snaps me from my thoughts when we reach the back of the bar, and I watch as Sav hugs and high fives a group of people. Three guys and a girl. The guys are wearing ripped skinny jeans and torn band tees. One has a short green mohawk, one has a buzz cut, and one has shaggy brown hair falling into his eyes. The girl has long black hair with pink streaks, and she's wearing leather pants and a black mesh top with a neon pink bra underneath. The bright pink eyeliner lining her almond-shaped brown eyes matches her bra and hair perfectly, and when I glance at her feet, she's wearing a pair of bright pink Chucks.

I immediately feel out of place in my khaki shorts and polo shirt, but Sav fits right in.

Savannah steps back so she's standing next to me once more, then introduces me to her friends, gesturing to each person like she's Vanna White and they're a car I just won.

"Levi, this is Torren, Jonah, Sean, and Mabel. Everyone, this is my friend Levi."

"What's up, man," Jonah, the guy with a green mohawk says, putting out a fist for me to bump.

His nails are painted a sparkly pink and he's wearing about a dozen colorful friendship bracelets. I nod and bump his fist with mine. The contrast between my hand and his is almost comical.

I turn to the other guy, Torren, expecting the same sort of hello, but he just looks me over with a stony face. I nod awkwardly. Sean gives me a nod and a smile, and then I turn to Mabel.

"Hey." She smiles and gives me a small wave. "Nice to meet you, Levi."

"You too, Mabel." I turn back to Savannah and find her beaming up at me with a look that tells me she's got a secret, and she's excited about it. "What?" Her smile grows. "Sav, what?"

"This is my band."

My reaction must be exactly what she was hoping for because the triumph she's exuding almost knocks me over.

"Your *band*?"

She nods, then gives my shoe a nudge with her black boot.

"We got a gig tonight." Her tone is steady, unbothered, as if this is just another day at work, but I see the excitement sparkling in her eyes. "If anyone asks, you're a roadie."

"Wow." I blink a few times and pan my attention back to her bandmates. They look the part. "Wow, Sav. That's really awesome. What's y'all's name?"

Torren snorts, and Mabel smacks his arm. He raises a pierced eyebrow at me.

"*Y'all*? So, you're a good ol' country boy?"

I jerk my head back, screw up my face, then dart my eyes to Sav.

"Savannah and I grew up together," I say slowly.

It's not like I expected them to know who I am, but the fact that they don't know where Sav grew up gives me pause.

"Southeastern North Carolina. So, I guess you could say country?"

Torren's eyes fall to Savannah and the way he looks at her makes me clench my fists. He looks at her like she's more than his bandmate. He looks at her like she's just *his*.

"North Carolina, Savvy?"

Savvy? I roll my eyes at the nickname on impulse but wipe it away quickly. Savannah shrugs at him with a flirty grin that pisses me off even more than the look on his face.

"Never came up," she says. "You're the one who assumed I was from Miami. Had you asked, I'd have told you."

"I'll be sure to ask more questions, then."

He smiles when he says it. It's a kind smile, a little suggestive, but it doesn't seem predatory. Just interested. And I want to punch that smile right off his face. My jaw hurts from how hard I'm gritting my teeth, and if they don't break eye contact soon, I'll break it for them.

"Would you two stop eye-fucking," Jonah says with a groan. "We have shit to do. Eye-fuck later."

"Maybe just real fuck and put us out of our misery," Sean adds.

He rolls his eyes like he's disgusted, and it tenses my shoulders. I'm staring daggers at him when Mabel nudges my arm. When I glance at her she's grinning, then she jerks her head toward a door behind her.

"Want to help us set up, roadie?"

I glance once more at the guys. Sean and Jonah have disappeared, but Torren is is watching me closely. Then I return Mabel's grin.

"Just tell me what to do."

I follow her to an alley behind the bar and find a van packed full of stuff. I want to turn around and see what Sav is doing with Torren, but I don't. Instead, I watch as Mabel opens the back of the van, pulls out a bass drum with a grunt, and gives it to me.

"We don't have a name yet," she says, stacking a tom drum on top of the bass that I'm holding. Then she grabs some metal poles—drum stands—and nods for me to go back inside. "Torren wants to call us The Eff Em. Like, as in FM radio, but spelled out e-f-f-e-m so it looks like fuck them."

Our eyes meet and we share a grimace.

"Yeah, we don't like it either," she says with a laugh. "Right now, we're on the fliers as Savannah Alt. and everyone just assumes we're from Georgia. But really, it's just 'cause when we got the gig, the bartender filled out the paperwork with Sav's name and our music genre as a placeholder, and we never changed it."

"Savannah Alt. actually isn't a bad one."

I follow her lead as she heads to the stage area and sets up the drum stands, then I put my haul down and trail her back outside for more.

"It's not bad, but Savannah doesn't like it." Mabel laughs. "Sav even wanted to use her stripper name because she didn't want people to think we named the band after her, but we told her that was stupid."

"Vixen Viper," I drawl with a smile, my mind drifting back to our interaction at the club.

"That's the one." Mabel hands me a guitar case and another tom drum, then hops out of the van with drumsticks in her back pocket and cymbals under her arms. "C'mon. We'll get these in, and then you can help the guys with the rest."

"So how long have you known Savannah?" I ask as I help her set up the drum set. And by "help," I mean I hand her things when she asks for them and try to stay out of the way otherwise.

"A little over a year. We met in Nashville."

"Nashville?"

My curiosity is piqued. What has Sav done since she left? Where has she been? How did she end up here, in Miami, working as a stripper and playing in an alternative rock band with an idiot named Sean and a fuckboy named Torren? I want to know everything.

"Yeah. We were, uh, *staying* at the same place." Mabel flicks her eyes to me quickly then darts them away. "Anyway, we hit it off and when she decided to come to Miami, I came with her."

I stare at her for a moment, willing her to say more. When she doesn't, I go back to playing roadie.

Soon, laughter brings me out of my thoughts, and I catch sight of Savannah and Torren coming back in from the alley. They're both smiling, and he's giving her that *look* again. The one that makes me see red. When he says something that makes her smack him playfully in the side, I force myself to look away.

"Anything going on between them?" The question doesn't faze Mabel at all. It's almost like she was expecting it.

"He wishes," she says with a scoff. "But Savvy would never. This band is too important to her. She doesn't want to fuck it up."

I want to bristle at Mabel's confirmation that Torren wants something from Sav. Then I want to heave a sigh of relief at knowing Sav isn't interested. But what grabs my attention is the last point Mabel made. *The band is too important.*

I never knew Savannah to be musically inclined.

I was the one in band despite being terrible at it. Sav never showed any interest in playing an instrument or singing. I don't even recall her mentioning popular musicians or songs. The fact that she's in a band is extremely unexpected.

The moment the thought forms, I have to smile.

I suppose that's Savannah. Everything she does is unexpected. She's as unpredictable as a hurricane. Forget Vixen Viper as her stage name. She should have chosen Tempest.

"Done?" Jonah asks, stepping up onto the stage and handing me a drink.

I take it and nod my thanks. I don't want to be rude.

"We're done," Mabel says, coming to stand next to me as Savannah, Torren, and Sean join us. "No thanks to you losers."

Sean laughs. "It's not my fault your instrument has a gazillion parts. Should have learned to play something that comes in fewer pieces. Easy in, easy out."

"Just how you like it," Torren drawls, and Sean sends him a wink.

"Exactly."

Savannah sighs loudly and shoves past the guys, then snatches my hand. Without saying anything, she tugs me off the stage and over to a table against the wall. She pulls the high-top stool out, then puts her hands on my torso and maneuvers me backward until I'm sitting. The whole thing is awkward and silly, but that doesn't stop me from fixating on the way the heat of her hands seeps through my thin shirt and warms my skin.

"Is this where you want me?" I ask, setting my drink on the tabletop.

She nods, then raises a brow at the glass.

"What are you drinking? How'd you get it?"

"Jonah."

I study the mystery beverage. Something caramel brown on ice with a twist of orange rind floating at the top. I'm not old enough to get anything from the bar on my own, and I've only tried alcohol a few times, so when he handed it to me, I took it.

"Is it safe?"

Sav laughs. "If you're asking if it's good booze, the answer is probably no. If you're asking if you'll die from drinking it, the answer is also probably no."

I start to laugh with her, but the sound dies on my tongue the moment she moves into my space. On instinct, I widen my legs so she can step between them, and she leans her hip against my inner thigh. I inhale deeply and fix my eyes on hers, refusing to let them wander to her purple bra and bare stomach. For the briefest moment, I catch a spark of nerves in her gray eyes.

"Is this your first show?"

She nods and sinks her teeth into her lower lip.

"Our first big one, yeah." She reaches out and fidgets with the hem on my t-shirt. My ab muscles tighten on impulse, and I do my best to keep my cool. "We've played some house parties. A few dive bars. Once we played at some random illegal rave thing in a parking lot. But this is the first gig where we're actually getting paid more than a hundred bucks. They've advertised us. We're on the marquee. We're even on their social media page."

"This is awesome, Sav. You're going to be great."

She clicks her tongue sarcastically and cocks her head.

"How do you know? You've never heard us. For all you know we could suck hardcore."

I smirk at her attitude, then reach out and give a strand of her dark brown hair a light tug.

"Because you're a star, Savannah Shaw. A force of nature. A tempest. You'll knock them all on their asses, and they'll be begging you to do it again before the night is over. It's just the way you are. You can't help it."

Her cheeks tint pink and her full lips curve upward, but she doesn't say anything. She just locks me in with those swirling silver depths. When she opens her mouth to speak, feedback shoots through the speakers on the stage, making us both jump, then someone is saying "sound check" into the microphone. We look toward the stage and find Torren standing at the mic glaring at us.

I'm not surprised he's the frontman. Lead singer. Probably lead guitarist, too. Jealousy surges when Sav gives my thigh a little squeeze, then walks away from me without another word.

Savannah steps onto the stage, and I watch in awe as the lights illuminate her every feature. The girl was made to be under a spotlight. I think part of me always knew it. She was always meant for something bigger than a dingy bedroom and a joyless life in our nowhere hometown.

For some reason, I expect Savannah to head to the small keyboard, away from centerstage, the mic, and the attention. Instead, I'm taken aback when Torren makes a show of stepping away from the lead microphone and presenting it to her. My slack jaw falls wide open when she not only takes her place at the mic, but then turns and takes a white electric guitar from Jonah.

She slings the strap over her head, strums the strings once, then finally looks in my direction. I know I'm gaping. Her grin makes my heart pound and my dick harden. Then, she licks her lips and leans in close to the mic.

"How's everyone doin' tonight?"

I'm shocked by the way Savannah's voice transforms through the microphone. She evolves underneath the stage lights. It's still Savannah, but it's like I'm experiencing her on an entirely different plane. Sure, she looks hot as hell and twice as sinful, but it's more than that. She's magnetic. Her voice is sexy, lilting and raspy with a sharp edge. You can *hear* the smirk. You can *hear* the mischief. It's damn near hypnotizing.

I glance around the packed bar and find I'm not the only one who's felt it.

People who were playing pool before have put up their sticks. Bodies at the bar have turned all the way around so they can face the stage. Even the bartenders are fixated on Sav because no one is bothering them for drinks. The crowd cheers. Someone whistles. Everyone claps. She's spoken four words and has them wrapped around her finger.

"Now that's what we like to hear, isn't it guys?" Savannah drags her eyes off me to glance over her shoulder at Mabel, and Mabel pounds out a quick beat in agreement.

More cheers. More whistles.

"Thank you. We're Savannah Alt. We've got Jonah playing lead guitar over there, Sean on the keyboard, Torren rocking on the bass, Mabel beating on the drums, and my name's Savannah. Let's fucking rock."

Following Sav's lead, they launch straight into a rendition of a 90's alternative rock hit, and all I can do is stare. I had no idea she could sing. It's just as sexy as her speaking voice, but ten times more powerful. She's not just reciting lyrics. She's *becoming* them.

Her delicate fingers work the strings on the guitar with practiced ease. A few times, when she's not singing, she plays a lead guitar riff that absolutely blows me away, and I don't know where I want to settle my attention. Her fingers playing the instrument, or her mouth crooning the song.

She's amazing. The whole band is great, but Sav is the star. Sav is the magic.

They go through a handful of covers, each one just as good as the last, when the music fades and Sav turns to speak to Mabel. They exchange a few words, then Sav looks at the guys and nods before turning back to the mic.

"Alright, South Beach, how 'bout a new twist on an old favorite?"

People go nuts, and for the first time since she started singing, I glance back at the crowded bar. I'm floored.

The place is packed. The number of people in here has doubled since the set started, and everyone, I mean everyone, has their eyes on Savannah. Not the band. Sav. When I swing my attention back to the stage, though, the woman everyone's eyes are on is looking right at me.

"I have a good friend visiting tonight," she says slowly into the mic, her impish grin stretching over her face. "Leviticus, told ya the universe wasn't done with us. This one's for you."

She starts to play something on the guitar—some riff that sounds vaguely familiar, but I can't quite place—before Mabel joins in on the drums. When Torren, Sean, and Jonah start to play, the melody pulls at a memory just out of my reach. I know this song, but I don't know what it is yet.

Sav glances at me and laughs, then sends me a wink I feel in my gut. When she starts to sing, I can't stop my smile from taking over my face. It's "Wagon Wheel" by Old Crow Medicine Show, but they've tweaked it. Made it less Americana folk and a little more rock and roll, and it's good. Really good.

If nothing else solidified it tonight, this does. The way she can take this song and make it something else entirely. The way she can make anything better just by touching it.

Savannah Shaw is going to be the reason this band goes anywhere, and before she finishes the song, I know. I can see it, crisp and clear as if it were playing out in front of me.

This is going to be something. Something big.

Savannah Shaw has always been made for something better than our hometown, but I didn't realize just what that meant until this moment.

It creates a tight, sinking feeling in my chest, and suddenly I'm back outside my childhood bedroom, listening to her footsteps fade into the darkness.

"What did you think?" Sav asks after her show, her voice mixing with the sound of the ocean breaking on the shore. From her smile, she already knows what I'm going to say.

"You were brilliant," I say honestly. "Absolutely amazing. When did you learn to play guitar?"

Jonah hands Sav another shot, and she swallows it back quickly, swaying a little on her feet. I've been holding the same drink since we got here. At the bar, I nursed the strange whiskey and orange beverage Jonah gave me for the whole set. When we left the bar and came to the beach, he miraculously produced another one for me in a red plastic cup.

I don't even know where he's getting the liquor from.

"Busking in Nashville," Savannah says after wincing through her shot. "That's how I met Mabes. Me and her were part of this group. Like a little community of misfit delinquents."

She giggles and turns her head to Mabel, who is currently making out with her girlfriend in the sand. I look away. Mabel introduced me to her, but I don't remember her name. Some kind of gemstone. Diamond or Crystal or something. The single whiskey drink I've had has fogged me up a bit.

"We lived with this guy named Oscar—me and Mabel and probably twelve other kids. The number was always changin', ya know? Hard to keep runaways in one place. Anyway, Oscar was like fifty, and he had this old house that we all stayed in, and he taught me how to play the guitar so I could busk. Everyone did something different, and that's how we bought food and paid rent and stuff."

I blink at her.

"So, he basically exploited kids who had nowhere else to go?"

She grins, then calls out to Mabel without taking her eyes off me.

"Hey Mabes. You think Oscar exploited us?"

Mabel doesn't miss a beat. She pulls away from her girlfriend long enough to shout, "Definitely."

Then she and her girlfriend laugh before going back to making out.

Sav chuckles, then shrugs.

"I don't mind. I learned to play the guitar, which I love, and I'm one hell of a pickpocket now, too."

"You're a pickpocket?" I ask incredulously, and she rolls her eyes.

"Don't be such a weenie."

I work to hide my smile as I shake my head.

I'm working up the nerve to ask another question when Torren and Sean sidle up next to Savannah, and Torren throws his arm around her. My shoulders stiffen, and I grit my teeth as I watch the exchange. He pulls her into his body, and she leans against him. I tell myself it's just because she's had a few shots.

"Want to have some fun, Savvy?" Torren holds out his palm, flashing a few white pills, and Savannah grins up at him, then flashes a trouble-making glance my way.

"How straight edge are you, exactly, Leviticus?"

She cocks her head to the side as she watches me, taunting me just like she would when we were kids, and I shake my head slowly, biting back a smile.

"Still pretty straight edge."

She hums, her Cheshire smile taming to something sweeter, and her eyes soften. She bites her lip, then laughs lightly.

"Good."

"Good?"

"Yeah." She kicks a little sand onto my barefoot. "I like you how you are."

The way my stomach jumps is so unexpected, and all I can do is stare at her with a stupid half-smile on my face.

I'm about to open my mouth to speak, to tell her I like her how she is too, when she smiles back up at Torren, and opens her mouth for him. I watch, jealousy clawing at my chest and rage burning the butterflies that were lapping my insides seconds earlier, as Torren places one of the white pills on her tongue. She closes her mouth, swallows, then tips her head back to the night sky. Then Torren hands something to Sean and Sean puts it in his mouth.

The whole scene shocks me, so I just stand there and watch. I want to ask Sav what the hell she's doing. Drugs? After everything she went through with her mom and her mom's boyfriend, how could she be okay with doing drugs? I want to scold her. I want to pick her up and take her home. Make her spit out whatever it is she just took.

But then Torren runs his hand down Sav's back, and I grow angry for a different reason. I clench my fists when he leans down and says something in her ear. Her eyes pop open and a smile stretches her face.

"Okay," she says to him, then swings her attention to me.

I stand a little taller when she steps out of Torren's hold. Briefly, I let myself glance at him, and my pride bolsters when I see him scowling.

Good.

Savannah takes both my hands in hers. "Let's dance."

Despite my disapproval, my lips curve upward. "There's no music."

She laces her fingers with mine, then starts to step backward, steering me away from Torren and closer to the surf. My fingers tingle wrapped up with hers. I feel it running up my arms and into my chest.

"So?" She releases one of my hands, then twirls herself in a circle before spinning into my chest in a way that wraps my arm around her. "We can pretend."

Once again, we're so close that I can feel her breath on my skin. If I bent down just a few inches, I could kiss her. I'll do anything she wants to in this moment. I'll dance for hours with no music, just the memories of her on stage replaying in my head. Anything she asks. I'm that tangled up in her.

We both jump when actual music starts to play, and we look up the beach to see a Jeep rolling slowly toward us, stereo turned all the way up. Jonah jogs to the vehicle and slaps hands with whoever's driving, and then I look back at Savannah.

"Now we don't have to pretend," she says.

Her body starts to sway back and forth to the music, and something about her movements tells me whatever Torren gave her is already starting to take hold. She lifts her arms above her head and rotates her hips. It's languid and hypnotic, and when she reaches out and places my hands on her waist, I almost feel high, too.

"Now we can do it for real."

10

My body tingles.

For hours or minutes, I can't tell. I'm humming, buzzing. A neon sign. A flowing web of kinetic energy. Every movement creates waves of color. Every touch an explosion of sensations.

The delicate skin at my waist vibrates where he rests his hands, emanating to every sensitive, intimate spot. Behind my ear. The nape of my neck. Between my legs. My hard nipples rub at the fabric of my bra, and I want more.

A giggle bubbles out of me.

I laugh and laugh, blissful, then press closer, needing his skin on mine. Needing to erase the colorful waves that separate us.

"Are you okay?"

His voice is low. Low and so, so sweet. He's always been so sweet. His concern for me. His care. His deep timbre echoes around me, blanketing me, and I breathe it in. I press my hands to his chest, feel his skin mold with mine through thin cotton, then wrap my arms around his neck.

"Sav."

He's at my ear. Inside my head. I lean my whole body on him. I want to melt into him. He laughs, his chest rumbling against mine, and I moan. The way it feels against my nipples. My pussy. Everything pulses in the most delicious way.

"Do you want to sit?"

"Mmmm." I press my nose into his neck. "You smell good."

His throat contracts. I can hear his hard swallow. I kiss his Adam's apple, and his body quakes. I want more.

I gaze up at him. His halo of stars is bright, making his handsome face glow. His eyebrows are slanted. His full lips are downturned, and I run my fingers over them.

I remember this mouth.

"So stern." I rub my thumb back and forth over his plush lower lip. "But so soft."

Out of curiosity, I push my thumb into his mouth, and mine opens on a gasp when he sucks, the pad of my thumb caressed by his hot tongue. His fingers dig into my sides, sinking through the soft flesh and tickling. Something firm presses into my hip, and I press back. I drag the pad of my thumb over his bottom teeth and a whimper escapes. Mine? His? I'm not sure, but I *feel* it.

Slowly, smoothly, I slide my thumb from his mouth and into mine. I want to taste him. Want to feel what he felt. I imagine my thumb as his. My mouth as his. My head clouds with more colorful waves—a thicker, more liquid sensation—and I rise on my tiptoes, fusing our lips together.

He opens, and I'm awash in the flavor of him.

Citrus lips. Whiskey tongue.

So soft. So soft.

I'm spinning around him. We're spinning together. The breeze tickles my skin, cooling every place that he heats. I seek out his tongue, in and out, to the tune of the surf ebbing and flowing. I latch onto his body. I pull him close. Closer. Closer still.

"Slow down."

The soft words dance over my face, leaving me cold, and I hear him chuckle.

"I don't want to go slow," I tell him. "I want to make it all up."

The time. I want to make up the time. What we've lost. What we'll lose. I try to explain but the words stick to my tongue, and all I want to do is breathe them into him.

"C'mon."

His warm hand encases mine, and I close my eyes and let him lead me. The sand feels gritty and strange between my toes, and I flex them back and forth as we walk, sending electric shocks up my calves and thighs. I squeeze his hand and press my thighs together. My stomach jumps. My pussy throbs.

I open my eyes as the music gets louder, wrapping me up with sound.

"Why are we back here?"

I roll my head to him and his smile glows. I put my fingers on his lips again, seeking out his heat. When he speaks, his mouth drags over the pads of my fingertips, burning my fingerprints. I think they're altered forever.

"We can't have you running off into the surf, Sav. We should stick close to your friends."

I shake my head no, the motion slow and heavy. I smile back at him as he laughs, rumbling my chest and between my legs.

"I want to go home," I tell him. My voice sounds wistful and dreamy in my own ears. "I want to go home with you."

"Okay. I can get you home. Wait right here. Don't try to wander off again. I'll be right back."

He lets go of my hand, and I frown down at it. It's empty and alone now. I close my eyes. He's gone, but I'll wait. I hum along with the music, swaying back and forth to the tune.

Hands wrap around my waist, and I sink into him. Lips press into my neck, and I tilt my head to the side, reaching for him, wanting more. His mouth moves to mine, and when it lands, I pull away.

It's wrong. Spicy. Not citrus. Tequila. Not whiskey.

I open my eyes, and instead of brown, I'm met with blue.

"Sean?"

"Want to get out of here, Savvy?"

He leans back in for my lips, slow motion cutting through the color, and I dodge him.

"Yeah."

I do want to get out of here. I'm leaving with Levi. I open my mouth to say that, but I'm smothered with spice and tequila and someone else. I shove at his chest, twist my body to make room between us, but it doesn't work. I swing through the color, but nothing happens.

"Sean. Get off," I mumble against his mouth, trying to shake my head.

"Savvy."

His voice is a moan. I feel tentacles or ropes or hands on my hips, my ass, my chest. I push and push, and my shoulders burn.

"Off, Sean. No."

It's wrong. It's all wrong. The taste. The feel. The man. I twist again, bring my knee up into something soft, and he grunts. His weight is heavier, suffocating, and then...

He's gone.

I shake my head, open my eyes, and watch as Levi shoves Sean. Sean swings at him, and I yell. In my head? Out loud? Stop. No. Don't hurt him. Then Torren comes out of nowhere and shoves Levi. Levi stumbles backward, but rights himself quickly and lunges at Torren.

"She said no."

Levi growls, throwing his own fist and landing it on Torren's jaw, then kicking at Sean on the ground. I see the colors explode, shock waves flowing outward from the impact. Red. Deep red.

"What the fuck," Torren yells. Throws his body into Levi. "Get the fuck off of him."

Levi twists. Torren hits the sand. I feel the Earth quake. He yells something, vulgar and rude, then tries to stand.

"You're a damn pathetic mess."

I can hear the patronizing tone in Levi's voice, the disgust, and my lips turn down. My eyebrows grow heavier. He's stern again. Scowling and angry.

"What the fuck?" *Jonah.*

Jonah falls to the sand next to Torren, looks at Sean, then looks up at me. His jaw drops, and he whispers my name, then turns an angry face back to Sean and Torren. Angrier than I have ever seen Jonah.

I glance down at myself. My shirt is off one arm. My bra is askew, barely covering me. The button on my shorts is undone. The ocean breeze dances over bare skin—more than there was before—and my cheeks are cold. Wet. Like I'm crying.

Sean did this?

I look at Levi, but he's staring daggers at Jonah, Torren, and Sean. He flings a finger at all of them.

"Get him out of here before I kill him," he says, and I shiver. He's not lying. I can feel it in his tone. "He's fucked up. She said *no*. He *hurt* her. He tried to—"

"I wasn't hurtin' her," Sean defends, at the same time Torren shouts, "dude, calm down."

I feel eyes on me, but I keep mine on Levi. My chest aches at the look on his face. Anguish. Fear. Rage. He whirls on Torren.

"Calm down? You're trying to fucking protect this fuck when you should be protecting, Savannah," Levi growls. "Do you see what he did to her?"

Torren looks at me.

"Savvy, I—"

"Don't fucking talk to her. Don't look at her. Go home. Go the fuck home and take that guy with you."

I don't hear anything else from Torren, Jonah, or Sean. I don't look at them. I just watch as Levi stalks toward me and then stops in front of me, shielding my body from the guys. Carefully, with a touch that's impossibly soft, he buttons my shorts back up, then rights my shirt and buttons it up to my neck. His skin never touches my skin. The colors remain swirling thickly between us.

"You okay?"

I look into his eyes and breathe a sigh of relief. Dark, dark brown. I nod.

"Yes. Thank you."

His eyes search mine. His eyebrows still slanted and harsh. I reach up and smooth my thumb between them, erasing the lines there before tracing my fingers over both eyebrows, down his jaw, over the cute little dimple in his chin, and back to his lips.

Softly, he presses a kiss to my fingertips, then nods. He pulls my body under his arm, and I sink into his warmth once more.

"I'll take you home."

I follow him, through the sand and up the beach. He finds my boots and slips them on my feet. We step onto pavement. We walk on a sidewalk, then stop at a curb where a car waits, exhaust mixing with the briny, humid air. Levi opens the back door, maneuvers me inside, then climbs in next to me. I rest my head on his shoulder and keep my eyes shut for the drive. I focus on the way his hands feel on my arm, trailing sparks up and down. The weight of his cheek resting on my head.

When the car stops, he slides out, then helps me out to stand next to him. I look up at a familiar building and smile. My house. We walk to the door, and he turns the knob.

"Damn."

My foggy brain knows it's locked. My roommate is working tonight.

"The frog," I say, and raise a heavy hand to point at the little ceramic frog holding a pin wheel to the right of the door. Levi looks where I'm pointing, then bends down and lifts the frog.

"Thank you," he mumbles as he fits the key into the knob, then swings the door open slowly.

He shuffles me into the house, and I cling to his hand, leading him to my room.

"Will you be alright?"

He stands in my doorway, arms folded across his chest, eyeing me with concern that makes my heart squeeze and my stomach flip.

"Are you going to leave?" I hear myself ask, and he shrugs. I shake my head. "Stay."

I start to unbutton my shirt and he turns around. Another giggle.

More laughter. He's laughing, too. I can tell. I strip naked while his back is turned, then slip a large shirt over my head before stepping into a pair of underwear.

I'm still wobbly, but not as much as before. The colors are still here, but muted. My senses are dulling, my energy draining, but the pulsing at my core is still strong. I climb onto my mattress.

"Levi," I say softly.

He turns toward me, and I pat the bed. He doesn't move except for a twitch in his jaw. I smile and roll my eyes, then pat the bed again.

Slowly, he kicks off his shoes, then closes the distance between us. He lowers himself down next to me, and I lie my head on the pillow. He does the same. For a moment, we just lie there, gazing at each other. I listen to him breathe. I watch the emotions battle in his eyes as I feel my own eyes drifting shut.

I don't want to fall asleep. I don't want this to end.

I scoot closer and put my lips on his once more. He still tastes like whiskey. Like citrus. I whimper as his tongue tangles with mine. When he groans, I put my hands on him, tugging at his belt. Fumbling with the buckle.

He wraps his hand around mine, firm but gentle, and halts my movements.

"Sleep, Sav," he says against my lips. I pull back to look at him, but my eyes won't open. "Sleep."

My body starts to obey despite my protests.

"I want you." My voice is a rasp, my words thick and heavy. Lust. Exhaustion. The come down. "I want you, Levi."

Gently, he moves his hand to my shoulder and turns me, then wraps his arm around my body and pulls me to his chest. His breath tickles my scalp. His palm rests on my hip. My body relaxes, like it used to when he'd hold me like this. Safe and warm and finally able to rest.

"I want you," I mumble again through tired lips.

His arms tighten around me. His heart thunders against my

back. When he speaks, it's a whisper. Almost a plea. I barely hear it, but it's there.

"Then still want me tomorrow."

When I wake, it's nearly dawn.

My sad little window AC unit whines under the weight of the humid heat, and my bedsheets stick to my bare legs. Levi's arms tighten around me, the steady rhythm of his breathing catapulting me backward into his childhood bedroom.

I still can't believe he's here.

Slowly, careful not to wake him, I roll over, so we're face to face. In the semi-darkness, I can barely make out his features, but I don't need to see them to know them. Even three years later, I could draw him from memory. When we're old and wrinkled, I'll still recognize him. Age doesn't change the way a soul feels.

When we were fifteen, I'd lie like this and watch him sleep before I had to slip out the window and leave the safety of his room. I'd study him, memorizing every freckle, every eyelash, every dream-filled pout and pained whimper. Even when he was close, he felt unattainable. Too good. Too pure. I'd tease him about it, but deep down, I agreed with his mother. I knew I'd ruin him. I'd dirty him up, tarnish his shiny gold halo, and set fire to his perfect angel wings.

Flashes of memories flicker in and out of my head, pictures of scenes from hours earlier. I close my eyes and try to bring them into focus, but everything is blurred on the edges. Like I was a witness, not a participant, watching through thick, colorful smoke.

My fingers burn, and I remember running them over Levi's lips. Remember kissing him. Citrus and whiskey. Did it really happen, or was it just another one of my intoxicated dreams? Drunk or high, every time, I've dreamt of him.

I snake my hand between us, raise it to his mouth, and lightly trace his lips. His brow furrows in sleep and his nose scrunches up, and I stifle a laugh. Then I do it again, running the pads of my fingers over his lower lip.

"What are you doing?"

His gruff voice makes me jump, and I let out a startled squeak. He smirks, but he doesn't open his eyes, and I huff, giving his chest a shove.

"You scared me, you ass."

He tightens his arms around me and peeks one eye open.

"Why are you feeling me up like a creep?"

I wipe my face of expression, then raise a brow slowly.

"Just seein' if you were real."

He opens his other eye and smiles softly.

"I'm real if you're real."

My eyes bounce between his. His face becoming clearer with every minute of the sunrise.

"How are you feeling?" he asks, his voice still rough from sleep. I shrug.

"Fine. Why?"

"You were pretty out of it last night..." He lets the statement trail off, and he studies me, searching my face for I don't know what. "What do you remember?"

I sift through my brain before speaking, then list everything I know was real.

"A party on the beach. A bonfire. Wading into the ocean. Losing one of my earrings. Dancing with you. Mabes and Crystal got into a fight, then made up, then left together after Jonah told them to stop boning on the beach."

I giggle and Levi's lips quirk up. He nods. Mabel was so mad at Jonah, but that's nothing new. Those two fight like siblings. I'd be worried about how it would affect the band if I wasn't sure it came from a good place. Jonah is a protector and a planner. Mabel is the opposite, so they butt heads.

When Levi's smile fades, the back of my neck prickles.

"What?" He doesn't answer right away, so I press again. "*What*, Levi?"

"Do you remember anything with Sean?"

I want to fidget under his focused gaze. I want to look away, but I don't. Instead, I search his eyes as I fumble through my memories of the night before. Torren. The molly. Then Sean...

My head jerks back, and my eyes widen. Levi folds his lips between his teeth and nods slowly. I shake my head back and forth.

"No..." I breathe out. No way. That couldn't have been real.

"Yeah, and your fucking bassist tried to defend him. Was going to let him do it."

No. Sean would never. He's always been flirty, but he flirts with everyone, and Torren would never let anyone hurt me.

"Yeah, Sav," Levi says slowly. "You were telling him no. You were struggling. If I hadn't..."

He clamps his eyes shut and his nostrils flare, his jaw so tight it could slice through me.

"And then Torren fucking tried to fight me for pulling that sleazeball off you."

"He was probably confused," I say quickly, and Levi's eyes pop back open. I don't know why I need to defend Torren, but I do. "He probably didn't understand what was going on. He was tripping. He was on drugs. He was confused. Sean is Torren's brother. He didn't know."

"Savannah," Levi says, and his dark tone sends a shiver down my spine. "There is no excuse. None. Definitely not for what Sean did, and not for Torren either."

I bristle at the authority in his voice, the patronizing attitude behind it. I want to argue with him, to tell him he doesn't know Torren or Sean. It's none of his business. He needs to back off.

But then I remember something else.

The careful way Levi buttoned up my shirt and refastened my shorts. How he brought me home and stayed when I asked. *Get him out of here before I kill him.* The way my heart races...

So, I nod.

"You're right," I tell him. "There's no excuse. I'm going to talk to him. To all of them."

He's quiet again, searching my face with a furrowed brow, trying to find the lie. I roll my eyes and shove his chest again.

"I'm serious. I'm bein' honest. You are right, and I will talk to them."

The sun is up now, and my room is filled with the early morning glow. It hasn't escaped my attention that Levi's arms are still around me despite the rising temperature. He's still holding me, and I'm still letting him. It's unnerving. I can't get this close if I'm just going to have to say goodbye again.

"I'm never up this early," I say with a forced grin. "Want to go get pancakes?"

11

"HOW ARE you going to eat all of that?"

Levi eyes my gigantic stack of chocolate chip pancakes curiously. His head is cocked to the side, his mouth quirked up in a cute little bemused smile. I shove another forkful into my mouth and talk to him while I chew just to watch his nose scrunch in disgust.

"I jus' am," I mumble, then have to stifle a giggle because he looks absolutely appalled. I swallow, then take a drink from my water glass. "I'm hungry and these are delicious. It's better than that."

I flick my eyes to his plate—an egg white veggie omelet and dry wheat toast—then match his look of disgust. He laughs, and I roll my eyes, shoving another huge forkful of pancake into my mouth.

"So, how's school? You like it?"

He finishes chewing, swallows, then takes a sip of his orange juice and wipes his mouth with his napkin before responding. I narrow my eyes at him, and he smirks. What a proper little weenie.

"Yeah, I guess." Levi shrugs with a genuine smile. "I mean, it's school, but it's been great living on campus and meeting people and stuff."

I want to ask what *kind* of people. *Girl* people?

I want to ask if he has a girlfriend, but I don't actually want to know the answer, so I don't let the question leave my mouth. I think we kissed last night. Or, at least, I think I kissed him. Call me a selfish bitch, but I don't want anything to ruin that, even if it was just another figment of my drunken imagination. So instead of saying what I want, I do what I do best: I tease.

"You sure you're okay being away from Father Cooper? Has your momma moved into your dorm yet?"

"My dad's not a priest, Sav."

His tone is exasperated, but it's fake. He's amused. It makes me sit a little taller.

"Whatever." I take another bite of pancake and chew through a cheeky grin. "Same difference."

Levi chuckles and shakes his head.

"My mom has adjusted, but it doesn't matter anyway. I like where I'm at, and it's not up to them."

My eyes widen with surprise, and my lips part slightly. Not to be dramatic, but I have to swallow back a gasp. Levi was never one to disobey his parents. At least not so openly.

Actually, now that I think of it, I'm pretty sure *I* was the only rule he ever broke. And broke it repeatedly, despite the consequences.

I take another sip of my water before prodding.

"I'm surprised you're at UNC, and not some fancy private Jesus college learnin' how to follow in Father Cooper's footsteps."

"They tried. I said no. UNC has the better engineering program, and I got a scholarship, so I didn't need their money."

I stare openly, blinking. When he looks up from his plate and sees my face, he barks out a laugh.

"What? Stop looking at me like I've been body snatched."

"I'm just surprised, is all. Openly defying the parents? Turning down a life for Jesus so you can go party it up with co-eds? Who even are you, Levi Cooper?"

He rolls his eyes, an amused smile on his lips and a pink blush dusting his ears.

"A lot has changed since you left, Sav."

I watch as he cuts another perfectly bite-sized piece of boring vegetable omelet with his knife and fork. He puts the fork in his mouth, chews approximately twenty-four times before swallowing, then wipes his mouth gently with his napkin and places it back on his lap.

I snort. So polite. So dainty. Such a proper, well-mannered weenie.

A lot might have changed, but not everything, and that makes my cheeks warm and my heart twist up in my chest. I make sure my next forkful of chocolate chip pancake is extra big before I speak to him again, and from the way his lips twitch, fighting a smile, I'm pretty sure he's thinking the same thing I am.

"Architectural engineering sounds cool," I say. "You wanna do what? Build houses?"

"Yeah, maybe." He shrugs with a grin, then his eyes grow wide with excitement. "But big houses. Mansions in Hollywood for celebrities, or giant beachfront summer houses in the Hamptons for those rich bankers and politicians and whoever else lives up there. Grand, sprawling art you can live in."

My smile matches his, his energy and excitement fueling mine. I can see him practically buzzing with it. These plans, these dreams. He's talking about building houses the way I talk about writing songs. It's not just a future career. It's a future *life*. One he can't wait to begin.

"When I get famous—when I can actually afford your grand, sprawling art—you gonna build me a house?" I nudge his shoe, then shove another bite of pancake into my mouth.

"I'll build you one anyway," he says, and his eyes lock with mine. His smile softens. "Something special, with a recording studio for you to make music, and a closet for your skateboards, and a pool so you never have to go to the beach. A chef's kitchen for making gourmet chocolate chip pancakes. Big windows so you get all the natural light. Maybe even a room with a pole so you can practice if you want."

The last sentence is said playfully, and I roll my eyes with a shaky laugh.

"I'll design every inch of it just for you, Sav," he says, voice low and serious. "Only for you."

My cheeks heat as he looks me over, and I pull my lower lip between my teeth. His eyes caress my face, his soft smile is so inviting that I can almost imagine his lips on mine again. My heart is racing, my fingers trembling. I don't even know why I'm so emotional, except maybe the idea of a house built just for me, a real-life actual *home* of my own, means more than I let myself realize. And maybe the fact that he still knows me that well shocks me in the best way.

I swallow, lick my lips and force myself to speak. It's a rasped, shaky whisper.

"And you're going to be my neighbor?"

He waits, brown eyes boring into mine, lips twitching ever-so slightly. I can see his pulse thrumming in his neck. He taps his finger slowly on the table.

"Maybe. Or maybe I'll live there with you."

My heart squeezes in my chest, so tight that my lips part on a small gasp. God. I didn't know I wanted that until right now.

A waitress startles us, and we break eye contact as she drops the check on the table and refills our waters.

"Can I get you guys anything else?"

"No, thank you," Levi says, giving her a smile.

I return my attention to my food, but watch her walk away in my periphery, before taking a deep breath and changing the subject.

"So, I guess you have to get back to your friends soon."

I say the words into my plate, forcing a lightness into them I don't feel. I make work of using my fork to cut some pancake and I wait for his answer, but then his shoe nudges mine under the table. I look up and meet his eyes. He's smiling at me. A stupid and lopsided smile that has my lips turning up to match.

"I don't have to get back to them."

That's all he says, but it fills me back up with a giddy excitement

I haven't felt in a while. In three years, probably. Not since the night outside his bedroom window when he asked if he could kiss me. I swallow back my desire to dance in my seat, to giggle like an idiot, and instead, I tame my smile and nod.

"Cool."

After we finish our breakfast, I call Jonah.

I have a few missed calls from him, and I texted him this morning that I was fine, and I'd call him later. When he answers, he sounds rough, like I just woke him up.

"What?"

"Ooof. D'you go hard last night?" I say with a laugh, but he doesn't answer me.

Instead, he perks up and starts talking a mile a minute. The exhaustion in his tone is gone, and it's replaced with panicked concern.

"Are you okay, Savvy? I'm so fucking sorry. Torren says Sean feels like shit, but I still kicked his ass. How are you feeling? Shit, Sav. We can find someone else to play keyboard tonight. I swear, we c—"

"Whoa, slow it down, Jonah," I say, cutting off his breathless tirade. "I'm okay. I'm fine. Levi brought me home and filled me in."

"Sean's banned. He's not allowed around again. I called around to some friends. I got someone who can fill in for the show toni—"

"Dude, chill. We can't get a new keyboard player before tonight's show. That's crazy. It'll fuck everything up."

I flick my eyes to Levi. He's watching me intently, obviously eavesdropping. I pull an annoyed face at him and gesture for him to give me some privacy. He scowls but does as I ask. I lower my voice when I continue my phone call.

"Look Jo, you know Torren and Sean are the ones with the connection. If we want to play those shows up the coast, they have to be with us. We'll never keep Tor if we kick out Sean."

"That's bullshit, Savvy. We can find someone else. We'll make it work."

I sigh and close my eyes. Jonah is right, but he's also wrong.

Sure, we can find someone else, but only if we're okay giving up our chance at a tour. We can get rid of Sean as long as we're also okay getting rid of Torren. Torren won't stay if we kick out his brother. We'd have to replace half the band, and if we do that, there's no way we'll catch this break.

Fuck, this sucks.

More scenes have been clearing up in my memory. The way his hands felt, the forceful way he touched me. I think it hurt. I think I cried. I know I was scared.

I breathe through my nose and my shoulders fall.

Why does it always come to this bullshit? My plans and life always being upended by a man who can't keep his fucking hands to himself.

First Terry with his nasty comments and threats, thinking just because he could pimp my mom out for drugs, he could do the same to me. Then Mr. Oglesby, watching me shower and sleep. I woke up once with him standing over my bed in the middle of the night. I stopped sleeping after that.

Oscar was the worst. He wasn't sneaky or secretive. He was loud, his desires obvious. He didn't care who saw because he knew he could get away with whatever he wanted. He'd touch me—squeeze my boob or butt or put his hand high on my thigh—and if I pushed him away, he'd withhold food or allowance. When he started to mess with Mabel, though, that's when I knew I had to get out. I couldn't stand the thought of him punishing her just because I didn't want to give into his advances. If he started starving her the way he was trying to do to me, I might actually have given in.

God, and now this mess with Sean.

Miami was supposed to be my escape. I'm supposed to be in control now.

I'm so sick of being vulnerable. I'm so tired of being looked at as prey. Just once, I'd like something to *be* good and *stay* good. I deserve that, right? Not everything should have to be this difficult.

"I'm going to talk to him," I say finally. "We'll play tonight, and I'll talk to him after. Then we'll decide where to go from there."

Jonah grunts on the other end, but he doesn't say anything, so I change the subject.

"Anyway, that's not why I was callin'. What size shoe do you wear?"

Levi is terrible on rollerblades.

Luckily, Papa Jonah insisted he wear a helmet; otherwise, his head would look as beat up as his palms right now. Couple that with the bruise he got from Bobby, and Levi looks like he had quite the Miami spring break experience.

"C'mon," I say with a grin, rolling slowly on my skateboard down the boardwalk. "We'll never get there if you keep letting gravity make you its bitch."

Levi scowls at me, sweat dotting his forehead and making his arms glisten. He's wearing a black tank top I borrowed from my roommate's boyfriend, and the way his sculpted shoulders and biceps have tanned makes my throat tighten.

Definitely *not* fifteen anymore.

"Didn't Jonah have a bicycle I could borrow?"

"Yeah."

His eyes widen and he wobbles again on the rollerblades. "You did this on purpose."

I smirk. "Wanted to see if your balance had gotten any better."

He growls and makes a lunge for me, and I laugh before pushing off on my board. When I'm a distance away, I pop a kickflip and flash him a grin.

"Show off," he calls as he slowly and unsteadily closes the distance between us. I shrug.

"If you got it, flaunt it."

He tries so hard to fight his smile. He wants to act irritated, but it's the fact that he's not that makes me take mercy on him.

"Ohhhhkaaaay. Take 'em off. You can walk the rest of the way."

"Bless you," he breathes out, then falls to the ground.

As Levi takes off the rollerblades, I swing the backpack I'm wearing off and dig through it for his pretentious ass boat shoes. I toss them on the ground next to him and he slips them on. When he stands, I step off my board, stomp on the end and pop it up into my hand before slinging it under my arm. When I look at him, he's staring at me with one eyebrow raised.

"What?"

"You just can't help it, can you?"

I narrow my eyes.

"Help what?"

"Never mind." He shakes his head, a small secret smile on his lips. "Let's go."

We talk as we stroll down the boardwalk, and I find myself wondering if we'd be holding hands if ours weren't otherwise occupied. Him holding the rollerblades and helmet, me toting my skateboard. I've never really had a boyfriend, but this feels like something you'd do with one. Exploring the boardwalk together on a pretty afternoon.

I sneak glances at him from my periphery as we walk and a few times I catch him glancing back. My cheeks hurt from the number of smiles I'm trying to tame.

"We've got another show tonight," I tell him after we get ice cream and settle at a table outside the shop under a big blue sun umbrella. "If you want to come, I mean. It's at the same place."

He takes a bite of his strawberry ice cream, and I watch as his lips close over the white plastic spoon. I lick my mint chip off the cone and wait.

"I'd love to come, but I don't think I'm up for another after show beach trip."

He locks his eyes with mine and I see the anger there. He's still mad about last night. I think he might hate Torren and Sean.

Honestly, I don't blame him. I'd probably feel the same. But Levi is supposed to go back to North Carolina tomorrow night, and I'm not ready for him to go.

I'm trying to keep him with me as long as I can.

"No post-show rager, I promise."

"Okay, Rockstar. I'll be there."

12

"THANK YOU SO MUCH, South Beach. We've had a blast playing for you guys this weekend."

Clapping. Whistling. Cheering. It's just a popular beach bar, but it feels like Hard Rock Stadium, and I can't hide my happiness. I glance over my shoulder at Mabel, and she's grinning just as wide as I am. I lean back into the mic slowly, panting to catch my breath. I've never been this full of energy, and I try to keep my cool when I speak.

"Once again, just so you don't forget us, we're Savannah Alt. That's Mabel on the drums, Jonah on the guitar, Torren on the bass, Sean on the keyboard, and my name's Savannah. Have a great night!"

This show was phenomenal. It was the best one yet. I'm bouncing with excitement at how well it went. The bar was at capacity, and the guy who has been talking to Torren and Sean about possibly putting us on a small tour up the coast sent some random guy to come and record bits of the show on his phone.

That's got to be a good sign, right?

We played six originals. That's five more than we usually do, but the crowd clapped so loud after the first that we decided to try another one. After the second, they kept asking for more. My songs were a hit.

Lyrics and music *I* wrote.

Songs *I* sang.

The crowd loved them, and I loved it. I've got a notebook filled with more to share.

I've never been the focus of so much positive attention before, and it's been growing with each show. Even when I was busking in Nashville, I always had to read the crowd. Watch for cops or annoyed pedestrians. Once I had a whole soda dumped on me by an angry businessman in a suit.

Such a prick. It's always the ones who appear respectable that turn out to be the biggest assholes.

When the lights shut off and I put my guitar back on the stand, the only thing I want to do is jump off the stage and rush to Levi. No matter what happened during our show, every time my eyes landed on him, his were on me.

And his attention?

It was better than anything else.

I want to run straight to him, but I need to talk to Torren and Sean first. I have shit to say, and they need to listen. I chug the rest of my water bottle, hold up a *give me a minute* finger to Levi, then turn to face the stage.

I can't find Sean, but Torren is standing just off the side of the stage, texting someone on his phone. His hair is sweaty from the set and pushed back on his forehead, exposing dark eyebrows slanted in concentration. I don't know if the black eye and fat lip he's sporting are from Levi or Jonah, but I'd be lying if I said it didn't make me feel a little better about this whole thing.

I take a deep breath and walk up to him. We haven't spoken since I got here. He tried to apologize, but I shut him down. Told him we'd talk after, so here I am.

"Hey," I say, making him look up from his phone. "Got a minute?"

Torren nods and puts his phone in his pocket. `"Yeah. Want to talk out back?"

He looks so sad and nervous. Like a scolded puppy. It almost makes me feel bad. Almost. I tell Torren to lead the way, and I follow him through the door and into the alleyway where Jonah's van is parked. When the door shuts behind us, muffling the sounds coming from inside the bar, he puts his hands in his front pockets and lowers his eyes.

"I'm so fucking sorry, Savvy," he says, but he's talking to the ground.

It pisses me off. It feels like a cop out. I use my booted foot to kick some rocks in his line of sight.

"Say it to *me*, Torren, not the damn gravel."

He drags his eyes to mine, and I keep my face hard. When he doesn't speak, I wave a hand between us, prompting.

"I'm sorry. I don't even know what happened. I just saw Levi wailing on Sean."

I scoff and roll my eyes, my irritation flaring hotter.

"What happened is that you got us high, and then Sean tried to grope me. I trusted you guys. I know he's your brother, but you're supposed to be on my side."

"I am, Savannah. I swear. But it wasn't like that with Sean."

"Yes, it was! He twisted up my shirt and bra. He had my shorts undone—"

"He thought you were into it—"

"I said *NO*! I remember. I said *no*, Torren."

He drags a hand over his face, embarrassed or ashamed, I can't tell.

"God, Sav, I just...Sean says you said yes. He says you wanted it. He wouldn't do this."

I gasp, and my jaw drops.

"I tried to shove him off me! I kneed him in the gut. I was *crying*."

The words strangle my throat, and I feel like I might start crying again. It's strange, saying all of this out loud. Watching him react. Realizing that it actually *did* happen. I didn't misremember it. I was high, and someone I trusted took advantage.

"Savannah, I'm sorry. He would have stopped."

"That's a lie. He stopped because Levi made him stop, and now you're defending him? Even after I'm telling you what happened? You're taking Sean's word over mine? God, Levi was right. You don't care about me at all."

Torren's face turns angry, and he shakes his head.

"No, I didn't even know what was happening. I just saw your friend attacking Sean, and Sean is my fucking brother. He practically raised me, Savvy. But now, this Levi dick has to come in and pretend to be some gallant hero saving you from danger. It's *Sean*, Savvy. He's not a rapist. Your friend overreacted."

I take a step toward him, pointing right at his chest. It's taking all of my strength not to yell. Not to smack him. I've never been good at curbing my temper. Now's no exception. When I speak, my voice is shaking.

"You don't get to rewrite what happened, just so you feel better about it. You sure as hell don't get to talk shit about Levi. I don't care Sean's your brother. The truth is the truth. Sean forced himself on me, and Levi did what he did to protect me. Unlike *you*, and you gotta sit with that."

Torren's jaw pops as he clenches his teeth. His nostrils flare. He closes his eyes briefly, then opens them and sets them on me. I don't know what to expect. If he's going argue some more or apologize again, but I'm fifteen seconds from saying fuck it and leaving him in this alley. I'm so busy glaring at him, that when his phone rings, I actually jump.

His face wipes of the irritated expression and it's replaced with excitement. A bit of fear. He goes a little pale as he pulls his phone from his pocket, locking his eyes on me as he answers.

"Mr. Hammond. What's up, sir?"

My ears perk at the name. Hammond. That's Torren and Sean's contact. The man with the phone camera's boss. I watch Torren's face as he listens. I read into every muscle twitch. Every eyebrow dip. When his lips start to curve into a smile, I find mine mirroring his.

Oh my god.

Oh. My. God.

"Thank you," Torren says into the phone. "Thank you so much, Mr. Hammond. We'll be there first thing Monday morning. Yes. Okay. See you then."

He hangs up and slides his phone into his back pocket, then turns his smiling attention on me, one eyebrow arched playfully.

"Hey Savvy. Wanna go on tour?"

"Oh my god, are you kidding me?" I yell, then clasp my hands over my mouth to smother my uncontrollable giggles. "We're going on tour? We're really going on tour?"

Torren nods, looking like an excited doggy bobblehead on a dashboard.

"Starting next week if we can get our shit in order. Three months. Miami all the way up the coast to finish in New York City."

I squeal, move to launch at him in a hug, and then halt myself. His face falls, the picture of remorse, and I wince. I feel bad, but not enough to follow through with the hug. I clear my throat and gesture to the door that leads back into the bar.

"I'm gonna go tell Mabes."

I don't wait for his response. I just rush into the bar and tackle Mabel in the hug I almost gave Torren.

"Whoa, babe, what's up?" Mabel rasps with a laugh. I pull back and give her shoulders a shake.

"We're fucking goin' on tour, Mabes, that's what!"

"What? Tour?"

"TOUR!" I kiss her cheek and move to step away. "Go find Torren. He'll tell you about it. I'm out of here tonight, though. Levi leaves tomorrow. I'll call in the morning, okay?"

Mabel groans and grabs my hand, tugging me back in for another hug.

"Don't be lame! Come hang and celebrate with us!"

"I can't," I say with a laugh. "Tomorrow, okay?"

"Ugh, fine, bitch. Tomorrow."

I smile and start walking backward.

"We're going on tour," I call to her, and she squeals, clapping her hands.

"Tour!"

13

I'M BOUNCING and grinning like an idiot when I get to Levi's table.

He's frowning down at his phone, so I pluck it away and shove it in my bra. He turns his body to face me and when his brown eyes meet mine, they're full of amusement and mirth and something else I can't quite name but want more of.

It's because of that last thing that I don't tell him about the tour.

"Brat," he deadpans. It's a term of endearment disguised as an insult, I've decided.

"Leviticus," I croon, stepping between his widespread legs so our faces are only a foot apart. "Want to get out of here?"

I don't let him answer. I just grab his hand and lead the way, and he follows behind. He never lets go. When people stop me to tell me how much they liked the show, his fingers tighten around mine and my heartbeat kicks up. When I look up at him, he's looking back at me. Always.

"Where are we going?" he asks once we're outside in the humid night air.

"Where do you want to go?"

He shrugs and gives me a small smile.

"I want to go wherever you're going."

I roll my eyes playfully to try and hide the way I want to melt into a quivering puddle of goo.

"What time do you have to leave tomo—"

My sentence cuts off as another memory from last night fades into focus.

Tomorrow. Levi's voice. Whispered and warm. Goosebumps prickle my arms and legs.

I want you.

Then still want me tomorrow.

My gaze flies back to his, and he's watching me curiously. I bounce my eyes between his. Silvery gray dancing with chocolate brown. *Then still want me tomorrow,* he said.

"Let's go back to my place," I say, nerves racketing in my chest and throat.

He can tell something's up, but he doesn't ask. He just nods and takes my hand once more as I order up a ride on my phone.

"You guys were great tonight." His low voice cuts through the silence as we wait, and I beam at the honesty I hear in his words. "I can't get over how good you are, actually. You're really talented, Sav."

I can feel the tips of my ears heat under his praise. I bite my lip and shrug it off, elbowing him in the side.

"Don't sound so surprised. I'm capable of being good at something," I tease, and he sighs.

"Trust me, I am well aware you can be good at something. You've always been able to master anything you touch. Skateboarding. Drag racing. Kickboxing. Pickpocketing, apparently, too. Hell, even math, despite the fact that you refused to let it show."

I scoff playfully.

"I was a C student."

"You were a C student by choice, not ability."

I wave him off and he chuckles as the car pulls up and we climb inside.

"What I'm saying, though, is that when you're up on that stage, you're beyond normal good. You're just, kind of, I don't even know how to put it."

"Mega good?" I offer with a laugh. "*Super* good? Fan-freaking-tastically good?"

He rests his head on the car seat, then looks at me. His expression is serious enough that my smile slips a little. I lock eyes with him and wait.

"You're good enough to be something big," he says slowly, his voice full of emotion. "I can feel it. You, with your electric guitar and your raspy voice—you've got star power. Just don't forget all about me when it happens, okay?"

I nod and swallow back a lump in my throat, my tongue suddenly tied and heavy. I bump my leg into his and give him a small smile.

"I could never."

The minute the words leave my mouth, Levi's grin grows until it's stretched over his face, and for a few seconds in the back of this car, he looks just like the boy I left behind.

We sit in comfortable silence the rest of the drive, and when we're pulling up to my house, my head is resting on his shoulder and my hand is clasped in his. He slides out of the car first, then holds out a hand to help me. I let us into the house using my key and we walk to my bedroom. The house is quiet because my roommate is probably staying at her boyfriend's place. It's so quiet that I wonder if Levi can hear how fast and hard my heart is pounding.

He turns to me awkwardly and leans on the doorframe to my room.

"Well, what did you want to do?" He glances at the watch on his wrist. "It's pretty late, and I'm leaving with the guys tomorrow afternoon, so maybe you and I can—"

"It's tomorrow," I blurt, cutting him off. He looks at me quizzically as I lick my lips and try again, more softly this time. "It's tomorrow...and I still want you."

The moment what I'm saying registers in his head, the confusion is erased. His jaw tenses, and he swallows hard. His eyes burn on my skin as I walk slowly toward him.

"*Savannah*," he warns, whispered low and full of need.

I stop in front of him, six inches apart, and look up into his handsome face. I take my fingers and run them over his lips, and his eyes flutter shut as he sucks in a shuddering breath.

"It's tomorrow, and I still want you."

His eyes fly open, and he searches my face, the lingering disbelief making my mouth turn up into a smirk. I've said it twice, and he's still surprised.

"Ask me," I tease, and I know the minute he understands.

He takes one hand and places it on my hip, then cups his other hand around my neck so his fingers thread into the hair at my nape and his thumb caresses my jaw. I bite my lip, shivering a bit at his touch.

"Savannah. Can I kiss you?"

"Yes."

His lips are on mine in an instant, soft and tentative at first, then harder and more urgent. I open for him, inviting him in, and I moan when he once again tastes like citrus and whiskey. It makes the memories from last night—the kissing and touching—more real, and I revel in it. I fist my hands in his shirt and pull him into me, then pull him with me as I walk backward toward my mattress.

I'm a hurried, fumbling mess. Feeling everything everywhere. I tug at his shirt, and he leans back just enough to pull it over his head and toss it on the floor. Then he makes sure mine follows. My torn and cropped AC/DC t-shirt already exposed my stomach and flashed my red bra, but Levi still presses hot kisses to my collarbone as if it's a new discovery.

I put my hands on the waistband of his shorts, and a low groan rumbles in his chest as I undo the button. Slowly, with his forehead pressed to mine and his rapid breaths ghosting over my lips, I push his shorts over the curve of his ass and down his thighs until I hear them drop on the floor at his feet. Then I take his hands, drag them down my heated skin, and place them on the band of my pants.

"Are you sure?" His question is whispered, and he lifts his eyes just enough so he can peer into mine. "We don't have to."

God, the way my heart squeezes at his words. At his concern and care for me. No one has *ever* cared about me the way Levi did. *Does.* The way Levi *does*. I force a smirk to hide just how emotionally wrecked I am.

"Just take off my pants, Leviticus."

He huffs a laugh, then does as I say. He slips his thumbs into the band of my skin-tight distressed jeans, and carefully shimmies them down over my ass. When he gets my jeans to mid-thigh, I have to take over or risk toppling backward. I stifle a squeak as I struggle, and when I finally get the pants to my ankles and kick them to the side of the room, I'm heated through with embarrassment.

"Talk about sexy," I groan jokingly, but when I meet Levi's face once more, the sarcasm dies on my tongue.

He's staring, devouring every inch of my body with his eyes, and then I turn red for a different reason.

Men look at me lustfully all the time. It's quite literally my job. I dance and get half naked while they watch. I don't care about their opinions. I don't care how they see me. But with Levi? It's an entirely different experience. I care how he sees me. I always have. And the way he's looking at me right now?

It's completely and utterly reverent.

Spurred on by his reaction, I undo the front clasp on my red bra and let it fall to the ground. The breath he sucks in goes straight to my toes. My clit throbs. My nipples harden the longer he stares, to the point that it's almost painful. I need to be touched.

"You're absolutely beautiful," he rasps, eyes roving my body and hands clenched at his sides.

I glance down at his gray boxer briefs and my eyes widen, nerves and butterflies warring with each other in my stomach. I knew from the lap dance that he was probably going to be big, but this? I worry my lip and furrow my brow.

"Are you okay? We can stop."

"No," I say quickly, forcing a smile. "It's not that. I'm just nervous, is all." He huffs out an awkward laugh and nods. I slip my fingers into the sides of my thong, then meet his eyes. "Together?"

"Yeah."

Levi matches my movements, sliding his fingers into the band of his underwear and pulls them down his body. I stare. I can't help it.

I can't *stop* staring.

As if in slow motion, a tuft of dark blond hair comes into view followed by the thick base of his dick. My mouth goes dry as more and more of his shaft becomes visible. It looks smooth and solid, with light purplish veins that make my throat tight and my core throb. And it feels like it never ends. When the head of his dick springs free from the fabric, my breath catches. It's just as smooth and solid and pulsing as the rest of it. It's intimidating, but also really fucking sexy, and I don't know what to do with that.

"Fuck," I breathe out, dropping my panties to the floor, eyes still trained on his hard dick.

"Fuck is right."

When I drag my eyes from Levi's cock to his face, he almost looks like he's in pain, stuck somewhere between pleasure and agony. He forces a hard swallow, his attention on my pussy, which is already throbbing and wet. When he wraps his hand around his shaft and squeezes, I have to press my thighs together to relieve some of the ache.

"Can I touch you?" he asks, and I nod.

"Please."

He steps forward and runs his palms down my arms, then up my torso. He thumbs the undersides of my breasts, making me whimper, before brushing featherlight caresses over my nipples. I drop my head back, and his lips find their way to my neck.

"Yes," I whisper, gripping his biceps before dragging my hands to his waist, working up the courage to grip him *there*.

Levi's hands move from my breasts to my ass, squeezing, then he brings one hand between my legs and cups me. I gasp.

"Yes."

"Fuck." His voice is a low rasp as he runs two fingers through me. "Fuck, Sav."

He closes his mouth over mine, swallowing a cry as he rubs lightly on my clit. Desperate for him, for more, for all of it, I wrap my hand around his hard dick and stroke. I groan into his mouth at how silken his skin feels, how hard he is. As his tongue attacks my mouth, I rub my thumb over the head of his dick, swiping at something wet, and rubbing it over the tip.

When Levi growls into my mouth, I almost lose it.

"*Fuck*, Savannah."

"You like that?" I pant against his lips, and he thrusts in my hand.

"I'll like anything you do."

I smile against him, then squeeze and stroke some more, loving how ragged his breathing gets. How rough his soft lips treat mine. I press closer to him, so my breasts graze his body, rubbing my hard nipples over him. He drags his mouth from mine, bites and sucks on my neck, then drops to his knees in front of me and takes my nipple into his mouth.

I cry out, the sensations of his lips on my nipple and his hand on my pussy is more than I have ever felt before. He laves his tongue around me, sucking and grazing me lightly with his teeth, as his fingers move from my clit lower, circling my entrance, already soaked and tingling.

"Oh my god."

He hums around me, then looks up at me with eyes that take my breath away. I swallow hard around the strange desire to cry and run my fingers through his hair. He presses a kiss to the dip between my breasts, then licks around my other nipple, eyes never leaving mine.

"Do you have a condom?"

His voice is so rough that for a moment, all I can do is nod. I bend down and kiss his lips, then step away, walking backward toward my door.

"Just, um, stay," I say with a giggle.

God, he looks so fucking sexy, naked and on his knees, hard cock jutting out from his body.

"Don't move. I'll be just a second."

His expression is confused as I turn and rush into the hallway. Thank god no one is home. I sprint into my roommate's room and go straight for her top dresser drawer. Please, please, please let there be condoms in here. When I open the drawer, my shoulders sag with relief.

"Jackpot."

My roommate teases me all the time. *If you ever decide to bring someone home, don't forget a condom! I don't want to have to rent the room to you AND a baby. I've got some if you don't.*

I always laughed her off until now. I grab one, then turn to leave, but stop myself. I turn back to the dresser and survey the box in the drawer. I think it over for just a second before I snatch the whole box and take it with me. Better to be safe, right?

When I get back to the room, Levi is sitting on my mattress with his long legs stretched out on the floor in front of him and his upper body propped on his forearms. Even in the darkness, he looks like sculpted perfection. To say I'm shocked would be an understatement.

I walk to him and toss the condom box on the bed, then climb onto the mattress next to him. He wastes no time, kissing me once more with a hunger I've only heard about in songs. His palms caress my skin, tugging and rubbing, as he lays me down on my back. I part my legs so his body can fit between them, and when his hard cock rubs against my wet, sensitive skin, I moan.

"You're so perfect," he rasps against me. "You're so beautiful."

I reach between us and palm him. When he thrusts into my hand with a groan, my chest tightens. When I speak, my words are whispered against his lips, into his mouth.

"Levi. You're so...Is it...Do you think it will hurt, much?"

He pulls away slowly, surprised eyes scanning my face.

"You're a virgin?"

I bite my lip and try to shrug off my immediate embarrassment. I huff out a fake laugh.

"I mean, don't look so surprised."

"No," he says quickly, kissing me again. "It's not that. I'm just...I'm honored is all. To be your first."

I dig my fingers into his sides and lick my lips, bouncing my eyes between his.

"Have you, um, have you done this already?"

The way he winces guts me. Disappointment I never expected shoots from my head to my toes and makes my eyes sting. I want to double over from the force of it.

"Once. Just once."

"Oh."

Before I can stop, I picture her. The girl he gave his virginity to. His *once*.

Someone from college. Someone from a good family. Someone who doesn't strip for money. Someone with a halo and wings to match his. I bet his mom would like her. Blonde-haired, blue-eyed, and perfect in every way. Like him.

"If I had known..." he says, pulling me from my thoughts. "If I had even thought there was a chance—" he cuts off and kisses me again, then presses his forehead to mine.

"I wish it was you, Sav. I wish it was you."

That whispered confession does enough to loosen all my muscles, to calm the pain in my chest and soothe away my need to cry. I tell myself the other girl meant nothing. Pastor's kid rebellion. This time is what counts.

I nod and give him a small smile.

"I'll get you ready, okay? I'll make sure it feels good for you."

Slowly, he kisses his way down my body, leaving goosebumps in the wake of his lips, until he's situated between my thighs and his hot breath fans over my pussy. I'm wet and throbbing, and when he licks me the first time, my whole body jerks. He uses his forearm to press down on my hips and does it again, this time circling my clit with his tongue and sucking.

"Oh, Christ," I groan. "Oh, Jesus Christ."

He chuckles against me, intensifying my arousal.

"I thought you weren't religious, Shaw?"

"I thought good Christian boys weren't supposed to do wicked things with their tongues," I pant back, tightening my thighs around his head.

He licks and sucks again, and I buck against him.

"Oh my god, are you all like this?"

He stops and lets out a low growl, vibrating from his mouth over my pussy.

"You don't talk about other guys when my mouth is on you. Understand?"

The authority in his voice, the absolute dominance in the command, shocks me in the most delicious way. I usually find this side of Levi irritating, but right now, I'm melting for him. I'll do anything he tells me to. I clear my throat before answering.

"Yes. Understood."

"Good."

He quirks his lips, glistening with my arousal, into a sinful smile.

"Now stay still so I can make you come."

I laugh, but it quickly transforms into a moan. Levi's mouth and tongue have me seeing stars. When his finger probes into me, I release a strangled cry.

"Relax, Sav," he croons against me, rotating his finger and sliding in deeper. "Relax for me."

I feel a sting, a tightness, and then he's lapping at me again, flicking and sucking at my clit in a way that makes the pressure feel blissful. When he presses another finger into me, I move against him. Against his face and hand, until I'm panting.

"Oh shit, Levi," I say, tightening my grip on his hair and my thighs around his head. "Oh my God, is that...is this..."

And then I'm detonating, sparks of electric sensation shoot through my body, turning me to a panting, twitching mess. I don't even realize he's moved back up my body until he's kissing me again. I can taste myself on his lips. He's propped on one arm, his other hand resting on my rib cage and caressing me with gentle strokes of his thumb.

"Are you good?" he asks as I gasp for breath.

"Oh my God. Just once? You sure just once? Because that was...that was..."

He laughs.

"This was actually my first time doing that."

I pop my eyes open and gape. I can't tell in the darkness, but I would bet money that he's blushing just from the smile he's sporting. Adorably bashful, yet full of pride. He laughs again and jerks his shoulders in an awkward shrug.

"Porn."

I bark out a laugh, and he rolls his eyes.

"Leviticus Noah Luke Paul Jesus Cooper! You perv! You do not watch porn!"

He buries his face in my neck and blows a raspberry on the sensitive skin below my ear, making me giggle and squirm. I shriek and push at him.

"Ewww!"

He pulls back up and looks down at me, smile stretched wide.

"You're such a brat."

I bite my lip, then slowly arch my hips upward, bumping his hard dick with my wet pussy. Immediately his smile disappears, and it's replaced with hunger. Lust. Need. He flexes his hips, so he rubs against me, and my breath hitches.

The way he's looking at me, searching my face, like I'm the only thing worth seeing. I'll never find anyone else who will look at me that way. I know it for certain. It makes my heart ache.

"I'm ready."

Levi nods and reaches for the box of condoms. I watch as he fumbles with tearing one open and rolling the latex down his shaft. He's so big that my fear spikes again. He must see it in my eyes because he presses a slow kiss to my lips.

"I'll make sure it feels good for you," he says against me, and I believe him.

I trust him wholly. He's the only person I've ever trusted.

So, when he positions himself above me and kisses me, I relax. I get lost in the way his mouth moves over mine. I feel him swipe the head of his hard cock through me, pressing lightly on my clit before doing it again.

I grab onto his biceps and breathe deeply through my nose as slowly, gently, he presses into me. I wince at the sting, at the tightness of the stretch, but it doesn't hurt nearly as much as I thought it would. When Levi reaches between us and rubs my clit, the discomfort almost disappears, until he's fully seated inside me.

"How do you feel," he grinds out, breathing hard.

I wiggle a little, mentally taking inventory of my body parts and the shape they're in. When I flex my pussy, Levi groans.

"Fuck, Sav, don't do that yet, okay?"

"Are you alright? Did I hurt you?"

He chokes out a laugh and drops his forehead to mine, eyes squeezed shut.

"The opposite of hurt. But if you want me to last more than two seconds, you have to give me a moment to adjust."

I giggle, and he groans again.

"Sorry," I say, but I flex again anyway.

"Brat," he chokes out, and his amusement is mixed with enough pain that I take mercy on him.

This time, tentatively, I start to move on him. Little thrusts upward to get used to the feel, testing it out.

"I feel good," I say honestly, answering his earlier question. "I feel really good."

"Yeah? Can I move?"

"Yeah. You can move."

He starts to thrust into me, slow and gentle at first. When I start to thrust back, marveling at the way his face twists in pleasure, he speeds up.

"Better," he says as he moves. "So. Much. Better."

My voice is raspy and breathless, somewhere between a whimper and a moan, when I respond.

"Better than what?"

"Everything."

He drops his head to my shoulder, speeding up until he's hitting me somewhere inside that makes sparks flash inside my head and every sensitive part of my body throb.

"You're better than *everything*."

I kiss him. His cheek. His neck. His ear. I kiss every part of him my mouth can reach as he pounds into me until he finally brings his lips back to mine. I hum, tangling our tongues in time to the rhythm of our bodies, every movement a perfectly-orchestrated chorus, until he speeds up.

"Sav. Touch yourself for me."

It's a plea as much as it is a command, and I obey, snaking my hand between our bodies, flattening it on my pelvis as his grinds into me, and I rub my clit the way he did. I moan and feel myself clench at the contact, and he grunts.

"I'm going to come," he blurts out.

It sounds almost apologetic, but I don't say anything. I just clench harder around him and match his thrusts in a way that makes his mouth fall open and his eyes clamp shut.

"Oh, fuck."

Levi's movements turn jerky, and he captures my lips once more, moaning into my mouth as he comes inside me. When he starts to slow our kiss, I follow suit. I'm covered in sweat, my thighs and butt are wet and sticky, and I've never felt so exhausted, but I've never felt so happy, either.

He pulls out of me and props himself back up on his arm beside me.

"How do you feel?" he asks, and I grin at him.

"Perfect."

"Sorry you didn't....that I didn't..."

He closes his eyes and shakes his head, lips turning into a rueful grin.

"Next time, I'll make sure you come first."

I laugh. It's airy and giddy despite my exhaustion. I don't point out that technically I *did* come first because the idea of there maybe being a next time already has me squirming.

"It's a deal."

Levi rolls off the bed with a "be right back" and wanders down the hall to the bathroom. When he comes back, he drops down on the mattress next to me and scoops me into his arms. I snuggle into his chest in spite of the heat, his breath tickling the naked, sweat-slicked skin on my collarbone.

I have to swallow back a giggle.

I just gave my virginity to Levi Cooper, and I've truly never been this happy. I've never felt this cherished. This important. This *loved*.

I've never trusted anyone enough to even care much about sex. I've never felt safe enough. But with Levi, it's different.

He's special. He's gentle and kind, and he cares about me. He'd never hurt me. I trust him more than anyone else in the world. I trust him more than myself, even.

The fact that he was my first makes me giddy, and even though I wasn't his first, I know that this was just as important for him.

This time, with me, is the one that matters.

It was perfect. *He* is perfect.

I'll never, ever forget it.

14

"WHAT TIME DO you have to leave tomorrow?"

I try to hide the sadness I feel at losing him. I don't want him to go. I want there to be a next time, and I don't want to have to wait three more years for it. He's quiet for long enough that I think he's fallen asleep, but then he tightens his arms around me and speaks into my hair.

"Our flight leaves at four."

"Oh. At least you don't have to be up too early."

I make myself smile so maybe he won't be able to hear how badly this hurts. I force a laugh.

"I gave you a pretty decent goodbye gift, yeah?"

He doesn't laugh at my joke. Doesn't call me a brat or get patronizing with me. Instead, he puts his arm on my shoulder and turns me so we're facing each other. He takes his hand and wraps it around my neck, so his thumb is brushing lightly over my jaw, and his brown eyes lock onto mine as he speaks.

"I don't want this to be goodbye," he says clearly.

My chest tightens, but I don't let myself get excited. I keep cool and smile.

"Yeah. Of course. We can keep in touch."

"No, Sav. I don't want to just keep in touch. I want to be together."

Butterflies swarm my belly as his words sink in. Together. He wants to be *together*. Excitement and uncertainty battle inside my head.

"Like, you want to, what, date me? Be my boyfriend?"

I raise an eyebrow and purse my lips. He gives me a lop-sided grin in response.

"Yeah, I guess. I want to talk to you every day. I want to see you as much as possible. I definitely want to do *this* again—" he gestures to our naked bodies "—so yeah, I want to date you. I want to be your boyfriend."

I don't even bother trying to fight my smile. I just let it take over my face and giggle when he does the same.

"But how? You're in North Carolina, and I'm here."

"We'll make it work. We can talk on the phone, and I can come visit and you can come visit. We can do it. We'll just be one of those long-distance couples."

He looks so hopeful and excited, and I feel the same. I'm two seconds away from agreeing when I remember how hectic and unpredictable my next three months will be. I groan.

"Shit. Tour."

"Tour?"

"Yeah, we're going on tour," I say tentatively. I'm excited, but I'm terrified this will ruin everything. "We leave next week, actually. Three months up the coast and ending in NYC. Playing dive bars, probably, but it's something."

Instead of getting angry or telling me he's changed his mind about dating me, Levi just looks at me. He bounces his eyes between mine, drops his gaze to my lips, then back, and his brow furrows.

"Is Sean going? Torren?"

My spine goes ramrod straight and I grit my teeth, but I don't back down. I should have expected this.

"Yes."

"Savannah—"

"Don't," I cut him off. "Whatever you're going to warn me of or scold me for, just don't. I already know." I close my eyes and breathe through my nose. "I talked to Torren. Things aren't fixed by any means, but I talked to him. I'll talk to Sean. Jonah kicked his ass. Mabel's on my side—"

"So then find a new fucking keyboard player and bassist."

"I can't just replace half the band," I snap. "Torren and Sean are the ones with the connection to this guy with the money who is funding our tour."

He sits up abruptly and rakes his hands through his hair. I feel cold without him beside me, even though it's 80 degrees outside. I sit up and drape the bedsheet over my shoulders. Levi shakes his head and hits me with an exasperated glare.

"That's bullshit, Sav. You're the talent. You're the one people will pay to see. No one gives two shits about who's standing behind you."

"Yes, they do. The guy with the money does. And that's the only person whose opinion matters right now."

He stares at me, and I stare back, neither of us willing to back down. When he opens his mouth to argue, I press my fingers to his lips, silencing him.

"This could be the break I need, Levi. This tour is going to change everything. I can feel it. I can taste it, even. Is it ideal? No. But it never fucking will be ideal. Nothing ever is for me. Fuck, man, I had to pickpocket and busk just to get out of a house where I was abused. Then I had to leave Nashville because fucking Oscar kept trying to get handsy with me. Nothing *ever* works out for me, Levi. Ever. But I think this might. So just...can't you just be happy for me? Please? I need you to be happy for me."

We stay silent a moment longer. His eyes stay hard, and his eyebrows stay harshly slanted, but he nods and presses a kiss to my fingers. He reaches up and grips my wrist lightly and brings my hand to his chest.

"I *am* happy for you. I'm so damn proud I could burst, and I would never want to hold you back from something like this. I hate that you have to do this with that skeezy asshole, but I'm happy for you. You're seriously so damn talented, and I'm going to be at every show I can be. I'll even pretend to be your roadie if you want me to."

"Really?"

He chuckles and takes my lips in a kiss that makes my toes curl.

"Really. Maybe..." he breaks off, then purses his lips.

"Maybe what?" When he doesn't answer, just smirks a little, I give him a shove. "Maybe what?"

"Maybe, after my semester is out for the summer, I can join you..."

"Join me on tour?" My excitement is through the roof. I can't hide it. I'm vibrating with it. "You want to join me on tour for the summer?"

"If you think you and your band will be okay with it, yeah. But if you think I'd be—"

"No! I mean yes," I cut him off with a laugh, tackling him into a hug so we're falling back down on my mattress. "I think it would be great. I don't think they'd mind at all. A free roadie? They'll love it."

He rolls his eyes, but his smile matches mine, and I'm so stupidly giddy. I don't know the last time I was this excited. I wasn't even this excited last night when we found out about the tour.

"So, you still want to date me, then?" I ask, giving his shoulder a nudge.

He laughs again, does that exasperated sigh thing he does when he thinks I'm being ridiculous, then kisses me once more.

"Will you be my girlfriend, Savannah Shaw?"

I bring my finger to my chin and tap, pretending to think it over, and he squeezes my side, making me giggle.

"Okay, okay. Yes," I say through laughs. "Yes, I will be your girlfriend, Levi Cooper."

Sometime before noon, Levi wakes me with soft kisses pressed to my chest and neck. I roll to him and wrap my arms and legs around his body, and he laughs.

"I don't remember you being this clingy," he jokes, hugging me tightly.

"It's the sex. I'm a changed woman."

Levi smirks and kisses my lips.

"Is it okay if I use your shower? My phone is blowing up. I overslept and have to meet the guys. Grab my stuff from the hotel and head to the airport. Checkout is in an hour."

My stomach sinks, and I can't hide my disappointment. I was hoping to spend more time with him today, but we slept too late. I was also thinking I'd get to meet his friends...but I guess there's always next time.

"Yeah, okay." I force a smile. "There are towels in the cabinet under the sink."

"Hey." He kisses my nose. "Don't be sad, okay? This isn't goodbye this time. I'm going to see you soon. Let me know your tour schedule, and I'll find out which shows I can come to, and then in like two months, I'll be yours for the whole summer."

This time, my smile is real, my heart racing happily once more. Two days ago, I never would have guessed I'd end up naked in a bed with Levi Cooper.

Levi Cooper who is now my boyfriend.

"What are you grinning about?"

I shrug. "I just never thought I'd lose my virginity to such a huge weenie."

I widen my eyes for emphasis, and he groans, grabbing a pillow and shoving it onto my face. I'm gasping with laughter as he climbs off my bed, lips twitching from the force of the smile he's trying to hide. He snatches his boxer briefs from the floor and steps into them.

"You're a brat."

I don't respond. I just watch with a dopey smile, and when he dips out the door to head to the bathroom, I drop my head back onto the pillow and squeal.

This was definitely unexpected.

I'm trying like hell to turn off the doom and gloom mindset that keeps circling my brain, but it's hard when good shit never stays good for long.

When the shower kicks on, I roll off my mattress and open my "dresser," digging through it for clothes. I throw on some underwear, jean cutoffs, and a t-shirt, then toss my hair into a ponytail. I need to head into the club today and let Mack know about the tour. See if she'll let me pick up a few more shifts this week before we leave.

I'm putting on eyeliner when an incessant buzzing comes from the floor by my bed where Levi's shorts still lie discarded from last night. It must be his phone. He did say the guys were blowing him up.

I go back to finishing my other eye when the buzzing starts again. I glance at the shorts, then at my door. The shower is still on, and my curiosity is getting the better of me.

I walk to my mattress and sit down, then reach for Levi's shorts. The buzzing has stopped by the time I pull the phone out of his pocket. It's on 10% battery, and it's locked in that annoying way that doesn't preview what calls and texts you get. I tap the screen and the passcode prompter comes up.

I'm debating trying to break into it when the phone buzzes again, and my restraint snaps.

It's only four digits.

I try 1-3-1-6 first and smirk to myself, but it's not the winner. I didn't actually expect John 3:16 to be his passcode, but how hilarious would it be if it was? I'd never shut up about it.

I think for a minute, then punch in his birth date.

Bingo.

What a square. I broke into his phone in two tries. Doesn't he know you're not supposed to use your birthday? I snicker as I pull up his contacts and put my phone number in. I save it under *Sexy Girlfriend,* then snap a selfie to save as my contact.

Then, because apparently, I'm one of those nosy girlfriends, I open his messaging apps.

The first thread is one titled Spring Break Boyz and there are fifty unread messages. I roll my eyes with a laugh as I open it and scroll through it. Messages from guys named Dalton, Dylan, Josh, Scott, and someone saved as B-Ramz have been blowing him up the last two days. A lot of pictures of beer and the beach. Lots of messages calling him a dick for ditching them, and him responding with middle-finger emojis.

I smile so big my cheeks hurt when I see he sent them a picture of me on stage last night. I look good, too. Quickly, I forward the picture to my phone number. The last several texts are telling Levi to hurry the hell up because he's going to miss check out and they need to get to the airport, and him apologizing and saying he's on the way.

It's so weird seeing this side of him. The college guy side. I feel like a wildlife photographer in some remote corner of the world researching a new species. Eighteen and nineteen-year-old frat boys are certainly an interesting bunch.

When I finish that thread, I close it out and go to the next. It's his mom. I sneer at it. I wonder if she's still a judgy bitch.

I open the thread and scroll. It's just a bunch of check-ins. Mostly one- or two-word responses from Levi, assuring Mrs. Cooper that he's alive. I snort a laugh when I get to a long paragraph she sent last week preaching to him about the importance of modesty and purity. Apparently, she was not down with the Miami trip and was worried it would corrupt him.

Too bad photos aren't allowed in the club, because then someone could send her a video of me giving her precious angel baby a lap dance. Damn, she'd flip her top. Just the mental image has me smiling.

I close out of her thread and go to the next.

This one makes me sit up straighter. Some person named Jules.

I click open the thread without breathing, and the most recent text is from her asking Levi to call her. I check the time stamp. Friday morning. He read it but didn't respond.

JULES

Please call me when you get a chance. It's important.

I scroll up. Their exchanges are pretty basic. Wishing luck on exams and stuff like that. Then I get to one where Jules mentions Levi's mom. Calls her *Ms. Judy* and everything. She's on a first name basis with Levi's mom?

I click on her contact and pull up her photo. She's a blonde girl who looks vaguely familiar. The longer I stare, the more I think I know her. *Jules*. And then it clicks.

Julianna Lark.

She went to Levi's church, I think. She was a year older than we were. She was always nice enough. Never treated me like trash like everyone else did. Never called me crack baby or sneered at me in the hallway.

But still.

Why the hell is Julianna Lark asking Levi to call her? Why the hell is she even in his phone at all?

The hairs on my arms stand up and my throat tightens. This couldn't be the 'one time,' could it? Was he dating her? She's definitely someone old mommy dearest would approve of. My jealousy spikes and I scowl at the phone.

Then I feel like an asshole.

This is so dumb. I've been a girlfriend for all of a few hours, and I'm already becoming a psycho. I snort. I have to check myself if I want this long-distance thing to work.

I go to close out of the phone when a new text from Jules comes in.

When do you get back to town? I need to see you, Levi. It's important, and I think we need to talk before we go to our parents.

I can't breathe. Something dark and slimy coils in my stomach. Something telling me that this is bad. I know it is. My instincts are never wrong when it comes to shit like this.

Before I can think better of it, I send a text as Levi.

Just tell me now.

The chat bubbles pop up, then disappear. Pop up again, then disappear again. Then she tries to call, and I silence it.

I think it's better we talk in person

That irritates me. My temper flares hot, and my annoyance skyrockets.

No. Just text it.

More chat bubbles. Appear, disappear. Appear, disappear. And then a photo comes through. It takes me a minute to realize what it is. When it finally registers, I can't breathe. I can't speak. I can't do anything except stare.

This is it, I think. This is the hidden punch. This is the *joke's on me* moment. This is how the rug gets pulled out from under me.

"What are you doing?"

Levi's voice makes me jump, heart in my throat, and when I look at him, standing in my doorway wrapped in a towel, the smile he was wearing falls right off his face.

"What's wrong?" he says, rushing to me. "Why are you crying?"

I didn't even realize I was crying.

"Who is Jules?"

The color drains from his face, and his eyes fall to the phone. He meets my eyes again, and I want to throw up. I don't know if I want to sob or murder him. The sorrowful look on his face just makes it worse.

"Is she the 'just once?'" I ask, already knowing the answer. He nods. "Did you know she was pregnant?"

I turn the phone to him, showing him the grainy ultrasound picture. His eyes fall shut, and I gasp. I can taste my tears on my lips.

"You knew? You knew, and you slept with me anyway?"

"No," he says quickly. "I didn't know for sure. She told me last week that she'd missed a period. Had a positive pregnancy test she got from the drug store, but those aren't always accurate. I thought it was a false positive or something...."

I blink.

"I thought you weren't dating anyone."

"I'm not, I swear. I didn't lie to you, Savannah. I slept with her one time. Once. We used a condom. I didn't think....Fuck, I didn't think it was anything."

"Didn't *think*, or didn't *want*?"

He lifts his shoulders in a heavy shrug. "I don't know. Both?"

A dark laugh escapes me, and I close my eyes.

"Well, sorry to tell you, but it's definitely something."

"This doesn't have to change anything," he says quickly, and my eyes fly back open. "I still want to be with you. I don't want to be with anyone else. I don't love her. I want you, Sav."

The desperation on his face, the plea in his words, makes my stomach churn and the tears fall faster. My anger spikes again. At him. At Julianna Lark. At the situation. At my fucking shitty luck.

"How is this not going to change anything? She's having your kid, Levi," I force out through gritted teeth. "You're going to be a *father*."

Another thought pops into my head and I jerk my head back.

"She goes to your church," I whisper, and Levi nods. "Her dad is friends with your dad. Your families are close, right?"

His eyes clamp shut. "Yeah. That's her," he croaks.

"They're going to make you marry her," I say flatly, and his eyes fly back open.

"No way, they wouldn't."

"They will."

"It doesn't matter what they want. I won't do it."

"She's having your child. You are having a child with her," I shout at him.

"I don't care," he shouts back. "I don't care, Savannah. I don't want Jules. I don't want to marry Jules. I want you. I want only you."

"And what about the baby, then? You can't be traipsing around the country on your girlfriend's shitty band tour while the mother of your child is raising your kid. You can't do that. How would that even work?"

"She wouldn't...I don't think she would...."

His voice is strangled and pained, every bit a reflection of how I feel. His shoulders fall. I can actually *see* the defeat washing over him in the way each muscle sags and his cheeks grow wetter. And then it hits me.

"She wouldn't have the baby yet..." I say, almost to myself. "You'd be with me on tour, and she'd just be pregnant and waiting for you when you get back in the fall?"

He doesn't say anything. Doesn't confirm or deny my suspicions, but I can't stop now. Speculating. Guessing. They don't feel like guesses, though. They feel real.

"She messaged you Friday," I say. "She told you she missed a period. You knew she'd had a positive pregnancy test. She messaged you Friday to call her, said it was important, and you ignored her."

"I didn't ignore her," he says. "I got the message when we were in the club. Right before..."

He brings his palms up, gesturing at nothing. He doesn't have to explain. I know. I snatched his phone. He got the message right before I snatched his phone from him, then essentially kidnapped him for the weekend.

"Why didn't you call her back, Levi?"

My voice is deathly calm. He had to have known why she wanted to talk. He's not an idiot. He had to have known what she would say.

"Why didn't you call her back, Levi!"

"Because I didn't want her to ruin it," he shouts back. "Because I was here and you were here and I've missed you for so fucking long, and I just—"

"You wanted to enjoy your spring break with the stripper before going back to UNC and your baby."

"Jesus Christ, Savannah, you know that's not true."

"You wanted to slum it. You wanted to make plans for the summer until your baby was born, and then you'd go back home to Julianna Lark and be a daddy. You used me—"

"I didn't."

"You used me!"

"I didn't! I swear I didn't. I really, truly, didn't think it was anything. We had sex one time. Once! I used a condom. She's on birth control. Do you know the statistical probability of her getting pregnant? It's just..."

He drags a hand down his face then pinches the bridge of his nose.

It's just my shitty fucking luck.

"It's just impossible. I thought it was nothing."

"If you really thought it was nothing, then why were you worried she'd ruin it? Why not just call her back on Friday?"

He swallows hard, the silence screaming louder than anything he could say. He takes a deep breath, then tilts his head to the ceiling.

"I don't know, Sav," he whispers. "I don't know."

A cyclone of raging thoughts cloud my head. He wanted to slum it with me. He wanted to forget about his real life and fuck around with me before he had to go back home and face the music. Before he could go home and be a fucking father. I try to silence them, try to tell myself that this is Levi, and he would never treat me that way, but then another one comes barreling in, louder than the others.

I was going to be the homewrecker.

I was going to be my mother.

I squeeze my eyes closed and shake my head, trying to quiet the thoughts, but they won't go away. They just get more persistent.

Levi is going to be a dad. Levi is going to have a baby with Julianna Lark. Perfect, kind, respectable Julianna Lark. Her momma works at the bank. Her daddy isn't a drug dealer and backwater pimp. Her family is active in the church. She calls his mom *Ms. Judy*.

And who am I?

I am my mother's daughter.

I'm the stripper he fucked on spring break. I'm the girl tarnishing his shiny halo. Setting fire to his perfect angel wings.

I don't know which feelings hurt more, the inadequacy or the jealousy. The fact that it isn't me that fate chose for him. It isn't me the universe wants him with.

I wish it was you, he'd said.

God, I wish it was, too.

"Get out," I whisper. I stand up and gather his clothes, then put them in his arms before repeating myself with more force. "Get out."

"What? Savannah no, stop. This is ridiculous." I shove at him, until he's stumbling backward through my hallway. "Would you just stop? Let's talk about this."

"No amount of talking is going to change this." My tears have stopped. I've willed my anger to burn through them. "Get out."

"Stop it, Savannah. I'm not leaving you like this."

He stands tall in the middle of my small living room. In just a towel, clothing balled in his arms. He looks furious and determined, and that just pisses me off more.

"Julianna Lark is now your priority," I say, my voice shaking. "Julianna and whatever child she pops out. *They* are going to be your number one focus. She's not just your *once* anymore, Levi. She's your *one*. *They* are your one. They are where all your attention will have to go, because that baby deserves good parents Levi, and you're going to be a good parent."

I pause to take a breath. I'm going to start crying again.

"And that's not even what upsets me," I say, my voice breaking. "What upsets me is that you *knew* all of this. Maybe you didn't want it to be true, maybe part of you thought it couldn't be true, but you knew. You knew I couldn't fit into your future, and you still let me believe we could be something. You still let me believe I could be your one."

He doesn't speak. He just stares, and I clench my fists.

"Tell me I'm wrong," I rasp. "Tell me I'll be your number one. Tell me I'm fucking wrong, Levi."

If he tells me so, I'll believe him.

If he says I can be a priority, if he calls me his one, I'll be okay with not being his only. I'll keep him in any capacity possible, if it means there will be a place for me in his world. If he tells me it can work, I won't question it. I'll live it.

"Tell me, Levi," I beg. "*Please.*"

He doesn't.

He doesn't because he can't. He knows I'm right.

I close my eyes and nod. I wipe my face, smearing my eyeliner on my cheeks. Always such a mess.

"Get out."

I turn and walk back into my bedroom, then shut the door. I stand with my back to him, to his presence in my living room, and though there's three inches of wood and ten feet of raggedy carpet between us, I can still *feel* him. His hands on my skin. His breath on my neck. Him moving inside me.

I wish it was you.

I wish it was you.

I wish it was you.

I'm never going to forget it.

I'm always going to be his, but now he has to be hers.

It fills me with so much anger that I can hardly breathe.

Girls like me don't get guys like Levi Cooper. Girls like me get guys like Sean. Or Oscar. Girls like me get guys like Terry, just like my mother.

The Levi Coopers of the world always end up with the Julianna Larks.

I stomp to my clothing bin and flip it over, dumping out all the contents, then I dig around in the clothing pile until I find what I want. A small clutch purse. Without overthinking it, I pop it open and snag the key, then I stand and go back into the hallway.

Levi is dressed now, but he's still standing in the middle of the living room looking lost. I bite my cheek as I stand across from him. Close enough to touch, but too far away to ever have.

"I don't want her," Levi whispers, his voice a broken, bleeding thing. "I never wanted her. I want you. I've only ever wanted you. I *love* you, Savannah. I don't want Jules."

I whimper, biting my cheek harder until I taste blood. I try to fight the tears, but I'm just not strong enough.

"Well, that's too bad," I say, closing the distance. "Because she's who you get."

"The universe isn't done with us yet, Savannah. It can't be. I know it."

I stop in front of him and shrug before taking his hand.

"Maybe it's not," I whisper, pressing the key into his palm. "But I am."

I don't look him in the eyes. I can't. Instead, I stare at his chest. I clear my throat, then speak with as much certainty as I can fake.

"I never want to see you again."

Then I turn around and go back to my room. When I come back out an hour later, Levi is gone.

NOW

PART THREE

Just one more, baby.
Just one more.
What are we waiting for?

15

26 Years Old

"THANK YOU SO MUCH, New York City!"

My voice booms through the Garden, mixing with and melting into the collective noise of the crowd, and not for the first time, I wonder if I'll miss this.

Not all of it, certainly. Not the ice baths or the IV drips. Not the drugs or the paparazzi. Not the absolute nonexistence of privacy and free time.

But this?

The way my songs sound when sung back to me 20,000 voices strong. The way the stage lights heat my sweat-slicked skin, making it sparkle. The lime green bra hanging from my mic stand that someone threw on stage. The giant posterboard sign that reads ***Sav Loveless, You Saved My Life*** beaming at me from the lower bowl seating area. In the front row of the pit, there's a little girl with bright pink noise cancelling headphones sitting on the shoulders of an older man, and her t-shirt says *The Hometown Heartless #1 Fan.*

This? I think I'll miss it.

Part of me already does.

"As always, you've been absolutely beautiful. The Garden has always been one of our favorite places to play." I glance over my shoulder at Mabel. "Isn't that right, Mabes?"

She pounds out a beat in agreement, and I send her a wink before looking back at the crowd.

"Thank you for always making us feel welcomed. For always bringing the energy. For making every single fucking show a memorable one."

I swallow back a lump of emotion I didn't expect when the audience starts to chant, "Just one more. Just one more." It's more than just our first hit song. It's more than just our debut album.

It's a plea.

One more song. One more show. One more *year*.

The chant started in Atlanta, right after our announcement that this tour would be our last. It's gotten louder and louder since. But tonight, when it's our actual last show until god knows when, it's damn near deafening. I can feel my organs rattle with the force of the emotion they've tossed behind their words.

I smile as tears start to well, and I strum out the opening chord to "Just One More," laughing when the chants turn into screams and whistles. I've already played that song tonight, but there's no doubt in my mind that I could play it again and they'd sing along just as passionately.

"From the bottom of our hearts, New York, we will never forget you. Even though this might be goodnight..."

"It's not goodbye!" the crowd shouts back, and I laugh.

"But just in case, so you don't forget us, we've got Mabel on drums, Jonah on guitar, Torren on bass, my name's Sav Loveless, and we are The Hometown Heartless. Thank you so much for *always* showing up to rock with us, New York. We love you. Have a great night."

The crowd roars as the stage lights dim. I take off my guitar and hand it off to a guy in all black, then snatch the set list off the floor.

I walk to the edge of the stage, untying the black sequined scarf from around my waist, then gesture to Red to come help me down. I'd told him after the first song to make sure the little girl and her dad don't go anywhere, and he's already pulled them aside. Red grabs my hand and steadies me as I jump off the raised platform, and when I turn to the little girl, she has big fat tears streaming down her face.

"Oh, baby girl, don't cry," I say with a smile, crouching down to my knees so I'm at eye level with her. "What's your name?"

"Jessica," she hiccups out, wiping away some of her tears with her hands. Her dad reaches down and runs his hand down the back of her curly red hair. "I'm six."

"Hey Jessica. My name is Sav. I love your shirt. Did you make it yourself?"

"Yes! My daddy helped. And I have this, too."

She lifts up the necklace she's wearing with pride, and I have to force back more tears. It's a pink plastic string tied to a little heart-shaped padlock; the kind you'd find attached to a child's diary.

"I love that," I say, grabbing my own padlock and lifting it to show off the similar necklace that I'm wearing. Sometimes I forget that it's even there. "Did you enjoy the show?"

She nods, sniffling and leaning into her father.

"I'm so happy you came tonight, Jessica. You made my last show very special, and I wanted to give you something. Is that okay?"

"Yes. Yes, it is."

The excitement that takes over her face, her chubby little cheeks and bright green eyes, fill me with warmth. Her tears haven't stopped falling, but she's smiling so big that my heart squeezes.

This. I will definitely miss this.

I hold my hand out to Red and he slaps a black marker into it. I use it to autograph the set list and hand that to her. Then I take my scarf and drape it over her shoulders. She squeals, and I wink before taking her hand and pressing one of my guitar picks into her palm.

"Oh my gosh thank you! Thank you. Oh my gosh."

"You're welcome," I say with a laugh. "Is it okay if I hug you?"

She doesn't answer. She just launches herself at me, knocking me back so I have to catch myself with one hand before I can wrap my other arm around her.

"Thank you," she says again, crying onto my shoulder. I rub her back and squeeze her tightly.

"Thank *you* for being such a wonderful fan."

She squeezes me tighter. "Please don't be done," she whispers into my ear. "Please don't. I'll miss you."

I clamp my eyes shut against the sting, forcing back tears. I take a deep breath. She smells like baby lotion and sugar. What do I even say? Sorry kid, but I can't do this anymore? I have to save myself? I swallow down the lump in my throat and tighten my hug.

"I'll miss you, too, Jessica."

It's as honest as I can be for both of us.

She releases me, and I stand. Her father shakes my hand, thanking me for 'making Jessica's whole year.'

"Of course," I tell him honestly. "On your way out, stop by a merch booth, okay? It's on us."

Red escorts me to the suite the Garden put me up in. The band used to share one, but we haven't for a while now.

"It was a good show, Savannah," Red says as I grab a bottle of water from the mini fridge. "One that'll go down in history."

I roll my eyes.

"We're not Fleetwood Mac, Red. We're not the Stones." I drop myself down on the couch and tilt my head back on the cushions. I need to shower, but I need to breathe first. "In a few years, The Hometown Heartless will only exist in the occasional Where Are They Now internet search."

"You don't give yourself enough credit, kid."

Red's told me this before, but I still listen respectfully. He might be my personal security, but he's become something more like a dad over the last eight months. Bringing him on as my personal security after my last rehab stay was one of the best decisions I've made since getting out. Adopting Ziggs was another.

"You've created something big. You built something amazing from nothing. That little girl out there? Everyone in that audience tonight? You gave them a show they will never forget."

I roll my head toward him and watch as he picks through my

fruit tray, popping a few grapes in his mouth. I hate grapes. The only reason I ask for them is because Red loves them.

"You think I'm making the wrong decision?"

He furrows his brow in thought, but he doesn't look at me when he speaks.

"I think six albums and six world tours in six years is a lot for anyone," he says slowly. "I think your body needs the break...But to make it permanent?" He pauses and shrugs. "I don't know, kid. Only you can be sure of that."

I sigh and close my eyes again.

That's the problem. I don't know that I'm sure of anything anymore.

Six albums, six world tours, six years. I don't even know how it all happened. It's a blur. We were "discovered" at the end of the summer after our makeshift tour up the coast. We spent the next year or so playing smaller gigs and opening for larger artists. Writing and recording. But then it just blew up and never slowed down.

We're quiet for a few minutes. Long enough that I could probably fall asleep if I let myself, but there's a knock on the door followed by an unwanted guest that has me groaning.

"What do you want, Hammond?"

"Just seeing if you've come to your senses yet," he grumbles. Hammond's been pissed at me since Atlanta. They all have.

"Not changing my mind. I told you that already."

He taps something out on his phone and doesn't say anything right away. The way he does this—makes you wait for a response—used to make me nervous, but after a while, I came to see it for what it was: plain old manipulation.

He can't make me squirm anymore, but he's not willing to accept it.

A minute later, my door opens again and in strides the rest of my band. Hammond sticks his phone back in his suit pocket and gestures for them to sit down. Mabel plops onto the couch next to me, Jonah throws himself into a chair, and Torren leans on the wall and scowls, ever the broody, misunderstood rockstar.

I wish I would have known we were having a meeting. I would have showered and changed. I'm still in my body suit, and it's hard to be serious when your top half is nearly see-through and you're sticky with sweat. These people have seen me in worse conditions, sure, but it's different now.

"So glad to have you all here," Hammond says with a fake smile. It takes every ounce of strength left in my body not to sneer at him. "Great show tonight. You played your hearts out. The label appreciates it."

I roll my eyes, but he doesn't notice. When it's obvious none of us are going to thank him, he loses the smile and lets his true intentions show.

"Here are the facts. You can't break your contract with the label."

I groan and shoot upright, but he points at me and gives me a *shut your mouth and let me speak* look. I bite my tongue, but only because Mabel puts her hand on my knee.

"You've recorded six albums. Your contract is for eight."

"Bullshit, Hammond," I spit. "You know that contract is predatory as hell. We were kids, starving and fucking desperate. Who the fuck requires eight albums from a breakout artist? We didn't know what we were signing."

"That contract is legally binding. It doesn't matter if you were ignorant and didn't read the fine print. I told you not to sign it, Savannah, but you didn't listen, and now you are legally bound to it."

Torren chuckles darkly from his place on the wall.

"But the princess gets what she wants, Ham. Did you forget?"

"Shut *up*, Torren." I turn my body to face him. "Just shut *up*. This isn't about you—"

"It sure as fuck affects me. It's fucking up *my* life."

"I can't keep killing myself for your dream!"

"Used to be your dream, too," Jonah says, and when I look at him, his eyes are closed. I'm surprised he hasn't passed out yet.

Guilt and worry churn in my stomach, and that just makes me angrier. There's no telling what he's taking, anymore. I've stopped trying to babysit him.

"That was before the dream turned toxic, Jo," I say through my teeth. "What the hell are you on tonight, anyway? You willing to fucking die for this?" I turn my attention back to Torren, gesturing at Jonah's hunched over, drugged-out form. "This is what you want to save?"

Torren's jaw tenses and he stares me down, but he won't look at Jonah because he knows I'm right. Pretty sure he also thinks it's my fault.

I look from Torren to Mabel and sigh.

"I can't do this anymore. I'm sorry. But I can't."

"Well, then you don't have to," Hammond says, and the cheeriness in his tone makes my skin crawl. When I look at him, he's smiling. "I talked to the label. We can replace you."

My jaw drops, and I bark out a laugh, but he's not joking. He's serious. When I look at Torren and Mabel, the way they won't meet my eyes, my breath gets lodged in my chest. I open and close my mouth twice before I can finally force out words.

"You agreed to this?" I look at Mabel. "You want to do this without me?"

She raises her eyes to mine, anger tinged with sorrow.

"You're the one who decided you didn't want to do it with us."

I shake my head. I look from Mabel to Torren, then back at Hammond, skipping over Jonah's passed out body.

"So, you're just going to hire some knock off Sav Loveless? To sing the songs *I* wrote? To front the band that *I* formed?"

"The label will do what it has to to make sure the contract is fulfilled." Hammond's voice is clear and steady. No remorse. No emotion. All business. "If you want to buy your way out, fine, but it was selfish of you to assume the band would want to do the same."

I gape. "You can't just bring in someone new to sing my songs—"

"They are the label's songs—"

"They are *my* songs, and you damn well know it. *Mine*, Hammond. Those songs are my story. My whole fucking heart. I won't let you just pimp them out to some wannabe rockstar so the label can recoup a buck. I won't allow it."

My voice cracks, and I hate myself for it. The thought of someone else behind my mic fills me with rage. The fact that my bandmates—people I used to consider family—are okay with it, cuts me in half.

"Savannah," he says with an irritated sigh, "you don't have a choice."

"So, these are my options? Be forced through another album, another world tour, or watch someone else take my place?"

The devastation in my voice is palpable. The Hometown Heartless was my life. It's my legacy. I can't just hand that over to a stranger. It's not supposed to continue without me. When I said I was done, it was supposed to be done, too.

Hammond doesn't answer my question. He doesn't confirm or deny. He doesn't have to. We all know the label has me backed into a corner.

"You don't have to make the decision right now," he says curtly, pulling his phone from his pocket and typing on it once more. "The label is going to run with the hiatus story for the time being. Your new movie role works out nicely for that headline. Take the four months to film. Think it over. We'll use that time to scout—"

"To *scout*?"

"Discreetly," he adds, raising a brow at my outburst. "You can't expect them to sit around and wait for you without covering their bases."

"You can't just replace me, Hammond. I *am* this band. This band would be nothing without me."

The moment the words are out of my mouth, I regret them.

I hear Torren scoff. Can see Mabel staring daggers at me from my periphery. I regret saying it, but it's not a lie. It's my voice that sells out arenas and breaks streaming records. It's my face they want to see. My music they want to hear. My lyrics they want to sing. The

Hometown Heartless wouldn't be the same without Sav Loveless. They wouldn't even exist.

Hammond stares at me for a moment, gaze scanning my face before locking back onto my eyes.

"You're right. To an extent. This band wouldn't be what it is without you. You are why The Hometown Heartless is such a global phenomenon. We all know it. But you're also wrong."

He slips his phone back in his pocket, then smooths the lapels of his suit jacket.

"They *can* replace you, Savannah, and they will. And if they have to, they will remold and repackage this band—the band that you put your blood, sweat, and vomit into—until it's something they can resell to consumers to make back the money they will lose when you walk. To your fans, you're Sav Loveless. But to the label? You're a dollar sign. And as far as you need to be concerned, the label is all that matters right now."

I feel like I've been kicked in the stomach.

And he's right. I know he is. Just another Where Are They Now internet search.

I don't say anything. I pick a spot on the floor and stare at it, processing everything that's been said. Trying like hell and failing to regain my footing.

"Take the four months. Maybe a little vacay from the band will do you some good. Shoot your movie. Think it over."

I take a deep breath, drop my eyes closed, and concede, "Okay."

He turns to leave. I listen to his steps as he crosses the floor. He reaches the door, and I listen as it opens, but before walking out, he shoots one last bullet through my heart.

"And during that time, wear the ring."

My mouth drops, and I whip my eyes to Torren, but he's gaping at Hammond. I turn my glare back to the devil at the door, and he's already staring back at me.

"It's my job to know these things," he says pointedly. "If you wear the ring, it will keep the press interested—"

"But I didn't say yes," I butt in.

Hammond doesn't even acknowledge me. He just keeps on talking.

"The tabloids won't run the stories about a lovers' quarrel breaking up the band, and the fans are more likely to buy into the hiatus. It will also give the label time to find your replacement without a media shitstorm."

"I didn't say yes, Hammond!"

This time I shout it, and he sighs again, exasperated, like I'm a tantruming toddler.

"You will wear the ring, or we will move forward publicly about the replacement. And if I were you, I'd think for a minute about how that news will affect your movie press. I know you've been working hard to clean up your image, Savannah. Wouldn't want all that effort to go up in smoke."

Hammond turns and walks out the door, and I watch as it closes slowly behind him, sealing us inside with a soft *click*.

My blood is rushing in my ears. My heart is pounding out of my chest. I clench my fists and feel my nails bite into my palm. I am so sick of this shit.

"You fucking proposed," Mabel sneers at Torren. "When the fuck did you propose, Torren?"

I drop my head between my knees and let them lash out at each other. For years I was the mediator and ringleader, but I'm too fucking exhausted to do it anymore.

"Cleveland."

Torren's voice is resigned. Cleveland was right before Atlanta. Right before everything blew up.

"In fucking Cleveland?" Mabel scoffs and turns her attention on me. I can feel her eyes burning giant holes in my back. "Is that why you decided to quit? Is that why you decided to pull the plug on everything we've worked for?"

I shake my head as I slowly sit my body back upright.

"It wasn't just one thing, Mabel."

Her disbelieving snort has my teeth clenching and my nostrils flaring. I stare her down and give her some hard fucking truths.

"I've had three failed rehab stints in as many years, Mabel. Three. One of them, the label made me check out early against medical advice because we couldn't disrupt our tour. It took Jonah almost dying for me to try to get clean, and the only reason he isn't dead yet is because I hired him a 24/7 babysitter with a briefcase full of fucking Narcan."

She rolls her eyes, as if Jonah's OD was no big deal, and that just pisses me off more.

"Everyone in this band is a fucking mess. We're on a fast track to burn out. To the goddamned grave. And what about you? Do you even know the name of the guy you screwed in your suite before the show tonight? What about last night? It's been two years since Crystal dumped you, and you're still on a downward spiral. Am I just supposed to wait until you crash at the bottom? Want me to wait around and see how you'll self-destruct, too?"

I pull at my hair and kick the coffee table to keep from screaming. I look at Torren, still standing with his back to the wall, jaw tight and brows slanted. His chest is rising and falling with his rapid breaths.

No one is listening to reason.

Everyone is so fucking afraid of change—afraid of what comes after this—that they're willing to hold on to the death. But I don't want to die. I don't want them to die. I want us to live.

"I don't need you telling me how to live my life, Savannah," Mabel seethes. "At least I'm coherent. At least I'm not waking up face down in a ditch reeking of whiskey."

"I'm not either," I yell back. "Not anymore."

She narrows her eyes and curls her upper lip.

"Have the track marks between your toes healed yet?" she asks, almost sweetly, and it makes me want to vomit.

"I am *trying*," I grind out. "I don't want to be that person anymore. Jesus, don't you get it? We won't survive another year like this. *I* won't."

"Then move on to your fancy new Hollywood career and let us replace you. We won't be your problem anymore."

She stands and walks out the door without another word, and the ice in her demeanor chills me to my marrow. Mabel used to be all laughter and sunshine. She was my best friend, and now she can't stand me. She can't even look at me without hatred and jealousy coloring her vision.

It started slow at first. In the beginning, she was just excited the band was getting the attention. It wasn't until the label started making me front and center on all the posters, giving me all the interviews and magazine covers, that it really started to eat away at our relationship.

Her and me, we're hanging by a rapidly fraying thread. I thought putting an end to The Hometown Heartless was the only way to repair it. Now I have no idea.

"I didn't tell him," Torren says, deep voice slicing through the silence. Jonah is still passed out in the armchair. I have no idea where Red went. It's just me and Torren. "I didn't tell anyone, Savvy, I swear."

"I know." I sigh. "I know, Tor. It's fine."

Slowly, he walks toward the couch, then takes a seat on the cushion next to me. When he takes my hand in his, I let him, relaxing into his warmth.

"Why won't you say yes?" His voice is brooding and steady. "Would it be so bad? Marrying me? I thought we loved each other."

"I do love you, but not like that. And you don't love me like that either."

I let go of his hand and stand up. For all the bullshit everyone is unfairly placing on me, this one actually is my fault. I used him. I lead him on. I tried to force myself to feel something, tried to pretend, but all it did was ruin him. I'm unmoved, and he's collapsing.

"You didn't propose to me because you love me, Torren. You proposed because you're desperate for a life preserver, and I can't be that person for you anymore."

"That's not true. You know it's not."

"It is, though. It *is* true. None of it was real. None of it."

16

"Morning, Boss. What's the word?"

I glance down at Brynn as she skips up to my office manager's desk.

"Ingratiate. Verb. To gain favor or acceptance by deliberate effort."

Sharon purses her lips and looks at the ceiling for a moment, then gives Brynn a smile.

"I ingratiate myself with the boss by recognizing how intelligent she is."

Brynn smiles back and flashes two thumbs up. "A-plus, Miss Sharon."

"Thank you, Boss." Sharon hooks her thumb over her shoulder toward the coffee station. "Donuts."

Brynn darts to the donut box, and I pour myself a cup of coffee.

"Late start for you today," Sharon says, and I grunt. "I suppose she had you up late?"

"It's summer break, Miss Sharon. My bedtime is nine now."

"How late did you keep him up doing puzzles?"

Brynn giggles. "Only 10:30, but it was Scrabble, not a puzzle."

Sharon looks at me. "She kick your butt?"

I raise an eyebrow, and Sharon barks out a laugh. She knows

Brynn kicked my butt. I stopped letting her win at six. She hasn't needed it. I take a sip of my coffee and get to business. As Sharon pointed out, we got a late start.

"What're we dealing with today?"

"Luke is at the Pine Avenue site. He checked in with me this morning. The crew is on schedule, but the HVAC company is delayed again."

Fuck. Of course, they are. This is the third job this year they couldn't meet deadlines.

"I went ahead and pulled some comps," she says tentatively. "I can call 'em today for quotes, if you want."

I take a minute to think it over. I hate to have to go somewhere else. I prefer to source locally whenever possible, but we can't push this end date anymore. This family wants to be in the house before school starts back up in the fall. I sigh and take another sip of my coffee.

"Give them another week. If they don't come through by then, you can start making the calls."

She jots something down on a sticky note and sticks it to her computer, then glances back at her paper agenda book.

"I sent Gemma with Mark to the Birch Isle restoration. Figure it will be good training for her since they're ripping up the rotted floorboards today."

I nod. "That was a good idea."

"I also sent out invoices and checks. Balanced some of the books."

When I glance at her, she's staring right at me.

"S'not as bad as you probably think it is," she hedges. "This bid you won with the studio is already helping."

I down the rest of my coffee and pour another cup, then rake my hands through my hair and down my face. I think I'm starting to get an ulcer.

The cost of materials has skyrocketed, but I can't bring myself to raise our prices enough to make a profit. Most of the work we're doing are repairs from the last hurricane. What was supposed to be a tropical storm turned Category 3 and hooked on us. We'd barely had time to board up, but the next town over got hit bad and so did a lot of places farther inland. The flood damage is the worst our state has seen in decades. Businesses were lost. Homes were lost. Lives were lost.

I can't charge these people more than what I already do. I feel bad enough charging them anything at all.

My company has been part of the stage workers union for a while now, but winning the bid for the production at the studio was the best luck we've had in two years. Or, at least, it was. Now I don't know if it's luck or punishment.

I glance at Sharon and raise a brow, seeing if she's going to address the elephant in the room. She raises an eyebrow right back, telling me the answer is *hell no*. Fine. We can ignore it for now. But in a few weeks, it will be impossible, and she knows it.

"How's the rebuild project?"

An hour inland, in the town where I grew up, an entire neighborhood was destroyed by the flooding. The houses in the River View neighborhood were mostly older, poorly structured single-wide prefabs, and not a single one was up to code for the floodplain. It was a local zoning oversight that resulted in dozens of people displaced after the hurricane, and several people injured or killed. When I took on the rebuild project, I was furious to see how irresponsibly the whole thing had been done. The families that lived there had no idea the danger they were in. It was just a matter of time before they lost everything.

"Moving right along nicely," Sharon says. "Honestly, if we could have a private bank roll like that for all our projects, we'd never have any problems."

I nod. She's right. Most of the cost of the rebuild is covered by the emergency relief fund, but I'm refusing to cut corners, and it was a non-stop fight to get quality materials approved on their budget. Then, about eight months ago, the town was contacted by a private donor—the estate of some wealthy philanthropist—who offered to cover any additional costs of the rebuild. Since then, it's been smooth sailing. I'm not making any money off the job, obviously, but my crew is paid, and those families will have safe, quality homes to move back into soon.

"You're going to the studio today, then?"

Sharon scribbles something else on another sticky note, then glances up at me for confirmation. I nod. I've been spending most of my time at the rebuild, but now that we've got the studio job, I have to bounce between.

"Is Brynnlee staying with me today, or is she going with you?"

"I'm going with Dad!" Brynn chimes in from her place in front of the donut box.

She's got chocolate icing on her face and a strawberry donut in her hand. The girl is going to be on one hell of a sugar rush.

"She wants to see the set before filming officially starts next week—"

"And you said you'd take me to the book shop!"

"*And* I said I would take her to the book shop."

Sharon smiles at Brynn, then looks to me and raises an eyebrow.

"Try to have some fun," she drawls. "Maybe smile a little. I hear it releases dopamine, endorphins and serotonin, which can lower anxiety and increase happiness."

Sharon sticks out her hand, and Brynn slaps it as she skips past the desk.

"A-plus-plus, Miss Sharon," Brynn cheers, then grins up at me. "She's a good student. You should be more like her."

My lips twitch into a small smile, and I drop my hand to Brynn's head and ruffle her hair. This kid is too damn smart.

"Go get in the truck, Einstein."

"Bye, Miss Sharon! See you later!"

Sharon waits until the door closes behind Brynn before she lets the smile drop.

"Everyone is paid. Crew, contractors, all of it." Her brow furrows. "Things are getting better, Levi. The first installment from the studio job brought the business almost entirely out of the red."

I don't miss that she said almost, and I don't miss that she specified the business.

"Did you pay yourself?" I ask, and she waves me off.

"Enough."

I sigh. I'm not going to argue with her again. She's stubborn. It's in her DNA.

I wait to see if she'll ask me anything more about the studio, or the plans for the on-site filming that starts in a few weeks. She doesn't, so I don't bring it up, either. We'll live in denial a little while longer.

"Alright, Sharon," I say gruffly, opening the door and stepping outside. "I'm out. We'll see you tomorrow."

"See you tomorrow."

I walk to the truck and climb into the front seat. Brynn is already buckled into her seat in the back. I turn around and reach into the back, tugging on her belt to make sure it's secure. She rolls her eyes and sighs loudly, so I give her side a tickle before turning back around.

"Ready to roll, Boss?"

"Ready to roll."

I pull out of the parking lot and onto the main road that will lead us out of town and to the highway. The film studio is a forty-minute drive up the coast, and the ride is an easy one. Minimal traffic and clear skies.

"You think she'll be there?" Brynn pipes up from the back, and my shoulders stiffen.

"Probably not," I say, more hopeful than certain. "They don't start filming for a few more days."

I glance in the rearview mirror to find Brynn frowning out the window, her little index finger tapping out beats of four on her thigh.

"I'll get to meet her, though, right?"

I pause before I answer, thinking over the best way to say it.

"I don't know, Brynn. She'll be working."

"But you can ask?"

I glance at her again. Her finger is tapping faster, her frown more pronounced.

"Yeah, Boss. I can ask."

Her shoulders visibly relax, and when her frown eases away, I bring my eyes back to the road. All the tension she'd felt moments before has left her and entered me. I consciously unclench my hands from around the steering wheel, then turn on some music. It only takes ten minutes before a song by The Hometown Heartless comes on, and Brynn sings along loudly in the back seat. I try to focus on her voice and not the one on the radio.

I'm a wreck. I haven't slept, and when I do, I dream of Savannah. Savannah then and Savannah now.

I do my best to ignore the click-bait surrounding The Hometown Heartless, but it is literally everywhere. Television. Radio. Hell, even my favorite podcast has discussed it.

Rumors have been soaring since the band announced their "hiatus." Early headlines cited drug use and the tumultuous relationship between Sav Loveless and the band's bassist, Torren King, as the reason behind the split. My teeth grit at every mention of Torren King. My last encounter with him wasn't a good one. I can still picture him fucked up and scrambling in the sand after I ripped his brother off Savannah. I haven't been able to stand him since.

Which makes the newest headlines even harder to digest.

The band released a joint statement debunking break-up rumors and saying relationships within the band are strong as ever.

We are taking a break to work on individual projects, but we still have the utmost love and respect for each other, the statement said.

Then, last week, Sav Loveless was spotted in L.A. wearing a giant emerald on her left ring finger. They haven't confirmed or denied the engagement rumors swirling, but I feel it in my gut. My hypocrisy is so loud it's nearly deafening, my own ring finger feeling itchy and uncomfortable for the first time in years. The silicone ring on my left hand can usually be ignored. I barely feel it, and it's not a hazard on a construction site. But recently? It's felt just as heavy as it did in the beginning, when it was brushed gold and strangling.

"Dad," Brynn says, shaking me from my thoughts.

I can tell by the frustration in her tone that she's called for me more than once. I reach up and turn down the radio.

"Yeah, Boss?" I meet her eyes in the rearview mirror.

"After we go to Penn and Paige, can we get smoothies?" I nod and she grins. "Thank you!"

I turn the radio back up and we listen to it the rest of the drive. Thankfully, another one of The Hometown Heartless songs doesn't come on before we're pulling up to the security gate at the studio. I roll my window down and grab my badge from the dashboard. It's more of a formality than anything.

"Gonna be seein' a lot of you for the next few months, I guess," Tucker says as he signs me in on his clipboard.

"Long as they're shooting, my team has to be here."

Tucker grins then glances to the back seat, giving Brynn a wave before opening the barrier gate and letting us through.

"Have a great day, Levi."

I nod and pull through without another word.

When I put the truck in park outside the sound stage, Brynn is already unbuckled and ready to run. She hops out and jogs up next to me, eyes scanning the parking lot for I don't even know what.

"You think she'd drive a big fancy car? She wouldn't be here with a tour bus," Brynn chatters to herself, skipping along next to me as we walk toward the building. "I bet she had to fly in a plane. Do you think she has a private plane? I hope not. The pollution is bad for the environment. That's a lot of carbon emissions. She wouldn't have a private plane, right? Maybe she flew in a regular plane and then took a limo. I don't see a limo, though."

I reach down and smooth back Brynn's hair, escorting her through the door I've already opened.

"I don't think she's here yet, Boss."

She glances at me and opens her mouth to respond, but then her eyes go wide when she catches sight of the set we've built.

Two of the soundstages have been combined to create a 40,000 square foot area. The flats have all been fully erected, the paint is dry, the textured details have been added, and I have to admit, it's pretty fucking cool. With the lighting, sound, and camera crews rushing about, it feels much more alive and real than it did two weeks ago.

"Wow," she breathes out, taking it all in. "You guys built all this?"

"We did."

My chest puffs out at the awe on her face, and I try to see the soundstage through her eyes as we walk past the sets we've constructed. There are several fancy New York offices, a cozy studio apartment, a coffee shop loft, an art studio, a jail cell, a few rooms that resemble an Italian villa, and a ballroom that looks like something straight out of a multi-million-dollar mansion. When we step in front of another structure, Brynn's jaw drops. She whips her head to me, then back to the set.

"Dad! This looks just like our kitchen!"

I watch her eyes dart around to every detail—the refrigerator, the island, the double oven—and I let my eyes follow. Even the backsplash is the same. It's actually eerie, and I worked directly with the props and designs crews. All that's missing are dishes in the sink, Brynn's artwork on the fridge, and our dry erase board calendar on the wall. Everything else is nearly identical.

"Oh my gosh, I can't wait to tell Cameron. You're so cool, Dad."

"Want to see the back lot?"

She jumps and claps her hands. "Yes!"

I lead her to the open lot where we've constructed what looks like buildings, a courtyard and several small roads in a coastal Italian village. I read a lot about this movie when we got the job, and it's predicted to be quite the blockbuster. An action thriller that takes place in New York City, a coastal village in Italy, and the Hamptons. Conveniently, though, it will be almost entirely shot here in North Carolina.

"Cooper," someone calls, and I turn to see Jerry, the studio construction manager, heading my way. I lift a chin in greeting, then turn to Brynn.

"Go look, but don't touch. And keep an eye out for some of my guys. They're out here somewhere."

Brynn salutes me, then skips off just as Dustin, a member of my crew, pops out from behind one of the fake Italian buildings. He waves at me. I point to Brynn, and he throws me a thumbs up just as my daughter bounces over to him.

"Hey, Boss."

"Hi, Dustin!"

I watch them give each other a low five, then Dustin leads her toward the courtyard fountain, just as Jerry steps up next to me.

"Everything is looking good." He grunts, shaking my hand. "Your guys did a great job. Some of the best work I've seen in all my years here, and you worked quick, too."

"Thanks."

He waits for a breath, but when he realizes I'm not going to say anything else, he looks toward Dustin and Brynn.

"You showin' your daughter around?" I nod in response. "She's welcome here anytime. We'll get her a badge if you like. Just keep her away from the equipment. Shit's expensive."

I raise a brow at him, an unspoken yet sarcastic *no shit*, and he laughs. We talk a bit more; I get some information about filming, then we say goodbye with another handshake and a nod.

Jerry has been great to work with. I'm pretty sure the only reason we got this job was because he's seen the work my company has been doing in the area since the storm. I also think he can guess how much we're *not* making on the reconstruction and rebuilds. It's been an unspoken favor, and I won't let him down.

These towns along the coast are small and tight knit. We all know or know of one another, and word spreads quickly. It's where small town nosy and southern hospitality meet. For as annoying as it can be, it can also be really nice.

I check in with Dustin, then grab Brynn and take her around to the trailer lot. Usually, the studio crew would be driving golf carts to get from one lot to another, but Brynn and I hike it on foot, so when we make it to the crew trailers, we're damp with sweat.

"This is where she'll be," Brynn whispers, walking slowly.

"This is where the cast will be during filming, but they'll be living somewhere off-site."

"Do you think we'll s—" Brynn halts in her tracks, and when I follow her gaze, I find what she's staring at.

It's a trailer just like all the others, but this one has a sign on the door that says SAV LOVELESS in giant black letters. The moment my eyes land on that sign, I'm just as frozen as Brynn. I can't move. I can't speak. Something like excitement or fear clamors in my chest, and I frown at the feeling. I scowl at that trailer. That door. That sign.

I scowl at the name.

Something about that sign makes all of this feel more real than it did ten minutes ago. The set, the crew, the studio. It all existed in my head separate from Sav Loveless. Until now. My muscles ache with tension and my fists clench tightly. Come Monday, I'll be better prepared to see her. But right now, I need to get the fuck out of here.

I clear my throat, then gently put a hand on Brynn's shoulder.

"Penn and Paige and smoothies."

17

"Fifteen minutes," Red says from the driver's seat, rousing me from my nap.

I glance out the window, noting how the scenery has changed just in the two-hour drive from the airport. I bet if I roll down the tinted window, I'll be able to smell the Atlantic. We've played in Raleigh several times over the last few years, but this is as close as I've gotten to my hometown since I was fifteen. We passed the exit for it about an hour ago. I was asleep, but I still knew. I could feel it.

"Should we go to the studio first, or do you just want to head to your rental? I already have the entry code."

Red flips the turn signal and glances at me from behind his dark aviators.

"Rental, please."

We're not expected at the studio until Monday, but Red and I decided to sneak into town early hoping to avoid a paparazzi swarm. They always show up where I'm supposed to be. We took a red-eye flight from LAX and rented our own car instead of flying the chartered jet and being shuttled by the studio limo. It's worked out pretty well so far. The flight attendant asked me to sign a barf bag for his kid sister, and I got a few curious glances in the airport but that always happens when I bring Ziggy with me. Mostly, we've gone unnoticed. No one has ratted me out to the press yet.

I watch as Red pulls the address for the rental up on the GPS, then turns the car toward the downtown area. We pass cute little shops, restaurants, and bars, and I watch the people strolling down the sidewalks eating ice cream and sipping on iced coffees. I see glimpses of the estuary and the riverwalk, and then the shops are replaced by historic houses and brick buildings. Red turns down a brick alleyway, then pulls up to a wrought iron gate. He rolls down the window and punches in a code, then pulls forward into a private cobblestone courtyard once the gate opens. We're not even inside yet and I'm already happy I chose to have the studio put me in the rental instead of the hotel suite. I'm tired of living out of hotels and tour buses.

"Well, this is fucking charming," I say, taking in the stonework and the tiled art detail on the garage door. "I never would have guessed this was back here."

"Let's hope it takes the paps a while to figure it out, too," Red says, hitting the garage door opener they'd sent us and pulling the car forward.

He puts the car in park and pops the trunk, then climbs out and grabs our suitcases. I sling a backpack over one shoulder and snag my guitar.

"Let's go Ziggs," I say, opening the back door and letting my rescue pup hop out.

She's wagging her tail so hard that her whole body serpentines, and I just watch her for a minute with a dumb smile on my face. She runs around and sniffs everything in the garage, then heads out into the fenced yard and finds a place to pee.

"Good girl, ZeeZee," I croon, and she bounds back up to me and attacks my hand and kneecap with sloppy kisses.

I can't believe I almost left her in L.A. with a dog sitter. In the eight short months since I adopted her, my Ziggy Girl has become family. Hands down, the best impulsive decision I've ever made. This weird little mutt ball of energy has become the sober companion I didn't know I needed. Red loves her too, even though he doesn't show it. I crouch down and scratch her behind her ears and above her tail like she likes.

"Good job, girl."

Red clears his throat, and I glance up to find him waiting in the open doorway. I roll my eyes and push myself to standing.

"C'mon Ziggy Girl, we can't leave the old man waiting."

Red grunts, then heads into the house and I follow with Ziggy trailing me.

As soon as I step through the door, I love it immediately.

What was an unassuming brick building from the street is luxurious and quirky inside. Everything about it is the perfect blend of chic and cozy with the most adorable trendy details mixed in. Exposed brick on accent walls, colorful shag area rugs, and funky light fixtures dot the entire first floor. It's open concept with a staircase on the far wall leading to what I know will be two more floors and then a rooftop terrace that overlooks the water. I was intrigued when I saw the photos of the house the studio had emailed, but I'm absolutely enamored seeing it in person.

I drag my fingers over the white and gray marble countertop, the matching island with a built-in sink and wine fridge, then make my way into the living room. I drop myself onto the large overstuffed dark purple couch, and Ziggy jumps up next to me, resting her head on my thigh as I tilt mine back into the cushion.

"This has to be one of the comfiest couches I've ever sat on," I say, and I hear Red chuckle from somewhere behind me.

I sit back up and look at the coffee table book—historic photography of the area—then push myself to standing despite my body's desire to stay sunken into the plush couch cushion. Ziggs doesn't even budge, and I don't blame her. I think she's found her favorite place in the house. I look at Red and point to the ceiling.

"I'm going to check out the upstairs."

Everything looks how it did in the pictures. The primary bedroom has a giant king bed and an ensuite bathroom with a spa tub and steam shower. The second bedroom is slightly smaller, but also has an attached bathroom, which makes me feel better about making Red stay in there. He's a big guy, but if I offered him the primary bedroom with the king bed, he'd never accept it.

Then I find the door to the rooftop terrace.

It's fucking beautiful. Twinkle lights strung around the perimeter, stylish patio furniture, a small fire pit, and an outdoor kitchen make the area beyond impressive, but my favorite part is the unobstructed view of the estuary and riverwalk. I want to watch the sunset and rise from this terrace. I want to light up the fire pit and play my guitar under the stars.

The whole scene lifts me up and excites me briefly, and then I'm hit with a wave of sadness.

It makes me miss the band.

A few years ago, we would have loved this set up. Mabel's laughter would carry, and I can close my eyes and imagine us jamming around glowing embers under twinkling lights. Jonah would make sure we had everything we needed, filling our drinks and stoking the fire, ever the mother hen. Torren would brood, smirk, and crack the perfect jokes at the perfect times.

The image brings a smile to my lips and a sting to my eye.

I miss that kind of fun. Fun like we used to have before we blew up and lost all semblance of normalcy. When they were my chosen family instead of my contracted business partners. When we actually *liked* each other.

I sigh and bring my attention back to the estuary. It's a thirty-mile-long stretch of the river that's become mixed with the salt water of the Atlantic before the two waterways meet, and the riverwalk is teeming with energy. Restaurants, coffee shops, boutiques, all of it. There's even an area a few blocks down for bands to play during the warmer summer months.

I grew up just about an hour from here, but I was never able to visit. Never saw this riverwalk. Never stepped foot in the ocean at the end of it. Never even thought about this town until that very first tour. When we played here, we were still Savannah Alt. It wasn't until our first show outside of D.C. that we became The

Hometown Heartless. Right on time, too, because our second D.C. show is when we debuted "Just One More," and it changed everything.

We were asked once in an interview why we named the band The Hometown Heartless, and Jonah answered for us.

"The concept of a hometown can evoke visceral emotions. People either love their hometown, or they hate it. They embrace it, never want to leave, or they run as far away as they can. But for us, the idea of never leaving means shunning growth and avoiding change. Those things—new things, different things—don't fit into the 'hometown' mold, and a hometown can be real cozy until you try to break out of the mold. For people like us, people who don't really *fit*, a hometown can be stifling. It can be heartless."

We all sat in silence for a moment, nodding and soaking in Jonah's answer. I remember feeling glad he answered because I wouldn't have been as eloquent. I would have said my most debilitating heartbreaks still reside in my hometown. Jonah's answer was better.

He was so much more vocal and charismatic in the beginning. The boy who always had a classic novel in his duffle bag. Who did crossword puzzles for fun between books he was reading. What a contrast to how he is now. My heart aches at the memory, and then I smile.

In that interview, after his answer stunned us all speechless, he laughed, then said with a smirk, "plus it just sounds fucking cool."

And that was Jonah. Insightful and deep, with a cool wit that always took the edge off.

I walk to the railing on the edge of the rooftop and brace my hands on it, leaning forward and breathing deeply. The air smells better here than it does in L.A. It's quieter, too. I hear the river lapping at the rocks from the boat wakes. I hear faint chatter and laughter and music. It's peace in a form I've never known. Calm and relaxing. Content.

Sometimes, I wonder where I'd be if the band hadn't hit it big. It's a delusional game I play with myself. I romanticize the hypothetical. I attempt to fool myself into thinking I'd be healthier and happier. I try to picture myself as one of those normal people on the riverwalk, sipping iced lattes and chatting about their daily lives.

The image never lasts, though. The reality always crashes in, reminding me just who and what I was before I was Sav Loveless. A broke stripper with a budding substance abuse problem. A runaway teen from a fucked-up family. Vulnerable prey for disgusting, vicious people.

I have to laugh at myself otherwise I'll cry.

It's not that I'm not grateful for where I am now. I am. For the fans, the success, the money. I have a fucking Grammy. This movie role is one actors go their whole careers trying to land. I'm lucky, and I know I'm lucky. That label rep in the D.C. dive bar who heard "Just One More" and saw potential in The Hometown Heartless changed my whole life.

But recently...

Damn if sometimes I wish he'd never showed, and I don't know what that says about me.

"Kid."

I startle and turn toward the door to find Red standing on the terrace, arms folded across his chest, assessing.

"No coverage at all," he says, glancing around to the neighboring rooftops. "Anyone with their phone camera could get you. The right lens will do it from one of the boats on the river, too."

I snort and shake my head.

"You're a fun sucker," I say, walking toward him. "You just suck the fun out of everything."

He raises an eyebrow.

"You still know how to have fun?"

I punch him in the stomach, and he acts like it hurts, then quick as lightning, crouches down, swings his leg out, and sweeps my feet out from under me. I land hard on my ass with a thud.

"Could have at least tried to catch me." I groan, lying myself flat on the ground and throwing my arm over my face.

"Could have but didn't want to suck the fun out of it."

I grunt and kick at his foot.

"You're a dick."

Red chuckles, then sticks out a hand.

"Get up. Your mutt is getting restless. I don't want her to eat the couch."

I reach up and let him pull me to my feet, then I make my way to the door.

"She wouldn't eat the couch," I say with confidence I don't feel.

He doesn't say anything because he knows I'm full of shit.

I pound down the stairs until I'm on the first floor and find Ziggs doing laps around the kitchen island. Definitely only a matter of seconds away from eating the couch.

"Want to walk downtown?" I ask Red and he shakes his head no like I knew he would. "C'mon, Red. We're in town days early. No one knows I'm here yet. I want to explore a little before I'm inevitably being stalked with every step."

He pauses a moment before nodding reluctantly. I flash him a grin, then rush to my backpack and pull out my baseball cap. I throw my hair in a loose bun at the nape of my neck and pull the hat low on my head, then slip on my aviator sunglasses.

"You still look like you," Red says, and I sigh loudly.

"Fun sucker."

I call Ziggy over, clip her leash onto her collar, and grab my handy little wristlet of dog poop bags. Then, just to be an ass, I toss the wristlet at Red and smile sweetly. He slips it onto his hand without expression, and I roll my eyes.

"C'mon, Ziggy Girl," I say, giving her some head scratches. "Let's go for a walk."

She's spinning in circles and panting like crazy, which has me smiling, but then Red has to go and ruin it.

"The ring," he reminds me, and my shoulders bunch with irritation.

"No."

"Yes, Savannah." His voice is stern, using the *father* tone that I have a love/hate relationship with. "You agreed. Until you make a decision, wear the ring."

"This is so dumb, Red. This move is low and skeezy, and you know it."

He nods.

"It's bullshit. But unless you want to announce that you're being replaced, you need to do it. And Savannah, I really don't think you want to be replaced."

I sigh, then groan and stomp my foot like a child. This whole mess has me wanting to rage and throw an epic tantrum. But Red is right, so reluctantly, I dig back through my backpack until I find the velvet box with the engagement ring. I slip it on my finger without looking at it.

It's a gorgeous ring. That almost pisses me off more than the proposal. Torren knows me better than most. This three-carat teardrop cut emerald on a simple gold band is the ring I'd pin on a wedding vision board if I were the type to do that. Makes me wonder if I described it to him once when I was high and forgot about it.

Red is already standing at the door with Ziggs, so when I step up to him, I act like I'm going to take the leash. When he reaches out to give it to me, I grab his arm, throw all my weight into him, and pull a perfect foot sweep, spinning out of the way so he lands hard on his ass. I bark out a laugh, then point at him while bouncing my eyebrows.

"You're getting slower in your old age."

He pushes himself up to standing.

"You're getting faster in your sobriety."

I grin, ring on my hand almost forgotten.

"I know."

18

I WALK OUTSIDE with Red trailing behind me.

He punches in the security code for the wrought iron door that leads from the courtyard to the street, and I hear it snap open.

"Gotta use the code to get in and out?"

"In and out."

"Hm. Security on lock," I say, and Red grunts.

He won't bring it up, but I know he pushed for these extra measures because of the stalker I had last year. Some forty-something-year-old man had delusions of me being his wife and managed to break into our tour bus and steal a bunch of my underwear. We saw him on the cameras but didn't catch him until three weeks later when we found him in my hotel shower.

Showering.

And jerking off with my bodywash.

I shudder at the memory. Guy ended up in a facility for mentally unstable people, and I didn't press charges because the label didn't want a media frenzy. I still double check my locks on the doors and windows before I go to bed.

Red and I stroll down the street toward the riverwalk, stopping every few feet so Ziggy can sniff at something. She's not very good on a leash yet. She pulls. She's not very good at all, honestly. She's house trained and that's about it. Absolutely no manners. I love it.

The riverwalk is busy, but no one looks our way other than to say hi to Ziggy. I think people are scared of Red because he's a giant covered in tattoos. It works out in my favor. I'm able to enjoy the scenery and the walk. The breeze tickles my skin and sets my nerves at ease. When I see a coffee shop, I flash Red a grin. I can't see for sure because of his dark sunglasses, but I can feel his side-eye.

"Can't bring the mutt in," he states, and I shrug.

"Just stay out here with her. I'll be like five minutes."

"And when you get recognized?"

I shrug again. It's a matter of time before it happens, anyway, and then my life will be a madhouse of bulb flashes and paparazzi tails for a few weeks. Then, hopefully, the excitement will die off and the mob will shrink from double to single digits.

"You want one of those frozen kid drinks?" I ask him instead of answering. He doesn't say yes, but I know he wants one. Caramel flavored with whipped cream because my big scary ex-Marine bodyguard has the tastebuds of a five-year-old.

I give him a smile, then walk into the café.

It's absolutely adorable, and it smells amazing. Like coffee and baked goods. The place looks like it used to be a car repair shop or something, because on either side of the doorway there are old garage doors. They're currently up, making the front walls of the café open to the sidewalk, with just a metal railing separating the inside from the outside. There are a few tables and chairs placed along the railings, too, for a cute little indoor/outdoor dining experience.

There are a handful of people sitting at the mismatched tables. One guy has a giant textbook open in front of him, but he's wearing headphones and scrolling through his phone. A woman at one of the front tables is working on a laptop with a half-eaten scone sitting on the tabletop next to her. Someone in the corner is reading a newspaper.

No one is paying any attention to me, and my body sags with

relief. I may have been ready for the attention, but that doesn't make it any easier.

I walk up to the register and the kid behind it greets me with a confused smile. I'm still wearing my aviators, so I know all he can see is his reflection in the mirrored lenses.

"Hey," he says with a cock of his head. "Welcome to Port Town Beanery. What can I get started for you?"

I scan the menu again, then order a large latte with an extra espresso shot for me, and a caramel frozen coffee for Red. With whipped cream on top.

"And can I get six blueberry muffins to go, too?"

The kid nods. "Sure thing. Name for the order?"

"Priscilla," I say, giving him one of the aliases I use in public, then walk to the bulletin board on the wall and look it over while he makes the coffee.

I'm reading a flier about the town's summer concert series on the water—a bunch of tribute and jam bands, including one that probably plays covers of my songs—when my phone chimes. I pull it out of my pocket but can't read the screen with my sunglasses on. I pull the sunglasses down the bridge of my nose and unlock my phone screen.

RED

Your mutt has to pee.

So take her to go pee?

Come out here.

I roll my eyes. I'm not leaving my coffee just so I can walk down the block and be babysat while my dog pees in the grass.

Coffee isn't ready yet. Just take her before she pees on your shoes again.

You'll be right back. I'll be fine.

The text bubbles pop up, then disappear, then pop up again, then disappear. I glance out the window and find Ziggy doing the puppy pee wiggle around Red as he frowns at his phone. I smirk. Just as I'm about to text him again, his response comes through.

I'll be right back. Don't go anywhere.

I send him a poop emoji, then he puts his phone in his pocket and stalks away.

I bring my attention back to the bulletin board and scan some more fliers—a garage sale tomorrow on Chestnut Street, a lost cat named Nibbles, some kid home from college for the summer who wants to babysit, pet sit, house sit, or clean your pool—then a small gasp startles me. I glance toward the sound and find a little girl, maybe seven or eight, with wild brown curls staring up at me through wide, bright blue eyes.

I flick my eyes to the barista, then bring my finger to my lips. "Shhh."

I point to the hallway with the bathrooms, out of sight of the barista and most of the customers. She nods quickly, then turns and skips toward the hallway. I follow.

As soon as we're alone, she starts bouncing.

"Omigod are you? You are. You are, right? I mean you are but omigod, omigod."

I laugh and nod. "I am."

"Prodigious," she whispers, and I laugh again.

"Prodigious? How old are you?"

"Seven and three quarters."

"That's a big word for a seven-year-old."

"And three quarters," she corrects, then grins wide, showing off two missing teeth. "I'm smarter than my dad."

"You're probably smarter than me, too," I tell her, and she smiles bigger. "What's your name, Miss Genius?"

"Brynnlee. You can call me Brynn. Some people call me Brynn. 'Cept my dad. He usually calls me Boss."

"I like Boss. Are you the boss?"

"Yeah, pretty much." She glances over my shoulder. "There's my dad! Can you sign one of my books? Dad! Can she sign one of my books?"

I'm all smiles when I spin to greet the girl's dad, but the smile disappears immediately the moment my eyes land on the man in front of me.

He looks different, yet exactly the same, and for what feels like years, we just stare at each other. His shoulders are broader, his short sleeves snugger around his biceps. His sharp jaw is covered with a dark, neatly trimmed beard, but I can still see the little dimple in his chin, and a memory flashes through my head of pressing my index finger into it. His hair is shaggier than I've ever seen it, and the dirty blond has darkened, but the stern slash of his eyebrows is just like I remember, and his mouth is the same one I still see in my dreams.

He's holding a bag full of books, and I open my mouth to speak just as he places his hand on Brynn's shoulder and moves her behind him. My stomach drops. The action is such a parental thing to do. Like he's protecting her. I furrow my brow. Is he protecting her from me?

And then it hits me.

This is his daughter. Brynn is *his* daughter.

I do the mental math, and it all adds up.

I have to force the image of him standing in the middle of my raggedy Miami living room out of my head. I grit my teeth and breathe slowly through my nose, trying like hell not to spiral into that memory. The cell phone. The ultrasound picture. The *just once.* But then a third surprise grabs at my chest and squeezes, and it's all over for me.

There's a ring on his left hand. It's black, and looks like it might be made of silicone, but there's no denying what it is. A wedding band.

"They're going to make you marry her."

"No way, they wouldn't."

"They will."

"It doesn't matter what they want. I won't do it."

I almost want to laugh. Levi Cooper is standing in front of me, shielding his daughter from me like I'm some dangerous stranger, and he's wearing a wedding band. My eyes fly behind him, scanning for someone who could be a wife. The *once* who became the *one*. When I see no one, I look back at his face, but he's not looking at me.

He's staring at my hand.

My left hand.

And suddenly, my emerald sham of an engagement ring feels like my own sword and shield. I flex my fingers, watch his jaw tense, then bring my hand up slowly and press it to my chest. His eyes follow, stick for a breath, then rise to my face.

"Uh, Dad, can you hear me?" Brynn says, and I watch as she tugs on his shirt and pokes her head out from behind him. "Can she, Dad? Please?"

Without saying anything, without taking his hard eyes off me, he hands the bag of books to Brynn, and she drops quickly to the floor and digs through it. She pops back up with a magazine in hand.

"Oh, no." Brynn looks at me. "I don't have a pen. Do you have a pen?"

"Priscilla," the barista calls, and I blink, shaking my head slightly to rid myself of the fog that came with Levi's reappearance.

"My coffee," I say lamely before looking back at Brynn, forcing a smile.

I scan her face, looking for Levi, but the curly brown hair and blue eyes must come from her mom's side of the family.

"I'll get a marker from the barista, okay, Boss?"

She nods, showing off her toothless smile, and I give Levi a wide berth as I pass him. I release a shaky breath when I round the corner back into the café, but then gasp when I see what's waiting for me.

There she is. It's her. She's here.

Flash.

Sav, when did you get into town?

Flash.

Are you here with Torren King?

Flash.

Sav is it true you're engaged now?

Show us the ring, Sav.

Flash. Flash. Flash.

"Fuck."

There have to be ten to fifteen paparazzi on the sidewalk, plastered to the metal railings and leaning into the café with their cameras pointed at me. I don't recognize any of them, but that doesn't mean some of them didn't trail me from L.A.

Thankfully, a barista is standing by the front door, and it looks like she's locked it, but it's only a matter of seconds before one of these idiots realizes he can just hop over the railing and come inside. Damn it.

Is this really a hiatus, Sav?

Did the band break up because of your relationship with Torren King?

Did he cheat on you again? Did you cheat on him again?

When did you get out of rehab, Sav?

Sav, what do you have to say abo—

I turn and head back into the hallway, reaching for my phone to call Red for an escape plan, and run smack into a hard chest. His hands wrap around my upper arms, and even though it's only for a split second—barely enough time to get a full inhale of his spicy, clean scent—it feels like he pulls me closer. Like his hands tighten. Like he doesn't want to let go.

"C'mon." He growls, then spins and shoves me down the hall.

I don't ask. I just do as he says. He grabs Brynn's hand and hurries past me, and I follow him to an exit door that leads out into the alley behind the café.

"White truck," he says, gesturing to a vehicle parked at the end of the alley. "Run."

So, I run.

Me, Levi Cooper, and Levi Cooper's daughter sprint through the alley, dodging rocks and potholes, until he's opening the back door of a beat-up old pickup truck and tossing Brynn inside while I climb into the passenger seat and shove myself onto the floorboard between the bench seat and the glove compartment.

Levi cranks up the truck just as my phone starts to buzz, so I twist my body awkwardly until my hand can reach into my pocket and pull out my cell.

"Red," I pant into the phone.

"Where are you?" His voice is steady, no hint of panic, but I know it's probably there.

"I'm okay. I'm with a..." I flick my eyes to Levi. He's staring straight out the windshield. "I'm with a local. They showed me the back way out. Has anyone seen you?"

"No," he says, and then it sounds like he's running. "Can the local bring you back to the rental?"

I swallow and look back at Levi. He nods once, confirming he's been listening, but he still doesn't look at me.

"Yeah."

"I'll be at the gate. Have them drive in."

I tell him okay, and then I hang up.

"Where's the rental?" Levi asks, voice hard and cold. No warmth. No fondness. Nothing but steel formalities and thinly-veiled anger.

I tell him the address and he flips the turn signal, turning the truck around and heading back to my side of town.

"Those men were reprehensible," Brynn says from the back seat. I almost forgot all about her. "They were so rude."

"Shit," I grumble, squeezing my eyes shut. "I'm sorry, Brynnlee. Are you okay?"

"Oh yeah, I'm fine. But that was simply atrocious."

I snort out a laugh. This kid is a trip.

"Sorry you didn't get your coffee," she says, and even though I can't see her because of how I'm squished on the floor, I can hear the sincerity in her voice.

"That's alright, Boss," I tell her cheerily, "I'll get my latte later."

I'm trying like hell to act like this whole incident hasn't made me feel extremely unsettled. Just another day in the life of an infamous rockstar. Just another nightmare in the brain of a scorned lover. No big deal. I'm not rattled. Just as calm and cool as ever.

I feel the truck slow and see the wrought iron gate of my rental looming in the windshield. It opens slowly, and Levi rolls the truck into the courtyard. I unstuff myself from the floorboard and reach for the door handle, making eye contact with Red through the window.

"He'll need to talk to you," I say to Levi.

He says nothing to me as he shuts off the truck, but he turns to Brynn in the back.

"Stay here."

"But Dad, can't I—"

"Brynn. Stay. Here. This isn't up for discussion."

I glance at her, her brow furrowed, and her lip poked out in a pout. This is the first time since I've met her that she actually looks her age. She huffs and crosses her arms over her chest.

"Fine."

Levi opens his door and steps out, so I do the same, taking a moment to send Brynn a smile.

"It was nice to meet you, Boss."

Her lips twitch into the smallest smile, then she looks away, still pouting. I temper my chuckle and shut the truck door. I don't see Ziggy, so she must be inside. I'd ask after her, but Red's already in a heated discussion with Levi when I walk to them. He's got some papers in his hand and my shoulders tense.

"I'm not putting my name on anything," Levi says with a snarl.

"This is for your benefit as much as Ms. Loveless," Red snarls back.

Both of their jaws are tense, their biceps flexed. Red has a couple inches on Levi, but I actually think Levi could hold his own—at least for a few minutes—if they ended up having to throw down.

Levi's bigger now. More sculpted. Not bulky, not the kind of big you get from lifting heavy weights in a gym, but lean and hard. Defined in all the best places. A manual labor build. Before I can stop it, a visual of him braced naked above me flashes through my mind, and I can't help but wonder how he'd look now. Same position. Same act. Older Levi.

"What's going on?" I ask, squaring my shoulders.

"The local doesn't want to sign the NDA."

I whip my eyes to Levi, but he won't stop staring daggers at Red.

"Why not?"

"I don't want my name on anything regarding Sav Loveless," Levi says to Red, and my fury flares. I grit my teeth and breathe through my nose before speaking, burning my glare into the side of his face.

"If you think you can take this to the press for a payout—"

Levi barks a sinister laugh, and when he finally looks at me, it takes all my strength not to flinch. Instead, I straighten my spine and narrow my eyes. Fire with fire.

If he can be an asshole, so can I.

"I said I don't want my name on *anything*. I don't want the association. I sure as shit am not going to take this to the press."

God, that hurts. I grind my teeth harder, my pulse point in my neck is thrumming so rapidly that it feels like it might explode.

"If you don't sign this NDA, we will be forced to get ahead of it. Contact the label. Who knows what they'll do to spin the story in my favor—"

"What fucking story?"

"Whatever bullshit one you're cooking up for the media paycheck."

It's a bluff. I'm bluffing. He says he won't go to the press, and I believe him, but I'll be damned if I'm going to let him win this. I take a step forward.

"I'll be protected regardless. Signing the NDA just makes this easier for everyone."

He raises a brow and tilts his head to the side.

"Because the label has done a great job keeping your name out of the tabloids so far, right?"

His implication is like a punch to the gut. I want to gasp. I want to wince. I want to hit back harder. I do none of it. I tilt my head to the opposite side and arch my own brow.

"You want to take that chance?"

We stare at each other for fourteen seconds. I count them out in my head, waiting. I blink once and then I see him give. A flare of his nostrils, an almost imperceptible growl that makes my toes curl, and then he turns to Red.

"Give me a fucking pen."

Red slaps the papers in his hand, then a pen, and Levi signs without reading anything.

"You can't t—"

"It's not a problem." Levi cuts Red off, then shoves the freshly signed NDA back into his tattooed hands.

Levi turns to leave, and I direct my attention to the little girl in the truck. I force a smile for her sake and wave goodbye, just as a broad chest moves into my view. My head jerks back and my eyes fly up to meet Levi's. Once again, his are filled with barely restrained anger, and it makes me want to slap some sense into him.

Why in the actual fuck is he treating me this way? If anything, I should be the one giving him attitude. Not the other way around.

"What?" I spit out, and I watch a muscle in his cheek twitch.

"Stay away from my daughter."

My jaw drops open on a gasp, my eyes flare wide. For a breath, I'm actually speechless. I force a swallow and fist my hands at my sides. There's no way I heard that correctly.

"I'm sorry, but what did you just say?"

"I said stay away from Brynn. She's a good kid and unfortunately, she idolizes you."

I blink, waiting for more, but he says nothing. He doesn't have to. I recognize that tone. I recognize those words and the sentiment he's so loudly hurled behind them.

"And you're worried I'm going to, what, corrupt her? My unsavory ways might rub off on your seven-year-old?"

His face doesn't change with my statement. He doesn't even flinch. No remorse or shame. I hit it dead on.

"I don't want reality to ruin the image she has in her head. She's too young for that kind of disappointment."

"Right," I force out, "because Sav Loveless in reality is so terribly disappointing. You don't even know me."

"I know enough."

"Tabloid fodder?"

He drags his eyes down my body, stopping on my ring, then back to my face.

"So, you're saying you haven't been in and out of rehab? Dating half of Hollywood? In a toxic relationship with your trashy bassist? That's not you? It's some other Sav Loveless? Some other band?"

His questions are rhetorical, and his voice is damn near mocking, so I don't say anything. I keep my shoulders straight and my face blank. I could defend myself. I could list all the positive things I've done and ramble off my successes. But what's the point?

"She's a good kid," he says again. "She doesn't need your influence."

I huff out a laugh and shake my head slowly.

"God. You sound just like your momma, you know that? Guess the apple didn't fall far after all."

The muscle in his cheek twitches again as we stare at each other. It's a new tell, I realize, but I'm not sure yet what it's giving away. I wait for him to make the same jab—bring up my mom's drug use and rotating list of bedroom guests—but he doesn't. I resist the urge to let my eyes scan his face and instead I hold his hard gaze. I have a lifetime of experience shielding myself from the judgment of others. It stopped bothering me a long time ago.

No one's opinion of me could ever hurt worse than my own.

Until now.

The distance between us seems to shrink as he leans forward, looming over me.

"Stay away from her," he repeats, and the protectiveness in his tone gives me chills that I don't want him to see.

I take a giant step back, cock my head to the side, and bring my left hand up in a mock salute. I force a sweet smile and flutter my eyelashes, a pleasant picture of obedience.

"Whatever you say, Sir. Any other requests before I kick your pompous, patronizing ass out of my courtyard?"

The corner of his mouth twitches, a whisper of a ghost of a smile. His eyes drop to my smirking lips and stick there for long enough that my breath catches. Then they land on my emerald engagement ring again. He jerks his head *no,* a response to my question, then starts to stride toward his truck. As he passes me, his steps slow. He's so close I can feel his heat even though we aren't touching.

"Welcome to town, *Ms. Loveless,*" he says, his deep voice curling around my stage name in a way that feels almost indecent. "See you Monday."

It takes a moment for his last sentence to register in my mind. When it does, he's already backed out of my drive and Red is closing the gate.

See you Monday?

I hear Red's boots on the cobblestone as he comes to stand next to me.

"Is he the guy from—"

"The lap dance and the Perv Pen," I confirm with a nod.

Red hums in surprise but doesn't say anything else. When I feel his eyes on me, I glance up at him and scowl.

"Ms. Loveless? Really?"

Red shrugs. "Professionalism."

I snort and roll my eyes. Professionalism my ass. He just wanted to be intimidating, as if being 6'5", jacked and covered in tats isn't enough.

I turn and walk toward the house. I need to find my dog and my guitar.

See you Monday?

Damn it. I'm almost afraid to find out.

19

My hands grip the steering wheel so tightly my knuckles are white.

She looks good. Really good.

I've seen her picture in magazines and on the television, but there's something different about seeing her in person. Before, I could pretend she was just another celebrity. The silver hair made it easier. I could separate the lead singer of The Hometown Heartless from the wild brunette girl with laughing eyes in my memories. But in the coffee shop today, with her long hair pulled back and hidden beneath a ball cap, she was Savannah, the girl I still consider mine.

Who I've always considered mine.

Her voice is a little deeper, a little raspier. It's sexy in a way that shoots right through me. I can't stop thinking of what it would sound like now compared to then. Telling me secrets in the dark, or ribbing me with a mischievous grin, or coaxing me into doing something we both know I shouldn't. Moaning my name.

Would she still own me the way she did? Still rule my heart and my head completely?

I already know the answer.

I squeeze the steering wheel harder and flick my eyes to the rearview mirror.

Brynn's got her arms crossed and is frowning out the window.

She hasn't spoken a word, and I feel like an asshole. But in my defense, I wasn't prepared for her to meet Savannah today. I sure as shit wasn't prepared for the paparazzi mob. I'll need to scour the internet tonight to make sure Brynn and I didn't make it into any of those fucking photos.

"Want to have a sleepover with Ms. Sharon tonight?"

Brynn shrugs. She usually loves sleepovers with Sharon, which shows just how pissed she is. Ms. Sharon has even started decorating the guest room the way Brynn likes. She's become something like an adopted grandmother to Brynn, and I've been grateful to her for the last two years despite the guilt.

It used to eat me up, seeing them interact. Seeing Brynn grow closer to her. When I hired Sharon as office manager, it never occurred to me that she and Brynn would spark up a relationship. I wanted to shut it down—even had a talk with Sharon about it—but then I realized Brynn deserves more people in her life who love her, and Sharon definitely loves her.

"I can take you to the house and let you pack up a bag and your tablet? I bet Ms. Sharon would order pizza and let you have a movie night."

I watch Brynn's nose scrunch as she shrugs again, so I sigh loudly.

"Alright, you can stay home with me, then."

She sits up straighter and whips her eyes to mine in the mirror. Her brow is furrowed, and her lips are twitching. I can practically see the struggle going on inside her head. She's determined to give me the silent treatment, but she really loves movie nights with Ms. Sharon.

"What do you say, Boss?"

She purses her lips, shrugs once more, then groans loudly. "Okay, fine."

I grin and nod. Brynn doesn't say another word for the rest of the drive, but she's not frowning anymore, either.

When I pull up to our house, she jumps out and sprints inside, so I give Sharon a call.

She's excited for Brynn to stay over, just like I knew she would be, and tells me she'll bring her to the office tomorrow. Sharon gives me a quick rundown of the job progress on our sites, then we hang up with the plan to drop Brynn off in an hour. When I walk up the stairs and into the house, Brynn is waiting for me with her magazine in her hand.

"I didn't get her to sign it," she says, and my stomach sinks. Her eyes are misted and she's trying hard not to cry. "I wanted to get her to sign it."

I step up and pull her into my side.

"I'll get it signed, Boss."

"Are you sure?" She sniffles into my shirt, so I tighten my hug.

"I'll take the magazine with me on Monday and have her sign it," I promise.

Fuck. I was hoping not to have to interact with Savannah again. Maybe I can pawn the job off on one of my guys.

"Thank you!" Brynn shrieks, then turns and runs back up the stairs, shouting at me as she goes. "I'm almost done packing!"

Then I hear her door shut, followed quickly by loud music. Through the door and the floor, the music is muffled, but I can still tell what it is.

The Hometown fucking Heartless.

I literally cannot escape Savannah Shaw.

"Thanks for doin' this, Sharon."

I shut my truck door and walk up to the porch where Sharon is standing. Brynn's already barreled her way into the small house. I kick at the step, making sure my repair job from last summer is holding up, then give the stair railing a shake, testing its sturdiness.

"It's no problem at all," Sharon says. "You know I love having her here."

I glance at the shutters and window trim. The house could use a clean now that the worst of the spring pollen is gone.

"I'm going to have Lucas come by this weekend with the power washer and get—"

"You will not, Levi Cooper. I can take care of this stuff myself."

I raise a brow at her.

"Then why isn't it done?"

"Because my hardass boss has had me working overtime while he tries to single-handedly repair every last bit of destruction from the hurricane, that's why."

I flick my eyes past her toward the house and call for Brynn. She comes running back out of the door, jumps off the porch and throws her arms around my waist in a hug. I can't get over how much taller she's gotten in the last few months. She was barely four feet at her school physical last August. I run my hands over the back of her head, smoothing down her wild brown curls, and return the hug.

"Be good for Ms. Sharon," I tell her, and she laughs as she drops her arms and steps back.

"Duh, Dad."

I smirk and then look to Sharon. "Call if you need me."

"We'll be fine. See you tomorrow."

"Have fun, Boss."

I give Brynn's hair one last ruffle before walking to my truck. The moment I'm in it, I send a text to Lucas telling him to power wash Sharon's house on Monday. Sharon might be stubborn, but so am I.

I back out of the drive and head to one of my favorite bars on the harbor, SandBar. It's right on the water, the kitchen is open late, and they have live music on the patio most Saturday nights in the summer. No one big—just local musicians and bands—but it's always a good time. After the day I've had, I could use a cold beer, a sea breeze, and music that isn't Savannah related.

It's about as busy as you'd expect it to be on a Friday. Some of my guys are at the pool tables in back and they spot me walk in. They call my name and I give them a nod of acknowledgement, but I don't walk toward them. Instead, I lean into the bar.

"Hey there, stranger," Molly says after a minute, already sliding me an open bottle. "Haven't seen you in a bit."

I take the beer and grunt out my thanks.

"Works been busy," I say, after taking a drink from the bottle.

She leans her forearms onto the bar top, pressing her tits up so her cleavage is damn near falling out of her low-cut tank top. I let my gaze run across her collarbone and over the swell of her breasts before I bring them back to her face. I didn't come here for this, but now that I'm here...

"I suppose being a saint and a savior is hard work," she says.

I take another long pull from my beer, bouncing my eyes between hers, and she brings her bottom lip between her teeth.

"I don't see Brynn," she says after a moment. "Are you flying solo tonight?"

I nod once and she smiles softly, her pink lips curving flirtatiously upward in a way I know intimately. Usually, I don't hook up with women from my small town. If I want someone for a night, or a week, I do it outside the county. But Molly and I have an agreement. She knows the deal, and she keeps it quiet. Just sex, no strings. She doesn't come around the house when Brynn is home. We don't call or text each other unless it's to confirm a meet up. We don't stay the night. We don't cuddle. We don't pillow talk.

Just sex. No strings.

"I'm off at eleven tonight."

I let my mouth turn upward on the side, a half-smile that tints her exposed collarbone pink and quickens her breathing. I set my bottle on the bar and lean forward, bringing my lips to the shell of her ear.

"Eleven-oh-five."

I pull back and she winks at me, then goes to tend to the other customers. I take my beer and head out to the patio seating to snag a stool at the outdoor bar. Just as I'm sitting down, another beer bottle is set onto the bar top, and I look up to find Chet, another bartender.

"You're getting low there," he says.

"Thanks."

"On your tab?" he asks, and I lift my beer bottle in confirmation, then turn my attention to the waterway.

This town is right at the mouth of river before it connects to the Atlantic, so the water is salty and at night you can still hear the waves crashing on the distant shore.

Boats are docked up for the night, and I watch their silhouettes sway with the gentle movement of the current. There's classic rock playing on the jukebox inside and the music streams on the patio through the speakers. On nights when there's live music, the jukebox is turned off, but tonight it's on and free to use.

I close my eyes and inhale deeply, consciously relaxing my shoulders and jaw, then imagine exhaling all of my tension. It's something the support group social worker used to have us do, and I've continued doing it even after I stopped attending support group. I still take Brynn to her sessions with her counselor, but after the hurricane, I stopped making the time for mine.

I've got more important things to do, and I usually left the support group feeling worse, not better.

I finish my first beer and swap it out with the new one Chet dropped off, then lean back on the bar and refocus my attention on the dark horizon. I try to lose myself in the sound of the water, but I just keep coming back to Savannah.

Seeing her was like a punch to the chest.

Seeing her with Brynn? Unbearable.

She smells like vanilla and peaches, which is fitting for a name like Savannah, but it's a shocking contrast with her appearance. Vanilla and peaches suggest southern sweetness, but nothing is sweet about Savannah. With her long silver hair, chunky black boots, and bright red lips, Savannah looks like she'd smell like cloves or cardamom. Cinnamon and ginger. Cigars and whiskey. Something spicy. Something tempting. Something dangerous.

I flex my hands at my sides. The feel of her biceps is still stuck to my palms, the memory relentless and refusing to fade. Her skin was hot. Savannah was always warm to the touch. I remember from the nights she'd sleep in my bed. She was like a personal furnace. Everything felt colder after she'd leave.

I'm hot blooded, she told me once. *That's why I have a such a temper.*

I believed it then. Even now, I think I believe it still.

It's weird to think that even after everything that's changed, something has stayed the same.

I finish my second beer and flag Chet down for a third. Despite myself, I'm smiling when I bring it to my lips. The way she smiled and saluted me in the courtyard. Her saccharine tone of voice. The bratty way she cocked her head and sized me up.

Any other requests before I kick your pompous, patronizing ass out of my courtyard?

It took everything in me not to laugh outright.

I was a dick to her. I had to be. But the way she fired right back at me? Fuck, if I didn't want to grab her and kiss her.

Whatever you say, Sir.

I chuckle at the memory. Her voice is playing on a loop in my head. That sexy, raspy voice. *Whatever you say, Sir.* I swallow a groan when the visual of wrapping her silver hair around my fist flashes through my mind. Her, on her knees.

Whatever you say, Sir.

Fucking Savannah Shaw.

Molly appears in front of me at the perfect time. Her smile is seductive, her eyes hooded and playful. I check my watch.

"Eleven-oh-five," I say.

On the dot. Molly is never late.

I widen my legs, and she steps between them, running her hands up my thighs. The sensation hints at the alcohol in my blood stream, everything is surface-level and muted.

"Want to get out of here?" Molly asks, using her head to gesture to the side door that leads to the staff parking lot. I mentally count the beers I've had and blink a few times at one of the bar signs on the wall.

"I can't drive," I tell her honestly, and she giggles.

"It's fine." She takes my hand then steps back. I stand and follow her out the side door.

The music from the bar is just as loud in the parking lot, and she starts to dance a little, swaying and shaking her ass, flashing me flirty grins over her shoulder as we walk toward her car. She spins herself out, then back into my chest and presses her ass into me. I'm still half hard from imagining Savannah on her knees calling me Sir, so I groan at the contact, my hips jerking forward on impulse.

"Jesus, Levi," Molly whispers, reaching back and palming me. "Were you ready for me?"

I don't say anything.

What could I say?

Actually, my dick got hard thinking about the girl who broke my heart?

Nope.

I keep my mouth shut and let her stroke me over my pants, my dick growing with each press of her hand. I drop my head into her hair and inhale, but she smells like hairspray and lavender. I grab her hips and spin her around so she's facing me, and she throws her hands around my neck. When she kisses me, I kiss her back, and she tastes exactly how she usually does. Her tongue tangles with mine the way it usually does. She whimpers into my mouth the way she usually does.

But nothing *feels* the way it usually does.

I run my hands down her back and squeeze her ass cheeks before picking her up and setting her on the hood of a car. It's not hers. It might be Chet's. She wraps her legs around me as I kiss her jaw, her neck, the swell of her breasts.

"Levi," she gasps, and I flinch.

Not low and raspy. High and soft.

Not Savannah. Molly.

I growl in frustration and bring my lips back to her mouth, then move my hands to her chest and pinch her nipples through her thin shirt. She moans again and threads her fingers through my hair.

"My place or yours," she pants out, and I open my mouth to

answer, but the words die on my tongue the moment the opening chords filter into the parking lot, lyrics following quickly behind.

Just one more, baby.
Just one more.
Whiskey and orange.
What are we waiting for?

"What the fuck?" I groan, stepping away from Molly and raking a hand down my face.

"What's wrong?" I can feel her concerned eyes on me, but I can't focus on anything except the sexy as fuck voice crooning through the speakers right now.

I'm the one who said we were done,
but you're the one who left.
Which one of us is hurting more now?
C'mon let's place our bets.
Just one more, baby.
Just one more...

"The Hometown fucking Heartless," I say, as if that explains everything.

"Oh yeah, I love this song," Molly says, her voice quickly changing to excited. "I heard Sav Loveless was spotted in Port Town Beanery today. There are pictures all over online. The kid who works behind the counter was even interviewed about her coffee order."

"What?" My eyes fly open, and I immediately reach for my phone.

"Yeah. A regular latte and a caramel frozen coffee. And six muffins. Weird right? I mean, the latte seems right. But a caramel frozen coffee? For some reason that just doesn't scream *Sav Loveless, badass rockstar*, ya know?"

"No," I shake my head, typing into my phone browser, "you said they were online?"

She says something else, but I don't hear her. I'm too busy flipping through the tons of paparazzi photos of Savannah from today. There are hundreds of them, most of which look exactly the same with just slight differences in her facial expression or body position. There are several zoomed in on that fucking flashy ass ring on her hand.

Molly starts singing along to the song, and I grit my teeth, trying to force the lyrics and melody out of my head so I can focus on the pictures.

There are a few shots where you can kind of see me in the background, but I'm grainy and out of focus. I wasn't the target. The moment I realize Brynn isn't in any shots, my shoulders relax briefly, only to tense up again as the song's bridge starts to play.

"Molly, I'm sorry," I say on a sigh. "I'm just going to walk home."

"Oh... Okay, then. Are you feeling alright? Do you need some ibuprofen or something?"

I'm relieved that I don't hear hurt in her voice. Disappointment, yeah, but I didn't hurt her feelings.

"I'm fine," I say with a shake of my head. "Just tired."

"Do you just want me to drive you?"

"No. I need the walk."

I step back up to her and press a quick kiss to her cheek.

"Have a good night," I tell her, then I turn and walk away with the bridge playing over and over in my head.

Did you ever pray for me?
Every day. Every day.
Did you ever pray for me?

Every fucking day.

20

"FUCK."

I groan as I roll over in bed. My head pounds and my eyes burn.

I've never been much of a drinker. I'll have a beer or two after work, or I'll whip up an old fashioned at home sometimes, but I never mix the two.

Usually.

I close my eyes and think back on my evening. Beers at SandBar. Making out with Molly in the parking lot. *Leaving* Molly in the parking lot. Whiskey at home. Lots of whiskey. And a few too many internet searches.

I fell down a Sav Loveless and The Hometown Heartless rabbit hole. Video clips of shows. Official interviews with entertainment magazines. Tabloid articles and gossip blogs. I even read that interview with the Port Town Beanery barista. It's more Savannah than I've had since I was eighteen. I honestly don't know if it's that or the hangover that has me feeling like I've been hit by a fucking bus.

At least I'm confident that there are no pictures of Brynn from the café circulating online. Just Savannah, looking gorgeous and stunned, and wearing that fucking engagement ring.

I force my heavy body off the bed and make my way to the

bathroom. I brush my teeth and take a quick shower, trying to revive myself so I can get some shit done. We've been working a lot of Saturdays since the hurricane. There's too much to do for a five-day work week, and I've got to head out to the River View neighborhood rebuild today. We're running on schedule, and I want to make sure we stay that way.

When I walk into the office, Sharon and Brynn are already there. Sharon's frowning at the computer, her glasses perched on her nose, and Brynn is sitting on the couch in the corner with a book.

"Morning," I say, nodding to Sharon, then glancing at Brynn. "What's the word, Boss?"

"Contretemps," Brynn says without looking up from her book. "Noun. An inconvenient or embarrassing situation."

I walk to the coffee pot and fill up my thermos, then turn and look at Sharon.

"The famous rockstar found herself in a *contretemps* when she was mobbed by photographers and had to flee with the town grump and his intelligent daughter."

I stare at her, unamused, and her laughter is joined by Brynn's.

"A-plus, Ms. Sharon!" Brynn calls out between giggles.

"How'd she look?" Sharon whispers. I fix my eyes on the floor and swallow back some hot coffee.

"Fine," I lie. She looked good. Great, even. Fucking breathtaking. "She looked fine."

"Did she say anything...?"

"Had me sign an NDA and called me a patronizing ass. 'Bout it."

Sharon doesn't say anything for a long time, long enough that I force myself to bring my eyes to hers. She's watching me with a furrowed brow.

"When do they start the on-site filming?" she asks, and I clench my jaw.

"Three to four weeks."

"Still want me to keep Brynn?"

I jerk out a nod, then turn to my daughter, ending the conversation.

"I'm heading to the rebuild today, Boss. You comin' with me or stayin' with Ms. Sharon?"

She looks up at me and purses her lips, thinking it over.

"Can I video chat with Cameron?"

Brynn's best friend Cameron is visiting family in Connecticut for the summer. It's been a huge adjustment for her since she's used to seeing Cameron every day, especially since Cameron is really Brynn's only friend. For a while, I was trying to set up playdates and get her into more activities, so she'd meet people, but Brynn put me in my place pretty quickly.

Even though she loves school, she doesn't like most kids her age, and they don't like her. I think she's too smart for them. I don't tell her that because I don't want to raise an arrogant kid, but she knows. Brynn's happy with Cameron, Ms. Sharon, me, and her books. She says she's not lonely, that she doesn't want or need any more friends. I get it, but I still find myself hoping she'll branch out eventually.

"Yeah, you can video chat Cameron."

"I'll stay here, then."

I make sure I don't let her see my relief when I agree, then I say goodbye and head out.

The drive to my hometown takes about an hour and I keep the radio off. When I pull into town, I go straight to the River View build site. My guys are already working hard when I park along the curb and climb out of the truck, shoving a hard hat on my head as a good example.

The project is about 75% complete. The neighborhood is eleven houses and we've finished eight of them. If all goes as planned, we should be done with everything by mid-fall.

"Levi," Marcus, my project manager, greets me, then gestures to the build in front of me. It almost looks like a house. "They're finishing up the plumbing here today."

I follow him into the build and nod a hello to the subcontractors installing the plumbing. Marcus takes me through the rooms so I can see the progress, and I type notes on my phone to send to

Sharon. Rough electrical looks good, plumbing so far looks good and should be done by end of day, and if we can get the inspectors out here early next week, we should be able to start insulation before the weekend.

I give Marcus the okay, and then follow him to the build next door to do the same thing. This one isn't as far along, and the team is still hammering away, getting it ready for electrical, but we've been lucky. Weather has been favorable, and thanks to our private donor, money's been doing the talking, so the construction is moving along quickly.

"It's looking good, right?" Marcus says as we step back out into the sun. "Movin' fast."

I grunt my approval, check my watch, then tell him Sharon will have lunch sent around noon. I do a quick walk through of some of the finished houses, and then I make the drive to the last place I want to be, but where my conscience and guilt won't let me avoid.

I park my truck on the curb, then walk up the sidewalk to the door. The shrubbery is neatly trimmed, the flower beds weeded and freshly mulched. The landscapers must have been by recently. I step up unto the wrap-around front porch and knock, then wait.

It takes my mother thirty seconds to open the door, another two to check behind me and then meet my eyes with a frown. She doesn't say anything as she opens the door wider and gestures for me to come in.

"Mom," I say with a nod, kicking off my shoes and following her into the kitchen. I take a seat in a chair at the kitchen table as she starts a pot of coffee. "The landscaping looks nice. Who'd you have do it?"

"Beverly Windsor's son came by and did it for me."

She flicks her eyes to me, then looks back to the task of counting out scoops of coffee and dumping them into the filter. She wants me to feel guilty that it was Beverly Windsor's son who did her landscaping and not her own. I don't.

"He did a good job," I say.

She scoffs and pulls two mugs from the cabinet, then brings

them to the table. She sets one down in front of me, then the other in front of the chair where she always sits. I meet her hard eyes, and I brace myself for what I know is coming. When she speaks, her voice is steel.

"You could have brought my granddaughter."

I inhale slowly. Not even a *hi, how are you*. She's just going to dive right into an argument. I'm not surprised.

"Brynn didn't want to come," I say clearly. Aside from the slightest flinch in her brow, there's no sign she heard me.

"I haven't seen her in over a month."

I give her a single nod. I'm aware of how long it's been.

"She's only seven," my mother snaps. "She's a child. You give her too much say in the day to day. She shouldn't be dictating when or how often she sees her grandmother."

I drum my fingers on my thigh. Turn my head from side to side to try and relieve some of the tension that's building.

"She has her own mind," I state. "I won't make decisions for her."

"She's a child—"

"She's a *person*," I cut her off. "If Brynnlee isn't comfortable around you, I will not force her to be around you. You're my mother, but that doesn't entitle you to anything."

I hold her gaze as she blinks furiously. She huffs a few more times, then stomps to the coffee pot. She takes out two new mugs and fills them in the silence. When she brings the mugs to the table and sees the other two mugs she'd already brought out, she huffs yet again. She sets the full coffee mugs down, then snatches up the empty ones and takes them back to the kitchen.

"Do you need any help with cleaning out Dad's office?" I ask, trying to change the subject. She waves her hand in my direction but doesn't look at me.

"No. It's just a bunch of files and paperwork. Sermons. Counseling notes. A lot of shredding."

She doesn't say more. She won't be redirected—her mind is still firmly on Brynn. On my daughter and how I choose to raise her. The oddest thing about it is how I know my mother doesn't want a relationship with Brynn. She just wants something to control. She can't control me anymore. She can't control my father. She's alone and bored.

I grab my coffee and take a drink, watching silently.

Some people might think I'm being harsh, or that I'm wrong in letting Brynn decide not to see my mother. That's fine. Other people aren't raising her. I am.

And I also know my mother, and none of the arguments in favor of forcing Brynn to spend time with her will ever outweigh what I know. She might be my mother, and she might be old, and she might be lonely now that my father has died, but so what? She's also judgmental, hateful, rude, and downright mean, and that's not the kind of energy I want around Brynn.

Brynn asked not to have to see my mother anymore. I will respect that.

When my mom turns her attention back on me, it's clear she's not going to back down.

"Is this because of what I said about her little friend? Is that it?"

I tilt my head to the side and raise a brow. She knows damn well it's because of more than that, but the body shaming comments she made about Cameron were the icing on the cake.

"What about the Larks," my mom tries. "Is she going to see them? Helen and William haven't seen her since Julianna's funeral."

I take another sip from my mug before answering.

"The Larks have made it more than clear that they don't want anything to do with Brynn if they can't dictate how she's being raised."

"Well, they are right that you should be taking her to church."

"She goes to church."

My mom's eyes go wide.

"You take her?"

I shake my head no.

"Sometimes she'll go with Sharon."

My mother's face turns murderous, full of disgust and anger.

"That woman," my mom sneers. "How dare you let my granddaughter around that horrible woma—"

I slam my hand on the kitchen table, silencing her. She flinches and grits her teeth, nostrils flaring as she glares at me. I glare right back.

"I did not come here to be berated," I say firmly as I push myself up from the chair. "I did not ask for your advice or input on how I should parent my child. Brynnlee has asked not to see you anymore. Those are the consequences of your actions."

I turn and walk toward the door, my mother hot on my heels.

"You are raising a wicked girl. She's been corrupted by the company you keep. That child has no respect! She has no discipline! You spare the rod, you spoil the child, and Levi, you have spoiled that girl. She is—"

I whip my body around to face her, halting her words once more, and shake my head slowly.

"Do *not* finish that sentence. I don't have to come see you. I do it for you, not me. But I swear, if you continue to spit that bullshit at me, I'll never come here again. You are my mother. That doesn't entitle you to anything."

She doesn't agree. She doesn't apologize. She doesn't even nod. But she also doesn't open her mouth to argue.

"Goodbye, Mother."

I let the screen door slam behind me out of spite, and I walk calmly to my truck. My hands are fisted at my sides until I have to unclench my fingers to open my truck door, and then I drive off without looking back at the house.

I question a lot of things when it comes to parenting—whether or not I'm doing it right—but I have no doubts about this. My youth was miserable because of my mother. It took me years to find my own voice because my parents constantly silenced me. I'm a grown man and still have the occasional scripture-and-belt related nightmare.

I will not make those same mistakes with Brynn.

I made a promise to her mother, to myself, and I keep my promises.

I swing through the grocery store and pick up more water for my crew, then drive it back to the River View build. I do another walk through, talk to some of the subcontractors, make a few calls. When I'm confident everything is under control, I head back to the office.

Brynn asks if she can stay one more night at Sharon's so they can go to church tomorrow, and I tell her yes. I drive by one of the local builds and do a walk through to check on that progress. I make a few more phone calls. I keep myself busy right until quitting time, and then I drive myself back home alone.

Normally, with a free Saturday night, I'd hit up SandBar for a beer and the band, but I'm not in the mood for a crowd. I also want to avoid Molly for reasons I refuse to admit. I know I'd be shit company, anyway. I could try to fish, but that's not interesting to me either.

I don't want to do anything except brood, so that's what I do.

Despite this morning's headache, I make myself an old fashioned and take it out to the back deck. I light a small fire in the fire pit and take a seat on the lounger. I sip my drink, then lean my head back and close my eyes.

I focus on the water.

On the breeze.

On the faint laughter and music carried on the night air from the downtown area just a few blocks over.

I focus on everything else except what's really plaguing my heart and head for as long as I can, but when the drink is gone and so are my defenses, Savannah Shaw is all I see.

She's all I ever see.

And then I let the guilt consume me.

21

I've never been on a real movie set, but I assumed it wouldn't be too much different from the music videos I've shot with the band.

I was wrong.

I didn't expect to get a full trailer to myself, complete with my name on the door and everything. Honestly, it's nicer than the house I grew up in about an hour from here. There's a couch, a television, a bathroom, a kitchenette, a desk, a small sleeping area with a bed, and there's even a little doggie corner with a bed and toys for Ziggs. I don't know how Red got them to approve her being on set with me, but I don't even care. She's here, and it makes me happy. He's such a good bodyguard.

As I poke around the space, opening cabinets and drawers and checking the mini fridge, Red shuffles through the fruit on my fruit tray, picking out grapes one by one and popping them in his mouth.

The fruit tray I expected. It's on my basic rider along with my favorite brand of electrolyte water in the glass bottles, extra guitar picks, citrus-scented candles (one for each night we play at a venue), dark chocolate caramel truffles with sea salt, cucumber eye masks, and a package of dental doggy bones for Zigaroo. What I didn't ask for, though, was the gigantic bouquet of flowers or the welcome basket of pastries.

I dig through the pile of baked goods, pull out a muffin, and take a giant bite.

"Oh, yum," I say through a mouthful. "This is pretty good."

Red hums. I take another bite, then am shoved forward by my mannerless dog and her bulky body. She nudges my leg again and hits me with her big pleading puppy eyes, so I laugh and break off a piece of the muffin to feed her.

"You're just going to make her worse." Red grunts. "The mutt will never stop begging if you keep feeding her like that."

I make eye contact with him and hold it as I feed Ziggy the rest of my muffin. He shakes his head, and our grins slip at the same time.

"You're a brat," Red grumbles, and my smile falls.

A brat.

Levi.

See you Monday, he'd said. Well, today is Monday, and now I'm on high alert. I'm already a mess of nerves, and Levi's cryptic statement is just making everything worse.

Asshole.

There's a knock on my trailer door, so I open it wide and find a girl with a clipboard looking up at me. It's only dawn, so it's still fairly dark out and I can't really make out the fine details of her features, but she looks youngish. Younger than me.

"Ms. Loveless, I'm Dakota, one of the production assistants," the girl says, her voice steady and clear. "I came to see if you'd want an escort to makeup."

Red pushes past me and sticks out his hand, and Dakota slaps her badge into it without a word. As he studies it, she continues talking to me.

"I've already signed the NDA you provided to the studio. I've been assigned to you in case you need anything." She reaches into her back pocket, then hands me a business card. "That's the cellphone I use for the studio. If you need anything, you can call me."

I nod, then glance at Red. He nods, then hands Dakota her badge.

"Cool," I say, and she gestures to a golf cart parked behind her. "You can call me Sav, though."

I follow her to the golf cart, sliding onto the passenger seat as Red grabs Ziggy and sits on the back bench. Red will probably trail me a lot the first few days before he finally backs off and gives me some space. It's how he does things. It's what I pay him for, honestly. Once we're in a routine and the new wears off, Ziggy will decide to stay behind with Red because she loves him just as much as she loves me. Even though Red refuses to admit it.

"Have you had a tour of the studio yet?" Dakota asks as she puts the golf cart in drive and pulls away from my trailer.

"I've explored a little, but not much. I was going to come in yesterday, but since everyone in North Carolina knows I'm here now, I stayed in and ran lines instead. I'll poke around today."

My face in the coffee shop has been everywhere. I'm used to the attention, but I'm nervous about Levi. I don't exactly want my relationship with him, or some elements of my past, to be dragged through the tabloids.

The paps are cutthroat, and the media is ruthless. I even stand next to someone in a crowd, and they find a way to twist it into headline material. Potential love interest? Drug dealer? Cheating on my "fiancé" again?

It's disgusting and fascinating to witness. The lengths they will go to sell magazines, the backflips they will turn to get clicks. Their detective skills are top notch, but their understanding of ethical journalism is lacking. It makes for a pretty dangerous game. I never know what I'll get anytime I step foot in public.

"I can take you around after filming wraps for the day, if you want," Dakota says, navigating through trailers in the lot like a seasoned pro. "And of course, I'll be here to escort you anywhere you need to go during the day."

"Thanks, Dakota," I say, then rub my hands down my thighs to hide my slight trembling.

God, I'm so fucking nervous.

We're filming scenes in the back lot today, and I made Red run lines with me until my speech was slurred with exhaustion. I could probably recite the dialogue in my sleep at this point, but that doesn't mean I'll be any good at this. I didn't even audition for this role. They came to me. What if I'm a terrible actress? What if I end up another washed-up rockstar with a failed film career?

I might puke.

"You're going to be great at this," Dakota says, and I glance at her with a raised eyebrow.

"You think?"

"Yep." She pulls the golf cart up to another trailer and puts it in park, then turns to me. "I've been working in this industry since I was eighteen. I've seen all sorts of stuff, and I can predict an Oscar winner from the casting call. And you? You're going to crush it."

I purse my lips, then slowly release a smile.

"We're going to be friends," I tell her, and she smiles back.

"I know."

I hop out of the golf cart and Ziggy is at my feet immediately. I give her head a scratch and wait for Red to step up next to me.

"I'll be back when you're done to take you to wardrobe," Dakota says, and then she drives off.

I take a deep breath, give Red one last glance as he posts up like some secret service guard next to the door, then step up the three metal stairs and pull open the trailer door. My menace of a dog rushes in before I can, and I hear a *whoa there* shouted from inside.

"Shit, sorry," I say as I step into the trailer then turn my attention to my dog. "Ziggy, no. You go back outside with Red."

"Oh, she's fine, hun," a man says, crouching down and addressing Ziggs while giving her tons of scratches. "What's your name, precious?"

"Her name is Ziggy," I answer awkwardly, bouncing my eyes between the man petting my dog and the woman sitting at one of the vanities behind him. "But she also answers to Ziggs, Zigaroo, Zigalicious, ZeeZee, and Mutt."

The man and woman both laugh, then he pushes back to standing and hits me with a grin.

"Ziggy, as in Marley?" he asks, and I shake my head.

"Stardust," I tell him, and he nods.

"My next guess." He puts out his hand and I shake it. It's soft and warm. "I'm Pax and this is Tatum. We'll be working you over every day. Chanel will be here in about an hour, but we've got to get started earlier since we've got to install your wig and tattoos."

"Sure," I say on an exhale, then glance around the space.

There are three large vanity stations with big lighted mirrors and salon chairs, and there's a skylight in the ceiling through which the first lights of the sunrise are peeking through. A water cooler, mini fridge, and coffee pot stand in the corner, and then on the back wall are built-in cabinets and shelves full of *stuff*.

"Where do you want me?" I ask, and Tatum stands and waves to the salon chair she was just sitting in.

I walk to it and plop down while Ziggy shoves herself under the table and curls up at my feet. She's so sleepy, poor thing. I kick off my shoe and use my toes to give her a few more pets.

"Have you seen this beauty yet?" Tatum asks, and I watch in the mirror as she opens one of the cabinets and reveals some mannequin head things and random hair pieces. Then carefully, she lifts a brunette piece off one of the heads and turns to face me. "It turned out great."

"I haven't." My eyes scan over my wig in awe. "Wow. It looks so real."

"It's real hair, babe," Tatum quips. "Wait 'til we get it on you. You won't even believe it."

The wig really is beautiful. Long, dark, silky strands that fall in soft waves. It's got a natural, healthy shine that my own hair no longer has without tons of conditioning products since I bleach it to high heaven to keep it silver.

After I accepted the role in this film, I attended a fitting appointment to have my head measured and molded so the production company could create a custom wig for me. It was a really weird process that involved wrapping my head in cellophane and tape, then tracing my hairline with a black marker. Very strange, but since I refused to dye my hair back to my natural brown, it was the next best option, and they assured me it would look better than something you pull off a rack at a Halloween store.

"Ready to get started?" Pax asks, and I nod.

"Ready as I'll ever be."

The whole process takes about four hours, with most of that time dedicated to applying my half sleeve of fake tattoos. Chanel shows up after about an hour and gets to work on my face, and when that's done, Tatum finishes up the final touches on my wig.

It's unsettling how real it looks.

It's been years since I've seen myself as a brunette, and while my makeup is heavier than anything I'd wear back then, I can still see the younger me staring back through the vanity mirror. It's so overwhelming that I almost want to cry.

The things I would tell her if I could. The warnings. The encouragement.

I smile at my reflection, and I have to swallow back a sob. The resemblance is unnerving. If you didn't know any better, you'd almost think I was the same person as that girl back then. But I know better.

"Oh hun, don't cry," Pax says, and Chanel attacks my face with a cotton swab.

"You're not supposed to cry until later," Chanel grumbles, dabbing under my eyes.

Chanel purposely used non-waterproof eyeliner because the final scene we're shooting today requires an ugly cry, and the script wants me to look like a hot ass mess, all streaky eye makeup and snot. Weirdly enough, I'm more terrified of the crying scene than I am of the sex scenes. There's only one crying scene, thank god, but there are three sex scenes.

I'm glad I'm getting the sobbing out of the way on the first day. Then I can focus on the shit I'm comfortable with—sex and betrayal.

"Alright, hun," Pax says, standing back and clapping his hands.

"Off to wardrobe you go. Try not to touch your face or hair, okay? But if you do, we'll be around to touch you up."

I push up from the salon chair and Ziggy stands with me, barreling through all our feet and skidding to a halt at the trailer door.

"Sorry," I say, flashing Ziggs a scowl as I make my way to the door. "She's rude."

I reach for the door just as it swings open, revealing my co-star, Paul Northwood, standing in all his broad-chested glory. Paul is a seasoned pro with two Oscar nominations, and he won an Emmy for the few years he spent on one of America's longest running soaps. We met briefly, albeit digitally, for the table read a few months ago, but I haven't talked to him since.

"Sav," he says with a smile, stepping backward off the trailer steps and offering a hand for me to climb down.

I take it even though I don't need it.

"I was hoping to run into you this morning. Have you been here long?"

"Since about 4:30," I tell him honestly, then laugh at his grimace. I gesture to my tattoos and hair, and he nods.

"Almost didn't recognize you. Brown hair suits you."

"I'd hope so," I say with a smirk. "It's what I was born with."

"Huh." Paul drags his eyes over my hair, then my face, taking note of my dark eyebrows and eyelashes, before landing back on my eyes. "I can see it."

"I'm headed to wardrobe," I tell him.

He's already dressed in suit pants and a button down, so I'm assuming he's already been. I gesture to the door I just came out of.

"You in here long?"

"Not as long as you," he says with a chuckle. "No ink or wigs for me."

"Okay, well, have fun. See you out there."

Paul gives me another of his charming smiles, reminding me again why most of the world is in love with him. He really is a beautiful man. Very rugged in build and stature, but his facial features are softer. His skin glows. His lips have the perfect pout. His dark brown hair has that attractive tousled look, and his dark brows and eyelashes make his bright blue eyes pop.

The girlies go gaga for him, and I can honestly see why.

He also has a reputation of being a perfect gentleman. Vocal about human rights, respectful of his castmates, and loves his mom. He even graduated valedictorian from high school despite his budding acting career.

Like, damn. I'm basically co-stars with Hollywood's idea of perfection.

I snort as I slide into the passenger seat of Dakota's golf cart where she, Red, and Ziggy are already waiting. I wonder how long it will take the media to run a story speculating on my scandalous relationship with my new co-star. They'd love that—Sav Loveless corrupting Hollywood's Golden Boy. That article would break the internet.

I stay in my thoughts as Dakota zips to wardrobe, which is a much larger trailer than hair and makeup. This one almost looks like a giant shipping container, and there are no skylights.

I'm introduced to the crew and walked through my wardrobe changes for the movie. I relax when I learn that I'll be wearing the same outfit for most of filming. Or, one of the several identical copies of the same outfit, anyway. My time in wardrobe is much shorter than my time in makeup. I was already measured and fitted last month in L.A., so all they have to do is double check that everything is the same, dress me, and send me on my merry way.

When the golf cart rounds the corner and the set on the back lot comes into view, my jaw drops. It's absolutely stunning. It looks like a small Italian village just popped up out of the ground in eastern North Carolina. I've been to Italy six times, once for each of our world tours, but I never really got to visit. Not much time to be a tourist when you're playing shows every night and sleeping while in transit between cities.

"Oh my god," I breathe out, and Dakota laughs.

"It's beautiful, right? It's easily one of the best sets we've had in the studio the whole time I've worked here." She pulls the golf cart up behind some lighting equipment and throws it in park. "Plus, the guy who owns the construction company is just as beautiful as the set. Definitely didn't mind watching him work."

I laugh and smirk at her.

"Let me guess. Backwards ball cap, tattered blue jeans, and a tool belt with a—" I use my hands to measure out about a foot "—big hammer?"

She smirks back and raises an eyebrow, then reaches up and slowly moves my hands a few more inches apart. I bark out a laugh, and I hear Red sigh with annoyance.

"Fun sucker," I say over my shoulder, and he sighs louder.

"But seriously though, he's just a good guy, too," Dakota cuts in. "He does a lot for the community. Only mark against him is he's not very friendly. I don't think I've ever heard him say more than a few words at a time. I saw him smile one time and I about swooned, though, so it's probably for the best."

I climb out of the golf cart and give Dakota a wink.

"I think I like them better when they don't talk, anyway."

She laughs and nods in agreement before throwing the golf cart back in gear.

"Break a leg today, Sav," she says, then she zooms off, leaving me, Red, and Zigalicious in her dust.

"You ready for this, kid?"

Red's gruff voice is low and gentle, and I think it over. I've memorized all of my lines plus half of Paul's. But am I ready?

"I could use a shot of whiskey and a xanny," I say honestly. It's about all I'm sure of right now.

Red doesn't say anything. Doesn't even acknowledge what I said. What do you say to a recovering alcoholic and drug abuser, anyway? Silence them? Tell them, *oh no, I know you don't mean that*? He knows I mean it. He also knows that nothing anyone says can change it. Not him. Not Mabel. Not Torren or Jonah. Certainly not Hammond.

Only me.

I sigh loudly and reconsider his question. I pick up a strand of my new brunette hair and twirl it around my finger. My head doesn't itch as much as I expected it to with this wig on. Neither does my arm where they applied the fake tattoos. If I don't look in the mirror, I'd never know the difference.

I shrug.

"I guess we'll find out."

22

"ALRIGHT, let's take two hours for lunch, and then we'll try to get the next one in before the sun goes down."

My director, Karen Evans, addresses us from where she stands next to one of the large cameras. She's reading something on a tablet with a furrowed brow, and her long gray hair is currently piled on top of her head in a bun. She's given me direction and encouragement all day, but I can't help but feel like I've disappointed her.

I've been fascinated by Karen since I took this role and did an internet search deep dive on her credentials. At fifty-one, she's one of the most decorated and respected directors in Hollywood. Her very first film cost four grand to make, was twelve-minutes long, and took home a special jury award at Sundance. She was twenty-eight.

I freaking love her. Half the reason I'm trying so hard to get this right is because I don't want to fuck up royally in front of Karen Evans. I'm in the presence of greatness, so I need to step my shit up.

As if summoned, Dakota pulls up in her golf cart and waves me over. Red took Ziggs back to the trailer a few hours ago, so he's nowhere to be seen. I take one last glance at Karen, then head to my awaiting escort.

"Word on the set is that you don't suck," Dakota says as I plop into the passenger seat. I perk up immediately.

"Says who?"

"Some of the other production assistants, one of the sound guys, and basically every extra."

I glance over my shoulder. There are about fifty people being used as extras right now. I haven't spoken to any of them, and they haven't spoken to me. They've been watching me, though.

"Are they credible?" I ask suspiciously, and Dakota laughs.

"The extras might be a little starstruck, but the people who work on set are very credible. To them, you're just another actress. If anything, they're more critical. A little jaded, even. The fact that you've gotten good reviews after your first scene? That's pretty good."

I heave a sigh of relief and send her a smile.

"Thank you for telling me."

"Sure thing," she chirps, then smirks. "Don't get comfortable and start slacking, though. Their good favor is easily lost."

I smile and nod. "Noted."

When my trailer comes into view, I can see Red standing outside the door, arms crossed and Ziggy at his feet. His sunglasses are on, and he's as still as a statue. Very intimidating.

"Does he talk?" Dakota asks.

"Sometimes," I say wryly. "Usually, it's to tell me off for doing something dumb."

She hums, and I notice the golf cart slows down, but she doesn't take her eyes off Red.

"How old is he, exactly?"

I side-eye her. "Why?"

She shrugs with a smirk. "Got a personal policy not to sleep with anyone my dad's age or older."

"How old's your dad?" I ask with a laugh.

"Fifty-two."

"You're in the clear." My voice is lowered to a whisper as we pull up to the trailer, but then I raise it when I address Red. "Hey Red, how old are you?"

I see one dark eyebrow rise up behind his mirrored sunglasses.

"You know how old I am," he deadpans.

"Humor me."

"Forty-five."

I smile, darting my eyes from Red to Dakota and back. "Thanks."

I slide out of the passenger seat and Dakota tells me she'll be back in exactly one hour and fifty-three minutes before zooming off on her golf cart to do whatever it is that she does when she's not chauffeuring me around. I bend down and give Ziggs some love as she does her little excited body wag, then head into my new trailer.

There's a plastic tray on the counter that Red tells me was delivered a few minutes before I arrived, and I pop it open to find some delicious looking club sandwiches, chips, and more fruit. I throw myself down onto one of the barstools, snag half a sandwich, and take a bite.

"How were your first six hours of being an actress?" Red asks as I slide him the tray to grab his own sandwich.

"Fine," I say as I chew. I think it over and swallow before adding, "Dakota says people don't think I suck."

Red grunts and nods. It's about as much of a compliment as I'm used to from him.

I open my mouth to ask him if he wants to run lines with me, even though I have them memorized to the point of saying them in my dreams, when there's a knock at my door. Red turns and opens it, then uses his deep, intimidating voice to greet the visitor.

"Can I help you?" he grunts out, and I stifle a laugh.

I expect to hear Dakota's voice, or maybe Tatum or Pax, since I was told they'd want to touch up my hair and makeup before we start filming again, but instead, I'm shocked mid-chew by a new but familiar voice.

Brynnlee's voice.

"Hello, sir. I'd like to speak with Sav Loveless, please."

My lips twitch with amusement at just how *grown* she sounds.

Like a little thirty-year-old woman in a seven-(and three-quarters)-year-old's body. I can't see her, but I can picture her. I bet she's standing just as tall and fearless as ever.

"What do you need with Ms. Loveless?" Red booms, and I giggle into my sandwich.

His posture is just as rigid as it always is, and I bet there's not even a hint of a smile on his lips, but I can hear the humor in his voice.

"I would like to ask her to autograph my magazine," Brynn states. "I brought a pen with me this time."

Shit, that's right. The magazine.

I put my sandwich on the counter and push myself to standing, then walk to the door and tap Red's shoulder so he steps out of my way. When Brynn sees me, she beams and clutches the magazine to her chest. It's the same excited smile she gave me in the café a few days ago, and it relaxes my nerves even as I glance past her in search of her dad.

I don't see Levi anywhere, but there's a guy in a golf cart watching us nervously. I nod in his direction, then focus back on Brynn.

"What's up, Boss?" I throw my hand out so she can slap me a low five. "What are you doing here?"

"You forgot to sign this," she says, then holds out the magazine. I take it and the pen. "My dad said you could sign it today."

I raise a brow. "He did?"

"Yes."

"Did he tell you to bring it to me?" I ask slowly, and she shrugs.

"No. He was supposed to bring it with him this morning, but he forgot." She flings her hand behind her and gestures to the guy in the golf cart. "So, I had Dustin bring me."

Bring it with him this morning.

See you Monday.

I feel like there's a realization somewhere just out of reach. I'm fumbling around for it, but my fingertips just brush right past it.

I glance once more at the guy Brynn called Dustin. His back is ramrod straight now and his eyebrows are furrowed, like he never questioned her until this moment. She told him to bring her to the studio, and he just...*did.* I tilt my head and raise an eyebrow, and he purses his lips before speaking.

"Is this, uh, okay?"

The uncertainty in his voice makes me laugh out loud.

"You're asking now?" I ask incredulously, then glance down at Brynn. "You just told this poor guy to bring you by my trailer and he did, huh? No questions asked?"

She grins again, and this time it's impish and familiar in a way that I find unsettling.

"Told ya before," she says. "I'm the boss."

I return her smile, once again looking her over in search of some resemblance to Levi. They have the same nose. The shape of their faces is the same. Her hair and eyes aren't him, but her mouth could be. Her sass, though? That is something else entirely. I bet he doesn't know what to do with her half the time, and it makes me giddy.

Conflicting thoughts war inside my head. For reasons I'm too ashamed to say out loud, I don't want to like this girl. Part of me already doesn't. Never did. But another part of me, an annoyingly loud part, wants *her* to like *me,* and I don't know how to reconcile the two.

Levi's deep, menacing voice replays in my ears and I grit my teeth. *Stay away from my daughter. I don't want reality to ruin the image she has in her head.* Even as a memory, the statements still sting.

What a complete and utter asshole.

"Is your dad here now?"

"Yeah, somewhere. He's one of the builders," she chatters proudly. "His guys built all the sets for your movie. One of 'em even looks just like our kitchen."

His guys. It's all starting to make sense now. I look back at Dustin.

"You gonna get fired, Dusty?"

His eyes flare wide and he looks from me, to Brynn, then in the direction of the back lot. His reaction all but confirms it for me. Levi

Cooper is Dustin's boss. Levi Cooper owns the company that has built all the sets for my movie. Levi Cooper is the guy Dakota was talking about—good guy, not very friendly, big...*hammer*.

A *very* big hammer, if I remember correctly.

"Dad won't fire you, Dustin," Brynn says with an exasperated sigh, then rolls her eyes. "Don't look so scared."

I bite back another laugh. Damn it, I like this kid.

And since she's already here...

"Hey, Dusty," I call out, "how about you head back to work and let her dad know we're right behind you. I'm just going to sign this magazine for her."

"Uh, um, I can wait," Dustin says, uncertainty lacing his every syllable.

He knows he fucked up now, but what's he expect? Taking blind orders from a sassy seven-year-old. I bet she really is smarter than her dad. I bet she's smarter than a lot of people, Dustin definitely included.

I give him a suggestive smile, bat my eyelashes a little, and drop my voice a bit.

"It's okay, Dusty. You did great bringing her here. We'll be right behind you."

He blinks at me a few times, jerks his head in a nod, then looks at Brynn.

"Right behind me, okay, Boss?"

Brynn salutes him, and I can't hold back my laugh. I don't wait for old Rusty Dusty to drive away. Instead, I move to the side and gesture Brynn into the trailer.

"C'mon on in here, ya little troublemaker."

She just smirks and skips inside, then I turn to Red.

"Hey, text Dakota and tell her I need a golf cart, will ya?"

He eyes me suspiciously. "What are you up to, kid?"

I shrug.

"Just having a little fun, Red. Don't be a fun sucker, okay?"

From inside the trailer, I hear a bark that sounds like it came from my very excitable, rude dog, then a grunt followed by giggles that sound like they came from a sassy seven-and-three-quarters-year-old. I rush inside and find Brynn on the floor with Ziggy lick attacking her.

"Ziggy Lou Stardust, get off," I command, but she ignores me like a jerk.

"It's okay," Brynn says through giggles, "I like dogs."

I watch them for a few seconds, and when Ziggs starts to chill a little, I walk to the counter and flip through Brynn's magazine, finding the article on my band to sign. Red walks back inside, sliding his phone into his pocket, and gives me a scolding look. I narrow my eyes at him and resist the urge to stick my tongue out.

Fun sucker, I mouth. He just shakes his head.

"Whoa," Brynn says, and when I look up from finishing the final S in my name, I find Brynn staring at my acoustic in the corner.

My signature white custom Gibson is locked in a closet back at the rental, but the beat up acoustic in the corner has been with me since the beginning.

"Is this the guitar you debuted 'Just One More' on at your show in D.C.?"

My jaw drops and I flick my eyes to Red. He's eating his club sandwich, but has stopped mid-chew, just as shocked as I am.

"Yep."

That's all I can say. *Yep*. This kid was barely a toddler when we played that show. Plus, she said *debuted*. I don't know if I'm more impressed or flattered.

I watch as she reaches her hand out and hovers it over the strings, but never touches them. Like it's something holy, and that gets me. To me, it *is* holy. It's the closest to church I've ever gotten. That guitar.

I walk over and stand next to her.

"You know how to play?" I ask, and she shakes her head, glancing from the guitar to me and back. "You should learn."

She whips her eyes to mine and her question comes out so rushed that it sounds like one big word.

"Canyouteachme?"

My eyes widen with surprise. Well. I wasn't expecting that.

"Dunno, Boss," I hedge. "You'll have to talk to your dad about that one."

"If he says yes, will you teach me?"

I agree immediately. I don't even think it through. I recognize that desire, that pull to play. Something tells me she might need it just as much as I do, but for different reasons.

She squeals and claps her hands, and then I hand her back the now-autographed magazine.

"Let's jet before your dad blows a fuse."

23

Brynn, Red, and Zigalicious follow me out the door and I find a golf cart waiting for me.

No Dakota.

When Red moves to sit in the driver's seat, I dart around him and throw myself into it before he can get to it. He raises a brow, so I raise one right back. He sighs and reroutes to the back bench, patting the seat for my dog while Brynn climbs up next to me.

"Know where he's at?" I ask Brynn as I put the cart in drive.

"Yeah. In the back lot. They've got to add some New York thing."

That's right. Our filming schedule had to be moved around, so some of the on-location filming was changed to the studio. Something about contract negotiations. Now, instead of filming next week in New York, we're filming here before we have to film on location in Oakport. The turnaround is tight, but from the sound of it, the crew is going to be done in no time.

I head to the back lot, past the Italian village courtyard and into the downtown New York alleyway. I slow down when I see one of the builders, and he waves politely at me before turning his attention to Brynn.

"Hey, Boss. What's the word?"

Brynn doesn't miss a beat.

"Vicissitude," she says. "Noun. A favorable or unfavorable event or situation that occurs by chance."

She watches the guy expectantly, so I look back at him. His lips are pursed in concentration and he's squinting at his feet. When he speaks, it's slowly, as if he's trying to work something out in his head but doesn't quite know how to articulate it.

"Sometimes...life...Sometimes life can have a rude vicissitude."

"Ehhhh," Brynn says, tapping her chin. "C minus, Luke."

The guy grins.

"That's better than last time," he says proudly, and Brynn beams back.

"It is! Great job!"

I hear a chuckle come from Red, and I'm opening my mouth to inform Luke that I, too, was a C minus student, when a very angry, very booming voice, cuts through the set, and I get goosebumps. I have to temper my smile.

Showtime.

"Brynnlee," Levi calls, and Brynn's back goes ramrod straight.

"Oh, curse it," she whispers, and I can't hide my snort.

By the time Levi marches up to us, I've lost the battle with my smile, and he looks pissed about it.

Pissed, but also stupidly sexy. All rugged and roughed up. There's no tool belt, thank god, because if there were, I'd probably lose my nerve.

A plain blue t-shirt stretches across his chest with some sort of white logo on the breast pocket. His arms strain the sleeves. His beat-up blue jeans hang low on his hips and mold around his thighs, then taper off around brown work boots. And on his head, covering his light brown hair, is a fucking backwards UNC ballcap.

Kill me dead. Levi Cooper is even sexier than I remember, and I fucking hate him for it.

"Hi, Daddy," Brynn says sweetly, snapping me back to reality.

"Hi, Daddy," I repeat, matching her tone, and Levi's nostrils flare as he flicks his eyes to me.

"Ms. Loveless, may I have a word," he grits out, and my smile grows.

"No, I believe you may not."

"Savannah," he growls, and I have to keep myself from squirming. "*Now.*"

"Ugh, fine." I stand up with a fake huff and Ziggy immediately comes to my side. I give her head a pat, then raise my eyebrows at Levi expectantly. "Lead the way."

He turns and stalks off, so I follow him, but I take small, slow steps. He disappears behind one of the fake buildings, and I bend down so I can untie and retie my shoe. Slowly.

"Savannah," he shouts.

Oh, he's so pissed right now. Good. Asshole. I stand and follow his voice, and I don't bother trying to hide the bounce in my step.

The back of the set piece is just a bunch of two-by-fours and nails and unpainted space. It's crazy how real the other side looks.

"I told you to stay away from her," Levi says as soon as I set foot in front of him. His patronizing tone pisses me off, and I meet his eyes with equal fire.

"She came to me, Levi. What did you want me to do, kick her out? Be rude? I thought you didn't want me to disappoint her."

He's silent for a breath, and I give myself a tally in the ME column in my head. He steps closer, dropping his voice lower.

"You should have let her come back with Dustin. He shouldn't have brought her to you."

I wave him off and roll my eyes.

"Should've, would've, could've. And if I'd refused to give her an autograph? How do you think that would make her feel?"

He doesn't say anything again, so I plow forward.

"I brought her back as soon as I finished the last S in my name."

His eyes are still hard, his teeth still clenched, and my anger spikes higher. I take a step closer to him.

"I'm not a fucking bad influence, Levi," I whisper-yell, my voice shaking with fury in self-defense. He has the audacity to scoff in my face.

"Like I'm going to take the word of someone who's spent the last several years in and out of rehab. Someone engaged to Torren Fucking King."

He spits Torren's name like it's acid on his tongue, and I suppose based on what he thinks he knows, it's understandable. Doesn't mean I don't see red because of it, though.

"I am sober, you prick," I say through my teeth. "And I'm not fucking engaged to Torren King."

"And how do you explain this, then?"

His hand shoots down and takes my left ring finger, rubbing the base of it where my emerald would be if I were wearing it. The way his touch burns and sends sparks up my arm makes me suck in a breath, and I yank my hand from his grip.

"It's complicated," I seethe, and he fucking laughs.

He throws his head back and barks out a sardonic laugh that makes me want to knee him in the balls. When his eyes meet mine again, though, he goes silent.

He glares at me a moment, but then his gaze rises to my hairline. His eyes flare, he blinks twice, and his eyebrows furrow. I reach up and touch the place where his stare is burning into my scalp, and it dawns on me.

"It's a wig," I explain, and he nods.

"It looks so real." His eyes drop back to mine, searching for something I feel in my chest, then scanning my face. "It looks so fucking real."

I don't know what to say, and I hate feeling vulnerable, so I hop back on the offensive.

"Brynn's going to ask you if I can give her guitar lessons."

The weird emotions from seconds ago disappear from his features.

"Savannah," he says, but this time it's more irritated than angry. "You can't."

Now it's my turn to scoff.

"Fine. Tell her no, then. You can be the one to disappoint her, because I refuse. It won't be me."

I'm still grappling with the fact that I've disappointed hundreds of thousands of fans. Little girls just like Jessica from our last show at the Garden. Fans just like Brynn. I hate being the cause of it all, but I don't know how to fix it in a way that won't lead to my own permanent destruction.

A voice sounds out over a speaker, and we both look in the direction of the cameras. We're going to start shooting again. I have to go get my makeup touched up.

I glance down at my outfit. I probably should have changed out of it before break, but thankfully it looks fine. It's just jeans, a white tank top, and a black bomber jacket. I'm supposed to be running through the streets of Portofino in search of my sister who has been kidnapped, so it looks better a little rumpled.

"Break a leg," Levi grumbles, and part of me thinks he might mean it literally.

He turns to stalk off, but just before he disappears around the corner of the set, I let myself ask the question that's been bugging me since the café. It comes out bitter and hurt.

"Where is she? Your once. Your *one*. Where is she?"

He stops, but he doesn't turn around.

I watch every muscle in his back tense under his plain blue t-shirt. For a moment, I think he might answer me, but then he steps around the corner without another word. Without even looking back.

I feel just as small as I did in my dingy rental house in Florida. Only then, I told him to leave. This time, he's done it on his own.

It's not until Levi's gone that a wet nose nudges my hand, and I realize Ziggy followed me. My girl has been here the whole time. She probably sensed my distress. That or she smells club sandwich on me. Either way, I fucking adore this rude, mannerless, super loveable jerk of a dog.

"C'mon, ZeeZee," I say to her, scratching quickly at the spot just above her tail, and we head back to set.

Red takes Ziggy, Tatum and Pax take fifteen minutes to fuss over my makeup and "fluff" my hair, and Levi and Brynnlee are nowhere to be found.

Then, I nail my crying scene.

The sobbing, the snotting, the full-on ugly cry. I'm actually afraid to see it on the big screen. I know for a fact it looks authentic because it *was* authentic.

Levi is dredging up all sorts of shit I'd rather not deal with again. Shit that's always sent me on a fucking bender in the past. This is how it would begin. I'd feel inadequate and lonely, and I'd start to replay *everything*. Start to blame myself. Then, to shut it all up, I'd use.

I'd use drugs to make me think less. I'd use Torren to make me feel wanted and special. I'd use music to disconnect. I'd black out, write music, and play up the chaotic artistic rockstar angle because it was the only tangible thing I had.

I have to cut it off at the root before it takes me over completely.

Like I'm going to take the word of someone in and out of rehab.

God, what a prick. He's right, but he's still a prick. It makes me even more determined to keep it together. Out of rehab, yeah, but not back in. Not again.

I change, wash my face, then head back to my rental and take an hour-long shower. I make myself one of those mocktail old fashioneds with black tea that I hate, and I take it to the roof to sip as I sit around a small fire. I listen to the cars and the breeze and the cicadas and frogs.

Without overthinking, I pull up the nearly abandoned group text with the band and send a photo of my view. I make sure my drink isn't in it. It's a mocktail, but I don't feel like having to clarify that.

Mabel and Torren react immediately. Torren likes the photo and Mabel sends a text that says, "sick view." I wait a few seconds for Jonah's text, but it doesn't come.

And then, on a hunch, I go to my text thread with just Mabel.

Could you ship me my Yamaha?

The black one that's in the corner of my music room at my house.

MABES

Sure. What for?

I sit on the question for a minute, contemplating if I should lie. Mabel knows everything about everything. That's why it hurt so bad when she started to hate me. I keep fucking up the most important relationships.

I decide to go with the truth.

Levi is here.

It's a long story, but I'm going to teach his daughter how to play.

You good?

A smile curves my lips. She asked not even a second later. She's concerned for me. She cares.

For now. I'll let you know if that changes.

24

SHARON PUTS a thick manilla envelope on the counter and I curl my lip at the familiar cursive scrawled across it in black marker.

They just don't fucking quit. I don't even have to open it to know what's in it, so I pick it up, walk it to the trashcan in the corner, and drop it in.

"At this point I bet this could classify as harassment," Sharon says idly as I stare daggers at the envelope. If I were the dramatic sort, I would light it on fire and dance on the fucking ashes.

"They'll give up eventually."

I feel Sharon's eyes on me as I speak, but I don't look at her. She doesn't believe my words any more than I do. I try to act unbothered, but she and I both know that I'll be making a call to Clark Jessop, my lawyer, later just to double check that everything is still good. I have nothing to worry about. Just for the peace of mind.

"It's been over two years," Sharon states, and I nod.

Two years and five months. Just a few months before the hurricane hit.

That day is cataloged in my brain as both a blessing and a curse. Brynn was devastated and terrified, but also relieved, and she was far too young to have to grapple with such heavy things. Watching Julianna die slowly, withering away to nothing before my eyes, was impossibly difficult to handle. But watching Brynnlee watch it was worse.

Saying goodbye to your mom is hard at any age, but at five, Brynn had a more advanced understanding of mortality than most adults ever will. She will never have a memory of Julianna where she wasn't sick. Even the good times were tainted, jagged and dangerous around the edges. Brynnlee will never know what her mother looked like healthy without the help of photos from the years before her birth. She will never remember a time with her mother that wasn't shadowed by doctors' appointments, and monitors, and the ever-present promise of death. I know she'll never heal from that. She's already grown around it. It's part of her. It always will be.

My relationship with Jules's parents was never a good one, but once she died and everything came to light, it was beyond saving. That's fine with me. I expected it. I remind myself of that every time another of these fucking envelopes comes in the mail. But for Brynn's sake, I wish it could have played out differently.

"You think Brynn misses them," Sharon asks, and I glance at her out of the corner of my eye.

"She says she doesn't," I tell her honestly.

Sharon doesn't respond. She just continues staring at the envelope in the trashcan with a frown.

I know what she's thinking. Sharon loves Brynn as if she were her own granddaughter. I think part of Sharon even wishes she was. She's done more for Brynn in the last two years than any of the others have since Brynn was born, but Sharon struggles with the guilt. She thinks that she's not enough. She still worries that it's wrong for her to be this close to us.

I struggle with it, too, honestly, but I'll continue to struggle with it if it means Brynn can have another person in her life who loves her. She deserves that and more.

"The Larks are not good people, Sharon," I say clearly. "Their love is conditional. It always has been. It doesn't matter what they try to throw at her, the bribes or false promises or smoke shows, Brynn will never fall for it. She's a smart kid."

She nods and sighs, then brings her attention to my face.

"And the threats?"

I hold her gaze, and when I speak, my words come out angrier than I'd intended.

"I'll worry about that."

"You can't do it on your own, Levi," she replies, her voice lower and softer than before. "You should let me—"

"No."

I cut her off firmly, and she doesn't argue. I don't want money from Sharon any more than I want it from the Larks. The business is in the clear now. I'll pull ahead on the house soon. I don't want Julianna's life insurance money from her self-serving parents, and I won't take Sharon's rainy day fund. I don't want any of it.

"Thank you," I say more softly this time, "but no."

Sharon nods reluctantly, and I shift my focus to the stairwell leading up to the second floor of my house, then shout up for Brynn.

"Boss, I'm heading out!"

I hear Brynn's feet pattering across the ceiling and then down the stairs until she's skidding to a halt in front of me. She's already got her old backpack slung over her shoulder in preparation for the public library's STEM summer camp. I'm glad she's finally agreed to do something with kids her own age, but I'm not thrilled about the compromise I had to make. I managed to hold her off for a whole week, but she broke me down eventually.

"You promise you'll ask her?" Brynn studies me suspiciously, eyes narrowed and ready to argue in case I go back on my word. I don't know why she's doubting me. I've not broken a promise yet. I don't plan to start now.

"Yes."

"Say you promise," she insists, and I force a smile.

"I promise I will ask her."

"Thank you, thank you, thank you." Brynn wraps her arms

around my legs in a hug. I reach down and run my open palm over her glossy brown curls.

"Remember, if you don't finish out the week, then we don't have a deal."

She steps back from me and grins.

"Kay."

I tell Sharon thank you once more for agreeing to take Brynn to and from the library this week, and then I head to my truck. My feet are heavy with each step, and my stomach churns with nerves. I've managed to avoid Savannah, and it hasn't been hard. I think she's been avoiding me, as well. But now, thanks to the promise I made to my daughter, I can't avoid her any longer, and I can't tell if I'm dreading this or excited for it. The entire drive to the studio, I have to fight off the urge to press harder on the gas. But do I want to speed to the studio, or turn the truck around and speed back home?

I'm just not sure.

I go through the gates and flash my badge, then drive through the lot and park in my designated spot. Then I just sit. I sit and stare at my dashboard. Am I working up courage? Am I calming my temper?

I don't fucking know. It's the most confusing form of edging.

"Fucking grow up," I grumble to myself. "She's just a fucking girl you used to know. She's just a fucking girl."

I take a deep breath, then climb out of the truck and slam the door.

Filming has already started, so instead of going by her trailer, I head to the set. My guys are finishing up the job turning the dirt lot into a nondescript New York City street corner, and despite the rush at which we needed to construct it, it looks good.

It's crowded because we're having to share the space with the painters and designers, but it looks like we've figured out a system that's working. It also helps that we're able to use existing exterior set buildings, so we just have to transform the look a bit. They'll be able to start filming on it by the end of the week.

I inspect my guys' work. I check the blueprints. I do some work of my own. I check the blueprints again. I talk to Jerry, the studio construction manager. I keep myself busy until I hear an announcement come through one of the radios that the actors are breaking for lunch soon. Then I put down my work and head to the sound studio.

They're filming inside today, and right now, they're wrapping up a scene in the kitchen.

The kitchen that I built to look like the one in my house, which I also built.

Savannah is perched atop my kitchen island wearing an oversized button-down, and her brown wig looks perfectly tousled. I step around one of the lighting guys to get a better look. There are coffee mugs sitting next to breakfast plates. A morning scene.

"I hate that you have to go in so early on a Saturday," Savannah says dreamily, popping a piece of strawberry into her mouth. Then her co-star Paul comes into the room. He's fixing his tie, wearing a button-down that looks just like the one hanging off Savannah's body.

"I hate it, too," he says before stepping in front of her. "But you'll have me all day tomorrow, and then next weekend, it's you and me and the Italian Riviera."

"Mmmm," she hums. "I can't wait."

From where I'm standing, I have the perfect vantage point of Savannah's face, but only the back of Paul's head. I don't care, though. I can't take my eyes off her, anyway.

The scene is a tender moment, and I know from my script read-through that it's from the beginning of the movie before Savannah learns that Paul's character is involved in shady business dealings that ultimately lead to the kidnapping of her younger sister.

In this scene, Savannah's very much in love with Paul. She doesn't want him to leave. She wants to stay in bed all day so they can continue trying for a baby. She's looking at him with those big, lovey doe eyes, smiling flirtatiously with plump, mischievous lips, and I feel murderous.

It's acting, I tell myself. *It's for the fucking movie.*

But goddamn, it looks real. Just like her brunette wig looks real.

Savannah trails her hand down Paul's chest. He tucks a strand of her hair behind her ear. I can tell from the way she's looking up at him that they're about to kiss.

I clench my hands into fists. Grit my teeth so hard the muscle in my jaw aches. I watch as he brings his hand to her face, cups her neck and brushes his thumb over her jaw. I hold my breath as he leans down, and I memorize the soft way Savannah watches him as she brings her hands to his waist.

The moment their lips touch, I see red. If I could send daggers with my eyes, they'd be lining Paul fucking Northwood's spine. The kiss turns heated, and Savannah's hands tighten in Paul's shirt, and I'm practically shaking with jealousy and rage. When Savannah opens her mouth to welcome Paul's tongue, I lose my grip and growl.

A low, feral, rabid wild animal fucking growl.

I feel the lighting guy next to me jump, but no one else seems to notice.

Except Savannah. Her eyes pop open and land on me immediately. She doesn't even have to search. Like a magnet, our gazes snap together, and she freezes. It's apparent to everyone, though it feels like it takes a million years for anyone to notice.

"CUT!" the director yells, shaking me out of my trance, and then I turn around and storm off the set.

I can't do this. I can't. I power walk through the sound stage, out into the parking lot, and all the way to my truck.

I can't fucking do this to myself.

I brace my hands on the hood of my truck and drop my head. I squeeze my eyes shut and breathe. She's looked at me like that before. She's talked to me that way. She's kissed me with just as much passion. More.

It's acting. It's just for a movie. And me and Sav are in the past. It's over. It's done. It doesn't matter.

I kick my tire with every word as I scold myself.

"Fucking hell. Grow the fuck up."

It's that stupid fucking wig.

I refocus my attention. I think of the envelope that showed up in the mailbox this morning from Julianna's parents. I didn't open it, but I know it was filled with brochures for church camps and Christian therapy for Brynn. They probably threw in a bank statement, too. They usually do. Just to remind me of how much Jules's life insurance payout was.

And then, because Helen works at the bank and thinks she's above the law, there's probably a statement in there of my mortgage. The one I took out to pay for Jules's experimental treatments, despite knowing they likely wouldn't work. They gave her one more year with Brynnlee, though, so I try not to regret it.

If the Larks really want to fuck with me, they could throw in my student loan debt that's piling up. That one is especially frustrating because I don't have a degree to show for it. Or if they got their hands on the business books from a few weeks ago, they'd use those dismal numbers to their advantage as well.

I remind myself of the other things they'd use to their advantage if they could.

I remind myself of the promise I made.

I think of Brynn.

Then, like the fucking grown man that I am, I stand straight and head back to the studio. I walk through one of the side doors and weave my way back through the sound stage. When I get to the kitchen set, it's empty but for a few sound and lighting techs.

"She's in her trailer, if that's who you're looking for," a voice says, and I turn to find a girl with a clipboard and a headset. It's the same girl I've seen carting Savannah around the studio. I raise an eyebrow and she blinks. "I'm Dakota. I'm a PA. I'm assigned to Sava—I mean, Ms. Loveless."

I tilt my head to the side and narrow my eyes.

"What makes you think I'm looking for Ms. Loveless?"

The girl fidgets a little with the hem of her shirt and shifts her weight between her feet as she lets out a little laugh.

"Aren't you all?"

I don't answer. I blow a harsh breath through my nose, nod in thanks, then turn on my heel and head to Sav's trailer. *Aren't you all?* What the fuck is that supposed to mean?

I keep my head down and avoid eye contact. I walk right past everyone and keep my feet pointed in the direction of the cast trailers, until I'm stepping up to the one with Sav Loveless brandished on the door. I raise my hand to knock, but my knuckles never connect.

Instead, I drop my hand back to my side and listen.

Music. An acoustic guitar. And Sav's voice.

She must be playing inside, and I'm frozen in place, rocketed back to a dark corner in a dingy D.C. dive bar. My heart races, my throat tightens, and I have the urge to sink further into the shadows so I can listen safely.

Just one more, honey
Just one more
Whiskey and orange
What are we waiting for?
Your spicy lips.
Your citrus tongue.
My drugged regrets
What have I done?

I avoid this song at all costs, yet I could still recite the lyrics from memory. I can still close my eyes and picture her up on that stage, holding a beat-up guitar and wearing a ripped Joan Jett shirt and a short denim skirt.

I wrote this one for a guy I thought I loved, she'd said to the crowd, and it *awwwww*'d in response before she started singing. Every word was a vise around my heart, my windpipe. Every note was a knife to the chest.

Streetlamp silhouette,
wore my shoes out on that pavement.

Thought you were my safe place, baby,
look how wrong I've been.

"She's good, isn't she?"

Paul Northwood's voice comes from behind me, and I turn slowly to find him standing only a few feet away, carrying a craft services bag. I look from his face to the bag and back to his face. He grins and lifts the bag up.

"Came to see if she'd want to run lines. Brought her and Red some lunch."

The muscle in my cheek twitches with the need to sneer. I don't like that he knows Red's name. I don't like that he's bringing her lunch. I don't like that the scene he's likely wanting to run lines for is the one I'd interrupted earlier.

"How's your girlfriend, Paul?"

His smile falters, caught off guard by my question. When he doesn't answer, I raise an eyebrow.

"That model," I clarify, and his brow furrows.

"Oh, well, she and I aren't together anymore," he says slowly.

I look him over. He's changed out of the outfit he was wearing earlier and is now in a pair of athletic shorts and a plain t-shirt. The shoes on his feet could probably make one of my mortgage payments.

"Is there a problem?" he asks, and I bring my eyes back to his.

"You tell me." I hold eye contact for a few breaths. He laughs awkwardly, and I tilt my head to the side. "You're not her type, Paul. She's not going to fuck you."

Northwood's jaw drops open, then he sputters out a bumbling attempt at a defense.

"*What*? No, I didn't...I'm just running lines. I'm not—"

"Good. Don't. If you do, well, it sure would be a shame if one of these set walls came loose and just toppled over, wouldn't it?"

He blinks at me in shock. I keep my face blank. Then the trailer door swings open.

I step back and look into Savannah's surprised face. Her eyes dart from me to Paul, and she tilts her head to the side before raising a brow at me.

"Did you need something?"

Her curt tone makes my nostrils flare, and then she looks over my shoulder and gives Paul a smile that makes me consider elbowing him right in his American Heartthrob face. It's probably insured.

"Sorry, Paul. Give me just a sec, okay?"

She bats her eyelashes at him, all sweet and welcoming, but when she looks back at me, it disappears. We lock eyes, but she doesn't say anything else.

"Brynn would like it if you could give her guitar lessons," I say flatly, and the shocked look that flashes over Savannah's face gives me a spark of excitement.

"Really?" she asks, and then she narrows her eyes at me again. "What's the catch?"

"No catch. She agreed to go to the STEM day camp this week at the public library, and in return, I told her she could have the lessons."

Savannah smirks. "She played you."

I don't answer, but she definitely did.

"I've got some conditions, though," I say, and Savannah nods. "You don't take her off set. I don't want her anywhere near those paparazzi vultures that follow you around. And no photos on social media. I don't want—"

"The association to Sav Loveless," she finishes for me.

I don't confirm or deny. She's not exactly right, but she's not wrong either. With Sav comes media attention. I don't need that.

At my silence, Savannah lets out a humorless chuckle and rolls her eyes.

"Got it. When do you want to start? My filming schedule is weird, but we can figure it out."

Now it's my turn to smirk.

"Let's start middle of next week," I say, taking a step backwards. "I feel like it will be easier to coordinate then. See ya later, Rockstar."

25

"I'LL TALK to her tomorrow about coming up with a schedule," I tell Brynn, trying like hell not to act as nervous as I feel.

"Why can't I be here, too," Brynn asks with a pout. She gives her overnight duffle bag a kick and then scowls at it.

"You love staying at Ms. Sharon's."

"Yeah, but I want to be here instead. I want to watch. I won't even be in the way. You know I won't."

I shake my head.

"No. We've talked about this. You're staying at Ms. Sharon's while they're filming. That's final."

"But what if Sav can only give me lessons on her lunch breaks?"

"Then I'll call Ms. Sharon and you can walk back on the lunch breaks."

"What if she can only do it at night after shooting?"

"Then I will come get you and bring you back here after filming."

She huffs. "But I wanna watch—"

"Brynnlee, the answer is no."

Not only will there be a ton of expensive equipment around here, but this movie has scenes that Brynn isn't old enough to watch.

She's mature for her age, but I'm not about to let her watch sex or murder scenes just because her idol will be starring in them.

My gut twists. I'm especially not looking forward to the sex scenes.

"Go on," I tell her, and she huffs again before picking up her duffle bag. She starts to stomp down the front porch stairs, but I call after her. "Forgetting something."

She sighs loudly, then grumbles, "Goodbye, I love you see you later."

"I love you more," I say to her retreating back. "Be good for Ms. Sharon."

I lean on the porch railing and watch as she drags her feet the whole two blocks to Sharon's. When she reaches the house, Sharon steps out onto the sidewalk and sends me a wave. I wave back, then Sharon shuffles Brynn into the house.

Once Brynn and Sharon are out of sight, I walk the couple of blocks to Main Street. When I turn toward our small coffee shop, I notice a familiar man staring angrily at the sign painted on the large window. I step up next to him and take it in.

For the most part, Main Street looks the same, but a few of the businesses have been altered slightly for filming. Names and logos changed, fresh paint, etc. The coffee shop is one of them.

What used to be *Oakport Sugar and Cream* is now *Buongiorno Bakery*, and instead of the usual logo displaying a happy pink pig lounging in a teacup, there's a plain white outline of a coffee bean and a croissant.

"This is your doing," Joe Shultz grumbles before taking a drink from his cardboard coffee cup. Even the to-go cups have been changed.

"How so?"

He flicks irritated eyes to me before looking back at the window sign.

"You had to go and build that million-dollar house and now all these Hollywood folk want to take over our town."

I raise a brow at the sign, but I don't look at Joe.

"Movies have been filmed here before, Joe," I remind him. "Blame the studio up the coast."

Joe shakes his head and his nose twitches.

"Those were romantic films. Comedies. Not this explicit baloney crap. Not with that devil music making band girl."

Devil music making band girl? I almost want to laugh. Something tells me Savannah would get a kick out of that one.

"They're only here for a couple weeks, Joe. Two tops. In and out, and it's good for the economy of the town."

Joe snorts into his coffee, but doesn't say anything else, so I walk into the café without another word. Mary Lynn, the lady behind the counter, sees me walk in and smiles, then gets to work making my coffee. She's already setting it on the counter by the time I reach it.

"He's been out there for thirty minutes just starin' at the sign on the window as if everyone in here can't see him doing it," Mary Lynn says with a grin. "'Bout refused his coffee when he saw the cups."

I shake my head. Joe Shultz needs to find a hobby.

"Did the studio contact you about tomorrow," I ask her, and she nods.

"We're fillin' the order now. They've got us doing baked goods for the cast and crew for the next two weeks."

That's what I thought. They've got the café covering breakfast, and two different local restaurants alternating lunches and craft service foods. The film being here really is good for the town's economy. Joe's just an asshole.

"I want to add six of your blueberry streusel muffins." I take my wallet out, but she throws up both hands with a scowl. Mary Lynn's been trying to refuse my money for years. "Put 'em in a box by themselves, though, and write 'Ziggy' on the top of it."

"Ziggy?" she repeats curiously, and I nod. She waits for me to explain, but I don't.

"Okay, sure," she says with a smile.

"Thanks, Mary Lynn."

I take my coffee in one hand and drop a twenty-dollar bill in its place before turning and heading back to my house.

On the walk back, I let my mind sift through the memories I usually avoid. Memories of Savannah and me when we were young. I think of blueberry streusel cake and laughter, and the thrilling feeling of doing something wrong for the right reasons. The thrilling feeling I'd get when it came to anything that had to do with Savannah. I'd have stolen a hundred blueberry streusel cakes just to see her smile. Walked through fire to keep her safe.

Everything about her being here has me conflicted.

Brynn is my priority now. She has to be.

But Savannah Shaw has always been a part of me in a way no one else ever has. She took up residence in my heart when we were fifteen years old, and she's stayed there. I can't fucking get rid of her. I used to think I didn't want to. Her memories were the ones I'd visit anytime things got so difficult I couldn't breathe. Every time I felt fucking lost or trapped, I'd think of her. I'd think of how I'd had her once. How I'd loved her. Held her. How part of her would always be mine, and it always managed to soothe some of the ache.

I did that for years, until I couldn't anymore.

Responsibilities can be daunting. Sacrifices are painful. I question every decision I've ever made, except the ones I've made for Brynn. I love my daughter. I'd lay down my life for her. In a lot of ways, I have.

I just can't stop wishing I could have them both. Brynn and Savannah.

I can't stop wishing I could have my blueberry streusel cake and eat it, too.

The trailers start to line the streets around five in the morning.

I've been up for an hour already. They'll be mostly filming in the

outdoor space—our deck on the back of the house overlooking the waterway, the side yard, and the portion of our backyard that stretches out to the beach. The kitchen and dining area are directly connected to the deck, which is why the set at the studio was built to look just like mine. They film what they can on the set at the studio, but for the shots that require the beach-like backdrop, they'll be in my house.

She'll be in my house.

I'm not ready, I don't know if I'll ever be ready, but I can't back out now. If for nothing else, we need the money. When the location scout for the movie approached me and asked to use my house for the film, I was all set to tell them no, but then they told me how much they would pay, and I caved. Use the house or lose the house, and I worked too fucking hard on this house to lose it.

I let the crew in shortly after the trailers arrive. I'm told that if the weather holds, they should be able to get everything filmed in two weeks. There are several beach scenes that take place at the beginning of the film, and then a few at the end when Savannah's character returns home with the sister she saved.

Paul's character should already be dead by that point. The death scene is one that needs to take place on location elsewhere, so unfortunately, I don't get to see Sav kill him off, but I'd pay to see the film just for that part alone.

For the next two weeks, the outside and part of the inside of my house will resemble a set on the backlot. Film equipment will line every free area, and people will be rushing about with headsets and clipboards. My original plan was to try my best to stay out of the way, but now that I know Sav will be here, I'm not sure if that will be possible.

As I slip out the side door with the sunrise and walk to my truck, I hear her laughter carry on the salty breeze. It's throaty and full. She's always laughed with her whole body. The kind of laughter that makes other people want to be in on the joke. I stop walking and let my eyes drift toward the sound, finding her immediately.

She's talking to her security guard about something while

playing with her dog. She's not wearing her wig, so her silver strands sparkle with the rising sun. Instead of getting into my truck and going to the office, I change direction and walk right to her.

Savannah hears footsteps and turns her beaming smile on me, but the smile disappears when her eyes land on my face.

"What are you doing here?" She stands back up from where she was crouched with the dog. "You working on these sets, too?"

"Something like that," I say slowly.

I drag my eyes from Savannah's face to Red's and give him a nod in greeting, then put my hand out to pat the head of the dog that's now sniffing my feet and legs.

"The guitar lessons," I say, cutting to the chase. I thought she'd be easier to talk to without the wig. I was wrong. "Would on the lunch break or after shooting work?"

"Oh. Um, yeah, I think so." She looks at Red. "Have they given you the schedule for the day?"

Red nods. "Lunch should work. You film kind of late tonight."

When Savannah looks back at me, I don't miss the hint of excitement in her eyes.

"I don't know the exact time for lunch, but if you're going to be here, then you can just have her meet me at my trailer?" She points across the street. "They brought mine."

I turn in the direction she pointed, then look back at her.

"Remember what I said. Don't venture off set. Stay within the barricades. I don't wa—"

"I know, Levi. No paps. No photos. No association with big, bad Sav Loveless. I got it."

We stare at each other for a few breaths. Her eyes are hard, giving nothing away, and I'm working to make sure mine match. When I feel my skin start to heat under the pull of her attention, I break eye contact. I take my hat off, run my hand through my hair, then put my hat back on. I give the dog one last head scratch, give Red one last nod, then address Savannah one last time.

"She'll see you at lunch, Ms. Loveless."

I turn to leave, but she's always liked to fight for the last word.

"How'd a straightlaced Pastor's kid end up such a grumpy dick, Cooper?"

I turn and look Savannah over one more time.

What do I tell her? That she broke my fucking heart, and my pile of shit just keeps getting deeper? Do I tell her I'm jaded and guarded and she's part of the reason why?

No.

"Loss will do that to you," I say flatly.

Then I turn and leave.

26

"This house is fucking insane," I say to Red as I step into my trailer for lunch.

"The kitchen looks exactly like the one at the studio, first of all, and the view from the deck is just yard, then beach, then water. I guess it's not technically the ocean. It's the mouth of the river before it connects with the Atlantic, but the guy who owns it must be some sort of millionaire."

I throw myself down on the barstool and pull one of the lunch containers toward me, flipping it open to find some sort of green salad that smells of pepper and vinegar. I grab a fork, spear a piece of lettuce for a test bite, and shove it in my mouth. It tastes good, so I eat as I chat.

"I wanted to snoop around but we've been busy as hell, and then I didn't want to miss the kid, so I hustled back here when they called break."

I shove another forkful of salad into my mouth as Red steps up next to my stool and sets a white box in front of me. It's got Ziggy's name on it.

"This was at craft services," he says. "Dakota told me to bring it back here."

I set my fork down, then pop open the box to find six of the most delicious-looking blueberry muffins with streusel topping. They smell divine, and immediately my interest in the leafy green salad disappears.

"Oh my god," I say, pulling out a muffin and taking a bite.

I hum and tilt my head back while I chew. It's so damn good. Ziggy whines, so I reluctantly break a piece off for her. The box did say her name, after all.

"Did I ever tell you about the blueberry streusel cake?" I ask Red as I take another bite.

He shakes his head no, so I plow forward.

"The town where I grew up—well, the town that I lived in until I was fifteen and ran away, I mean—there was this horrible old lady, right? Just awful. She hated me with a passion, but most people in that town hated me, so whatever. But anyway, she made this amazing blueberry streusel cake. She'd bring it to all the town functions. Bake sales and fish fries and town hall meetings. Anytime there was some sort of event, I'd sneak in just to get some of her blueberry streusel cake."

I pop another piece in my mouth, then take a sip of water before continuing.

"She tried to get me arrested once for stealing an entire one of her cakes from the mayor's daughter's baby shower, but they couldn't prove it was me."

"Was it you?" he asks, and I smirk.

"Yep."

He shakes his head like he's surprised, but he shouldn't be, and I frown into the box where five more perfect muffins sit.

"She used to go to Levi's church," I say into the box. "She'd bring the cake once a month when they had this weird Sunday potluck, and Levi would always smuggle some out for me. He'd wrap it in a paper towel and stick that in a plastic cup, then bring it to me at school on Monday."

I close the white box and slide it away from me, but I don't take my eyes off it. I tilt my head to the side and consider it. I can't shake the feeling...the hope...

"Was there a note or anything? With these muffins, I mean. Did anyone say why these were set aside for me?"

I glance at Red, and he shakes his head, so I look back at the box. I stare at it, narrowing my eyes as if I can glean the answer from the cardboard.

"What happened to the lady?" Red asks, breaking me from my stare off with the muffin box, and I shrug.

I start to tell him that she's probably dead and that I don't really care either way because she was an evil bitch when there's a knock on the trailer door. I'm up out of my seat and turning the knob before Red can even move, and when I swing the door open, Brynn is grinning up at me.

"Hey Boss," I say with a smile.

I flick my eyes behind her, but there's no sign of Levi, so I step out of the way and gesture for her to come in.

"Thank you so, so much for teaching me to—"

Brynn cuts off mid-sentence with a grunt when my menace of a dog bulldozes right into her, and they both tumble to the ground. Brynn is a mess of giggles as Ziggs does another lick attack, so I just lean on the counter and watch with an amused smile until it's over.

"Sorry," I tell her once Ziggy has calmed down, but Brynn doesn't seem to mind.

"It's okay, I love dogs." She moves to the couch and sits down. "We had to get rid of ours when my mom got sick the second time. Oh wow, you have two guitars? Did you bring one for me?"

Brynn made the comment about her mom so casually before switching topics and asking about the guitars, but I find myself stuck. Her mom got sick? I look at Red to find him watching Brynn closely. I want to ask about it, have her elaborate so I can learn more, but she's already moved on.

"Yeah, I had my friend Mabel send me another one so I could teach you on it."

Brynn's head whips to mine and her eyes are just as big as they were the day she spotted me in the café.

"Mabel? Mabel Rossi? Your drummer Mabel Rossi?"

"The one and only," I say and her jaw drops.

"You think I can meet her too?"

She's so fucking excited that I don't know what to say for a minute. I just flick my eyes to Red, who is pretending not to listen, then back to Brynn.

"I dunno," I say slowly, then shrug. "Maybe."

Before she can say anything else, I change the subject back to guitar lessons.

"Alright, just have a seat on the couch and we'll start with your first lesson."

Brynn darts to the couch so fast. It's adorable. But what's even more adorable is that Zigaroo jumps on the couch next to her and crawls onto her lap. My sixty-pound mutt thinks she's a lap dog. I don't even bother trying to tell her to get down because Brynn looks like she's in heaven, and Ziggs wouldn't listen to me anyway. Jerk.

I grab my Yamaha from the stand in the corner and then sit down on the little table in front of Brynn and Ziggy. I already switched out the strings to a light gauge for beginners.

"First lesson, Boss, is that I'm the boss during class," I say firmly and ignore the light chuckle that comes from Red. "Dig it?"

Brynn nods seriously.

"Dig it."

"Good. Now we're going to start with the basics."

I lay the guitar across my lap and point out the parts. I do it the same way Oscar did when he taught me how to play. I hate that sleazeball, but I will always be grateful that he put a guitar in my hand. Headstock, tuning keys, nut (Brynn doesn't giggle like an immature idiot like me and Mabes did when Oscar said it), neck, strings, frets, body, pick guard, bridge, and saddle.

"There might be a test," I tell her, and she giggles.

"I'm really good at tests."

"I bet you are." I smirk. This kid is too damn smart. Poor Levi. I look at my dog. "Okay, Ziggs, you have to get down."

She doesn't budge.

"C'mon, you mutt." I give her butt a shove. "Boss can't learn to play if you don't let her hold the guitar."

I shove Ziggy again, and she grunts. Brynn giggles, and I sigh, glancing at Red.

"Can you take her out?" I ask him, and he nods and moves to grab her leash, but Brynn pipes up.

"Or you can just come to my house. We can use the music room. We never use it, and it's not by the kitchen so it won't be in the way."

I freeze. I glance at Red, and he jerks his head in the tiniest *no*. His eyes say *this isn't a good idea,* so naturally I glance away from him. Levi has a music room? I get a chance to be in Levi's house? Um, why would I turn that down?

"How far is your house?"

"Just across the street."

Across the street isn't far. Levi said to stay within the set barricade, but just across the street might as well still be in the barricade. And besides, I've only seen like three paps since we got here, and they've all been on the beach since that's the side of the house we're filming on. I make up my mind and plow forward.

"Yep, let's do it." I pop up and gesture to the door. "Lead the way, Boss."

I snag the Yamaha and slip the strap over my head, so the body of the guitar is resting on my back, then I grab my beat-up acoustic from the corner. Brynn shimmies out from under my dog, and Ziggy just rolls on her back like a giant dead bug.

"I think she's pouting," Brynn says with a laugh. I nod. She definitely is.

Brynn walks to the trailer door and says goodbye to Red, so I do the same, mimicking her wave and everything. Red stares at me.

"I know what you're doing," he says on a low voice. "Troublemaker."

I smirk.

"Fun sucker."

I follow Brynn as she walks down the street, then look both ways with her before we cross, which just makes me giggle because all these streets have been barricaded off to traffic. I suppose it's smart to watch out for rogue golf carts or frenzied PAs though.

When Brynn starts walking toward the house where we've been filming, my feet start to drag. It's almost comical how long it takes me to connect the dots.

Instead of heading around all the filming equipment to enter through the sliding doors from the deck, Brynn takes me through the front yard. Past the giant tree with a rope swing hanging from its branches, up the front steps, onto the front porch, then through the front door. Her movements are familiar and practiced, and I'm glad she's not talking to me because I don't know that I could form words.

I recall something Brynn said the other day. *His guys built all the sets for your movie. One of 'em even looks just like our kitchen.*

Our kitchen.

Because this house is her fucking house. It's *Levi's* house. Suddenly, I'm even more in awe than I was this morning; only now, I'm also excited and nervous. The cast and crew are only allowed in part of the house. Everything else is blocked off with green screens and portable wall partitions. To be honest, I couldn't stop myself from snooping now if I wanted to.

And I don't want to.

I marvel at every detail of architecture. The crown molding. The open layout. The high ceilings and large windows. It's absolutely gorgeous, and I know in my bones Levi designed and built this house.

I'll design every inch of it just for you, he'd said once. *Only for you.*

I stop in front of a framed picture hanging on the wall. It's Brynn and Julianna. Levi's once who became his one. Brynn is tiny in the picture, maybe four or five years old, and they're sitting on the rope swing hanging from the large tree in the front yard. Julianna looks thinner than I remember, but she's smiling brightly with Brynnlee on her lap.

I'll design every inch of it just for you.

I guess he took that promise and gave it to someone else.

I feel jealous, even though I know I have no right to be. This is his family. His daughter. The mother of his child. He made the right decision by choosing them. By making them his priority. I don't yet know what happened to Julianna but judging from this picture—a picture I'm sure Levi took—she was happy and loved.

I tear my eyes away and trail after Brynn as she starts to give me a mini tour.

"You've already seen the kitchen and the deck. This is the foyer. This is a dining room that we literally never use. This is a sitting room that we also literally never use. This is the living room, we use this all the time, and it's usually open to the kitchen, but they put all these walls up for your movie."

I nod and pretend to listen, trying like hell to reset my mood as Brynn blazes through the house. She stops at the foot of a large staircase, so I stop with her.

"The music room is down that hall, but do you want to see my room first?"

She gestures up the stairs, and I follow the movement. There's a cut-out banister that gives me a view of another wall full of pictures, and while I want to go inspect it, I don't think I can handle it just yet. I've known this is Levi's house for all of two minutes, and I'm already shook to the core.

"What all is up there?"

Brynn ticks things off on her fingers as she answers.

"My room, the guest room, the guest bathroom, my bathroom, the laundry room, the office, and Dad's room."

It's the last one that makes my mind up for me. I definitely am not ready to be that close to Levi's bedroom. The bedroom he shared with Julianna.

"Maybe later. Let's head to the music room and get to work."

Brynn nods and turns around, then skips down a hallway. I follow, keeping my eyes on my feet this time. She turns a corner and opens a door, and then we're stepping inside what appears to be a sound-proofed room. It's empty but for a glass-partitioned area that is the perfect size to hold recording and mixing equipment. I blink as I take it in.

"What did you say this is?"

Brynn plops down on the floor and crosses her legs at the ankles.

"Dad calls it the music room." I stare at her silently, and she bounces her eyebrows at me. "Okay, um, are we going to get started?"

I shake my head to loosen the sand that's taken over my brain. *A music room.* Why would Levi put a music room—that looks very much like it's meant to be a sound studio—in this house he built for his wife and child?

I sit down next to Brynn in a fog, then pull my phone out of my pocket to check how much time we have left on the lunch break. Instead, though, I get distracted by two missed calls and a text. One missed call and a voicemail from Hammond (barf), a missed call from Mabel, and a text from Mabel. I open Mabel's text first.

MABES

Hey call me back before you talk to Ham. Talk to me before you even listen to his voicemail. Labels on a rampage. I'll give you the deets so you don't pop off on his ass and get yourself in hot water.

My eyes narrow at the screen and my lips purse. I don't even know what I did, this time. I've been on my best behavior. What the hell is Hammond up to now?

How much trouble am I in?

Not much. Just call me before you talk to Ham. I'll explain.

The fact that Mabel is running interference for me warms my heart more than the idea of Hammond playing games cools my blood. She's looking out for the band, but it also feels like it's for me. I still feel like I am the band, and I file that feeling away for later.

Despite the irritation, I smile as I type out the thank you text and let her know I'm shooting until late, but I'll call her as soon as I get a free minute, then I stick my phone back in my pocket.

"Alright, Boss, we've got about forty-five minutes before I have to report back. First lesson starts now."

I set Brynn up with the guitar on her lap and show her how to hold it properly, then I sit across from her and mirror her position. I walk her through how to count the strings and frets and show her proper finger placement for a few chords. She's the perfect student and every bit Levi's daughter in how attentively she listens, and how perfectly she carries out each instruction I give. The grin that stretches wide across her face every time her strum sounds exactly like mine is so full of joy, and I feel like I'm reliving a crucial part of my life I'd forgotten.

Learning to play the guitar was thrilling. It was my first taste of freedom. Of control. It was my first healthy outlet, and it was like discovering the sun after a childhood locked in darkness. You'll hear musicians say it all the time, and it may sound cliché, but it's one of the truest statements that has ever passed my lips—music saved my life. It gave me a purpose and a direction. It was everything else that came with it that led to my destruction.

If I could take the music and leave behind everything else, I'd be set for life. I just can't figure out how to do that.

"How'd I do?" Brynn asks as we finish up.

"You did great. I think you're going to be a natural."

"Really?" Her eyes widen and she bounces slightly on her toes. "You think I could be good like you?"

I smile and answer honestly.

"Boss, I think you could be better."

I trail Brynn out of the music room and down the hallway, my mood brightened by the music lessons. My step is light despite the awkward weight of carrying my two acoustics, and my attention is no longer stuck to the floor for fear of seeing something I shouldn't.

And then I regret it.

Brynn weaves through the formal dining room and I halt in my tracks when I see a large canvas portrait on the wall. My mouth drops, my heart stops, and my eyes sting. I stare at the canvas without blinking.

"Oh, that's my mom and dad and me."

Brynn's voice comes from somewhere off to the side, and I see movement in my periphery as she comes back to stand next to me. I don't take my eyes off the canvas portrait, though. I can't. They're stuck. I might die here staring at this picture, and it's the closest I've ever come to worrying about going to hell.

My eyes scan, and though it hurts, I don't look away. Morbid fascination and my self-sabotaging tendencies partner up, and I'm nearly knocked over from the force of the shock.

"Is this..." I work to clear my now dry throat and form words with my now numb tongue. I swallow and lick my lips before trying again. "Is this their wedding?"

I know the answer. It's obvious. Levi's in a tux and Julianna is in an expensive looking white wedding gown. She's holding a bouquet of gorgeous flowers. His boutonnière matches. I knew they were married. Levi still wears the ring. That's not what has my brain addled and my nerves racing.

What throws me off is Brynn.

She's a toddler in this picture, not an infant.

It's not uncommon for couples to wait years after the baby is born to get married—there are a multitude of reasons why this happens all the time—but something about this seems significant in a different way. Knowing what I know about Levi's parents, and what I remember about Julianna's, something feels *off.*

"They're going to make you marry her."

"No way, they wouldn't."

"They will."

"It doesn't matter what they want. I won't do it."

Had he held out? Had he really told them no, but they wore him down? Maybe the delay had to do with college? Maybe it was venue-related or had something to do with aesthetics?

Maybe Jules wanted to lose the baby weight?

I study her. She looks beautiful. An absolute angel in that wedding dress. Maybe Levi said no at first, but he grew to really love her. Maybe he was excited to get married. Maybe—

"Yeah, that's from our wedding. From the first time Mom got sick."

I drag my eyes off the portrait and pin them to the side of Brynn's face. She's studying the canvas with a small, sad smile. When she speaks again, her voice is wistful, and I'm reminded that she's only seven. I keep forgetting that. She seems so much older, but she's still just a child.

"Mommy got sick, and Daddy didn't want us to be alone. He moved back here, and we got married, and then we became a family."

I swallow hard and try to process what she's said, but once again, my mind is moving in slow motion, and I can't seem to make sense of any of it. Brynn said only a handful of words, but my body feels like it might collapse beneath the gravity of what she's implied.

"What happened to your mom, Brynnlee?"

I ask the question, but I'm already certain I know the answer.

"She died."

"When?"

"Two years, five months, two weeks and three days."

She rattles it off, right down to the day, and everything in my chest hurts for her. For Levi. This poor girl lost her mother, and she was only, what, five?

The first time she got sick, she'd said. I glance back at the wedding portrait.

Brynn was five years old when her mother died of cancer, and she'd lived every year before that with the stress of the disease. I can't even imagine how something like that would color a childhood. How it could affect development. The way Brynn carries herself, so grown-up and serious, no longer amuses me. It pains me. Even her spark of mischievous humor makes me feel like crying.

This girl had to grow up way too quickly.

Not for the first time, I feel a connection to Brynnlee so powerful that it makes me flinch. My hands clench to fight off the desire to reach for her and pull her in for a hug. To brush her hair back and look into her eyes—eyes just like her mother's—and tell her, *I get it. I understand.*

I make up my mind to end the conversation here, to stop putting her through this, when she continues.

"Mom had osteosarcoma. That's a type of bone cancer. It's supposed to have a 74% survival rate, but when it came back, it was already everywhere. It was fast."

I don't know what to say. I'm sorry for your loss? That really sucks? Nothing feels like enough. I'm watching her, trying to pull something worth saying out of my head, when footsteps sound in the hall just outside the dining room, and I know who I will see even before his body graces the doorway.

"Brynnlee, you were told to stay out of the house during filming."

Brynn and I turn to face him at the same time. He's speaking to her, but his eyes are hard and set on me.

"Sorry, Daddy. Sav and I did guitar lessons in the music room."

I watch Levi's jaw tense and his eyes flare just slightly. To anyone else, he'd appear still as stone, but even after all these years, I can still read him.

He doesn't want me in that room.

He doesn't want me in this part of the house at all.

He probably doesn't want me to even know it belonged to him, and he definitely doesn't want me gawking awkwardly at his wedding portrait.

Any other day, in any other moment, I'd toe the line. Test the boundaries. I'd nudge and nudge just to see how far I could push him. But right now, with how off balance I feel, I just can't do it. I still need to do a half day of filming, and right now, I feel like I might throw up.

I want answers. I *will* get them.

But right now, I need to leave it alone.

I tear my eyes off Levi and bring them back to Brynn with a smile.

"Thanks for showing me around, Boss. Don't forget to practice, and I will see you tomorrow, okay?"

"Okay," she says quietly, just a small hint of a secret smile. She's definitely expecting to get in trouble when I leave, but she's not worried. I turn to Levi.

"Let's just plan on lunchtime lessons for the next week."

He jerks a single nod, but says nothing, so I wave awkwardly with the hand not holding my Yamaha, then turn and see myself out the front door.

This time, when I step off the porch, I head straight for the large tree with the rope swing. I peer up into the canopy of leaves, noting the thick, sturdy branch where the rope is tied. I turn to study the seat of the swing. It's just a plain, worn piece of wood. The ropes attached on either side have plastic guards the size of an adult hand right where you'd expect someone to grip when swinging. I reach out and run my fingers over one of them.

I imagine Brynn and Julianna on this swing together, like in the photo, but in action, like a home video. They're laughing and smiling with Levi watching happily from the porch. I have the strangest urge to sit on the swing, but I resist.

Instead, I take a step backward. Then another. I take one last look up into the canopy, then I turn around and walk back to my trailer.

27

AFTER FINDING HER WITH SAVANNAH, I brought Brynn straight to the office to hang out with Sharon.

The urge to interrogate Brynn about what she'd said to Savannah and what they talked about was too strong. If I'd been my mother, I'd have punished her with some archaic and cruel practice sure to leave lasting scars. I'm not my mother. I've sworn to never be my mother. But fuck if I'm not totally lost in this parenting thing sometimes.

Sometimes the only guidelines I have are how *not* to be. My mom and dad set great examples for that. Julianna's parents were worse, so together, Jules and I were often just fumbling messes, trying to navigate raising a kid while also dealing with the shadow of Jules's disease. It's been anything but normal, and Sharon tells me all the time that I'm doing the best I can. That should be enough, but sometimes...it's just not.

Sharon tells me that she and Brynn are going to attend the church fish fry tonight, which I totally forgot about.

I have to remind myself regularly that the church Sharon attends now is not the same corrupt organization that my father led. They're more accepting. They don't condone child abuse. They don't send "troubled young girls" to live in dangerous fake foster homes simply to get them out of the way. So, I promise them both that I will make an appearance at the fish fry, and then I make myself scarce.

I drive to the River View neighborhood to check on the rebuilds. We've run into a snag with the plumbing in one of our last houses, so I send a text to Sharon that she'll have to reach out to our private donor. We deal directly with the estate lawyer and accountant, and so far, they haven't turned us down once.

I go through the same routine for the next few days. Office, work inspections, office, sleep. But by Friday, my luck has run out.

When I get back to my house, the sun is setting, but the film crew is still hard at work. I sneak through the front door and into the part of my house that's been partitioned off before stepping out onto the deck.

There are dark clouds and flashes of lightning on the horizon, giving the water a rough, dangerous aura. From the way the crew is scrambling, they're rushing to get the last scene shot before they get rained out.

I can just make out Savannah down on the beach, the perfect silhouette of her body displayed starkly against the water, as if summoning the impending storm. I can't hear her lines, if there are any at all, but I stand on the deck and watch until someone shouts CUT over a loudspeaker. When the crew starts packing up and everyone begins to disperse, I should turn around and head inside. I should continue to avoid her like I have all day.

I don't.

I watch as her silhouette grows larger, until I can just make out the skimpy black bikini they have her in, showing off her sleeve of fake tattoos. I wonder if they've left the real tattoo on her back for the movie, or if they've covered it up with makeup.

I stare at her, willing her to turn around so I can see for myself. To assuage my curiosity and feed my craving. Instead, as if she can feel my gaze, she looks up and her eyes meet mine. She stops walking and stares up at me, face blank. I stare back. When she nods discreetly toward the side of my house, I don't question it. I just turn and walk down the deck stairs, meeting her in a matter of seconds. I know what's coming, and something inside me has been longing for this conversation for years.

When Savannah opens her mouth, her question shoots out quickly, like it's been sitting on the tip of her tongue for hours, fighting to get past her teeth, and she's finally released it.

"Did you marry her because she got sick?"

"Yes."

"Why?"

"I didn't want Brynn to be alone," I say honestly. "I didn't want Julianna to have to go through it by herself—raising a toddler while trying to go through treatments for cancer. She didn't deserve that. Brynn didn't."

"How old was Brynn when Julianna got sick?"

"Two the first time. Four the second."

She runs her eyes over my face, and when she speaks next, the question is softer. More tentative, like she's afraid of the answer.

"Did you love her?"

Savannah doesn't specify, but she doesn't have to. I know she's talking about Julianna. I shake my head once and answer without hesitation.

"Not like that."

I don't finish. I don't say what I want to. *I didn't love her like I loved you.*

"Why still wear the ring, then?"

I shrug.

"Keeps the Larks happy thinking I'm still mourning their daughter. Keeps people from trying to set me up."

And it keeps women from thinking I'll ever let them become more. Because the only woman I've ever wanted more with is standing right in front of me.

I keep my mouth shut, and the silence between us stretches.

I wait for her to say something, anything, but she doesn't. She just stares blankly and keeps her mouth shut for what feels like years. The more breaths I take in the quiet, the more tense my shoulders grow. The angrier I become.

I don't know what I want from her in this moment. An apology? A confession? Would anything even be good enough? I just want more than she's giving me. I want more than I've gotten over the last eight years. I want more than what I was left with in that small house in Miami when I was eighteen. A giant decision with no right answer, and the only person I'd ever loved walking away from me for the second time.

When Savannah finally speaks, I'm a lit fuse attached to almost a decade's worth of dynamite.

"Why didn't you contact me? I could have helped."

"And interrupt your glamorous rockstar lifestyle? It was too much for you when it was just a baby to deal with, remember? No way in hell you'd be willing to accept a baby *and* cancer."

She grits her teeth, and her nostrils flare.

"That's not fair, and you know it."

I scoff.

"What's not fair is you pushing me away when I was begging you not to. What's not fair is you hearing me say I loved you and then kicking me out of your house. I wanted *you*, Savannah. I wanted you, but you didn't want me enough to put up with everything that came with me."

My voice shakes more and more with each word, and it's difficult to keep from shouting. I'd have taken her with everything. With all of it. Even if she was still a stripper in Miami—if that was all she'd ever be—I'd still have wanted her to be mine. If she'd never left her mother's house. If she'd stayed in our small town, I'd have run away with her after graduation. I'd have kept her safe.

None of it would have happened at all if she'd have just stayed.

I did want her to be mine. She just didn't want me.

"I did what I had to do for the both of us," she spits out. "I didn't have a choice. You were having a baby. There wasn't going to be any room for me in your life—"

"That's bullshit. *You* didn't have room for *me* in *your* life. In your exciting new life. In your big, bright career plans. You didn't want to deal with me and my complicated future while you were on tour building yours. That wasn't for both of us. That was for *you*. You couldn't even—"

"I couldn't save you, Levi!"

She shouts the words, then immediately closes the distance between us while lowering her voice to a harsh whisper. I can feel her breath slam into my chest, words hitting like silent bullets, punctuated by a deluge of angry tears.

"Don't you get it? I couldn't save you. I was too busy trying to save myself. And yeah, I know that's selfish. But do you know how hard it was to go from not caring if I lived or died to actually trying to be something? To try and make myself into someone I didn't hate when I looked in the mirror? And then—"

Savannah chokes back a sob, swiping roughly at her tears, then reaching up and tugging on her brown hair. Her eyelids flutter, then clamp shut as she shakes her head.

"Jesus, Levi, I was in love with you. I loved you more than anything. More than *everything*. Do you know how much it would have hurt to watch you put them first? Do you know how hard it would have been for me to eventually, *inevitably*, be pushed out of your perfect life with your perfect new wife and perfect baby? It would have killed me, Levi. It would have fucking killed me. For eighteen fucking years, I'd been a punching bag. An afterthought. A burden and a fantasy and nothing important to *anyone* but you. And that was going to change, and I couldn't handle it. So, I'm sorry you had to deal with the consequences of your actions at eighteen. I'm sorry you think I failed you, that I was a bad friend, but I'm not sorry I saved myself. And if you've hated me for the last eight years because of it, well then—"

"I had to," I force out, and she startles.

For seconds, we stare at each other in silence. Just the sound of the wind, and the storm in the distance, and our rapid breathing fill the air around us.

When she finally speaks, it's a jagged, terrified whisper.

"What does that mean?"

"I had to hate you, Savannah."

I hold her gaze. Her eyes are filled to the brim and overflowing with tears, and in the darkening twilight, not even the moon can compete with her shimmering irises.

A hurricane. A tempest. A violent force of nature.

The only kind I've ever looked forward to.

"I *had* to hate you, or I would resent them. I would resent them for making me lose you, for taking away the only thing I ever so desperately wanted, and they didn't deserve that. Neither of them did, but especially not Brynn. For their sake, for mine, I *had* to hate you. I've thought of you every single day. Even when I didn't want to. Even when I tried not to. You're in my dreams. You're in my head and my chest and my fucking blood, Savannah. I *had* to hate you, or I wouldn't have been able to move forward. Not even a little. Not at all."

Our chests are heaving, our panted breaths mingle in the space between our bodies. The breeze kicks up, tousling the strands of her brown hair and giving her that fierce look I remember from when we were younger.

Swirling, slate gray eyes. Wild, untamed hair.

Savannah Shaw has always been my perfect storm.

As if on cue, the rain starts.

Soft sprinkles wet our bodies, reminding me that Savannah is in a swimsuit that leaves nothing to the imagination, before the sky opens up and blankets us in a downpour. I grab her arm and pull her under the shelter of the deck. The rain hits the wood slats above us and the stone pavers under our feet so loudly that I can no longer hear her breathing. Only the harsh, pounding rain, and my racing heart.

I glance toward the water, but the rain is falling in such thick sheets that I can barely make out where the grass of my backyard meets the beachy shoreline. When I bring my eyes back to Savannah, she shivers, rain dropping from her eyelashes and onto her cheeks. To her lips. I watch as a raindrop slides to her plush lower lip and rests there, sparkling. Taunting. Teasing.

I can't want her again. I can't awaken that desire. I can't unlock that fucking box inside my heart. I know all of this. I know how badly it will hurt when it ends, but like a man possessed, I don't think of any of it.

Without taking my eyes off that raindrop, I open my mouth and rasp the only words my brain can form.

"Savannah, can I kiss you?"

Her lips part on a gasp. The raindrop trembles.

"Yes," she whispers, and my mouth is on hers before the raindrop falls.

The moment we touch, my body sags with relief, eight years of tension burned away in the heat from this kiss. I groan and wrap my hand around her neck, holding her to me, keeping her close so I can taste her thoroughly. She whimpers into my mouth and fists her hands into my shirt, pulling and tugging. I coax her lips with my tongue, and she opens without hesitation.

I will never forget this moment. It will haunt my nightmares for years after.

I walk her backward and press her against the house. I move my mouth from her lips to her ear, then to the soft skin covering her pulse point. I suck, and she whines, pressing her body into me and tilting her head to the side. Giving me access. Granting my wishes.

When my name leaves her lips on a soft whimper, my restraint snaps.

I drag my teeth from her neck to her collarbone, then suck the swell of her breast into my mouth. I bite down, making her cry out, then suck hard enough that I know she'll need extra time in the makeup chair tomorrow to cover the mark I've made.

Her hands move to my hair, digging into my scalp, as I nudge the cup of her bikini aside and suck her nipple into my mouth.

"Levi," she pants out, moaning my name and tugging me closer with each breath. "Levi. Levi."

Quickly, I press kisses down the side of her torso, to her stomach, as I drop to my knees and bite at the soft flesh of her hips. I take one hand and wrap it around her bare ankle, then lock eyes with her. Without speaking, I push her foot out, widening her stance so I can move my body between her legs. She sucks her lower lip into her mouth, watching me with hooded, wild, lust-filled eyes, and tilts her pelvis toward me. An unspoken, unmistakable invitation, and I accept.

I cover her pussy with my mouth and her whole body shudders as my hot breath caresses her sensitive skin through the wet fabric of her bikini bottoms.

"Oh fuck," she whispers. "Oh fuck, Levi."

I hook my finger in the crotch of her bottoms and pull them to the side, then devour her naked pussy with my eyes. Her pale skin almost glows in the moonlight, shimmering and slick with the rainwater, and directly contrasted by the dark bikini. I blow lightly on her clit, just to watch goosebumps appear on her skin.

"Please, Levi."

I tear my eyes from her pussy and direct them at her face.

"Please what, Savannah?"

I take my finger and drag it through her, coating my fingertips in her arousal before bringing them to her clit and rubbing it in small circles.

"Yes," she says on a sigh, and I halt my movements. "No, Levi, don't stop."

"Please what, Savannah?"

I repeat the words slower this time, my voice so rough that I barely recognize myself, but it carries despite the sound of the rain pounding all around us. She gasps, staring down at me as her chest rises and falls rapidly with her pants. She tightens her grip in my hair and tilts my head back slightly.

"I want your mouth on me. Please."

Our eye contact doesn't break until my mouth covers her pussy and her eyes fall shut with a gasp. I groan the moment her taste hits me, and I lick her once before sucking her clit into my mouth.

She tastes of saltwater and rain and something decidedly her. My tempest. My chaos. I hum against her, flicking my tongue over her clit again before starting all over and licking her fully with the flat of my tongue.

"Yes. Yes, Levi."

She whispers into the air, pulsing her hips slightly. When I slip two fingers into her, she groans and tightens around me. My dick is straining hard against my jeans, pressing into my zipper in a way that's almost painful. I want to reach down and squeeze it, stroke it to relieve some of the ache, but I can't take my hands off Savannah. I rove one up and down her body, gripping her hip and pulling her hard against me, as the other makes slow, rhythmic thrusts in and out of her pussy.

I flick and suck her clit, grazing my teeth as my fingers work her from the inside. I slide my free hand up her body and palm her breast, massaging and then pinching her nipple. Three separate sensations, three separate motions, and if I could, I would give her more. I'd give her everything.

She whimpers louder and brings her eyes to mine. I feel her start to pulse around me. Her body starts to quiver. I bring my thumb to her clit and rub quickly and watch in awe as her mouth drops open with a gasped moan.

"That's it," I croon over her pussy between swipes of my tongue, never stopping the thrusting of my fingers. I hold her eyes as I speak, as I work her with my hands and mouth. "That's it, Sav. Give it to me. Give me your orgasm. This one is mine."

I pick up speed, thrusting and rubbing with more vigor.

"Give it to me," I say again, my voice a growl. "Give me what's mine."

She comes with a shaky, breathless cry, pulsing around my fingers and soaking my hand in her cum. Then she stills, breathing heavily, with her head dropped back on the wall of the house.

I pull my fingers out of her, adjust her bottoms so she's covered, then stand to face her.

When her eyes meet mine, I don't hide my smirk.

"What?" she asks breathlessly. "What?"

I raise an eyebrow, dragging my gaze down her body to her pussy and back, and then shrug.

"That might be the first time I've seen you do what you're told."

Her eyes flare and her jaw drops, and I watch as she tries to fight the upward turn of her lips. She loses the battle with her smile, but I can tell from the mischief in her eyes that she's already formed another plan to regain the upper hand.

She reaches for me and hooks her fingers into the band of my jeans, then tugs me forward roughly. Our lips collide, tongues tangling instantly, until she's moaning into my mouth and palming my dick through the denim.

"Fuck." I groan into her mouth as she strokes me, and I thrust into her hand.

My arms bracket the wall on either side of her head, and I pull back slightly to watch her talented fingers pop the button on my jeans, then tug down the zipper. I wait, chest rising and falling with my hard breathing, for her to do more, but she doesn't.

I bring my eyes up to her face and find her watching me with a smirk. I hiss as she drags her nails over the taut skin of my abdomen, teasing the band of my boxer briefs. She quirks a brow, then dips her fingertips lower until they just tease the base of my dick. I suck in a sharp breath, then meet the challenge in her eyes with one of my own.

"Don't be shy now, baby. If you want it, take it."

The way she parts her lips, then sinks her teeth into the plush lower one, fills me with need to take matters into my own hands. To guide her to her knees and push into her throat. To paint those sexy lips with my cum.

I take one hand off the wall and wrap it around the side of her neck, rubbing roughly at her jaw with my thumb before pressing it between her lips and into her mouth. She laves her tongue along the pad of my thumb then grazes it with her teeth, making me groan.

I drop my forehead to hers, and she wraps her delicate hand around my cock and squeezes. I'm fucking throbbing, aching for her. Her hands on my skin. Her mouth.

"Take me out."

She doesn't hesitate. She shoves the fabric of my boxer briefs down as she takes my bare cock in her hands. Her hot, soft palms and fingers encase my shaft, tugging in a way that threatens to snap my restraint. My hand moves to the nape of her neck and grips. I'm half a breath away from pushing her to her knees, when a voice cuts in.

"Ms. Loveless. You're needed at wardrobe and hair."

I flick my eyes to the intruder and sneer, shielding Savannah's body with mine. It's her personal security, and to his credit, his back is to us. Savannah sighs, and I feel her grip loosen.

"Give me five minutes," she says, and then she releases me, so I do the same.

I step back and give her space, shoving my hard dick back in my pants and doing up my jeans in the process. Her eyes are wild and pleading as they bounce between mine. We're still panting. We're still desperate and needy.

I want to tell her to come back. To go and do whatever she needs to do, and then come back to me. To this house that was meant to be hers before it wasn't. I want to finally know what it's like to have her inside, to feel her. How it was supposed to be. I want to possess every inch of her in the house I built for her memory. I want to *own* her.

"I have to go," she says quietly before I can speak. She gestures to her wet, tangled wig, then to her sleeve of fake tattoos. "They need to take care of all this."

I want to tell her to come back here to my house, but I don't. Instead, I jerk out a nod and watch her as she watches me. She scans my face.

"I have to go to L.A. tomorrow." I raise a brow in question, and she huffs out a small laugh. "There's an awards show. The band's nominated, and we're playing."

I fold my arms across my chest.

"L.A. with Torren King?" I try to keep my voice neutral, but I fail. I can't say his name without every syllable dripping with disgust. Savannah rolls her eyes.

"Yes, Levi, with Torren. Torren is in my band so he will also be there."

I stare at her, and she stares back, her brows slanted harshly over the challenge in her eyes. Torren King. Her bassist, her ex-lover, her supposed fiancé. He's been with her every day for the last eight years. He might know her better than I ever did now.

That thought, more than any of the others, makes me murderous.

I drop my gaze down her body, taking in every inch of exposed skin in the dim, dark night. The rain still pounds around us, and I can feel her security guard's presence looming off to the side, but I don't take my attention off Savannah as I close the distance between us once more.

I lock my eyes with hers, gripping her chin between my thumb and forefinger and tipping her face up to meet mine. She doesn't flinch. Doesn't bat me away. Her nostrils flare on an inhale, but her eyes stay on mine.

Slowly, with my other hand, I cup her pussy. I raise a brow in question, and she tilts her pelvis toward me in invitation. I slip my fingers into the side of her bottoms and swipe them through her pussy, coating my fingers in the cum that I coaxed from her moments earlier. Then, I bring them up and smear her arousal over her lips, pushing into her mouth and making her suck for good measure. I bend down and press my lips to the shell of her ear.

"When you're with him, remember how hard I made you come tonight. If he dares to try and kiss you, remember that this taste was my doing."

I drop my hands from her, take a step back, then leave her panting and speechless under my deck.

28

I'M MAULED by paparazzi the moment I exit the airport.

What should take ten seconds to walk from the automatic doors to my waiting car takes almost two minutes because Red and two more security guys have to pull me through the unruly swarm of camera wielding leeches.

Apparently, they've been starved for me this last month. Sav Loveless's return to L.A. is big news, especially since I was photographed in North Carolina last week out in public without my emerald. That was mistake number one. Mistake number two was flipping off the lone reporter who asked me why I wasn't wearing said emerald and suggested I was cheating on my "fiancé" with Paul Northwood. Mistake number three was ignoring Ham's calls so I couldn't properly ream his ass when he decided to schedule a surprise show to kick off the Music Choice Awards this weekend.

You're messing with the label's narrative, Savannah, he'd said, scolding me like I was a child. *To make up for it, you need to make an appearance with the band. If you don't, your replacement will. And wear the fucking ring.*

Once Red shoves me in the car and shuts the door, I roll my window down and flip everyone off with my left hand.

"Can't you just behave?" Red asks from the front seat, and I shrug, rolling the window back up and throwing myself against the soft seat cushion. I hear the click of the child window lock and snort. *Too late, old man.*

"Ham said make sure they see the ring. I just gave them a great photo op."

"They stalk you because of all those photo ops you so freely give them."

I meet his eyes in the rearview and smile sweetly. "You mean it's not my pretty face?"

He's unamused, and he stresses that when he turns on a country music station and cranks it. Asshole. I'm definitely body checking him at the next opportunity.

The drive to my house also takes longer than usual. Or maybe it just feels like it because I've been conditioned to small town North Carolina and its lack of traffic. Hammond tried to demand that I go straight to the studio and meet with him, but I told him hell no and then hung up on him. No way I'm meeting with anyone until I've showered the plane off me. I need a hot shower, a fresh change of clothes, and a fifteen-minute nap in my own bed before I can be expected to be even halfway civil with Hammond right now.

I'm so keyed up. So nervous and anxious and fucking pissed at always being told what to do. What I want is a drink. Or something stronger. Thank god I had Red hire someone to sweep my house for drugs and booze before we got here. Part of me doesn't trust myself not to take something if it were right in front of me.

But then wouldn't that just be letting them dictate my life for me? Wouldn't that still be letting others decide my fate? The label would probably love if I started using again. I'm more pliable that way. Who cares if my insides are rotting so long as they get their last two tours and albums.

Fuck.

If I'm going to succeed with this sobriety thing, it will be because I'm stubborn more than anything else. Do I want to be healthy? Yes. Do I want to live? Yes. Do I want to avoid becoming a member of the 27 Club? Yes.

But do I want to say fuck you to my label more? Hell yes.

What does that say about me?

Pulling up to my house, there are cars and cameras already staked out on the street. There are always a few stragglers hanging out when I'm home, but this is fucking ridiculous.

"How long have they been camped out here?" I ask Red as he punches the code into the gate and pulls into my driveway.

"Since they announced you'd be performing at the award show."

"Jesus," I grumble. "That was almost two days ago."

Red huffs in response and pulls the car into my garage. He parks between my Porsche that I never drive and my Harley that I never ride, and we climb out of his car at the same time. He walks to the trunk and pulls out my luggage, then trails me into the house.

I miss my mutt. Since this trip is such a quick turnaround, we had to board her in North Carolina. She's living her best doggy life in a damn puppy suite with a couch and a basket of new toys she's no doubt going to rip to shreds, but I'm selfish and want her with me. Rude, mannerless dog. I've been in L.A. a matter of hours and I'm already pouting.

When I round into the kitchen, I let out a startled scream, which makes Mabel scream and causes Red to rush forward and shove me behind him with one hand on the gun that I always forget he's carrying.

"What the hell! Why are you screaming at me?" Mabel shouts, then points her finger at Red. "Don't shoot me, for fuck's sake!"

"What the fuck are you doing in my house?" I shout back, panting with my hand pressed over my chest where my heart is threatening to burst out of my rib cage. "You scared the shit out of me!"

"I got here like two hours ago. I texted you."

Mabel barely gets the last words out before she starts to laugh, which starts me laughing. Red grumbles something unintelligible and leaves the room.

"My phone is on airplane mode," I explain through giggles. "Jesus, you 'bout took ten years off my life."

"Yeah, well Red 'bout took my whole life off my life, blazing in here with his hand on the metal. I thought I was a goner."

I roll my eyes playfully and climb onto one of my chairs at the kitchen island. It's a little weird how *not* weird it is to have Mabel in my house. Before everything went to shit, she'd show up unannounced all the time. She knows all my passcodes and everything. But it's been so long since we've actually wanted to be in each other's space that part of me thinks this should feel more awkward.

"What's up, Mabes? Why are you here?"

She hops up on the counter across from me and sighs.

"I guess I miss you."

My jaw drops and my head jerks back, and Mabel barks out a laugh that has me snapping my mouth closed again.

"Don't act so surprised," she says wryly. "I've spent nearly every day of the last decade with you. When you left to film your movie, it was like losing an appendage."

"Aww, Mabes. Are you saying I'm your right-hand man?"

"Nah, but maybe like a big toe. Apparently, those are pretty important for balance, so..." She waggles her eyebrows and I laugh as she continues. "Seriously, though, I know Ham is the worst, and the label sucks, and things with you and Torren are weird, and Jonah is, well, I don't know what the fuck is going on with him, but I'm glad you're back, even if just for this weekend."

I study her face and am almost bowled over by the sincerity I see there. A few weeks ago, I was certain she would hate me forever. It was nothing but scathing glances and snarky barbs between us. I hate to admit it, but maybe Ham was right when he said we just needed a vacation from each other. I'll never tell him he was right, but maybe he was.

"I've missed you too, Mabes," I say finally, then sigh. "I'm going to grab a shower and a nap before the chaos starts."

Mabel smirks.

"Why, Sav Loveless, don't you know? You *are* the chaos."

• • •

"Long time, no see, Los Angeles. How are you all doin' tonight?"

My voice carries through the outdoor venue, and the few hundred fans who managed to score seats to our last-minute surprise performance cheer back at me. We haven't played for an audience this small in years. It's still larger than the dives we played at in the very beginning, but after selling out stadiums on our last world tour, this feels more like an intimate family dinner than a rock concert.

I love it.

My leather skirt, vintage Blondie shirt, and ripped fishnets feel more right on my body than the clothes I've been stuffed into for the movie, and my silver hair is free and blowing around in the slight breeze. My lock and chain sit on my collarbone with a weight that I've longed for over the last few weeks. And the guitar in my hands, the roughness of the strap over my shoulder and the slide of my callused fingers over the strings, releases a tension in my body that I hadn't realized I'd been carrying.

I wasn't lying when I told Hammond that The Hometown Heartless is my band. It's my story. My legacy. It's *me*. And right here, with all these people in front of me, needing to hear my songs and sing along? This is as close to home as I think I'll ever get.

I knew I'd miss it. I just didn't realize how much until I came back.

It's like the first injection after a failed rehab stint. The first wave of euphoria after the third shot of whiskey. But for the first time in a long time, I'm not worried it will be the death of me. It feels like it's giving me life.

"Sounds like you missed us," I say with a grin, and when the cheers from the crowd grow louder, I feel lighter. Energized. I'm actually excited to play.

I wonder briefly if the rest of the band feels it, too, and as if in response, Mabel pounds out a quick beat on the drums behind me. I send her a wink over my shoulder before turning back to the crowd.

"We've got just a few songs for you tonight, but it's been a while since we've played, so you might have to help us out."

I strum out the opening chord to Just One More, and everyone goes nuts. It was our very first single, and years later, it's still our most streamed song.

"Sing along if you know it," I say with a smirk, then launch into the song.

Just one more, baby
Just one more
Whiskey and orange
What are we waiting for?

"That was amazing, right?" Mabel says to us as we hustle off stage.

We've got one hour to change and drive to the awards show so we can walk the carpet. I'm salty we have to give yet another show after already performing this one, but Mabel is right. This was amazing.

"I haven't felt that good in a long time," Torren chimes in, sidling up next to me and giving me a tentative half smile that I return.

I glance toward Jonah, but his head is down and he's texting. He hasn't said much at all to me. A *hey*. A *how's the movie?* And that's it.

I try my best not to stare at him, not to analyze his every move, but it's hard. My excitement at playing tonight fills me with guilt because I still think this is bad for him. I still can't stop seeing him in that hotel room. Just seconds later, and he'd be dead.

I give Torren a questioning glance, and he shakes his head once. My heart sinks, and I whip my eyes back to Jonah. What's happened since I've been gone? What's been going on with the security/babysitter I hired?

Torren reaches down and grabs my hand, giving it a squeeze, and I'm grateful for it.

"Hammond set us up in a suite to get ready for the awards show," Mabel says, cutting into my thoughts. "Since this was so last minute, he's already had stylists pick out our outfits." She scowls. "I swear to god if he puts me in another dress I will end him. I will stain the red carpet with his black, putrid blood."

I flare my eyes at Torren, who is grinning that lopsided grin that the fans are in love with, and even Jonah huffs out a laugh. It feels like before. I didn't know how badly I needed this.

Fucking Hammond.

We get to the suite, and my irritation with Hammond explodes. I might end him with Mabel.

He's got me wearing a black patent leather and lace number with a mostly see-through top and a ripped-up tutu-like bottom and shiny black knee-high faux snakeskin boots. It's not the outfit I'm pissed about, though. This is something I'd pick on my own. It's the fact that Torren's outfit fucking matches. Shoes of the same faux snakeskin, suit jacket of black leather and lace. He's not wearing a shirt under the jacket, and his pants are simple expensive black jeans, but it's obvious we've been dressed as a couple.

My fingers clench with the need to hit something. Someone.

Hammond.

I'm scowling at myself in a full-length mirror, contemplating flushing the ring down the toilet, when Torren appears behind me.

"I'm sorry."

I flick my eyes to him in the mirror and raise an irritated eyebrow in disbelief.

"Are you?"

"Yeah, Savannah, I am." He sighs, and the pain on his face makes me ache for a new reason. "This isn't how I wanted it to be. None of this is how I wanted it."

I spin around and face him.

"And how did you want it, Tor?"

His eyes search mine, and I leave myself open for him. I don't hide my anger. I don't hide my guilt. I wish I could make this how he wants it. I do. I wish I could love him. But I can't, and I don't, and that's just how it is.

"I just wanted you, Savvy," he says finally. "I've always just wanted you. But fuck, you're like trying to bottle lightning."

I smirk, but it's sad, and his lips curl up into something similar. He reaches up and runs a strand of my hair through his fingertips, then takes my left hand and runs his thumb over my emerald.

"It really is a beautiful ring, Tor."

He laughs and brings his eyes back to mine.

"I thought if I'd gotten it perfect..." He trails off, and then shrugs. "I'm sorry the label is making you do this. We all think it's fucked up. I think even Hammond hates it. It's just...it's not cool, and you shouldn't be forced to play along."

I scan his face and purse my lips. What happened to, *just take the four months?* What happened to, *think it over, you'll see?*

Torren sighs.

"Don't look so suspicious, Savvy. I meant it when I said that show was the best I've felt in a long time. I miss it. You guys are my family, you know? So, if there's any chance at all that...well...You can't bottle lightning, can you?"

The emotions in his tone are enough to break my heart into tiny pieces. Loss, hope, defeat. Even a little self-deprecating humor. I don't think I'll ever forgive myself for letting our relationship get so messy. It's caused us both so much pain.

Torren takes a step back, dropping my hand and fixing his face into a genuine yet subdued smile. I know what he's saying. This band, whatever magic we might be when we play together, isn't something just anyone can achieve. It's rare. It's worth sacrifice, even if the sacrifice hurts. But can we heal from the damage we've already caused?

Immediately, my thoughts go to Levi.

Levi, Brynn, and that little town on the east coast nearly three thousand miles away. *Where do I belong? Who do I belong with? Which sacrifice am I willing to make?*

"You look gorgeous. Ready to rock the red carpet?"

Torren sticks his arm out for me, so I smile and hook mine in his.

"Ready as I'll ever be."

I follow Torren into the main room of the suite where Mabel and Jonah are already waiting. Mabel's wearing a pink silk pantsuit with an open suit jacket and a black bra adorned with silver metal spikes, so it looks like Ham has evaded the grave for tonight.

I glance at Jonah. He's in a white suit with a Black Sabbath band tee under the jacket. He looks good. He looks sober, and it loosens one of the Jonah-related bands of anxiety that stay wrapped around my chest.

"Look at us," Mabel says, clapping her hands together. "We look like real fucking rockstars."

The drive to the venue is short, and the red-carpet walk is too long for my liking but still not as long as it usually is because Ham told everyone that we're not answering any questions. Photographs, yes. Interviews, no. Apparently, the label doesn't think they can trust me to not say something to make them look like assholes.

They're right.

When we reach the end of the carpet and step into the building, away from the larger crowd, I catch a rare moment where Red is distracted with his guard down, and I strike. In two practiced moves, I have him on his back in the middle of our group, and I don't bother trying to tame my triumphant smile. I really am getting faster with my sobriety. I fling my finger at him with a laugh as I loom above him.

"That's for the country music serenade, you assho—"

I shriek as he swipes my legs out from under me, and grunt when I hit the ground. Fast as ever. I didn't even see it coming. Damn it. I should have stepped back out of reach. Rookie fucking move.

"Ouch, fuck."

I reach out blindly and jab Red in the gut as he chuckles, tuning out the laughter coming from my band and the gasps from the few people milling about inside.

"What the hell are you doing? That is *Givenchy*," I hear Hammond seethe, quiet enough not to make any more of a scene, but loud enough that I can tell he is livid right now. "Jesus Christ, Savannah, if you ripped that dress I swear to god—"

"Oh, can it, Ham." I groan.

"Here," Torren says softly, and I open my squinted eyes to find him grinning down at me with an outstretched hand.

I slap both of mine in his and he tugs me to my feet. We're both laughing as he fixes my dress and tries to smooth my hair. No one is going to care if I look like a rumpled disaster. Usually, I'm high as fuck at these things. Sober and sporting some wrinkles on the *Givenchy* is a much better option, if I do say so myself.

"Stupid mistake," Red says over my shoulder, and I roll my eyes. "I still got you."

"Doesn't matter if we're both down."

I glance at him with a smirk.

"Agree to disagree."

The awards show is a decent time, surprisingly. I actually enjoy the performances, and one of the artists who opened for us on our last tour took home an award and thanked us in her speech, which is just really fucking cool. We don't win Video of the Year, but we snag the award for Best Rock Album, which is great. We usually dominate the genre categories. When we win Performers of the Year, though, I about pee my pants.

"Oh, my fucking god." I look at Mabel, whose jaw is dropped. "Oh, my fucking god, that just happened."

She looks at me, a smile taking over her entire face.

"That just fucking happened!"

I grab her hand and Torren's hand, with Jonah holding on to Mabel's other hand, and we walk to the stage in a long, centipede-type line. When we get to the mic, instead of taking turns like we usually do, Torren gives my back a nudge.

"This one is you, Sav," he whispers in my ear.

I couldn't tame my smile even to save my damn soul. I step up to the mic, the award heavy in my hand, and take a deep breath before speaking.

"I can't believe this just happened," I say excitedly. "Seriously, I thought I was going to pee myself; I was so shocked."

The audience laughs and claps, my bandmates behind joining in as well. I hear Mabel snort something like, "smooth, bitch," and I flash her a grin before continuing.

"Seriously, though, this is amazing. This is an honor we didn't expect, but we're so fucking grateful. Sorry for cussing. But, um, this couldn't have been possible without our fans. You all have shown up for us time and time and time again, and we owe all of this to you."

The audience claps again. I hear some whistles and cheers. I can't see much in the audience because of the harsh stage lights, but when the noise dies down, I find a camera and point at it, making sure whatever tech is calling the shots backstage knows to cut to this one for the live feed. Then, I look right into the lens for my next statement.

"I want to say a very special thank you to a very special fan. Boss, here's your word for today. Illuminate. Verb. To brighten with light. To make shine. You've illuminated my days, my hopes, my love for music. Thank you so much. This one is for you."

I hold up the award and blow a kiss to the camera, and then I practically float off stage and back to our seats. Another camera pans past us, and Torren takes my hand in his and leans in close.

"Who's Boss?" he whispers, and I smile.

"A really badass seven-and-three-quarters year old I've met in North Carolina."

That's all I tell him. For some reason, I don't want to tell him any more, and within seconds, the subject is changed.

We all finish the show, attend an after party, and crash at my house, and no one else brings up Boss or my cryptic acceptance speech. Before I leave for the airport the next morning, I run an idea past the band, and when I finally buckle into my seat for a long ass cross-country flight, I'm actually more excited than anxious.

I can't remember the last time that happened.

29

"WHAT THE FUCK?"

Red's irritated voice stirs me awake in the front seat, and I sit up to see the gate of my rental in front of us. We planned it so I would be getting back late to try and avoid too much attention, and from the looks of it, the plan worked. Except for...

"Oh my god, is that Levi?"

I try to open the car door, but Red hits the lock, and I turn and growl at him. He punches the button for the gate and pulls into the courtyard.

"Stay here," he commands, like Levi is some sort of crazy stalker.

I roll my eyes and try to open my car door again, but he hit the fucking child locks. Like I'm a child.

Well, if he wants to treat me like a child, I'll act like one. Gracelessly, I crawl over the center console and climb out the driver side door.

"Just let me fucking talk to her," Levi says, and he sounds drunk.

I hurry around the car and back toward the gate.

"Go home, or I will call the cops," Red says as I step up behind them.

"No one is calling the cops," I say, and Levi's eyes land on mine. "What are you doing here, Cooper? Are you wasted?"

Levi acts like he's reaching into his pocket, and in a flash, Red grabs Levi's hand and twists it behind his back. Levi hisses in pain and I gasp.

"I'm getting my fucking phone," Levi says.

Red does something that makes Levi grunt again, and a small smile curves my lips when a flash of memory reminds me of Levi, Bobby, Red, and the Perv Pen at my old dance club.

"Let him go, Red." I grab my security guard's wrist and tug on it. He drops Levi's arm immediately and steps back. "It's fine. Let me talk to him."

"That's not a good idea."

"Oh, for fuck's sake, Red, this is Levi. He's not going to hurt me. Just give me a minute with him."

The whole time I speak with Red, I can feel Levi watching me silently. I heard it in his voice that he's been drinking, but in my peripheral, he stands as tall and steady as ever. Arms crossed on his chest, eyes hard and focused on me. It's annoying, actually. Even drunk, he's still buttoned-up and straightlaced. Composed as ever.

"I'm staying right here."

Red is insistent. He won't leave me alone with this drunk idiot, no matter if said idiot is just this weenie from my childhood.

"Fine," I say on a sigh, then push past him, and face Levi. "What do you want, Cooper? It's two in the morning and you smell like a distillery."

That was a lie. He actually smells good. Like wood shavings and sea salt. He runs his fingers through his hair coolly, then shoves his hands in his pockets. He never takes his eyes off me.

"How was L.A., Rockstar? D'you have a good time with your band?"

I cock my head to the side. His question is unassuming enough. Friendly, even. It feels like a trap.

"I had a great time. We won two awards."

Levi nods. "Yeah, I saw. Brynn watched the whole thing. Real kind of you to give her a shout out."

"Is that what this is about?" I ask with a roll of my eyes. "I didn't say her name. You don't have to worry. There's no *association* with my infamy."

He doesn't comment. Not on my infamous reputation with the tabloids. Not on how important it is that he and Brynn aren't mixed up in it. He just stares, then takes a step toward me, dragging his eyes down my body slowly.

"How's your fiancé?"

My head jerks back at his sudden change of subject, but he continues, unfazed.

"Did you give him my message? Was my taste still on your lips when he kissed you?"

I flick my eyes to Red. He's acting like he's not listening, but I know he is. He's so nosy. I focus back on Levi and narrow my eyes. He's acting like a jealous idiot.

"I told you already, Levi, Torren isn't my fiancé."

He laughs a dark, humorless laugh.

"Sure, he's not. I thought you were supposed to be sober, Rockstar. Was that a lie, too?"

My jaw drops, but he still doesn't stop. He takes out his phone and starts to read out loud, his voice mocking and dramatic, like a newscaster giving a nightly broadcast.

"It says here, 'Is Sav Loveless due for another rehab visit? The Hometown Heartless made an appearance at the Music Choice Awards last night, but it seems their lead singer couldn't even make it off the red carpet without causing a scene. Has she failed yet another attempt to get clean? Judging from the drunk and stumbling, we sure think so. See our exclusive photos of Sav's despicable fall, even taking out her own bodyguard on the way down. At least her fiancé, Torren King, was there to lend her a hand. Let's hope she didn't ruin the *Givenchy*.'"

My heart is in my throat, and it takes all my restraint not to grab his phone and stomp on it. These tabloids are ruthless, and they don't care what lies they spread so long as they sell copies. Hammond is going to fucking kill me. I bet the moment I turn my phone back on, it will be nothing but scolding and berating and damage control attempts.

Fuck, if this fucks things up with the label...

I was feeling so good about this weekend, too.

"None of that is true. It's all bullshit."

I fist my hands to keep them from shaking, but I can't keep the angry waver from my voice. Or the hurt. For once, I actually do things right and I still get screwed over.

"I was sober. I didn't take anything. I didn't drink anything."

He raises an eyebrow.

"You just tripped over your dress, then? The one that barely covered your ass."

"That's not what fucking happened either. Jesus, Levi, give me some credit."

"The pictures don't lie, Sav. These photos with you on the ground. These pictures of you all cozied up with Torren fucking King."

"The pictures do lie, actually, and if you knew anything about anything, you'd know that. It's not what it looks like. It's *never* what it looks like. You're being a damn idiot."

Levi steps closer, his voice lowering to a sensual whisper. A lover sharing secrets, but his tone is menacing. He trails his knuckles up my arm, leaving goosebumps behind as he continues to speak.

"Am I, though? Am I reading too far into it? Matching outfits. Holding hands. Laughing. Cuddling in your velvet seats. Tucking your hair behind your ear."

His fingertips brush my jaw, then he takes a strand of my hair and runs it behind my ear, so gently I barely feel it. His breath smells faintly of whiskey and something sweet. Something citrusy. *Oranges.* When he wraps his hand around the side of my neck and rests his thumb on my lower lip, I expect him to kiss me.

He doesn't. Instead, he meets my eyes once more, and it's nothing but anger.

"That's how you do it though, isn't it, Rockstar. You come on my tongue then turn around and hang all over his arm. Did you think of me?"

"What?"

I shake my head slightly against the firm, warm grip of his hand, and his thumb moves over my lip. I'm so confused by his closeness, frustrated and angry and turned on, that his words don't make sense.

"What?" I ask again, and his answering smirk is almost cruel.

Cruel, but sad.

"When his mouth was on you. Did you think of me?"

I take a step back, my brows slanting and my jaw tightening. My heart is racing, hands itching to reach for him, but he's being an asshole.

"Nothing happened between me and Torren. I told you, he's not my fiancé. He's not even my boyfriend."

"That fucking flashy ring tells me otherwise, Sav."

He glances to my ring finger and back, and I mentally curse myself for not taking it off once we got out of the airport, but I was so tired. I've worn it all weekend, and I haven't taken it off just in case we ran into paps. I almost forgot it was there.

"It's a stunt, Levi. It's be—"

"Savannah."

Red's voice cuts me off, and I whip around to face him. He shakes his head once.

"You signed a contract."

I grit my teeth. He's right. I'm not supposed to tell anyone about any bullshit with my label or they could sue me six ways to Sunday. But what the fuck, man. I groan and purse my lips, tilting my head to the side as I stare off with Red.

"Savannah. Do not."

I sigh and turn to Levi. I meet his eyes once more, and I make sure he sees that I'm serious.

"It's a publicity stunt. The label is making me wear the ring so the media thinks I'm engaged to Torren so we can try to avoid any more negative press surrounding the band's breakup. It's not a hiatus. I told them I'm done, but they've given me an ultimatum like the money hungry, controlling douche bags they are."

I hear Red sigh. Poor guy. He deserves a raise. I glance at him.

"Sorry, Red."

He shakes his head, but he doesn't say anything else.

"Why would they do that? Why would *you* do that?" Levi asks, and I shrug.

"It's this or they announce they're replacing me. They want The Hometown Heartless to carry on without me, as if I'm not the whole fucking band."

Just saying that out loud makes my stomach twist up in knots. After this round of tabloid lies, I could have just fucked everything up, but I push that thought out of my head for now.

"They gave me until we're done filming to make a decision about leaving, but I gotta wear the ring to buy the time."

Two and a half months.

I have two and a half months left.

How are the days moving so quickly? How have I been here for this long already?

Levi's eyes bounce between mine as he considers my words. I can't read what's going on in his head. I used to be able to read his emotions, but right now, whether it's the darkness or the alcohol or the heightened emotions, I just can't tell, and it's making me nervous.

"Where'd you get the ring," he asks finally, and every muscle in my body goes rigid.

I don't answer, and his nostrils flare.

"He proposed, didn't he?"

When I still don't answer, he scoffs.

"That sleazy fucking loser has no respect for women. No respect for you. All he cares about is bro code. I knew the tabloids talked about you two all the time, but Jesus Christ. Do you really have no sense? Don't you care about yourself at all?"

My temper flares at his tone, at the way he's talking like he knows anything at all about the situation. He doesn't. He knows nothing. It's been eight years. Things are different now.

"Don't act like you know about me and Torren, Levi. You don't know him."

"I was there when he defended the guy who assaulted you, Savannah. You forgetting that? If I hadn't stepped in, his brother would have raped you, and Torren would have let him because he took that fuck's word over yours."

I don't believe that. Not anymore. I've had years to think it over, and I really believe Torren would have defended me if he'd seen Sean in action. God, it sounds so fucked up, but it was drugs and mixed signals and Torren struggled with going against his blood. Sean had been his protector since birth. Torren looked up to him his whole life. He'd only known me less than a year. He didn't want to believe it.

But how do I explain that to Levi?

I know he's right about Sean. I know what it feels like when someone has no plans to stop. I felt it in Oscar's forceful, painful touch. I felt it with that sham of a foster father and the sick rules he made me follow. I felt it in Terry's gaze every time he looked at me. I'm so conditioned to it now that I can sense it, and I felt it with Sean, but Torren has more than earned my trust since that night.

"What Sean did that night on the beach was fucked up. I agree. It never should have happened. I know that. But when I decided to kick Sean out of the band, Torren stood by me. He backed me even when our band was still sleeping in the van. Even when we had to rework all our songs to make up for losing the keyboard. We were nobodies, and he supported me. Turned his back on his older brother. His family won't even speak to him now."

Levi scoffs and shakes his head.

"Supported you and then moved in on you. Did he do the same as Sean? Did he—"

"Torren isn't Sean, Levi! They're brothers, but they're not the same. Torren didn't so much as touch me for two years after everything went down with Sean. And even then, he was adamant about being sober. About *me* being sober."

Levi's face twists up, and I have to close my eyes to keep from seeing the disgust that is sure to fill his after I speak the next truth.

"He wouldn't touch me until I made the first move. He wouldn't get high with me until I coaxed him. Until I *convinced* him. Until I reassured him over and over that it was what I wanted. Every encounter, every exchange, sexual or otherwise, was consensual, and most of the time, it was initiated by me. If anyone was disrespectful in that relationship, it was me, and that's the truth. Not everything is black and white. So much of life exists in the gray spaces."

Saying it out loud makes me feel even shittier.

I used Torren. I used him for comfort. For reassurance. I used him to make myself feel wanted. I used him so I didn't feel guilty for getting high and disconnecting.

Torren turned his back on his brother, on his whole family, for me, and how did I repay him? By messing with his head and his heart, and breaking up the band, which is the only family he really has. The only family any of us have. I've been so unfair to him. He didn't deserve it.

"And yes, he proposed," I force out. "But only because I led him on. I led him to believe I felt more for him than I do. He proposed, but I didn't say yes."

The silence between us is charged, and I wait, breathing heavily, for him to speak. For him to say or do anything to release me from this paralysis of guilt and shame. I hate what I did to Torren. To Mabel and Jonah. To myself. I want so badly to fix it, and damn it, I am trying.

Levi takes my left hand in his, and when I open my eyes, I find him staring at my emerald. He rubs the base of my ring finger, then toys with the stone on the ring.

"I don't care what led to it, Savannah. I don't care. It should have been mine. I have your first kiss. Your first fuck. And this? This should belong to me, too. This should have been mine just like the rest of you."

He holds my hand up between us as if I need a reminder of what he's referring to. I don't. I know exactly what he's saying. My blood roars in my ears as my heart races faster. My chest aches. *This should belong to me, too.*

"And what about me?" I rasp, tears starting to well in my eyes. "What about me, Levi? You can have all my firsts, and what do I get? The scraps? Whatever is left of you after you give everything else to another woman? I'm just supposed to be okay with always being your second choice?"

I flick my eyes to his left hand and the black silicone band he still wears on his ring finger. Julianna died two years ago. He says he never loved her, yet he still wears the ring.

When I bring my eyes back to his, the intensity I see there is enough to make me sway on my feet. For the second time tonight, I think he might kiss me, and it shocks me just how badly I wish he would. Even now, with everything muddled and confused between us, and the timing all wrong, I want to kiss him again.

I wait for it. I long for it. I know he'd taste like whiskey tonight. Whiskey and oranges.

Slowly, Levi brings my hand back up between us, unfolds my fist, and presses a soft kiss to my palm. I feel the brush of his lips on every inch of my body. It's such a sweet, featherlight touch, yet it sets me on fire. He holds my gaze, and when he finally speaks, the raw emotion in his voice breaks my heart.

"You may not have been all my firsts, Savannah Shaw, but you've always been my forever. You've always been my one. My only."

Slowly, he drops my hand and steps backward. I'm immediately colder with the distance.

"How will you get home?" I ask, and he smirks.

"I have a ride." He takes a few more steps backward until he's standing by my gate. "See you later, Rockstar."

Then he just turns around and leaves with me staring dazedly at his retreating back until the darkness swallows him and his footsteps have faded entirely.

30

I DON'T SEE Levi all week.

I've seen Brynn every day on my lunch break for guitar lessons, where we've stayed safely within the confines of my trailer, but nothing from Levi.

I watch for him on set like an obsessed teenager with a crush. I haven't been sleeping at night because I keep replaying what he said over and over in my head.

You've always been my forever. My one. My only.

But how?

I just want to see him. I want to see if it feels the same in the daylight. When he's sober and our emotions aren't in overdrive. It's tomorrow. Does he still want me?

At lunch, there's a knock on my trailer door, and I expect it to be Brynn, but I open it to find Dustin instead. He jumps back and gapes at me for a moment like he didn't expect it to be me behind the door that says my name. I'm sure seeing my silver hair is startling since they've all gotten used to the brown wig, but I'm still me. I quirk a brow.

"Um, Boss told me to tell you that it is with great regret and pent...penti...um, *penitence* that she must skip guitar lessons with you today."

His words shoot from his mouth like they've been rehearsed, and I give him an amused smile. This grown man is running errands and passing messages for a seven-year-old. She really wasn't kidding when she said she was the boss.

"She say why?"

He shrugs, mouth opening and shutting like he's surprised I asked. He wasn't prepared to say more. It's cute. I'm used to people being tongue-tied around me, but they're usually not 6'3" construction worker country boys wearing hard hats and American flag t-shirts.

"Something about it being the only time she could video chat with her friend in Connecticut, so she stayed back at the office. She does that sometimes. She'll be here tomorrow."

"Cool. Thanks for the message, Dusty. You did a good job. I'll make sure to pass it on to the boss."

His grin is adorable.

"Thanks," he says, then he just walks away.

What's he even doing here? The only person in Levi's crew I've seen around since we started filming at the house has been Levi. I think this man really came all the way here just to pass on the message from Brynn. When I turn my smile on Red, he's smirking too.

"That kid has everyone wrapped," he says, and I chuckle. She definitely does. "You got another request for materials, by the way. Did you want to approve it?"

"Yeah." I wave my hand at his change of subject. He knows I've approved everything without question. Then I have a thought.

"Hey, we have a longer lunch break today since we're shooting later. You want to take a ride and check it out?"

Red takes a deep breath and releases it slowly. I know what he's thinking. It's not safe. What if someone sees. Blah blah blah blah. But he also knows I'm going to do it anyway, so when he pushes himself to standing, I clap my hands, turn around, and skip out the door.

The drive inland is eerie. My nerves build with every mile

marker. I start picking at my nails. My leg starts bouncing. I start craving something to put my body at ease. Some chemical, artificial fix. I start missing my guitar. Even Ziggy snoring in the back seat isn't calming my nerves.

"We don't have to do this, kid," Red says, eyes never leaving the road. "We can turn around and just send the money."

I shake my head no, but I don't speak. I need this. I think.

We make the rest of the drive in silence, and when he finally turns down my old street, I'm sitting straight as a board and twice as stiff. The neighborhood comes into view, newer houses popped up in place of the old, beat to shit ones, and a bunch of white work trucks, a van, and some other vehicles are lining the streets. One says something about plumbing, one says something about HVAC, and several say East Coast Contracting.

Red pulls up to the curb and I flip down the visor, double-checking my ball cap and aviators. I'm wigless right now, so my silver hair could give me away, but my sleeve of fake tattoos is still decorating my arm. I guess if someone sees me, though, they see me. Too late to turn back now.

I glance at Red, nod quickly, then open my door and climb out. He cracks the windows, tells my dog to behave, then gets out after me.

I walk into River View and note that sidewalks have been installed. There were never sidewalks when I was growing up. No streetlights, either. I walk up to one of the first houses and stare at it. God, it looks so nice. So unlike anything that was here before the hurricane.

When I'd read about how the neighborhood was decimated after the storm, I went on a seven-day bender. So many people, my old neighbors, dead or injured or displaced. When I finally sobered up, I had Red do a search for my mom's name, but she wasn't listed as one of the casualties. I had him search every day for weeks, and the next month, the money I'd been depositing in her account went through without a problem. The deposits have been going through for the last two years, so I'm pretty sure she survived.

I'd felt lost for months following the storm. I followed news articles about clean up and rescue missions, rehoming and rebuilding. When I stumbled on a story mentioning that a contracting company had plans to reconstruct my old neighborhood, it was like I'd finally found a rainbow.

I had Red contact the company and offer to fund the rebuild—materials, labor, everything. We set up a dummy account and hired a lawyer, and we've been sending money blindly ever since. I'm as hands-off as possible. Before today, I couldn't even have told you the company doing the rebuild, but every so often, I'd worry whether the contractors were doing as promised. From the looks of it, my worries were unnecessary. The neighborhood looks amazing. Beautiful, even. I'm almost jealous of any little girl who will grow up here in the years to come.

"How does it compare," Red asks, stepping up next to me as I gawk.

"It doesn't," I answer honestly. "The houses that were here before were shacks in comparison. These are veritable palaces."

My eyes sting, and I have to reach behind my sunglasses to swipe away the tears that have started falling. I wasn't expecting to feel so moved by this transformation, but I can't help but think there's a sign in here somewhere. Some message from the universe about rising from the wreckage, about extracting beauty from something ugly.

Where I come from has always been a point of tension for me. Even my Wikipedia page lists Miami as my hometown. The only good memories I have from this small North Carolina town involve Levi, and after that summer when I was eighteen, those memories were tainted, too. Coming back here, though, I can't shake the idea that something is changing. A transition, or a revelation, perhaps.

"This feels significant," I whisper to Red. "It feels like healing."

I hear him hum in response, and I blink up at the house until my tears start to dry. I turn and face the rest of the houses, noting there are crews working on a couple unfinished ones toward the back of the neighborhood. I don't want to disturb them. I've seen what I came to see. I'm about to head back to our car when a voice calls my name and stops me in my tracks.

"Savannah," he says again, closer this time, and I turn around slowly to face him.

My brain tries rapidly to put together the puzzle pieces scattered in front of me. Levi in jeans, a t-shirt, and a hardhat holding a clipboard. Dark brown work boots on his feet. A basic, white logo on the breast pocket of his shirt. My eyes fall to it and focus.

East Coast Contracting.

I look back at his face to find him studying me with just as much surprise.

"Your company is East Coast Contracting," I state slowly. He jerks out a single nod.

"You're the anonymous donor," he says, and my nod mirrors his.

So many thoughts swirl through my head and I can't make sense of any of them, but I feel relieved. Warm. Buzzing, even. Levi has overseen the rebuilding of my old neighborhood. Levi is the one who insisted on not cutting corners—quality materials, quality labor, quality housing. Is Levi my message from the universe?

Before either of us can say anything, I hear a vehicle rumble up behind me and the engine cut off. I watch Levi's eyes flick over my shoulder and the color drain from his face as he brings his attention back to me. He looks like he wants to speak, but I turn to the vehicle on the curb.

I expect to see paps, but instead, it's another East Coast Contracting truck, and Brynn hops out of the passenger seat carrying two large fast-food bags. When she sees me, she smiles and I smile back, until a woman comes around the truck with more fast-food bags.

My stomach falls. My heart stops. I can hardly breathe.

"Dad," Brynn shouts, running up to us. "We brought you and the guys lunch."

"Thanks, Boss," I hear Levi say.

"Hey Sav!" Brynn says, but I don't look at her.

I can't take my eyes off the woman, and when she sees me, she halts. She doesn't move. She doesn't take another step closer. She just stares at me, and my foggy brain grapples for more puzzle pieces.

"Mom?"

My voice is nothing but a rasp, small and lost. I sound fifteen again. My mother opens her mouth but shuts it without saying anything at all.

"Mom? Ms. Sharon is your mom?" Brynn turns to my mother with a familiarity that almost knocks me over. "Why is Sav calling you mom, Ms. Sharon?"

My mom doesn't answer. She just gives Brynn a small smile, and then looks back at me. She stands still as a statue, and my eyes eat her up. She looks younger than I remember. Her dark hair is pulled back in a loose ponytail, her body finally has some weight and shape to it. Her cheeks aren't gaunt. Her eyes aren't sunken in. I zero in on her arms and as if she knows what I'm looking for, she turns her forearms out so I can see the inside of her elbow clearly.

No marks. No visible scars. No sign she's been using in that way.

Then I notice something else. She's wearing a shirt just like the one Levi has on. Just like the one Dusty and the rest of Levi's guys wear at the studio. East Coast Contracting is displayed proudly on her breast pocket. And when it clicks, it's like I'm being kicked in the side with Terry's steel-toed boot all over again.

Only this time, it's not Terry doing the kicking.

I drag my eyes to Levi.

"Does she work for you?" I ask quietly, and he jerks out another single nod. "Since when?"

He swallows before answering, but that's the only sign that he's worried about how I'll react. His eyes stay focused on mine, his face stays stern, his posture stays rigid. No hint of shame or remorse.

"Since after the storm."

I blink, clearing my eyes of more tears. This feels like a betrayal. This feels like a lie, or a maliciously kept secret. She's been working for him for two years.

Two. Years.

My mother has been part of Levi's life. Part of Brynn's life. And now, more than ever, I feel like an outsider. After everything my mother put me through. After being the reason why I had to run away. After all of it, Levi gave her a job? Welcomed her into his life?

My mother was the enemy. The villain. She's not supposed to have access to the thing I wanted most but couldn't have.

"Why?" I ask Levi, but he doesn't answer. I drop my voice to a whisper. "How could you?"

I turn and walk away, pushing right past my mom and Brynn without a word. I speed walk to the car, but when I reach it, Levi is right there behind me.

"Savannah, wait," he says, and I whirl on him.

"She made my life hell, Levi. She put me in situations that fucked me up so thoroughly I'm still not recovered. You said *I* was the bad influence. *I'm* the one who you're worried about with Brynnlee. But my mom is okay? Are you forgetting who she is? Are you forgetting who fucking made me this way? How could you do this?"

He was supposed to be on my side. My enemy is his enemy. How could he befriend her?

"It's not that simple."

"It is," I grind out. "It *is* that simple. She was a terrible mother. She made me miserable. I was abused, and she just let it happen because she cared more about getting high than she did about being a parent. She cared more about Terry than she did about her own kid. He would have raped me, and she would have let him do it. I know it. And you've just..."

How do I say it? He's forgiven her for what she did to me? How could he forgive her? It wasn't his place.

"You were supposed to be on my side," I whisper through clenched teeth.

I don't know which emotion is stronger, my anger or my sadness. Levi steps closer, until my back is against the car, and slowly spins my baseball cap around so the bill is at the back. Then he removes my sunglasses and sets them on the top of the car, so our eyes meet. He takes my hands in his and presses them to his chest. I can feel his steady heartbeat as he rests his forehead on mine.

"I have always been on your side. Always."

"Then how could you do this?" I shove at his chest, but he holds firm. "How could you forgive her for what she did to me?"

"It's not like that, Savannah."

"Then what's it like? Enlighten me. Because it definitely doesn't look like you're holding a grudge. It doesn't look like you're holding her accountable for what she did to me."

Levi sighs, then pulls back and meets my eyes again, but he still doesn't let go of my hands.

"I haven't forgiven her. But she's not the same person she was back then."

I scoff and try to look away, but he keeps talking, insistent and hushed. I can feel him still looking at me, and like a magnet, I look back.

"When I hired her, it was because she was displaced from the storm and trying to stay sober. She'd been sober for a year before she lost the house. She had been turning things around, and then the hurricane—"

"No. I don't care."

I shove at him again, and this time he takes a step backward giving me space to seethe. My temples pound from the force of my scowl, my jaw aches. If I look, I bet I'll find cuts in my palms from my nails because of how hard I was clenching my fists.

"You don't get to humanize her. You can't just make her a sympathetic character in my life story. She's not. She's not. She's the villain. She's the bad guy, Levi. And you just...you just...welcome her? You welcome her with open arms? You give her a job? You let her around your kid?"

Levi shakes his head.

"Don't bring Brynn into this. Don't judge my decisions as her parent."

"How can I not? You saw how Sharon was with me. How many nights did you hold me because my house wasn't safe? How many times did I cry myself to sleep in your bed? How many bruises do you remember seeing?"

"Savannah, please, just trust me when I say it's different. She's different. You spent all last night defending Torren, saying he's not the person I think he is. Why can't that be the case with y—"

"That's not the same thing!"

"It is! Not everything is black and white, remember? Sharon is an addict. She was a terrible mother to you. She was a terrible person when she was high, and you deserved so much better. Those are facts. But it's also fact that Terry got her addicted and kept her high, and he abused her and used her, and she was too fucked up to do anything about it. Your mom's situation—not yours, but hers—exists in the gray space. And she, *like you*, still somehow managed to pull herself from rock fucking bottom. That deserves recognition."

The silence stretches as we stare at each other. I hold, and I hold, and I hold, and then I crack.

"I can't," I whisper, closing my eyes against the sting of tears. "I can't forgive her, Levi."

I feel him close the distance once more, taking my hands back in his.

"I'm not asking you to. But she's important to Brynn, and Brynn deserves people who love her. My mother hasn't changed. And Jules's parents...They're worse. They're terrible, and even Julianna didn't want them around Brynn. But Sharon...Sharon cares about her. Sharon loves her. Brynn has already lost too much. She deserves more than just me."

My heart sinks. I know he's right.

And it doesn't matter anyway, does it? In two short months, I'll be back in L.A., and I'll likely never see these people again. No Levi. No Brynn. No Sharon. The thought makes my whole body ache. Why is it that every time I get close to Levi, the universe yanks him away from me? It's a sick fucking joke. A game. It makes me so angry, and all I want to do is lash out. I want to hit back harder. But I am so tired of being angry.

And yet...

There's got to be more to this, right? He's rebuilding my old neighborhood. He gave my mom a job when she was displaced. He put a music room in the house he built. He said he never loved Julianna. That he married her because she was sick.

Is it all just because he's a good guy with a savior complex?

But he said I was always his one. That I've always been his forever.

I once thought I would take Levi Cooper in any way I could if it meant there could be a place for me in his world. Is that still true now? Can there be a place for him in mine?

I take a deep breath and push at Levi's chest, forcing him back a step.

"The other night, you said I was your forever," I say bluntly, and his face goes blank. "Did you mean that, or was it just a drunken mistake? Pretty lies on whiskey lips?"

He doesn't answer. His jaw tightens and that muscle in his cheek twitches. I narrow my eyes at him.

"Got nothing to say now, Cooper? You make all these big declarations, stake outrageous claims, but in the light of day, you got nothing?"

He watches me like he thinks I'm trying to trap him. Like he thinks I'll try to make him choose between me or Sharon. Me or Brynn. I wouldn't. I'm just tired of lies and secrets.

"It doesn't matter what I said," he finally says. "It would never work. Once the movie wraps, you'll go back to Hollywood with your life, and I'll be here with mine."

Your life. My life. Not ours. Never ours.

"Did you design that house for me?" I ask, switching tactics.

Another blink. Another muscle twitch. No words.

"When did you build it, Levi?"

He swallows, and I can tell he's debating telling me. When he opens his mouth to speak, I brace myself on the car just in case I can't handle what he says.

"There was about a year when Julianna was in remission before she got sick the second time. I did it then."

"Did she help you design it? Since you were married?"

Levi shakes his head once.

"We were separated."

"Why does it have a music room?" He doesn't answer. "Were you going to divorce her?" Still no answer. "Give me something, Levi. Please. Just give me something."

Still no answer. I huff out a laugh. It's sad and tired. I open the car door behind me and swing it wide. I make sure when I meet his eyes again, mine are hard. I feel nothing. I give nothing away.

"You're a coward, Levi Cooper. You've always been a coward. There's no gray space about it."

I climb into the car and shut the door calmly, then stare forward until Red slides into the driver's seat. He waits until we're pulling back onto the interstate before speaking.

"You okay, kid?"

I keep my head tilted back on the head rest and my eyes shut. Levi still has my aviators. I sigh and answer honestly.

"No, I don't think I am."

31

I WATCH Savannah drive off with my feet planted on the sidewalk and a vise grip of guilt around my windpipe.

Give me something. Please.

I would give her everything if I could.

I've spent so long juggling everything, terrified to let even one responsibility slip, that I can't even begin to fathom stopping. I wouldn't even know how. The silicone wedding band burns my finger, and I flex my hand to ease some of the imaginary sting.

Another envelope came this morning. More brochures and pamphlets. More bribes. More not-so-thinly veiled threats. Since Helen works at the bank, I know she's seen that I'm finally pulling out of the red, thanks to the money from the studio. She's getting desperate, and desperate people are dangerous. Especially the self-righteous ones.

The most recent straw she's clawing at is threatening to take me to court. Saying my marriage to Julianna was a sham because I wanted her insurance payout, which is hilarious seeing as how I refuse to take it.

She's done this before.

She doesn't have a damn leg to stand on. Julianna and I made sure of it. Legally, Helen and William Lark have no claim to

Brynnlee. They can try to petition for custody, but they'll get nowhere. I dropped the envelope off at Clark's law firm this morning, and he reassured me that everything is fine, but it still makes me anxious.

I turn and walk back to Sharon and Brynn.

"I'm sorry," Sharon says, and I wave her off.

Sharon didn't do anything wrong. It was only a matter of time before Savannah found out anyway. I wasn't expecting it to be the same time I found out that she's our anonymous donor, but it's over and done with now.

"Is Ms. Sharon really Sav's mom?" Brynn pipes up, and I glance at Sharon before nodding. I don't lie to my kid. Sharon knows that. If Brynn asks, I give her the truth.

"Yeah, Boss, she is."

Brynn looks at Sharon with wide eyes.

"She's the daughter you were unkind to? Sav's the daughter who moved away because you were sick?"

"Yes," Sharon says. "That's her."

Brynn opens her mouth to ask another question, but I hold up my hand, stopping her.

"No more questions today, Brynnlee. They'll get answered, I promise, but not today."

I can tell Brynn wants to argue, but she holds her tongue, and I give her a small smile in thanks.

Sharon takes Brynn back to the office, while I finish the walk-throughs at River View, and then I meet the girls for dinner at SandBar. Brynn doesn't ask a single question. She holds true to my "not today" decree. Instead, we talk about her STEM program, the movies she's watched while staying at Sharon's, her friend Cameron's new crush in Connecticut, and how I'm not ready for Brynn to have any crushes at all, to which she said I don't have to worry because she thinks handholding is gross because palms touching is gross. Sharon thought that was adorable.

By the time I say goodnight to Brynn and Sharon and head home, I've almost forgotten about this mess with Savannah.

I haven't, but almost.

It's not until I reach my block that I remember tonight is a late shoot. I should just go to bed, but just like last time, I don't. I'm drawn to Savannah. I've always been drawn to Savannah. It's always gotten me in trouble, and when I see what scene they're shooting, I know this time won't be any different.

A sex scene, and it's taking place on my deck. The deck *I* built.

I watch from the sliding glass doors. They're open, allowing cords to run through the house and to a generator out front. I lean on the door frame, just out of the reach of the camera, with a perfect view of everything. I'm close enough that I can hear everything, too.

I knew this would be happening. I shouldn't be surprised, but seeing Savannah locked in a passionate kiss with Paul Northwood makes me want to punch something. Preferably Mr. Hollywood's insured face.

The way she's clawing at him as he picks her up and places her on the railing. The way she wraps her legs around his waist. Even the way she moans his character's name has me seeing red.

I hate every second of it, but I can't tear my eyes from her. I'm staring, scowling, when she pops her eyes open, and they land right on me. She freezes, long enough that she breaks character and the director calls cut.

"Sorry," Savannah says, then flicks her eyes to me before adding sweetly, "let's go again. I'll do it better this time."

"You don't have to be better, Sav. You were doing great. Just don't get distracted," the director says. "Just pick up where you left off. Ready? Action."

This time, she starts to play it up. Tugging Paul's hair. Thrusting her hips. Moaning louder. I keep willing the director to stop her. To tell her to tone it down, but she doesn't. Then Savannah directs her gaze at me, but she does it discreetly this time. She never stops moving. She never stops touching him. Kissing him. And with her eyes on me, moaning and whimpering and writhing, my dick starts to harden. It's painful, the way it presses into the zipper of my jeans. She knows exactly what she's doing.

When Savannah unbuckles Paul's belt, I've had enough, and I grab the first thing I can find—a framed picture on the wall—and toss it to the floor with a loud crash. Everyone looks toward the sound, including Paul, and the director yells cut. I don't take my eyes off Savannah.

"Apologies," I say loudly, but my feet are already moving toward the brat sitting on my deck railing. The closer I get, the wider her eyes grow, until I'm wrapping my hand around her arm and pulling her off the railing. "I need a word with Ms. Loveless."

The director yells something, but I'm already heading back through the sliding glass doors.

"I'll be just a minute," Savannah calls over her shoulder, and I don't release her arm until we're through the house, down the hall, and in the soundproofed music studio.

"What the fuck was that?" My voice comes out like growl, low and possessive and fucking feral. Savannah doesn't so much as flinch at my tone. If anything, she stands taller.

"Acting," she says flippantly with a raise of her eyebrow.

"Bullshit."

"So now you're saying I can't act?"

"I'm saying you did that to fuck with me."

"Oh, get over yourself. I was doing my job."

"You know damn well you didn't do that for your job." I take a step closer. I breathe in her scent. She smells sweet, like peaches and cream, and I inhale deeply, filling my lungs with her. "You know damn well you played it up to get under my skin. To get back at me for earlier. For the other night."

"And why would I do that, Levi? Hm? You don't care. It will never work. Your life and mine, remember? What the fuck does it matter?"

"It matters. It matters that you're driving me insane and you're doing it on purpose. You've never learned your lesson."

She drags her eyes over me suggestively, taunting me with her hands on her hips like she's unaffected. But I can see her chest rising and falling rapidly. I can see her jaw working as she clenches her teeth. She's affected. Just like me. She's always gotten a kick out of driving me mad.

"And are you going to teach me a lesson, *Daddy*? Hm? Just how are you planning to do that? You going to punish me? Put me in time out? Ground me? *Spank* me?"

I take another step closer, so we're nearly chest to chest, and my eyes drop to her lips. When she licks them with that perfect pink tongue, making them glisten, I have to force myself to bring my eyes back to hers.

"You've always been a brat, Savannah. Too wild for your own good. I think you'd benefit from a little discipline, but it's not your ass I'm interested in spanking."

That does it. Her lips part on a gasp. Her pupils dilate. Her chest and cheeks turn pink.

"You'd like that, wouldn't you? Do you crave that discipline?"

I drag my knuckles up her arm, over her collarbone, then wrap my hand around the side of her neck so I can feel her pulse.

"Would you let me spank your pussy, Savannah? How hard?"

She whimpers, and I don't bother hiding my smirk. I rub my thumb over her lip. It's still wet from her tongue, and I want to taste it. I want to suck the taste of her off my thumb. Off her lips.

"I think you would. I think you're already wet just thinking about it. Can you picture it? Me spanking your pussy. Would you let me fuck you raw after?"

"Fuck," she gasps, her eyes clenching shut. She's practically panting.

"That's what I thought." I drop my hand and step back. "Think about that during your next sex scene, Rockstar. Maybe you'll be more convincing next time."

I turn and walk out, my dick rock hard and my heart threatening to break ribs. Just before the door shuts behind me, I hear her release a frustrated scream, and then the click of the door brings silence.

Calmly, I walk up the stairs to my room, then lock the door. I don't even make it to the bed. I strip off my jeans and underwear and take my cock in my hand, hissing when I squeeze then stroke.

I'm leaking from the tip. It won't take long. All I have to do is think of Savannah. Of spanking that pretty pussy like I'd promised. Of hitting her clit just right, just enough to make her cry out in pleasure.

I don't know which of us would like it more, and it's her name on my lips when I spill my release into my hand.

"Filming is cancelled for today," the PA says. Dakota, I think her name is.

It's pouring outside, so I'm not surprised. It's a hot, humid rainstorm. All dark clouds and lightning. It's a fucking Savannah storm. They couldn't get a good shot if they tried, and it's supposed to go all day.

"You moving to the studio?"

She shakes her head. "They're giving everyone the day off since we're a few days ahead of schedule. Just a few more scenes until we're off to Portofino."

The news pisses me off for reasons I refuse to admit. I nod at her then turn to leave.

"Hey, wait," Dakota calls, and I turn back to face her. "Some of us are going on a float trip a few hours inland if you want to come. It's out of the storm. More mountainy, less beachy. We've got tomorrow off, too, so we're going to make a day of it."

I shake my head no and turn once more to leave, then stop.

"Who all is going?" I ask without facing her.

"Oh, um, a few of the other PAs and tech guys. Two of your men. Dustin and Luke, I think. Sav and Paul, too."

Sav and Paul. Mother fuck it.

"I'll grab a suit," I say, then head upstairs, leaving her standing in the doorway.

. . .

Everyone is standing under one of the equipment canopies in an attempt to stay dry, but the wind keeps kicking up and blowing the rain in sideways. I zero in on Sav's silver head of hair, and walk straight to her.

"You're riding with me," I say into her ear.

Her shoulders jump, and she flips around to face me.

"You're coming?" I raise a brow in response, and she rolls her eyes. "Where's Boss?"

"With Sharon."

I keep my face serious, and I don't miss the way she flinches. I know this is hard for her. I knew it would be. It's an obstacle we'll have to figure out how to overcome, but it's also something I don't think I can compromise on. Sharon is important to Brynn. I can't take that away from her.

Savannah's composure slips for just a second, then the wall drops, and she appears unbothered. She's not unbothered, but she's a better actress than she realizes. She shrugs and looks away, checking her nails dismissively.

"I'm not riding with you."

"You are."

"No, I'm riding with Dakota. She's taking me to Walmart to get a swimsuit."

I chuckle. "I don't think they sell Gucci at Walmart."

"Don't be an asshole, Levi."

I look over Savannah's shoulder and find Dakota.

"Dakota," I call, and she whips her attention to me. "You're riding with me and Sav. Good?"

She grins immediately, which makes me grin and Savannah scoff.

"Yeah, definitely. Sounds great."

Dakota punctuates her agreement with an enthusiastic thumbs up, and I give her a wink before looking back at Savannah. I keep my eyes firmly locked on hers, instead of letting them drop to her tank top and cut-off jean shorts like I want to. If she had the brown wig on, she'd look just like she did back in Miami when we were eighteen.

"It's settled. You can have shotgun."

I turn to walk away, but she grabs my bicep, halting me, and I look back over my shoulder at her.

"What the hell are you playing at?"

I hold her eyes for a moment, swirling storm gray and flashing with irritation. I force a smile and reach my hand up, grabbing hers and gently removing it from my bicep.

"Going on a float trip, Savannah. Having fun. Lighten up, would you?"

I hear her huff as I walk toward her bodyguard.

"Sav's riding with me," I say to him as I walk past. "You can sit in the back seat with Dakota, or ride in the bed. I don't care. But she's coming with me."

I climb into my truck and wait. I watch as everyone starts to pile into cars. It looks like there are three other vehicles, so we'll have quite the party on this trip. I'm already dreading it. I flex my hands on the steering wheel just as Dakota and Red climb into the back seat. We wait in silence until Sav finally climbs up into the passenger seat.

"Buckle up," I tell her, and she flips me off before doing what she's told. "Good girl."

Her irritated growl is enough to make me hard, and I feel a smirk curl my lips before I put the truck in drive and join our caravan of vehicles.

I follow everyone forty-five minutes inland to a small-town Walmart with Dakota talking Red's ear off in the back seat. I don't speak. Savannah doesn't speak. Red barely speaks.

When we pull into the parking lot, the sky is already clearing with the distance from the coast. This store is never very busy, and today is no exception. I can tell by the way Savannah's shoulders loosen that she's grateful for that. Still, she stuffs her long silver hair up under a black baseball cap and slides on a pair of black wayfarer sunglasses. Her aviators are in my glove compartment. I should give them back—they're twelve-hundred-dollar sunglasses, for fuck's sake—but I can't. Not just yet.

Once she's satisfied with her "disguise," Savannah is out the door without a word and slamming it shut behind her. I have to swallow back a laugh. It's always her irritating the fuck out of me. It's fun being on the other side for once.

Everyone from our group disperses with plans to grab snacks and beer to stock the cooler, sunscreen for once we're out from under these storm clouds, and a few more beach towels. I follow Savannah and Dakota, trailing a few feet behind with Red as they head to the women's clothing section.

Savannah's face twists up as she surveys the selection, and I let out a laugh.

"Told you. No Gucci." She ignores me, but Dakota laughs.

"I know what you're thinking," she says to Sav, and Sav raises an eyebrow.

"Try me."

"You're thinking that this is how the graphic tee business is still thriving."

Savannah snorts a laugh and shrugs, then pulls a swimsuit off the rack.

"I was actually thinking that I've never seen so many variations of animal print on one article of clothing before." She holds the hanger out and tilts her head to the side. "Is that cheetah, zebra, or tiger?"

Dakota laughs and digs through the rack, then pulls out a black one piece. It's perfect for Savannah. Simple and sexy, with a low-cut back that will show off her tattoo.

"This is your size," Dakota says to Sav, and just as Sav reaches out to take the suit, I snatch it from Dakota.

"This works. Let's go."

I don't look behind me as I walk to the checkout and pay for the swimsuit. I know Savannah's following me, though. I can hear her stomping and huffing like a child. When we reach the truck, I turn and toss the bathing suit at her. She squeaks and fumbles, catching it awkwardly against her chest.

"Real nice, asshole," she grumbles, and I smirk.

"You're welcome."

As we're climbing into the truck, the rest of our group comes out of the store and gets into their vehicles. We're on the road within fifteen minutes, back on the interstate and heading west.

Savannah reaches up and turns on the radio, flipping stations until settling on something that plays alternative rock. She kicks off her sandals, props her feet on the dashboard, and rests her arm on the window ledge of the door. The tension slowly melts from her body with every song, and mine disappears with hers.

I sneak glances at her. Mouthing along to the words of whatever is playing on the radio. Gently tapping her toes against the windshield to the beat. She's going to leave footprints up there, and I already know I will never wash them off. Footprints on my windshield. Footprints on my fucking soul.

Savannah Shaw is leaving her mark on my life in every single possible way.

I haven't talked to her since our encounter in the music studio. Since I overstepped and made a scene. I've gone back and forth in the last week about whether or not I feel bad for what I'd done. For interrupting the shoot and saying what I said.

I don't.

I don't feel a single ounce of remorse. I'd do it again in a heartbeat.

When we stop for gas, I snag a candy bar before paying. Sav used to steal this same candy bar from the small grocery store in our hometown. Always two of them. One for me, and one for her, but she'd usually end up eating half of mine.

She's standing next to the passenger side scrolling on her phone as I head back to my truck.

"Rockstar."

When she looks up at me, I underhand her the candy bar, and she catches it with one hand. She looks at it, then at me with a raised brow. I can almost see the rest of the ice thawing. She wants to laugh, but she's working so hard to keep her face blank. The corner of my mouth twitches with the need to smile, so I do. Just a little. I wink at her before climbing into the driver's side.

I spend the last hour of the drive watching from the corner of my eye as she picks at the candy bar, eating it slowly. Her delicate jaw muscles working as she chews. Her fragile, soft throat contracting as she swallows. Her perfect pink tongue licking chocolate and caramel off her lips.

Dakota and Sav chat. Red joins in when addressed. I stay quiet, keeping my eyes on the road and my attention on Savannah. When she puts her thumb in her mouth, sucking off chocolate, my hands tighten on the steering wheel. I stop breathing long enough to hear her quiet giggle, and when I glance at her, she's smirking at me.

It's so unexpected that I don't catch myself smiling until it's too late. She bounces her eyebrows, and I shake my head slowly.

Brat, I mouth, and she shrugs with a grin before looking back out the window.

This trip might have been a bad idea.

We drop two of the vehicles downriver where we'll end the float trip, and everyone piles into the other two vehicles for the drive back upriver to where we'll begin.

We already unloaded our tubes and coolers, so there's plenty of room for people in the bed of my truck. When I park, everyone climbs out, and Savannah snatches her swimsuit out of the grocery bag at her feet.

She looks at it and purses her lips.

"You can change in the truck," I tell her. "I'll stand guard."

She side-eyes me and pops a brow.

"And if you peek, perv?"

I shrug and tap my temple.

"Don't need to see it again. I've got it all up here in perfect detail."

Her eyes widen, and I can tell she's once again fighting a laugh. I am too. I didn't lie, though. I see her body on the backs of my eyelids, permanently tattooed there for life. Every dip and curve and freckle. Technicolor and lifelike. Absolute torture.

"Hurry up, Rockstar. We don't want to keep everyone waiting."

I hop out and round the corner, standing with my back to the passenger side door. I'm parked on the edge of the gravel lot next to the bank of the river, so the other side of my truck faces nothing but trees. I stare down everyone who even glances in my direction, including Red. My neck heats as I feel the truck move slightly behind me as she shuffles out of her clothes and into her suit.

When she knocks softly on the passenger window, I step out of the way so she can climb out. I keep my eyes on hers. I don't let them dip lower, but I can still see her subtle cleavage tempting me from the outskirts of my vision. She smiles and slaps a tube of sunscreen against my chest.

"Rub me down, would you?"

She's trying to unsettle me in that way she does. Trying to get me off balance, tease me. Taunt me. It's working.

I laugh softly, then grab her shoulders and turn her around so I'm looking at her back. I've been dying for a close look at this tattoo, anyway. This bathing suit is open to just above her ass, exposing the entire art piece to me, and as I squeeze sunscreen onto my hands, I can't take my eyes off it.

Dahlia flowers, one red, one white, and one purple, decorate the middle of her back down her spine, and at the base, just above the slope of her ass, is a black dahlia. It's stunning in the way they almost leap off her skin, appearing real and fresh. The photos I'd seen of this tattoo didn't do it justice. I want to run my fingers over each petal, each stem.

I rub my palms together briefly, warming the sunscreen, and then I slowly smooth it down her back, right over each perfectly inked flower. She sucks in a breath as I use my thumbs to massage around her spine, my fingers pressing gently into the tight, tense muscles.

"Relax," I say quietly. "Just relax."

I feel her exhale slowly, and her body grows loose as I use my palms to rub up and down her back, gliding with the sunscreen, while working every muscle gently. I let my fingers slip just barely into the sides of her suit, grazing the covered skin with my fingertips. It's 85 degrees out today, but she still gets goosebumps on her arms from my touch.

I move to her shoulders, massaging as I apply more sunscreen, and she hums in approval as my thumbs press firmly into the muscles of her neck.

"That good?" I ask, dipping my head low so I'm speaking into her hair.

"Mmmm, yes."

I keep massaging, and she drops her chin to her chest, giving me access and surrendering control.

"Didn't realize you were so tense," I say, and she chuckles in response.

I move from her neck, back to her shoulders, then down her arms, taking the time to drag my hands over every inch of goosebump-covered skin.

"Ready?" someone shouts, and my head shoots toward the voice the same time Savannah jumps away from me.

Dustin. My nostrils flare as I stare at him, but his smile doesn't slip.

"Got the tubes all set. We're good to go."

Savannah has already started walking toward the river, so I follow. There's a cooler already stocked with drinks and shoved into a tube, and I reach for a beer just as Savannah reaches for a water. Our eyes meet and she gives me a small smile before pulling her water from the ice. I watch as she uncaps it and takes a drink, then I put my beer back and grab a water.

"You don't have to do that for me," Savannah says, grinning. "I'm around alcohol and drugs literally every day. I can handle you sipping on a can of shitty light beer."

I uncap my water and take a drink, then shrug.

"I like water."

I turn my attention to the bank where our group is picking out their tubes and readying to start our float down the river. The water is higher than usual and moving quicker than I remember.

"Has anyone done this here before, in this part of the river?" I address the group as a whole, and Luke speaks up.

"I have. We do it all the time."

"This isn't a little high? Fast?"

Luke laughs. "It'll get a little choppy in parts because of all the rain, but you'll be fine. Ain't nobody died yet."

"That's reassuring," Red says, and I nod in agreement.

Savannah sighs loudly, and when I glance in her direction, she's got a hand propped on her hip and the hip popped out in a way that makes her look entirely too sexy. Her silver hair is piled on top of her head in a wild bun, pieces falling randomly around her face, and that black one-piece accentuates every single aspect of her body, while still keeping everything covered.

I take her in, head to toe, then back to her face. She smirks and a dark eyebrow raises up from her wayfarers. Before she even opens her mouth, I know it's coming.

"Don't be a *weenie*, Leviticus. It's just a float trip. Have a little fun once in a while."

The barks of shocked laughter that leave Luke and Dustin are almost enough to irritate me, but they don't. Instead, I feel charged, my stomach flipping in that familiar way it always used to when Sav issued a challenge. I match her smirk, and my lips twitch at the corners, wanting to turn up higher. I don't let them.

"Okay, brat. Let's have some fun, then."

32

THE WATER IS COLDER than you'd expect, given that it's in the upper eighties and humid as hell.

Luke and Dustin have already strung the tubes together, putting the cooler tube in the middle. I position myself on the end, right next to Sav, with her security guard on the other side of her, and we push out into the middle of the river, letting the current take us.

It's relaxing once we get going, and conversation flows freely. Everyone's talking about the movie and the rainstorm and their plans to jet off to Italy soon. I stay quiet and listen.

Paul Northwood's voice rises above the others, laughing and engaging like the good American Sweetheart he is. He calls out to Savannah, and she turns her body so she can see him better. I bristle, jealousy surging through me as she laughs with him. They make plans to explore Italy on their off days. She has places to show him. He has places to show her. She's much more well-traveled than I realized, which shouldn't be a surprise, but it is.

For some reason, it's hard for me to picture Savannah as a tourist in Italy. As a tourist anywhere. She's headlined six world tours at this point. Of course, she's been places I've only ever dreamed of. Of course, she's bigger than anyone ever could have imagined. That's Savannah, though. She's always been one to surprise people. You can't underestimate her. She'll just blow right past and leave you choking on her dust.

All of this doesn't upset me, though.

What upsets me is the idea of her doing any of it with Paul Northwood. Doing any of it at all *without* me.

Not for the first time, my need for her flares, my fists clenching around the handles on my tube. I've never been so set on having something, someone, as I am with Savannah. As I've always been with her. It will never go away. It's just as strong now as it was when we were kids. Maybe stronger, because now I understand it better.

Without overthinking it, I reach over and grab her thigh, pulling her slowly until she's facing me once more. She doesn't stop me. In fact, she's smiling when I finally see her face again. Without prompting, she stretches her legs, so her feet are propped on my thigh, then she wiggles her toes.

I chuckle and shake my head, but I grab her foot anyway. Pressing my thumbs into her arch and the ball of her foot, I massage gently, and she hums in approval. The sound ripples over me.

"You like that."

It's not a question, but she nods in response. I move my hand up her leg, using my fingers to work her calf, and I watch as her nipples harden, perfectly outlined in her swimsuit. I watch her chest as it rises and falls more rapidly and mine does the same.

"Were you getting jealous?"

Her voice is teasing, but breathy, and there's no hiding that she's turned on.

"Always. I'm *always* jealous when it comes to you, Savannah. And you know it."

She smiles, then slowly inches her body toward me.

"Hold this," she says, handing me her water bottle, and then I watch with amusement as she awkwardly maneuvers her body off her tube and into my lap.

My arm wraps around her waist to steady the tube in the quickly moving current, and I hear Red scold her. She ignores him, waving her hand behind her head, and I watch him sigh and turn his eyes forward.

"He's right."

My voice is quieter now that her face is inches from mine.

"This probably isn't safe."

"Too late now."

She wiggles, her ass rubbing up against my hard dick, and her eyebrows jump behind her sunglasses.

"Don't think you're upset about it, though, huh, Weenie?"

I tickle her side, and she squeals out a laugh.

"Definitely not upset," I tell her.

She reaches up and spins my baseball cap around, so it's sitting backward on my head, then slips my sunglasses off. She tucks the sunglasses into the front of her swimsuit, right into her cleavage, and smiles.

"I've missed your eyes," she whispers.

I reach up and gently pull off her sunglasses, then slide them onto her head.

"I've missed yours, too."

She smiles, then I smile, and I'm seconds from kissing her, when Dustin shouts to the group.

"Got some rocks up here and then the bridge, so hold tight, and stay upright," he yells with a laugh. "And avoid the supports. They hurt like hell if you hit 'em."

My stomach drops, and I glance forward just in time to see rapids. Angry, rushing rapids, dumping right into the supports under the old trestle bridge. It would be dangerous even alone in a single tube. Savannah and I are doubled.

"Fuck."

I look from the quickly approaching rapids to Savannah, and then to her tube.

"Savannah, get back into your tube," Red shouts, and I don't miss that his voice has to be louder to reach us over the sound of the river crashing into the rocks up ahead.

"She can't. It's too dangerous," I yell back, just as the water gets choppier. "You need to get untied."

I look at Savannah, gripping tightly to one of the handles of our tube. I brace myself in the middle, trying to use my core to center our weight on the tube.

"Can you hold onto me? Real tight, okay?"

"Shit," she says on an exhale, and she wraps her arms around me. "I swear to god if I quit using just for this to be how I die, I will rage," she says against my chest, and I laugh once.

Then we hit the rapids, and things turn to shit.

Our position on the end slams us straight into the rocks, and I curse myself for not untying us, or suggesting we go in clusters instead of this long fucking line. We hit another one, our tube jerking violently and tilting us heavily to one side. Savannah shrieks. My knuckles drag against something sharp. The pain tells me it's broken skin.

I can hear some of our group screaming. I can't tell if it's from fear or excitement. I hear Dustin or Luke whoop like a fucking idiot, but I focus on our tube. We slam into another rock, and I try to push us out of the way of another. We miss a few, but there's always another bigger one in the way. Sav is holding me so tightly I can barely breathe.

"Hold on," I shout to Savannah, the river roaring around us. "It's almost to the drop."

We hit another rock, toppling us sideways, then two more. I right us just in time to hit another, then just before we drop under the bridge, the tube flips.

It happens quicker than lightning.

My grip is yanked from the handle and my body smacks hard against something before I'm spun out and pulled under. Savannah isn't holding onto me anymore. I reach for her, all around me, but she's gone. I try to call for her but swallow a gut full of water. I can't die here in this river. I can't.

Pain ricochets through my hands and legs and head as my body hits rock after rock. My chest starts to burn, the need to breathe stronger than ever, but I know if I do, it will kill me. I try to stand but can't find a footing. The current is too fast, the water too deep. I manage to grab hold of something, rocks tear at my hands, but nothing stays. Everything is disorienting. I'm submerged and spinning. A washing machine. I can't die here.

I open my eyes and see brown—dark, muddy brown—and my thoughts flit to Brynn and the weekend we spent in the mountains a few summers ago. She caught a lake trout, and the lake was brown and muddy like this. Like this, but calmer. I can't die here. I can't leave Brynn. I can't lose her. I can't be another person she loses.

I kick and reach, grappling for a hold, straining for the surface. My lungs are on fire. My body aches. I think of Savannah. She's out here. She could be in pain like this. She could be scared. She could be dead.

That thought hurts worse than the need to breathe. It's more terrifying than death.

I kick more, reach more, clench my jaw against the burning, visceral, overpowering need to take a breath. And then I'm falling, like a roller coaster on the down track. The drop.

My head breaks the surface and I gasp, gulping down air and kicking to stay above the water. Not to get submerged again. The current is strong, but the rocks are smaller here.

White flashes. Silver. Up out of the water, then gone again.

Savannah.

"Levi," she screams as she crests the surface. "Levi!"

She disappears again. The rocks, the spinning. She's almost to the drop.

I swim. Sideways, away from the center, but against the current. Every muscle in my body burns, but I have to get to her. My head pounds. We can't die here. Not now. Not when I just got her back.

When she pops back up again, I put myself in the path of her body until she crashes into me, and for seconds that feel like hours, I crush her to me, holding tightly. Then we're both crashing into the cold, hard cement of the bridge supports.

I flatten myself against it.

"Climb up there," I command, shoving Savannah's body up so she can grab onto one of the iron posts and haul herself up and out of the water.

Once she's out, I follow, pulling myself out of the demon river and collapsing against the bridge support.

For a moment, we don't say anything, we just pant, sucking in deep breaths. My throat feels raw. My bearings are still confused. I still feel like I'm spinning, even though I'm finally still. My back is scraped to hell. I feel nauseous and dizzy. My head pounds, and I reach up to find a gash and a giant bump forming.

"Savannah! Levi!"

We look toward the bank and find Red, soaking wet and bleeding from his forehead. My vision is slightly blurred, but I can still see him.

"Are you hurt? Are you okay?"

Though his voice is steady and controlled, I can still hear the relief in it mixed with fear. Red thought we were going to die. He thought Savannah was going to die. He was terrified.

"I'm okay," Sav calls to him. "Scratched and bruised. Sore as fuck, but nothing terrible."

"I'm going to get help. Stay there," he yells, and Savannah gives him a limp thumbs up, then huffs out a tired laugh.

"Where does he think we're gonna go?" she mumbles, and she's right.

Getting back into this water is not an option, so until someone comes with a boat or a helicopter, we're stranded here.

"We're good," I shout. "But hurry."

Red turns and hustles up the riverbank, then disappears into the trees.

"Are you okay? For real?"

I look her over, my eyes surveying every inch of her body. Her suit is torn at her side. There's a large scrape down her arm and a bruise forming on her cheek. I take my fingers and lightly run them over each of the injuries.

"Do they hurt?"

Savannah's eyes flutter shut, but she smiles softly.

"I've had worse."

I can't laugh the comment off. She has had worse. I remember. The bruises on her arms and legs. The boot print on her side. The split lips and bruised cheeks. The emotional trauma. And possibly even more that I don't know about because she'd been lost to me for so long. When the urge to wrap my hand around the side of her neck comes, I don't fight it. I do it, and I feel her. She's cold, shivering, but her heartbeat is strong under my palm. Her breathing is steady. It's a load of bricks off my chest.

A water droplet slips from Savannah's eyelashes and trails slowly down her wet cheeks. I follow it until it's joined by another, then another. When more escape, flowing faster, I realize they're not droplets of lake water. They're tears.

"Hey," I say quietly, bringing my other hand to her neck and cradling her face.

I rub my thumbs over her jaw, caress her cheeks.

"Hey, you're okay. You're okay, Savannah. You're not hurt. You're okay."

She whimpers and closes her eyes tighter, shaking her head slightly.

"No," she forces out on a sob. "*No.*"

"Yes. You're okay. You're—"

"No, Levi. Not me. Not *me.*"

Her hands grip onto the band of my trunks and she presses her head into my chest.

"I thought you were dead. I thought you were gone, and I'd lost you. You were there—my arms were around you and you were right there and then—"

She hiccups into my chest, then pulls back and paralyzes me with gray eyes shimmering with tears. Liquid metal. Mercury. I can't move. I can't breathe. I can't look away.

"Then you were gone. You were just ripped from me, and I reached, and I reached, and you were just *gone.* God, I just...I just...You were gone, and I couldn't get to you. There was literally nothing I could do. I thought you were dead. I didn't care about me. I wasn't scared for me. I was scared for you. I can't lose you like that. I can't. Not like that."

I wipe the tears off her cheeks and crush her to me in a hug. I bury my face in her hair, and somehow, it still smells faintly of peaches.

"I know. Me too, Sav." I love her. I know I do. I always have. I never stopped. "Not in *any* way."

She pulls back and looks at me, brows furrowed and eyes questioning.

"What?"

"I can't lose you in *any* way, Savannah. Not like that. Not like anything. Do you get it? Do you understand?"

Her eyes shift between mine. She scans my face. My heart is in my throat. And then she nods.

"I understand."

I bring my mouth down on hers, and she meets me without hesitation. She opens immediately, letting me in to explore. Her tongue massages mine, and I squeeze her. I run my hands up and down her body, squeezing just to remind myself that she's real and safe and here with me.

The sound of a helicopter breaks us apart, then firemen appear above us on the bridge and on the bank of the river.

"They really aren't messing around with this rescue."

Savannah laughs, hugging herself tighter into my chest.

"Didn't you know? I'm a super famous rockstar. If I die, the tabloid industry will go bankrupt."

I don't laugh. I just hug her back and rest my chin on her head. If she'd died...

The tabloids would have recovered. But me? I definitely would not.

Savannah is sitting in the back of an ambulance wrapped in one of those silver blankets that first responders carry around for shock.

Red is with her, and they're talking quietly. He has a bandage on his forehead where the cut was. I heard someone talk about stitching it up, but I don't know if he let them do it.

Red says something to Savannah, and she shakes her head. He says something else, and she shakes her head again. He sighs and nods. I watch it all go down from my own spot in the back of a second ambulance, where I'm wrapped in a similar silver blanket and fighting dizziness, nausea, and a massive headache. When Red turns to talk to a paramedic, Savannah looks at me and stands. Keeping the silver blanket draped around her shoulders, she climbs out of her ambulance and walks to mine.

"I'm cleared," she says when she reaches the bumper.

"Are you cleared, or are you just refusing to let them take you in?"

She smirks. That's what I thought.

"What about you?"

"Possible concussion. They're worried about the bump and gash." I gesture to the back of my head. The scrapes on my back burn with the motion. "They want to take me in for some scans."

The concern that takes over her face about knocks me on my ass. She scans my body frantically, then climbs into the ambulance and gently turns my head so she can see the back of it. It's bandaged, but I'm sure there's still visible blood in my hair. She tugs down my silver blanket and looks at my back, then gasps.

"Jesus, Levi," she whispers.

I feel her hand hovering just above my skin, so I turn to face her and take her hand in mine.

"I'm fine, Sav. It's just precautions. I can't drive, though. I'll have to get one of the guys to drive my truck back."

"Do you have a ride home? From the hospital, I mean?"

I shake my head once, slowly, and the movement makes me feel like vomiting.

"No. Was going to ask Luke or Dustin to just wait it out with me."

"No. Don't. Red and I will come to the hospital. I'll take you home."

"That's not ne—"

"Shut it, Levi. I'm doing it, so you might as well just accept it."

I sigh, and she grins, then reaches down and presses her finger into the cleft in my chin. I bat her away, and she laughs quietly.

"Where are your keys? I'll drive the truck and Red can follow in the car."

I don't answer for a moment. I just look at her. She's a mess. We both are. But even after all this chaos, the fear and pain and everything with it, she's still fucking beautiful. Hair a tangled disaster. Cheek scratched and bruised. Red-rimmed eyes with shadows forming under them. She's pale and exhausted, but she's still the most gorgeous thing I've ever seen.

"I think Luke has them," I say finally, and she nods.

"I'll grab them from him and meet you at the hospital, okay?"

"Okay."

Savannah smiles softly, then slowly she bends down and kisses me. Her soft lips are warm and gentle, and despite everything, it all finally feels *right*. Nothing around us matters. Not the paramedics. Not her security guard's watchful eye. Not our friends milling about in the parking lot, awaiting instructions. It's just Savannah and me and this sweet, soft kiss.

Whatever is happening between us, it feels fragile. Fragile and valuable, but just as insistent. It won't be ignored any longer, and I want to protect it at all costs.

Sav pulls back and rests her forehead on mine. When she speaks, her lips brush over my lips in a ghost of a kiss. Her breath tickles my skin. Her nose grazes mine.

"See you in a bit," she whispers.

"See you in a bit."

She climbs out of the ambulance and disappears around the corner. I close my eyes and drop my head to my chest. I feel like I've been run over by a truck. Or like I got sucked into some rapids and hit every fucking rock on the way. I roll my shoulders slowly, noting the way each muscle aches and the cuts on my back burn. This is going to make sleeping miserable. Working even worse.

I just want to shower and sleep for a week.

I open my eyes when I hear someone climb into the front of the ambulance, then another paramedic shows up at the open doors on the back.

"We're going to get you strapped in," she says pointedly. "It's about a twenty-minute drive. Not bad."

I nod and maneuver my body on the stretcher cot. The paramedic comes over and checks my vitals again, then starts to hook up the straps across my body. She's doing one across my chest when Savannah appears at the back of the ambulance again.

She's looking at me like she's in pain, tears welling in her eyes, and my fear ratchets up. The heart rate monitor starts to beep, and the paramedic pushes a button to silence it.

"What's wrong? What happened?" I look to the paramedic. "Get someone for her. Get someone to—"

"What is this?"

Savannah's question is asked almost angrily, her voice is shaking with restrained emotion. I shake my head and open my mouth to tell her I don't know what she's talking about, when my eyes fall on my keys clutched in her hand. My breath is sucked from my lungs, and the heartrate monitor starts to beep again.

"Savannah..."

"Did you keep this? Is this what I think it is?"

She waves the key in front of her, the rest jangling with the motion. She brandishes it like a weapon, making sure I get a good look at it. It's tarnished and beat up, but it still sits on the key ring where it's been for the last eight years. I thought it blended in well. I don't know why I didn't think she'd see it. I nod.

"It is."

"Why? Why would you keep it?"

I stare at her. She knows the answer already. I know she does. She has to. I take a deep breath before I respond.

"The same reason you wear the lock on that chain around your neck when you perform."

She sucks in a breath, and she narrows her eyes. I watch her jaw clench as she swipes at the tears streaming down her face.

The lock Sav Loveless wears around her neck, at every concert and in every photoshoot, is the same lock I used to chain up my bike when we were kids. It's a small, cheap one that I'd bought from the hardware store with allowance money. It was a terrible defense against theft, which is why Savannah was able to steal my bike and hide it so easily.

That lock that adorns her collarbone, that she uses as an accessory to every outfit, that is considered an iconic staple of her image, is the only thing tying Sav Loveless to Savannah Shaw. It's the only tangible thing linking her to me.

"I've kept the key for the same reason you've kept the lock," I say pointedly. "Because the universe was never done with us. You know it, and I know it."

Silence stretches and we stare at each other, unblinking, until a second paramedic appears. He tells her to step back, that we need to get on the road, so she does, but she doesn't break her eye contact with me. There's a storm brewing in her gray eyes, and I'm ready for it. I'm welcoming it. I've craved it for too long.

When the paramedic shuts the ambulance doors, I can still feel her eyes on me.

The feeling doesn't leave until we've reached the hospital, and I'm forced into a CT scan.

33

It's close to three in the morning when Levi is finally discharged.

Three staples for the gash on his head, but his scans came back clean. Nothing to worry about. Just a mild concussion, and he was sent home with headache medicine and instructions to rest. No work until he checks in with his primary care doctor in a few days. I've volunteered to stay overnight with him, just in case, and then I have to turn him over to Sharon.

To my mother.

Listening to him talk on the phone to her was awkward as hell.

I could hear her clearly. She was terrified. She wanted to come get him from the hospital, but he told her to stay home and let Brynn sleep.

Sharon was concerned like a mother would be for a child, and I couldn't fight the jealousy that surged through me at that thought. But am I jealous of Levi, or of my mother? My thoughts are too jumbled to make sense of, and my adrenaline is starting to wear off, but I'm good at running on no sleep. I've had lots of practice. While Levi dozes in the passenger seat, I'm wide awake with my eyes on the road.

I keep glancing at him, though. Making sure he's breathing.

Every time we pass under a light on the highway, I check his face. His forehead is scrunched while he sleeps, his face stern. Every so often, he'll make a soft noise or stir slightly. I get the sense he's having bad dreams, and all I want to do is pull over to the side of the road and hug him to me.

It always used to be Levi taking care of me. Worrying about me. Holding me when I felt like I was falling apart. For the first time, I'm on the other side of that dynamic, and it breaks my heart. Is this how he always felt? All those times when we were kids, seeing me crawl through his window broken and beaten down? Did it hurt him like this? Did it make him feel angry and sad and guilty all at once?

The things I must have put him through.

My mind goes to the night on the beach in Miami. How he took care of me. He was so gentle. So loving. He never once judged me. Never abandoned me.

He would have stayed had I not kicked him out of my house. I know that. I've always known that. But I also know that it wouldn't have lasted. Eventually, he'd have left. He wouldn't have had a choice. Whether it was for Julianna or the baby or school, he'd have had to leave, and it would have broken me. It used to make me deeply, thoroughly sad. I used to get so lost thinking about it, and I always ended up finding myself at the bottom of a bottle.

Or worse.

When I think of Brynnlee, though, I smile.

For years, I hated her. I didn't know her—didn't know if she was a boy or a girl, what she looked like, what her name was. I knew nothing, but I hated her.

Or at least, I tried to tell myself I did.

But then I'd get high and dream of Levi as a dad. See him holding a small baby. Singing it to sleep. Feeding it a bottle. I'd see him pushing a young child on a swing, or reading it a story, and all I could think about was how *lucky* that child would be to have Levi as a dad. How safe and warm and loved he'd make that baby feel. In those moments, I couldn't pretend I hated that baby. I loved them with my entire being, simply because Levi loved them.

I still do, and it is a poignant adoration.

Brynnlee's happiness is the result of my own loss, and though it aches, I wouldn't change it.

When I pull up to the set barricade outside of Levi's house, Red puts his car in park and climbs out. He chats with the security guard, and the guard removes the barricade and lets us pull through. I park the truck in Levi's driveway and turn off the engine. The moment the radio quiets, he stirs awake.

"We're here," I say softly.

He nods and looks around, groggy and slow-moving from sleep. Red comes to his door and opens it, then helps Levi climb out. The doctor said dizziness will be normal, especially for the next twenty-four hours, so we need to watch him closely.

We make our way into the house, kicking our shoes off in the mudroom off the garage. Levi seems to be moving fine. I can tell he hurts, he's sore and aching, but he doesn't seem disoriented. I follow him into the kitchen and get him a glass of water so he can take some of the medicine the doctor gave him.

"You're staying here, then?" His voice cuts through the silence, and though it's subtle, I can hear the hope in it.

"Yeah, I am. Sharon will be here tomorrow, but tonight..." I shrug. "I'm all yours."

Red makes the decision to sleep in my trailer across the street. It took some convincing, but he finally caved when I pointed out that he could see the house perfectly through the trailer door.

Once Red leaves, I follow Levi up the stairs and when we reach the landing, he turns to face me.

"Stay with me," he whispers, and I nod immediately.

"Of course."

He takes my hand and pulls me into a small bedroom. The size would suggest it's a guest room, but it's obviously Levi's room. The bedding is rumpled. The closet is full. There's a phone charger plugged in by the side of the bed and a book lying on the nightstand. I look around for an attached bathroom, but I don't find one.

"Is this the primary bedroom?" I ask, and he freezes, swallowing once before he answers.

"No. The primary is down the hall."

"This is a guest bedroom?"

He shrugs. "It's my bedroom. The primary is the guest bedroom now."

I study him, lips pursed, as I try to untangle the meaning behind this. I wait for him to tell me more. He blinks slowly, and I can't tell if his pause is due to the concussion or a reluctance to explain further. Just as I'm about to ask, he speaks.

"The other bedroom was Julianna's. Once she passed, I just made it a guest bedroom. No point in me moving rooms. I like it here just fine."

"You and Julianna didn't share a room?" I ask in disbelief.

I let the rest of the question hang between us. *They didn't share a bed?*

"Never." Levi shakes his head. "I told you. I didn't love her. I married her to help out, to keep Brynn safe, but I didn't love Julianna, and she didn't love me."

I swallow, trying to force back the lump that's formed in my throat.

"Was that weird for Brynn?"

Levi chuckles once, and it's dark sounding. "Brynn understands."

"Wow. I guess I thought...well, I guess I don't know what I thought."

He was married to Julianna for almost four years, and they never shared a bed. Does that mean they never slept together at all? When I glance at him, the question must be written in my expression, because he gives me a sad smile.

"Just the once, Rockstar. That was it."

The once. *Just the once.*

"Come lie down with me," he says, taking my hand once more and leading me to the bed, and I follow. When he winces taking his shirt off, I stop him, and bring his hands to his sides.

"Let me."

I keep my eyes on his face as I untie his swim trunks, then push them down his thighs until they drop to his ankles. I put my hands on his waist and walk him backward until he sits on the bed. He spreads his legs wide for me and I step between them before reaching for the hem of the shirt he's wearing. Slowly, I inch the shirt up his back, careful not to bump the bandages covering his cuts, and work it over his head until I can pull it down his arms and drop it on the floor next to the swim trunks.

The desire to look him over is almost too much, so when he leans back, propping himself on outstretched arms, I don't fight it. I let my eyes take him in. I look over every single part of him, glowing silver in the moonlight streaming from the windows.

His chest, though marred now with scratches from the river, is sculpted to perfection. I want to trail my fingers down his abs, tracing the strip of hair that leads to his pelvis. When I get to his hips, I suck in a breath and my thighs squeeze together.

Levi is hard, dick jutting out proudly between his muscular thighs, and my fingers tingle. My mouth waters. None of my memories, not a single drunken dreamscape, did him justice. How long ago was it that I had him in my hands? In the rainstorm after he'd made me come on his tongue. A week? Two weeks?

It was too long.

I lick my lips and force myself to bring my eyes back to his.

"Your turn," he rasps, and I don't waste time.

I strip off my tank top, then my cut off shorts, until I'm standing in just my simple Walmart one-piece swimsuit. He sits up straighter, and I walk to him without a word. I know what he wants because I want it too.

I step back between his legs and drop my arms to my sides as he reaches up and hooks his fingers in my swimsuit straps. Slowly, he pulls them down my arms, then tugs the snug fabric down the curves of my hips and over my ass. It drops to the floor, and I step out of it.

Like he did for me, I let him look. My skin burns where his gaze touches. My nipples pebble. My pussy throbs. With a featherlight touch, he trails his fingertips over my skin. My collarbone, between my breasts, circling both nipples before brushing down my stomach to my belly button.

By the time he reaches my pelvis, I'm panting. My chest is rising and falling rapidly just inches from his face, and he slides his fingers through me. I gasp, and he drops his head to my chest with a groan.

I place my hands on his shoulders, squeezing tightly, as he swipes through me once more, then rubs my arousal on my clit. I moan.

"I want you so badly," I rasp out, moving slowly on his hand. "God, Levi, I want you so fucking badly."

He takes one of my nipples into his mouth, swirling his tongue around it as he presses a finger inside me. I cry out, squeezing his shoulders tighter and crushing his body to me. He presses hot kisses to my breasts, my collarbone, my neck, then uses the hand not working my pussy to grab my head and pull my lips to his.

He groans into my mouth as he kisses me. As he claims me. When he pushes a second finger into me, I cry out and thrust my fingers into his hair. He jerks at the same time my hands hit the back of his head, and I freeze. The cut on his head. Three staples.

"I'm fine," he says, kissing me again. "It's fine."

My inhale and exhale are shaky as I put my hands back on his shoulders and gently push him away from me. I smile, then take a step back, so his hands leave my body at the same time mine leave his.

"You need rest," I say firmly, and then I bark out a laugh when he pouts. Six foot two inches of lean muscle, dick still rock hard between his legs, and he's pouting at me like a child. I close the distance between us and press a soft, easy kiss to his lips.

"Hold me like you used to," I whisper against him. "Please."

He does exactly that. I crawl into bed after him, sliding under crisp, cool sheets, and curl up on his chest. Then I release an exhale that feels like eight years worth of hurt feelings and bad decisions. None of it matters anymore. Right now, I'm exactly where I belong.

Levi is right. The universe was never done with us. It was just biding its time.

I wake with the sun, blissful and wrapped comfortably in Levi's strong arms.

Twice in the middle of the night, I woke with lyrics and music in my head. I had to reach for my phone and type them out in my notes app. I'll transfer them to my notebook later, but I couldn't bring myself to leave the comfort of this bed. The comfort of Levi's embrace.

Our legs are tangled together, our bodies twisted so intricately that we might as well be one. I pull back and look at him. His breathing is steady. His face soft and peaceful. I trace a finger down his cheek, and he flinches, scrunching his nose up. I stifle a giggle and press a soft kiss to his lips. He kisses me back, tightening his hold on me.

"Where are you going?" he grumbles against my lips, and I smile.

"I'm going to go make some coffee, and when I come back, I'm going to help you shower."

"Hmmm." He kisses me again. "Coffee is in the cabinet next to the fridge."

Slowly, I untwine our arms and legs and scoot myself out of the bed. When I stand, his eyes track me. I raise an eyebrow and prop my hand on my naked hip.

"Seen enough?" I quip and he smirks.

"Never."

I roll my eyes and fight my grin.

Instead of putting my tank and cutoffs back on, I saunter to his dresser on the far wall, making sure to put some extra sway in my hips with each step. He growls. I arch my back and glance at him over my shoulder, sending him a wink before opening one of his drawers and pulling out a blue East Coast Contracting shirt. Without turning around, I raise my arms above my head and let the shirt slide down my body. I pull it down over my breasts, but pull it taut at my waist, leaving my ass on display.

"You think that's funny," Levi grinds out.

I look at him over my shoulder once more and shrug, making my eyes wide and innocent.

"I don't know what you mean."

I poke out my lower lip and bat my lashes, but my eyes grow wider as Levi slowly pulls the bedsheet off his body and exposes his hard cock. He wraps a hand around his erection and squeezes, before stroking himself once.

"Don't think just because I've got a concussion that I won't grit my teeth and power through just to feel you clench around my cock when you come. You keep flaunting that tight little ass around, Savannah, and I might just have to fuck it."

I gasp, tearing my eyes from his dick to his face. He smirks, tilting his head to the side as he strokes himself again.

"Have you done that before, Rockstar? Have you had someone take your ass?"

My core is on fire and throbbing. I'm wet, and my nipples are so hard they hurt. I answer him honestly with a slow shake of the head. I've never done it—never had the desire to—but right now? I might actually *need* it. The way my pussy clenches, the way my lower belly stirs, tells me I do.

Levi's brown eyes go nearly black, and I watch as his jaw pops and his nostrils flare.

"I'm going to take your ass," he says finally, his voice raw and rough.

I watch him move his hand up and down his hard cock as he speaks.

"I'm going to fuck your tight little ass with my cock, and your cunt with my fingers, and I'll make you come so hard you'll have tears streaming down your face from the force of it."

My lips part, but no sound comes out. My whole body is tingling. I want him. I want him more now than ever before. He raises an eyebrow, the sexiest and most wicked challenge in his eyes.

"Speechless? Is your pussy aching and wet?"

I blink. I am, and it is. He doesn't need confirmation. It's obvious.

"Good. Go make me some coffee, Rockstar."

My eyes narrow and I shake myself out of my lust-induced fog just enough to match his smirk and regain the upper hand. Sparring with Levi has always been fun. But *sexy* sparring? It might just be my new favorite thing.

"If I weren't so worried about the long-term damage of restricting the blood flow to your brain right now, I'd take your cock down my throat and suck you dry."

I snatch a pair of athletic shorts from his drawer and step into them, bending lower than necessary so he gets a full view of what exactly he's done to my pussy. I tie the drawstring, then give him a sweet smile.

"Coffee, coming right up."

He lets out a chuckle that sounds more like a groan as I skip out of the bedroom and down the stairs.

The house feels different without the crew and actors running around. It has a homey atmosphere that I couldn't appreciate before. I walk to the sliding glass doors and open them, letting the sound of the water filter through the house. I take a deep breath, then scan the view. It's beautiful.

"Off to the right, that's where I wanted to put the pool."

I jump at Levi's voice, turning to find him leaning on the doorframe with his arms crossed, watching me. Pajama pants cover the lower half that was exposed to me minutes earlier, and a tank top covers his top half. His biceps still bulge from his posture. His shoulders are still strong and stable.

To think I'd almost lost him yesterday. It makes me want to cry even now.

He drops his arms and pushes off the doorframe, then crosses the floor toward me. When he reaches me, he kisses my forehead, then slides his hands around my waist.

"I know you're not a fan of the beach."

It takes a moment to understand what he's saying, but when it finally registers, my eyes widen, and I glance back to the place in the yard that he'd mentioned. *A pool.*

"You were going to put a pool in for me?" I whisper, and he smiles.

I glance out at the water again. I feel warm and relaxed. Safe. It's like I almost belong here. Almost. Then I remember the primary bedroom. The wedding portrait in the formal dining room. The picture of Julianna and Brynn on the rope swing in the front yard. My shoulders tighten involuntarily, and I feel Levi stiffen as well. He sighs, then presses another kiss to my head.

"I know," he whispers, and it's sad. "I know."

We break apart and he makes coffee. I make him take the medicine the doctor sent home. We're about to take the coffee to the deck when there's a knock at the front door. Levi leaves to open it. I hear him grunt, a bark, and then my menace of a dog barrels through the kitchen and bowls right into my legs. I spill the coffee all over the floor and collapse with the damn dog on top of me.

"Ziggs, oh my god, get off. I missed you too but get off, you moose."

She doesn't listen. She never does. She just covers me in dog slobber and traps me beneath her giant paws.

Red steps foot into the kitchen and stares at me with a bored face. He's used to the lick attacks. I think he's jealous he never gets any, but Ziggs prefers girls.

"Picked her up from the boarding place. She'd eaten the heads off every toy and destroyed the doggy couch, but apparently, everyone loves her."

I snort. Red brought her to the boarder before the float trip because he didn't trust her not to destroy my rental or trailer. Appears his fears were warranted.

"Because she's so damn lovable," I say with a grunt as I try to shove her off me. "Get off, Ziggy Lou."

Red walks over and gives me a hand, pulling me to my feet. Ziggs licks my ankles, then freezes. Her ears perk up, and she looks back toward the front door.

"Oh shit," I say, just as Ziggy takes off running.

I hear another grunt, then a bunch of giggles, and I slide into the foyer just in time to see Brynn on the floor with Ziggy on top of her. Levi is standing with his arms crossed, observing, and I laugh just before my eyes catch on the other person in the foyer.

My mom.

My laughter dies, sucked from me immediately, and my body goes rigid. I stare at her, and she stares back. I imagine the contrast in our faces must be comical. We look almost exactly alike, but my expression is shocked and hard. Hers is open and soft.

"Savannah," she says quietly. Hopefully.

I swallow. I don't speak. I feel everyone's eyes on me, but the weight of Brynn's is heavier than all of them combined. I glance at her and find her wide-eyed with concern. I force a smile.

"Hey, Boss."

Levi's hand comes down on Brynn's shoulder, and he steers her out of the foyer without another word. Ziggy follows because she's a traitor, but Red gives me a look that asks if he should stay or go. I consider it. I go back and forth, then I nod toward the kitchen, letting him know it's okay to leave me here.

Once he's gone, I look back at my mom.

"You look good," she says with a timid smile. "You look beautiful. I've been following your career. You're so talented, Savannah. I'm so pr—"

"Don't. Don't say that. I don't want your approval. I don't need it."

My mom swallows hard and nods. "Of course."

I look her over in the silence, pressing my toes hard against the wood floor to keep my balance. I feel unstable. I had a therapist in rehab tell me to use the 5-4-3-2-1 method whenever I started to feel like this. Like I was losing control. Five things I can see, four things I can touch, three things I can hear, two things I can smell, and one thing I can taste. I only get as far as seeing my mom's face before I give up and decide to count my breaths until I get my bearings.

"You look good, too," I say finally. "You look healthy."

It's honest. She does look good. I never, in my entire life, remember seeing her like this. She was always messed up and miserable. Using and being used.

"I'm three years sober."

I nod. "I'm coming up on a year."

I had been sober for a month before I checked myself in for my last rehab stint. Struggled through the European leg of our world tour. I just couldn't do it after Jonah's overdose. Every time I so much as looked at a substance, any powder or pill or bottle or needle, I saw him on that hotel room floor.

I spent eight weeks getting my head straight in the facility. Called Red and brought him on to be my personal security as soon as I got out. My old guy would get high with me all the time, and I couldn't have that around me anymore. I tried to get back into performing after. I tried like hell to jump back in like nothing, to play our American shows with as much enthusiasm. But I couldn't.

I was tired and jaded and on the verge of breaking, and the label never gave us down time. We're not people to them. We're money-making machines.

As I survey my mom, I can't help but wonder what her reason was. It wasn't me. I wasn't enough for her to try and get clean. So, what did it?

"Why?" I ask. "Why three years ago, after I was gone, and not when I was here and needed you? What was more important than me?"

"Nothing has ever been more important to me than you."

I almost believe her. I scoff and shake my head.

"That's bullshit, and you know it. If that was true, you wouldn't have waited so long to get clean."

My mom closes her eyes and breathes deeply. I notice her hands shaking as she clasps them together.

"I have no excuse. I was a terrible mother, and I was weak. I let Terry control me. Let him do with me what he wanted, and I was too high to care what happened to myself. But I swear, Savannah, I did what I could to protect you. It wasn't enough. I know that. But I always loved you. I always tried."

She opens her eyes and looks at me with tears welling around her gray irises. Eyes just like mine. Weaknesses just like mine. Is she to blame? Are her parents? Where did it begin, this cycle of self-destruction? When does it finally end?

"I detoxed in the hospital after one of Terry's friends..."

Her voice shakes and she closes her eyes again, clamping them this time as tears finally break past her lashes.

"He let them do it. I think he encouraged it. I was in the hospital for three weeks recovering and detoxing. When I was discharged, I went to the police and tipped them off about the drugs in the house. Terry had been going to parties. Selling to the college kids. Getting them to deal for him. Terry was arrested, and I haven't seen him since. I followed the story for a bit. Eighty-eight months in prison. Potential for parole. Something about giving up his suppliers. Didn't really hear much after that."

She shrugs and silence surrounds us once more. I let her words wash over me, but I don't speak. I wait, and when she realizes I want more, I'm giving her the space to explain, she doesn't hesitate.

"Levi found me in one of the shelters after the hurricane. The house was decimated. Everything was gone. I was moments away from giving up, but he was delivering supplies and donations to the shelter and found me. Put me up in a hotel that day. Offered me the job a week later."

At that, I don't fight the smile that wants to break my lips. I don't question the way my heart aches.

"Levi's always had a savior complex," I say.

Saving me. Saving my mom. Saving half the town, from what I've learned. Even his marriage to Julianna was out of some sense of duty. I've always thought of Levi as saint-like. More charitable and giving and caring than his own good. Too good for me.

My mother nods.

"He's a good man, Savannah. I care about him and Brynn so much. I owe him *so much*."

I let that sink in before I speak again. This time, my words are calm and controlled. Curious, but not angry.

"What have you been doing with the money?"

The money I've been depositing in her account every month since we signed with the label. I always assumed she was using it for drugs, but I'd always hoped she would use it to get away. To get clean.

"At first, I used it for what you think. Terry had open access to the bank account. After he left, I saved it. Used a bit of it to help me buy the house down the street. And now I put it into a savings account. Sort of a college fund, I guess."

My eyes widen.

"For Brynn?"

My mom smiles softly, the love in her eyes undeniable.

"For Brynn."

I break eye contact and look at my feet. I flex my toes against the hardwood again. I think of five things I see, four things I can touch, three things I can hear.

I understand how addiction can fuck you up. I understand how it affects the people you love. How you hurt the ones closest to you. I get it. I've lived it. I'm guilty of it.

"I don't know if I can forgive you," I confess to the floor. "I know I can't just forget and move on."

"I know. I would never ask you to. But..."

She hesitates, grappling for words. When I finally look back at her, her brows are furrowed and she's crying silently again.

"I have always loved you. I hope someday you can believe that. And I hope...I hope that one day, you can understand that I'm different now. I know the damage I've caused. I'm so very sorry for it. I know it can't be undone. But I have changed, Savannah. I'm trying every day to be better."

I can see the honesty on her face. I can hear the truth in her words. I let them move from my head to my heart, and I will myself to accept them. Part of me doesn't. I don't know if it ever will. But another part of me? It already has.

"Okay," I say quietly. "Okay."

34

It's around noon when Savannah's phone rings.

We've spent the morning—me, her, Brynn, Red, and Sharon—lounging on the deck. It was tense at first. It still is. But it's getting better. The production has three more scenes to shoot before they head to Portofino. If everything goes as planned, they'll be gone by the end of the week.

I don't know where the time has gone.

I curse myself for dragging my fucking feet in the beginning. For avoiding the inevitable. I should have kissed her in that café. I should have been with her every day since the day her flight landed in North Carolina. Instead, I was a coward, just like she said.

"What's up?" Savannah says into the receiver. Her eyes widen and she whips her attention to the clock on the wall. "Oh shit. I forgot."

She laughs as the person on the other end says something.

"Yeah, well, I had a near-death experience yesterday, so I think I'm allowed." She pauses. "Chill. I'm fine. I'll explain later." Another pause. An eyeroll. "No, it wasn't anything like that." She quiets again, listening to the person on the other end, and then she smiles. "Sounds good. See you soon."

She hangs up and passes over Red and Sharon before setting her eyes on Brynn and me.

"What are you guys doing tonight? I have a little surprise for Boss."

Sharon parks my truck two blocks from the riverwalk, and Brynn can't stop bouncing. I have to remind her three times not to run as we walk to the downtown concert series stage.

According to the fliers, tonight is supposed to be an eighties tribute band, but I know Savannah has done something. I'm nervous as hell. Excited for Brynn, but terrified. I've checked the internet every fifteen minutes since Sav left my house this afternoon, but it's nothing new. Same speculations about Savannah's relationship with Paul fucking Northwood, but nothing else. Not even a headline about Savannah's mishap with the rapids or her late-night ER visit.

My back stings at the memory. The nausea and dizziness are gone, but the scrapes on my back still burn, and my head still hurts as soon as the meds start wearing off. It's been a little over twenty-four hours, but I'm fucking over it.

"Do you think she's playing?" Brynn says with another bounce. "Oh my god, I hope she is. That would be phenomenal. Iconic!"

"Prodigious?" I ask and she grins.

"Prodigious!"

When we get to the small stage set up on the riverwalk, I spot Red and Ziggy immediately. No Savannah. He waves us over and we follow him to a spot roped off next to the stage.

The hairs on the back of my neck raise. My muscles go rigid.

"What did she do?" I say to Red, and he shrugs.

"She does what she wants," he says pointedly.

Fuck.

My eyes dart around the space, but no one seems to be expecting anything other than an eighties tribute band. The signage is still advertising the scheduled show. Nothing mentions The Hometown

Heartless at all. But I know. Even before the familiar guitarist, Jonah, steps on stage, I know, but that's when the crowd starts to murmur.

"Oh my god," Brynn whispers. "Oh my god oh my god, Dad. Dad. Dad. Can I have your phone? Please? Please? Please!"

I take my phone out of my pocket and hand it to Brynn just as Torren fucking King steps on to the stage and picks up his bass.

"OH MY GOD," Brynn squeals, and I watch as she pulls up the camera app and points the phone at the stage. "Oh my GOD, Cameron is going to die."

The crowd around us gets louder. *Is that Torren King?* The *Torren King?* When Mabel Rossi takes a seat behind the drum set, everyone goes nuts. I hear The Hometown Heartless shouted, whispered, chanted all around me. Brynn is practically vibrating, and I hold my breath as I wait for Savannah.

She loves a dramatic entrance. She waits until the crowd starts yelling her name before she finally steps foot on stage, her signature white electric guitar in her hand and my old bike lock around her neck. She looks straight at Brynn and winks before speaking into the mic.

"Hey, Wilmington, how you doin' tonight?"

The crowd roars and shoves to get closer to the stage. The whole time, Red stands facing them, his back to us, like he's our personal security. And the dog? She lounges at Brynn's feet, like she's used to the chaos. Living with Sav, I'm sure she is.

"I know you were expecting to hear some eighties jams tonight, and you still will, but the band has been kind enough to let us open for them. I hope that's okay."

More screams and shouts. More applause, and Savannah laughs into the mic.

"It's settled, then. Wilmington, let's rock."

Briefly, I wonder if being in this noise is smart, considering I still have a concussion, but the moment Sav launches into a song I recognize, the worry disappears. The song is another angry alt rock track that dominated the charts when it first released.

Her voice, still raspy and sexy in a way that sets my gut on fire, becomes something even more powerful when she's on that stage. Her energy is electric. The most beautiful, controlled chaos. Her emotion is palpable with every syllable, every note. The pain is just as raw as when she penned the song. Everyone in the audience feels it, too, because you can hear it as they sing along.

Oh baby, place the blame on my name,
I know you're dyin' to do it.
You know you want to shame me, tell 'em all I'm crazy.
You know they will believe you.
Make me the only bad guy, no one ever asks why,
Drag me through the fucking dirt.
You know I deserve it, baby, I do too.
C'mon, make it fucking hurt.

I haven't been in this position, watching in awe from the audience, in years. Not since they played that show outside of D.C. and debuted the song that would launch their career into rock and roll stardom. Julianna was seven months pregnant, and I was still enrolled at UNC, but I'd make the drive home every weekend to be with her.

Every weekend, except the one when Sav's band played in D.C.

I watched from the back of the venue and left immediately after, but it gutted me. Seeing her up there, loving her from a distance, hearing how she'd forgotten me. Listening to the heartbreaking lyrics of "Just One More."

I wrote this one for a guy I thought I loved.

I was angry and jealous and proud all at once.

As I listen to her now, I know she's in her element. She's a born performer and a natural artist. She belongs on that stage. I've always known it. I used to hate it. But now? Now, I just want to be part of it, watching from the sidelines and supporting her as best I can.

I want to be in the eye of her storm instead of thrashing about with everyone else.

I don't know how. I know it's dangerous. I know it's risky. But I lost her once. I can't let her go again.

"She's brilliant, isn't she?"

The admiration in Sharon's voice is audible, but it's the tears in her eyes that make my chest tight. I take her hand in mine and give it a squeeze in response.

She is brilliant. She's so brilliant it fucking hurts.

The Hometown Heartless play five songs. During one, Torren King joins Savannah on the mic and the crowd loses their fucking minds. Everyone still thinks they're engaged.

"Thank you so much for having us tonight, Wilmington, and huge thanks to Biff McFly for letting us open for them tonight. We haven't been openers in a while, and we really enjoyed it."

Mabel pounds something on the drums and Savannah laughs.

"Now, this might be goodnight," Sav says with a grin.

"It's not goodbye," Brynn and the rest of the crowd shouts back.

"But just in case, so you don't forget us, we've got Mabel on drums, Jonah on guitar, Torren on bass, you can call me Sav, and we are The Hometown Heartless. We had a blast with you tonight, Wilmington. Have a great night!"

Red and Ziggy disappeared the moment Sav started her goodnight speech, and when Jonah, Torren, Mabel and Sav exit the stage, the eighties tribute band, Biff McFly takes their place.

"Never thought we'd get to say that *the* Sav Loveless and The Hometown Heartless opened for us," the lead singer jokes.

The audience claps, and Brynn nudges my side.

"Dad, your phone. You got a message."

I grab it from her and open it up.

SAVANNAH

Meet us at my rental.

All of us?

The text bubbles pop up, then disappear, then pop up again.

If Sharon wants to come, she can.

Okay

"Let's head to the truck," I shout over the music to Brynn and Sharon.

They nod and turn to follow me.

When we reach Sav's rental a few blocks from downtown, Red is already waiting at the gate. He lets us in and gestures for us to park in the garage. Sharon is nervous and fidgeting with her hands, but when I ask her if she'd rather leave, she shakes her head no.

It's two hours passed Brynn's bedtime, but you couldn't tell it from how energized she is. She's going to crash hard, though. I already know it.

"Hey guys," Sav says as we follow Red into the house. Brynn, then Sharon, then me.

Sav's leaning on the kitchen island, a notebook sitting open next to her, and Jonah, Mabel, and Torren are all hanging out around her. She looks happy. They all do, except for Jonah. He looks...blank. Tired.

Brynn takes a few steps toward Savannah and then—bam!—tackled by Ziggy. Savannah lets out a groan-like laugh as Brynn starts giggling. That dog is a menace.

"Good god, Ziggy," Mabel says. "Sav, you need to put that mutt back in obedience school."

"She got kicked out the first time," Torren says. "She'll just get kicked out again."

Sav shrugs.

"She does what she wants anyway." She looks at Red and winks. "Like her momma."

"Trouble," Red says and Sav laughs.

"Fun sucker."

Jonah bends down and shoves Ziggy off Brynn, then grabs both her hands and pulls her to her feet. Brynn's mouth is dropped wide open, her eyes the size of fucking dinner plates. She's starstruck.

"Thank you," she whispers.

Jonah smiles with a nod, then throws himself down on the couch without a word. When I look at Savannah, she's staring at him with a furrowed brow. Then she looks at Torren, and he shrugs. She's worried about Jonah. From the look of Mabel and Torren, they are, too.

"Is that *the* notebook," Brynn says, breaking the tense silence. "The lyric notebook?"

Sav laughs, then slides it behind her back on the counter.

"Sure is. No, you can't see it, so don't even ask."

Brynn's lips purse and Mabel gives her shoulder a nudge.

"She won't even let us see it, kid. Don't feel bad."

"Oh shit! I forgot to introduce you guys," Sav says suddenly. "Guys, you might remember Levi, but this is Boss, and, um, that's...That's Sharon. My, um, mom."

Savannah flinches on the word, but wipes it away quickly, and I can feel Sharon's discomfort radiating off her. She waves awkwardly. Luckily, Red breaks in and takes the attention off her with a question directed at Brynn.

"What's the word today, Boss?"

Brynn grins immediately.

"Gamut. Noun. A range or series of related things."

Jonah's voice rings out from the couch.

"The Hometown Heartless have run the gamut of tabloid headlines from praise to contempt."

"A-plus-plus, Jonah. Great job!"

Brynn is beaming at the guitarist, and he throws a thumbs up her way without looking up from the coffee table book he's flipping through. This isn't the Jonah I remember from Miami, and I can't help but wonder what bullshit he's been through since making it big. Whatever it is, it's changed him, and it doesn't look like for the better.

"Welp, I was thinking we could hang out on the roof," Sav says pulling my attention back to her. "We can jam on the acoustics. Maybe let Boss show you guys what she's learned so far."

"I can play 'i wanna be there' almost. G, C, D, G."

"I hear you're doing great," Torren chimes in, and Brynn grins up at him.

I clear my throat with my eyes on him, and when he looks at me, I make sure my face conveys the threat. *Don't mess with what's mine.*

When everyone heads to Savannah's roof, I hang back, positioning myself in front of Torren so he has to stay with me. For a minute, we just stare at each other, and when he opens his mouth to speak, I put my hand up, stopping him. When I speak, I keep my voice low and steady.

"Whatever is going on with you and Savannah—this publicity stunt of an engagement and the touching and any *unrequited* feelings you might have—let's get one thing straight. She's not yours. She was never yours. Get rid of the fantasies. Stop looking at her like she's your forever. She's not. She never will be."

He glares at me, eyes hard on mine. I watch his jaw pop with the way he must be grinding his teeth.

"I suppose you think she's yours?"

"I know it. So do you. But if you want to fuck around and find out, be my guest." I smirk. "I think I'd like seeing you humiliated, and it's been a while since I've busted my knuckles on your face. I kind of miss the feeling."

Torren scoffs and shakes his head.

"You have no idea what you're getting into with her."

My shoulders tighten, and I grit my teeth. It's not an insult or a threat. It's said reverently, and that makes it worse. He honestly thinks he's in love with her. I almost feel bad for him. Almost.

I step closer and cock my head to the side as I scan his face.

"You've had almost a decade with her, yet she's still mine. That ring she wears? Might as well be scrap metal. Know why? Because I know *exactly* what I'm getting into with her. I'm the only one who's ever known."

I take a step back and my face softens.

"You think you love her. Fine. I get it. But this is the only time I'm going to say it. Get over it. I won't say it twice."

I turn without another word and head up to the roof. Savannah raises an eyebrow when she sees me, and I wink, then sit in a patio chair next to Brynnlee. Ten minutes later, Torren appears, and I don't miss the way he keeps a distance between himself and Savannah. Good.

After Red lights a fire in the small firepit, they bring out two acoustic guitars and play some songs. It's even better than before. Even Jonah perks up, seems almost revived. He sings along when Brynn plays. He claps. He even plays a few songs on his own. By the time Brynn falls asleep in the lounge chair, it's two in the morning and the atmosphere feels charged with promise. Something positive. Even I'm excited, and I don't even know what for.

Sav tries to convince her bandmates to stay the night, but they insist on going back to their hotel because they fly back to LA in a few hours. Sharon tells me she's going to take Brynn back to her place. She doesn't even ask if I want to stay with Sav. She just assumes, and though I probably should, I don't correct her. Red carries Brynn to the truck and buckles her in, then disappears into his room with Ziggy after making sure the gate and the windows are locked up tight.

Then it's just me and Savannah in the kitchen. Alone. She nudges my foot with hers.

"Hi," she says with a grin.

"Hi."

"How are you feeling?"

"Alright."

"How's the head?"

"It's been worse."

"Hmmm."

She bounces her eyes between mine, a soft smile playing on her lips. She nudges my foot once again with hers.

"It's a nice night. Want to come back on the roof with me?"

I look her over, head to toe. She's in sweats and a tank top now, but she looks just as tempting—just as fame-worthy—as she did on that stage tonight. She exudes sex appeal and danger. It's a heady combination, and I am at the end of my rope trying to deny it.

"I don't want to go to the roof with you, Savannah."

Her face falls, and I take a step toward her, boxing her in against the kitchen counter. I wrap my hand around the side of her neck and use my thumb to pull her lower lip down. Her breath hitches and her lips part, then she turns her head slightly and takes my thumb into her mouth. She sucks on it, swirls her tongue around it, and I groan. My dick hardens and my heart threatens to beat out of my chest.

"I'm done denying myself. I'm done keeping my distance. I've been shit at it anyway, and it's driving me fucking crazy."

I inch closer and take her hand off the counter where she's bracing herself, then put it on my cock. She squeezes me through my jeans, and I thrust into her palm.

"I need to fuck you. Now. Are you okay with that?"

She gasps and nods quickly, before halting and furrowing her brow.

"What about your head?"

"Not concerned with the one on my shoulders." I smirk and she smiles back. "Take me to your room. Unless you want me to fuck you right here."

I slide my hand into the front of her sweats and to her pussy. I press on her clit, and she whimpers. I move lower and rub my fingers through the wetness dripping from her, soaking her panties.

"Fuck, you do want that, don't you? I can bend you over this counter. Or do you want me to carry you to the couch?"

I press two fingers into her and watch as her eyes flutter shut. Her hips jerk against me when I push on her clit with my palm, and she gasps. I move my lips to the shell of her ear, my voice a rasp, and she shivers.

"I can throw your legs onto my shoulder and hit you deep with my cock, Savannah. I can fuck you like the brat you are."

I thrust in and out of her slowly, and her breathing kicks up to a pant. She squeezes my dick through my jeans, and I groan into her ear.

"I want to spank that pussy the way I've been dreaming about."

I thrust faster, then move my fingers to her clit and rub roughly.

"I want to sink my cock into you. Rub on your clit. Fuck your ass with my fingers until you're ready for my cock. Do you want that?"

"Yes," she breathes out.

I move my mouth to her neck and kiss it.

"Say it louder."

"Yes."

I rub her with my fingers, then move my fingers back into her when I know she's close. I thrust faster, as deep as possible, massaging her. Making her clench around me.

"Say it again. Louder, Savannah"

"Yes, all of it. I want all of it," she cries out, then comes around my fingers, and I move back to her clit and rub, letting her ride out the shocks of her orgasm.

She shudders, then gasps out a low moan when I suck hard on the sensitive skin of her neck. Hard enough she'll need to cover it with makeup for a week on set. Hard enough that Paul Northwood and Torren King and everyone else around will know she's taken.

I smile.

"Good girl. Now take me where you want me."

She shoves at my chest, making me take a step back, then grabs my hand and pulls me up the stairs. We bypass her bedroom and head straight for the stairs leading to the roof. Logic, caution, self-preservation. It's all gone as we step onto the rooftop terrace, and she whirls on me, unzipping my jeans and dropping to her knees.

"Fuck," I groan, grabbing hold of her hair as she takes me in her mouth and straight down her throat.

No warm-up. No licking or toying with my dick. I have to brace a hand on the brick wall behind me from the way the pleasure makes me sway on my feet.

"Oh, fuck, yes."

I tug on her hair and thrust into her, making her gag around me before pulling her back up to her feet. She tries to protest, but I cover her mouth with a possessive kiss, hand still fisted in her silver hair. She claws at me and palms my hard cock, now slick with her saliva.

"I'm not coming down your throat right now," I grind out. "I'm not coming in your hand either."

I walk her backward until her legs are against the patio chair. She tears off my shirt, then I follow suit with hers, dropping them on the ground beside us. I tug her sweats and underwear down her legs, and she kicks them off her feet. I palm her pussy, growling into her mouth when I feel just how soaked I've made her. Just how wet she is from the last orgasm I coaxed from her.

She pushes my jeans down over my ass and I do the same with my boxer briefs, and then we're both standing naked under the night sky. I kiss her. Tweak her peaked, hardened nipples as she drags her long, black-painted fingernails down my chest. They don't break skin but I want them to.

I bite her nipple, she gasps, then I spin her around, so my dick is pressed against her ass. I tug her head back by her hair and kiss her lips as I thrust between her ass cheeks, and she arches into me.

She's so willing. So eager.

I want to claim her. To fucking *own* her. I want to ruin her for everyone else.

I've only ever felt this possessive over Savannah. No other woman. She's the only one who belongs with me.

She moans against me, and I use my feet to kick her legs apart, so she's standing with them spread wide. I use my free hand to swipe my dick between her legs, once, twice, until she's pushing back onto me, her body begging for the head of my dick to push into her wet, swollen pussy.

"Knees on the couch. Keep your legs wide."

My command is ragged and rough, and I see goosebumps prickle the naked skin on her back.

She scrambles to do as she's told, and I rub my hand up her

spine before pressing lightly between her shoulder blades, so she's bent over, forearms braced on the back of the couch. Her back is rising and falling almost violently with her sharp breaths.

"Press your ass into me, Savannah. That's right. Just like that. Push it hard against my dick."

She does it, and I grab onto her hips, clenching my teeth to keep from rushing this. To keep from taking her hard and fast.

"Fuck, Sav. Who knew you could be so obedient?"

She huffs. "I'm not a damn dog."

I give her ass a smack then thrust against her, watching my cock slide up and down between her ass cheeks. It's fucking erotic, commanding her like this. Possessing her body like it's mine.

"I think I can tame this brat. I think I can fuck the brat right out of you."

She growls but pushes harder into me.

"Stop talking and give it a try, then."

The anger and impatience in her voice light me on fucking fire, and I smack her ass again. Her groan is guttural, and I know her wetness is dripping from her.

"No condom," I say.

It's a question as much as a warning.

"I don't care. Fuck me bare. Skin on skin."

I don't wait for her to say more. I slam into her pussy, until her ass is pressed hard onto my pelvis.

"Oh fuck," she chokes out.

I pull back and slam in again just to hear that moan once more. She doesn't disappoint.

"Oh, yes. Oh my god."

I pull out slowly, watching with rapt attention as my dick slides out of her pussy glistening with her arousal until just my tip is inside her, then I slam in again.

"Faster." She groans. "Go faster."

I smack her ass again.

"I'm not rushing this," I tell her as I pull out slowly once more, then reach around her and press on her clit before slamming into her a third time.

The cry that falls from her lips is rapturous, and my groan matches.

"I want you red and swollen and unable to fucking walk when I'm done with you. You want to be a rockstar? I'm going to fuck you like one."

35

Levi's movements are controlled and steady. He thrusts deep into me as he rubs my clit, until I start to move against him. Forcing him to fuck faster.

"Jesus, Savannah. Fuck."

He stops moving and lets me fuck him, and it feels so good to be in charge, even if just for a few seconds. I throw my ass back on his dick with vigor, making him groan. Making him crazy. I clench my pussy around him until I'm just at the edge of an orgasm, then he grabs my hips hard and halts me. I growl.

"Levi!" I practically shout my scolding. "Stop teasing!"

He fucking chuckles, dark and wicked and low, and it's like my buttoned-up Levi is possessed by some kind of filthy-mouthed alpha sex god. I can barely handle it.

"I'll give it to you when you behave."

I let out a frustrated cry, and he slams into me again, so my cry changes to a groan.

"Fuck, like that. Please, like that, Levi."

I know I'm a panting, begging mess, but I don't stop. I'll get on my knees if it means he'll keep this pace and let me come. He keeps thrusting, faster now, giving me what I want. What we both crave.

"You're trying to sweet talk me with your sassy mouth, now? I'm in charge, Savannah, but it might work. Try again."

Fuck me. I'm going to die at the hands of Levi Cooper, sexed-up and exhausted, and I don't even care.

"Please. Please. *Please*, Levi. Keep doing that."

He grips my hips and picks up the pace, until it's punishing. Until I'm crying out with every thrust and my words become nothing but jumbled nonsense. My arms shove into the back of the couch, so it almost hurts. I might even bruise, but I barely feel the sting. I don't want him to stop. I don't want him to ever stop. He rubs my clit again, fast and hard, and when my pussy starts to clench around him, when my belly starts to do those telltale flips, and my toes start to curl, he stops.

"Levi!" I try to push against him, and he pulls away. "Levi. Fuck. Me. Right. Now."

He wraps his hand around my neck and pulls me to him, bending down to meet me and take my lips in a kiss. He palms one of my breasts and massages it with callused palms that make me ache in the most blissful way. When he rubs those callused fingers against my nipple, I whimper into his mouth. I tangle our tongues and clench around his dick. To torture him. To coax him back into fucking me the way I want.

I bite his lip, and he growls, then he slaps my wet, swollen pussy, sending a brilliant sting over my clit and through my body. I cry into his mouth, and he does it again, spanking my clit and making me throb. He starts to slap, hard and unrelenting as he fucks me from behind, and it feels so sinfully good that my whole body tenses. He could make me come like this, spanking my pussy with his hand while his cock thrusts in and out of me.

"I knew you'd like that. You like being spanked as much as I like spanking you."

His voice is gravel on gravel, the way he forces it out through clenched teeth. His restraint. His control. It's pure sex.

"Fuck, you're flooding your thighs. My dick is soaked with you, Rockstar. Soaked from being spanked like the brat you are."

I want to argue, want to snap back with something snarky, but I just can't. Anytime I open my mouth, only whimpers and pleas come out. Then he pushes me back down, ass out and back sloped, and I brace myself on the back of the couch for more of him.

"Fuck, you have no idea how sexy you look like this," he rasps.

I can feel his eyes on me, every part of me, and that turns me on almost as much as his touch. He drags his palms back down my sides until he's grabbing the globes of my ass. He squeezes them, massaging with those talented fingers, before spreading them apart and baring me to him. He spits, and I shiver when it lands right on my ring of muscle. Warm and wet. Filthy and fascinating. I whimper, pressing closer. Wanting it. *Begging* for it.

"This will be mine, too."

He moves his thumb and rubs around me, massaging his spit into my skin.

"Are you going to let me have it?"

"Yes. God, please, fuck it. Fuck my ass, Levi."

I'll give him anything. I'll give him *everything*. I want him to take it. I've always been his, anyway.

He spits once more and presses lightly, barely breeching my barrier, but when I push back against him, he pulls away. I whine, and he laughs.

"Not tonight. I'm too big to take you out here without prepping you, and I want you nice and ready when I claim your ass. Trust me. I'll make it good for both of us, but not tonight."

I whimper and start to protest, but he moves his hands back to my hips, and silences me by pushing his dick back into my pussy. The protest changes to a moan, and he starts to fuck me again.

"Please don't stop this time," I beg, and he groans like he's finally losing it like I already have.

"No more edging, baby. I promise."

Oh, thank god.

He pulls me back up, so he can kiss me as he fucks me. I leave one hand on the couch for balance, and he moves one hand to my clit. He thrusts into me, plays with my clit, and conquers my mouth with his tongue. I'm completely at his mercy until I'm convulsing with my impending orgasm.

"There it is," he says, never changing pace or pressure. "You're squeezing me so tight. You want to come on my cock, don't you Rockstar?"

"Mmhmm," I murmur through pants.

"Then you're going to let me come down your throat, aren't you."

"Yes. Yes," I manage to get the words out just before I detonate with a cry, Levi's name on my lips as I come around him.

He groans but doesn't stop his ministrations until my orgasm fades. Then he pulls out, spins me around, and guides me to my knees.

I take him into my mouth eagerly, lapping and sucking and working him with my hand. He gathers my hair out of my face, then pulls it back into a makeshift ponytail. With his grip on my hair, he starts to bob my head the way he wants, and I open wide for him, swallowing around his dick every time he pushes into my throat.

"Jesus, Savannah," he says as I gag on him. "You're going to look so fucking good swallowing my cum. You want it?"

I hum in response. I can't answer with my mouth stuffed full of his cock, and he smirks down at me because he knows it. Just because I can, giving him back a little taste of his own medicine, I bare my teeth and graze the underside of his dick. He hisses, tugging on my hair with a dark chuckle.

"Still a brat, then. Looks like I'll have to spank harder next time."

I hum again and his eyes fall shut. He tips his head to the sky and starts to thrust into my mouth faster.

"I'm going to fill this sassy mouth up, and you're going to swallow every drop of me."

I don't even have to respond. He knows I will. He knows I'll do whatever he wants.

He stops thrusting and pulls out, taking his cock in his hand.

"Open. Tongue out," he commands, and I obey.

He strokes himself roughly until he's shooting his release into my mouth and on my tongue. I keep my mouth open for him, my eyes wide and on his face, so I can watch his rapt expression, until he's finished.

"Show me," he grits out, so I stick my tongue out farther, his cum on display.

He smirks, his eyes molten lava, then he spits again. Right into my mouth, and I feel it land on my tongue mixing with his cum. He grips my chin with his thumb and forefinger and closes my mouth for me.

"Swallow."

I swallow, then I open my mouth once more, proving to him that I did as I was told. I swallowed every last drop of him, and the absolute adoration on his face is enough to make me want him inside me again.

He pulls me to my feet and kisses me, at first roughly, but then he slows, growing softer and sweeter. Reverent and loving.

"You're amazing," he whispers against my lips, and I blossom under his praise.

My chest heating, my heart thrumming for a new reason.

"Now take me to your bed so I can make love to you properly."

My head jerks back and my mouth opens, shocked, and he smiles. It's the happiest, most beautiful smile, and I haven't seen it on his face in a long time. He kisses me again.

"You heard me right, Savannah." He smacks my ass, making me yelp, and then smirks. "Now do as you're told."

I put my hands on his chest and shove him backward, then I take a few steps toward the door.

"I hope you enjoyed the upper hand. But now it's my turn. My bed, my rules. You better keep up."

Then I turn around and strut to the door leading back into the house. He's on my heels immediately, throwing me over his shoulder before I even hit the stairwell. I let out a shrieking giggle that bounces off the neighboring buildings and turns me crimson.

"Bedroom?"

"Second door at the end of the hall."

He carries me to my bedroom and tosses me on the bed, then puts his hands on his hips, dick already hardening once more. He smirks as I gawk at him.

"Well, Rockstar. Do your worst."

The incessant buzzing of my phone finally wakes me, and I roll out of Levi's embrace to grab it from my nightstand.

My whole body aches. I need a hot shower and some coffee to feel halfway human again, but god, what a night. I can't stop smiling. The moment my eyes pop open, a smile takes over my face and I have to stifle a giddy giggle.

Levi Cooper is a filthy, dirty sex god. I shouldn't be surprised. He's always had a subtle darkness under that good boy exterior. Understated and unassuming in the day to day, but absolutely fucking filthy in the bedroom. Or on the rooftop terrace. Or under his deck in a rainstorm. Or basically everywhere.

Yet, he can be sweet and soft, too. Sensual. Heartbreakingly attentive.

After the rooftop ravaging, by which it will now forever be labeled in my memory bank, I took Levi to my room and rode him until my legs gave out. He outlasted me, then put me on my back and slowed things down. I've only been loved like that once before, and it was in a ragged old rental house in Miami when I was eighteen.

Basically, he's perfect and I'm in fucking trouble. Because I've already decided I want to go back to the band. I talked things out with them last night, and I think we have a chance of throwing our weight at the label to renegotiate our contract.

But I want Levi too.

I don't know how I can have both.

I need the band. But I need Levi.

I've always needed him.

Next week I'll be in Portofino, and hopefully being away from him, Brynn, and my mom will give me a chance to gain perspective. I need to troubleshoot. I need to find a solution that will let me live both lives, have both the band and Levi, without compromising anything.

After last night, I'm not willing to say goodbye again. To any of it.

I roll back to Levi's chest as I unlock my phone and see a text and two missed calls from Mabel, along with twelve missed calls from Hammond. I check Mabel's text thread first.

MABES

SOS. Answer the phone.

Wake up. Urgent.

Fucking call me!!!

Shit. Shit. Shit.

I'm pulling up her contact when she buzzes through, so I answer before it gets past the first ring.

"What did I do now?"

"Have you been on the internet?"

"I just woke up, Mabes."

My phone beeps in my ear and I pull back to see an article from my least favorite tabloid. I close my eyes and take a deep breath, then I click on it. As soon as the webpage loads, my stomach falls to my feet, and I feel dizzy.

"Oh fuck," I whisper, and I hear Mabel say *no shit* on the other end.

It's grainy photos of me on the roof last night with Levi. It's blurry and dark, and thankfully you don't get enough of Levi to really ID him, but I'm obvious. My silver hair is like a fucking beacon. Then there's a link to a video, and like a dumbass, I click it. I watch the whole three minutes with my heart in my throat. I don't even blink until it's over, then I have to rub the sting out of my eyes.

The video is grainy and dark, and again, you don't see much, but the noises. Slapping and moaning and murmuring. At one point, you can very clearly hear me moan *Oh fuck*, but nothing else.

I put my phone back to my ear.

"I have twelve missed calls from Hammond," I say to Mabel, and she snorts.

"Because the label is fucking pissed. Literally your only saving grace right now is that the article assumes you're with Torren since we were with you last night, but Hammond knows that Torren came back with us to the hotel. He's trying to run damage control, but honestly, I think he wants to strangle you."

I groan and flop back on the bed, waking Levi. *Sorry*, I mouth to him. He raises and eyebrow, and I shake my head, then focus back on Mabel.

"At least they didn't get much. The pictures aren't too bad. And the video—"

"Savvy, I know you're used to scandal and all, but this is basically a sex tape. You have a sex tape now, and it's obviously you. You have one of the most recognizable voices in the world and now everyone knows what you sound like when you come. And if it gets out that that's not Tor..."

My phone beeps and I pull it back to see Hammond calling. Goddamn it.

"Mabes, I gotta go. Ham's calling, and I might as well bite the fucking bullet."

"Good luck, bitch."

"Hey, Mabes," I say, just before she hangs up.

"Yeah?"

"Thank you."

She's silent for a moment, long enough that Ham's call goes to voicemail before she speaks again.

"You know I love you, right? This band is the closest thing to family I've ever had. You're my sister. Things got so messed up, and we lost sight of what's important. But I fucking love you, Savannah, and I just... I don't want anyone to hurt anymore. None of us. Not me or you or the guys. Fuck not even Ham, even if he is a prick."

I laugh with her and then wipe away a few tears. I hear her sniffle on the other end and sigh.

"If you want to leave the band, I get it. I don't hate you for it, and I don't want to be in Heartless without you. I was just scared of losing my family, but I don't want it without you. So, no matter what happens here on out, I got you, okay?"

"Okay," I rasp. "I love you too, Mabes. And I love our family. Just..."

What do I say? I want us back? I want what we had? Let's just erase everything and start over? Is it even possible? I glance at Levi. He's watching me closely, and when we make eye contact, he forces a smile. I love him and Brynn. I love Mabel and the guys. But am I going to have to lose one to have the other? I sigh, and then my phone starts beeping with another incoming call from Ham. I groan.

"I gotta go. Ham again. I love you."

"Love you," she says, then I click over to Hammond's call.

I don't even have a chance to say hello before he blows up on me.

"Have you lost your fucking mind, Savannah? On a fucking roof? With someone WHO ISN'T YOUR FIANCE?"

"Not my fiancé, Ham."

"Savannah, this is serious! I am fucking working my goddamn ass off trying to cover yours, and you can't even stay out of trouble for a couple of months? Are you using again, too? Were you fucking high wh—"

"No, Hammond, Jesus Christ. I wasn't high. I wasn't drinking. I've been sober for almost a year. Give me some fucking credit."

"I've been *trying* to give you credit and then you MAKE A FUCKING SEX TAPE!"

I hold the phone away from my ear as he bellows some more. The label this. Covering my ass that. I feel fucking guilty, but it has nothing to do with Hammond or Torren. I've already made up my mind to go back to the band, so this fake engagement bullshit has about run its course. But this is going to piss Levi off.

He didn't even want to be photographed with me. He's going to lose his damn mind when he finds out the most popular skag mag in America has a three-minute video of him fucking me on the roof.

"Hammond," I shout, trying to stop his tirade. He doesn't even pause. "HAMMOND, shut up! I get it, okay? I'll figure out how to fix it."

"You better hope nobody finds out that's not Torren with his dick in you, Savannah. You won't be able to come back from that. Just lay fucking low until I can figure out how to clean up your mess *again*."

Then he hangs up on me.

He hangs up on *me*, and the role-swapping puts me even more off-center. I drag my hand down my face, then sit up and turn to Levi.

He's sitting on the bed with his bandaged back to me. His cuts are healing, but the skin is still red and swollen around the gauze. Two days ago. Three? How long ago was it that we were sucked into those rapids? And why does it feel like this, whatever is coming, might be worse?

"Levi," I say tentatively. He doesn't answer, so I inch toward him on the bed. "Levi."

I put my hand out to touch his arm, but he stands quickly, brushing off my touch and then showing me his phone. He has the article open, and he is literally shaking with anger.

"I'm so sorry," I whisper. "I'm so sorry, Levi. They don't know it's you. They don't kno—"

He hurls his phone at the wall and my words incinerate in the rage emanating from him. He turns back to me and grabs my shoulders.

"You think I'm mad about that? Is that what you think?"

My mouth opens, then shuts, and I shrug.

"Yes? You said you didn't want the—"

"Torren fucking King, Savannah. All of America thinks you were fucking Torren King last night, but you are mine. Mine. Do you get it?"

His chest is heaving, his nostrils are flaring, and his teeth are clenched tight. The way he's shaking should scare me, but his grip on my shoulders is still gentle. It could just as easily be a caress.

"I don't get it," I say honestly. "You don't want to be in that magazine. You were adamant. You didn't want to be in the press."

He drops his hands and steps backward, clamping his eyes shut.

"I know. Fuck, I know."

He drags his hands through his hair and pulls at the root, and I wince for him.

"Fuck, Savannah."

"I'm sorry. I should have been more careful."

He sighs, but he doesn't open his eyes, and his body doesn't loosen. Anger and something else are still surging through him, rolling off him in waves.

"No. No, this isn't your fault. I was an equal participant. I could have stopped it."

"I'll figure out how to fix it. I'll keep your name out of it, Levi, I swear."

"You shouldn't have to keep my name out of it. If anyone is going to be in a leaked sex tape with you, it should be me. Not Torren King. Not *anybody*. It should fucking be me, but—"

"But it can't."

He shakes his head in response. *It can't be him.*

"So, what does this mean, then? You can't be with me and avoid the media attention, Levi. Me and the press, we're unfortunately a packaged deal. Match made in hell. There's no escaping them. Especially not when...well..."

"You're going back to the band."

His statement is resigned and tired. Not sad, but hollow, and it guts me. He already knew, but he was hoping against all reason that he was wrong. I swallow hard and nod.

"I have to," I whisper, my voice shaking as I fight back tears. "I have to, Levi."

"I know."

He crosses the floor and pulls me into a hug.

"You belong on that stage, Sav. You do."

I feel him kiss my hair, tightening his hold around me.

"I know."

But I belong to him, too...

36

WE'LL LIE LOW.

We'll "lie low."

Keep our distance, avoid each other, until she jets off to fucking Portofino at the end of the week. She doesn't even want Brynn coming for guitar lessons anymore. And I fucking hate it, but she's right.

I'm trying to protect you, she'd said. *I'll figure it out.*

It shouldn't be her protecting me. It should be me protecting her, or at the very fucking least, me protecting myself. Me protecting Brynn. But it's only been two fucking days, and I'm already about ready to storm her trailer. I'm even staying at Sharon's on her fucking couch because I don't trust myself not to interrupt another scene.

"This is dumb," Brynn says from where she's sitting in the office.

She has a book on the table and her tablet on the seat next to her, but she's staring at the floor.

"I should be learning Blackbird right now."

"She gave you her guitar to practice," Sharon says. "You could be learning it right now and surprise her when she comes back."

"She's not coming back, Ms. Sharon."

Brynn plops down dramatically across the couch and sighs.

"After this week, she goes to Italy, and after Italy, they go to New York, and after New York, she's going to go back to L.A."

Sharon flicks her eyes to me, but I've got nothing to say.

Is Brynn right? Will Savannah be back? If not, do I want to be wasting this last bit of time I have with her?

"Boss, how about you see if Cameron can video chat."

Brynn sighs loudly, but she picks up her tablet anyway. The moment Cameron answers the video chat and squeals their hello, Brynn hops off the couch and out the door to sit on the stairs. I turn to Sharon.

"I'm going to tell them. I'm going to just put it out there so I'm not fucking hiding anything anymore."

She blinks at me, and her forehead creases as her eyebrows slant.

"And if they try to fight you?"

"Let 'em. I've got the money from the studio now. I've got Clark on retainer. Let them try."

She takes a deep breath and glances at the door, then back at me.

"A lot could go wrong," she says, keeping her voice low, and my stomach swirls with the truth of it all.

A lot *could* go wrong. It could fuck up the entire life I've managed to piece together. But...

"I have to try, Sharon. I have to get it over with."

She looks at me, peering into my eyes as if she's reading my thoughts. I didn't know her well when I was younger, but I remember seeing her from time to time. Her eyes were always distant, sunken. She always appeared lost. I remember thinking Sharon was like a ghost. I couldn't believe Savannah was her daughter, because Sav was always bursting with life and vitality, while her mother seemed the opposite.

Now, though, with her sharp wit and keen eyes, she misses nothing, and I can finally see it. The resemblance is almost unnerving at times. I had to do a double take the day I found Sharon in that shelter after the storm. I thought my eyes were tricking me. I thought it was Savannah sitting on that cot. It was such a mindfuck, but when I realized who she actually was, I couldn't just leave her there. I had to help. If for nothing else, for Savannah. It was a way to feel closer to her even when she was miles, sometimes even continents, away from me.

I really hope that someday Savannah and Sharon can sit down and talk. Maybe work things out. They're cut from the same cloth. From how it sounds, they've had a lot of the same experiences, the same vices, and they've both managed to haul themselves out of that wreckage. That takes courage. That takes a strength a lot of people only wish they had. I think that could forge a bond, foster forgiveness, or at the very least, an understanding.

"Does this have to do with Savannah?" Sharon finally asks, and I answer honestly.

"It's something I've thought of doing for a while now, but ultimately, Sav is why I'm making the jump. She comes with media attention that I need to be able to face. I'm tired of hiding shit, of always looking over my damn shoulder. And now that Sav is back...I can't lose her again."

She nods.

"If you need anything, you can always use the—"

"I don't want your money, Sharon. Quit offering it. I don't need it now, anyway."

She huffs out a laugh and throws up her palms.

"Okay, forget I said it."

She takes a deep breath then hits me with a pointed look.

"So, when will you do it?"

I drum my fingers on the desk, glaring a hole in the wood top, trying to ignore my growing anxiety.

"I've got an appointment with Clark on Thursday to make sure all my loose ends are tied up, and then if everything is still good to go, I'll do it the start of next week."

"After Savannah has left."

I nod.

"It's easier that way."

She opens her mouth to say something else, but the door swings open and Brynn stomps inside, so our conversation halts. But when

I glance back at Sharon moments later, I can tell she hasn't stopped thinking about it.

About all the risks. All the ways it could go wrong.

I look at Brynn sitting on the couch reading her book and eating a bag of chips. God, for all of our sakes, everything better go right.

Friday at noon, I find myself outside of Savannah's trailer.

Today is the last day of filming. She leaves first thing tomorrow and the studio will have everything packed up by the end of the weekend. My meeting with Clark has me jumpy, nervous, and I just need Savannah right now.

I knock, and Red opens the door. When he sees me, he glances over my shoulder quickly, then ushers me inside. Ziggy attacks my legs, so I give her some head scratches. I look around the trailer, but Sav isn't here.

"Where is she?"

I look at Red, and he's typing on his phone.

"On the way," he says without looking up from the screen. "It's not smart for you to be here. There have been cameras all over ever since the article."

The article. What he means is the fucking three-minute tape of me and Sav on the roof. I close my eyes and nod.

"I'll be quick."

Red grunts. He slides his phone in his pocket, then takes a leash off the counter and hooks it on Ziggy's collar before hitting me with a serious stare.

"She's been through a lot, and you're a big risk for her right now, but she cares about you. Don't fuck it up."

I blink at him. I open my mouth to tell him I won't. That she's a risk for me too, but she's worth it. That I'm working on fixing it. But the door opens, and in steps Savannah. Her brown wig is shorter now. It's a bob instead of long waves because they're filming the final scenes of the movie. She looks like how'd she'd look now, today, if she'd never left. If she'd never become famous and dyed her hair silver. If she'd never run away.

She looks how she would have looked if she could have stayed. If she could have stayed and survived.

Sav looks at Red, something unspoken passing between them, and Red nods.

"Let's go, mutt," he says, then takes the dog out the door.

When he's gone, Savannah closes the distance and throws her arms around me. It's the best hug, and the tension in my body evaporates. When she brings her lips to mine, everything else disappears, and it's just me and her. I kiss her slowly, despite wanting to rush. It's been a matter of days, but it feels like eight years all over again. She pulls back and peers up at me, lips swollen from my lips. I finger a strand of her brown hair, then trace my fingertips over her jaw.

"What are you doing here?"

"I wanted to see you before you left."

It's only half the truth, but it's still the truth. I'm terrified she won't return. I'm terrified this is goodbye. I don't say it, but she searches my eyes and her brow furrows. She kisses me once more, then whispers against my lips.

"I'm coming back, Levi. I promise."

I close my eyes and rest my forehead on hers.

"Even if you don't, even if this is goodbye, I need you to know that I love you. Do you understand?"

"I do." I feel her smile. "I have two hours."

She kisses me firmly, then leans back and pulls my shirt over my head. I let her. She undoes the button on my jeans, pulls down the zipper, then pushes my pants and boxer briefs to the floor before pushing me back on the couch. I'm hard as a fucking stone pillar before my ass even hits the cushions.

She smirks, then takes off her own shirt, followed by her bra and pants, until she's standing above me wearing nothing but her wig.

"Two hours now."

She straddles my thighs, taking my dick in her hands and rubbing it through her already wet pussy.

"Then in four weeks, I'll be back for you."

When she sinks down onto me, we both groan before our mouths collide. I grip her hips, moving her back and forth slowly, feeling her slide over me, grinding on top of me. Her breasts press against my chest, and when she starts to move up and down, her nipples graze my skin. We never stop kissing except to murmur our praises. There's never more than an inch between our faces.

"You feel so good," she whispers, her hot breath mixing with mine. "I love you inside me."

I thrust up into her and she moans.

"Oh, fuck, Levi. Oh, fuck."

I speed up, pulsing my cock up as she thrusts down, meeting in the middle in a way that hits deeper, tighter, than ever before. The trailer fills with the sounds of us. Our bodies moving, our skin rubbing, our breath coming in pants. Her legs start to shake, her mouth opens, and her eyes clamps shut, so I take over. Her body stills and I pound into her, hard and fast.

"Yes, yes, yes. Like that. I'm so close."

"Good, baby. Let me have it."

I dig my fingers into the soft skin at her hips. Kiss her again savagely, then growl into her mouth.

"Let go. Give it to me. Give me your cum."

She explodes with a cry, squeezing me tightly, digging her fingers into my shoulders. I don't stop until she's clamping her legs around my thighs, then I flip us so she's on her back beneath me.

"Inside me," she groans out, as I move in and out of her once more. "I want it inside me."

That does it. I don't question it. I give her exactly what she wants, how she wants it. I pump into her, her pussy clenching around me, until I lose it. I kiss her, groaning into her mouth as I spill into her pussy. I thrust into her until I'm spent, until there's nothing left, and then I collapse onto my forearms.

Our bodies, sweaty and exhausted, stay pressed together as we both try to come back down to earth, then Savannah laughs lightly. She reaches up and pats my ass twice before smirking against my lips.

"Good boy."

I grin and shake my head.

"You're such a brat."

She shrugs.

"Guess you'll just have to spank me harder next time."

I bark out a laugh this time, then bend down and bite her breast. She gasps and swats my ass again, so I push off her and move into the small bathroom. I grab a hand towel from the cabinet below the sink, wet it with warm water, then go back to Savannah.

Without a word, I kneel beside the couch and press the washcloth gently between her legs. She's red and swollen, and I can't help but stare as I clean her up.

"Tighten your muscles," I say, and she does.

I groan as I watch my cum leak from her, store the image in my memory for when she's gone, then wipe her clean.

When we're dressed, she disappears into the small bedroom and comes back seconds later with my old bike lock on her chain necklace. Then she reaches into the pocket of my jeans and pulls out my keys. I watch silently as she takes the bike lock key off my keychain and unlocks the bike lock, then she slides the key onto her necklace and secures the bike lock on my key ring.

"Now I have to come back," she says with a grin. "Sav Loveless can't perform without her lock necklace."

She walks me to the door and kisses me once more before I open it and step onto the stairs. Red is waiting patiently, arms crossed, right outside the trailer with Ziggy lying on the ground beside him. He has aviators on, but I can feel his eyes on me. I give him a single nod as I step onto the street. I get a few yards away before Savannah's voice calls out to me.

"Hey, Weenie!"

I turn back to the trailer to find her leaning on the frame of the door with that mischievous grin that used to own me. That still does, if I'm being honest with myself. I cock my head to the side and wait, and her grin stretches wider.

"Don't forget about me."

My smile is immediate, and I laugh to myself as I take her in. Beautiful and fascinating and wild. When I respond, I feel the truth in my words all the way to my toes.

"I could never."

She laughs, nods at me, then goes back into her trailer and shuts the door. I'm on a high when I turn back to my truck, but with each step, my smile fades and my anxiety invades. The obstacles I have to face are closing in on me. There are so many things in the way before I can have Savannah freely. Entirely. I know how I feel about her. I know I have to trust the universe on this one, but the universe has been a fickle bitch in the past. It's never been on our side.

And it's not lost on me that Savannah didn't say she loved me back.

That *don't forget about me* could just as easily have been a goodbye. Just like last time.

I get into my truck and drive back to the office. I take Brynn around to do some site checks. We're finishing up the final house in the River View neighborhood. Another connection to Savannah severed. I feel like she's slipping through my fingers.

By Sunday, my house is back in the same condition it was two weeks ago. It's like the film crew was never here. I got her back for a matter of days, and now she's been all but erased. Sunday night, I'm scouring the internet for any mention of my name when I find an article about The Hometown Heartless, and a slew of photos allegedly from Saturday night.

From what I thought, Sav would have been on an international flight to Italy, but according to these photos, she was in L.A. She's walking into her record label's offices with the rest of the band. Mabel in front, Jonah in back, and Sav and Torren in the middle. His arm is around her, and on her finger is that fucking emerald engagement ring. The next set of photos is of the band leaving the offices hours later. It's dark and there's no clear shots of Sav's hands, but Torren is still right beside her.

I don't read the article. I close out of it and pour myself a whiskey on the rocks.

This is for the best right now. Until my meeting on Wednesday with the lawyers and the Larks, my name needs to stay out of the tabloids. Keeping the attention on Sav and Torren is a good thing.

Even if I fucking hate it.

37

ON WEDNESDAY, my phone wakes me at five in the morning.

I groan as I roll over to grab it. In my haze of exhaustion, my eyes don't focus on the phone when I accept the call, so the video chat surprises me. I'm shocked even more to see a distraught Savannah on the other end.

I shoot upright in the bed.

"What's wrong? Are you okay?"

"Levi...I'm so sorry. It broke a few hours ago, but I didn't see it until just now. I'm so fucking sorry."

"What? What broke?"

She sighs and closes her eyes. She shakes her head.

"They know. It's all over the internet. Pictures of us at the ER. Pictures of you leaving my trailer on Friday. Someone came forward and said they saw Torren return to the hotel the night of the show downtown, so now they know it was you on the roof."

"Fuck." I push my hands through my hair and try to control my breathing. "Fuck."

"I'm so sorry."

"No...It's not your fault. It's not that big of a deal. I've got a meeting in three hours. I'll...it'll be okay. I wish I'd had a little more time, but it will be okay."

"Levi..."

Her voice breaks, and her eyes are so sad. They're filled with a regret I can feel even though she's across the world.

"What is it, Sav?"

"Levi, they're saying Brynnlee isn't your daughter."

The breath is sucked from my lungs, dread coiling around my windpipe and squeezing. I drop the phone on my bed and stand, going straight for my laptop. I open it and go to a web browser, then search Sav's name.

Every single headline that pops up in the search results is about me. Sav Loveless's newest "affair." They think she's still engaged to Torren, and they're using the photos from L.A. a few days ago as proof. The comments on some of these articles are vicious. Spewing vitriol at Sav. At me. Wishing death on us both.

I ignore those, though. Instead, I skim the article until I find what I'm looking for. It's all there. All of it, in bold font on the internet. Every article mentions it. There must be a dozen of them all saying the same thing.

Levi Cooper. Business owner. Widower. Single father to an adopted seven-year-old daughter.

"Fuck. *Fuck.*"

I slam the laptop closed and stalk back to the bed. I pick up the phone and take in Savannah's face once more. It's full of questions. Questions and sorrow. Remorse. I close my eyes and breathe.

"Is she yours?" Savannah asks, and my jaw tightens before I answer.

"Yes. In every way that matters, yes. She's mine."

"But...is she..."

"No."

The silence fills the room, and I wait for her to ask more questions. I want to tell her. I've been hiding it for so fucking long, but she doesn't say anything. Not a sound. So instead, I just start talking.

"It was Julianna who...initiated...the night we slept together. She'd just broken up with this guy a few weeks earlier, and I just assumed it was some sort of rebound thing. I just wanted to get it over with. Having sex, I mean. I was curious, and horny as fuck, and done doing what my parents wanted. But that's why I was so upset and confused in Miami. I did everything right. Wore a condom. She was on birth control. I looked it up. It's less than a 2% chance. Turns out, though, she was already pregnant."

Savannah gasps.

"She...tricked you?"

I shrug and sigh.

"It's not how you think. Fuck, this is such a mess."

She waits in the quiet while I collect my thoughts, then I make eye contact and I don't break it again.

"Julianna was at a party. She was drugged. She would never tell me who the guy was, but I think she knew. She knew, and she was scared. I think she felt guilty, too. Like the pregnancy was her fault. Looking back, there were signs, you know? But I didn't know."

I take a deep breath and fight the urge to look away. I've beaten myself up over it so much since I learned the truth. There were signs that something wasn't right. I should have picked up on them, but I thought she was a virgin and was nervous. She was uncomfortable even though she kept telling me she wanted it. Hell, I was uncomfortable. I thought we felt that way for the same reasons.

I was so fucking wrong.

I shake my head and plow forward. Even though it hurts, even though I feel so fucking ashamed, it's a relief to say it out loud.

"She didn't want her parents raising the baby, but she didn't think she could do it alone, so she tried to make it look like I was the father. We went to church together. We were kind of friends. She trusted me. I guess she knew I'd step up."

"She trapped you. She lied."

Savannah's anger mixes with her sadness, and I feel it, too. I felt the exact same thing for a long time. But it doesn't matter. Jules was right. I did step up, and I don't regret it. I'd do it again. I *nod*, because she did lie, but she didn't trap me.

"This one...." I sigh and close my eyes. "It exists in the gray space, Sav."

She scoffs, but I keep talking.

"I was there for every ultrasound. Every doctor's appointment. I was there for the baby shower. We got an apartment together off campus. We decorated a nursery. Fuck, I was in the delivery room when she was born. I picked her middle name. At first, I hated all of it. I did it all reluctantly. Out of duty. But then...I don't know. At some point during the pregnancy, I started to get excited. I wanted to meet her. I wanted to hold her. I meant it when I said I never fell in love with Julianna, but I respected her, and Sav, I *did* fall in love with Brynn. I fell in love with her before she was even born. I *wanted* to be her dad."

I breathe through the pain. The ache of betrayal rattles through my rib cage, fresh and raw. It's like ripping a scab off a wound. Tearing open stitches. It fucking hurts just like it did the first time.

"When did you find out?"

"About an hour after she was born," I say with a dark chuckle.

"How?"

I tap the cleft in my chin.

"I read once that it's a dominant trait, but Brynn doesn't have one. Once I noticed, I couldn't stop thinking about that statistic. Less than 2%. So, I tried to figure out the math of the pregnancy. I'd never done that before. I just trusted Julianna. Then I asked, and she told me the truth."

Savannah is gaping at me with her eyebrows slanted in concern. Her eyes have welled with tears, and she looks like she's feeling the pain with me. We're connected, and for once, I don't feel like I'm shouldering all this alone. Sav shakes her head in disbelief.

"But you stayed with her?"

"No. I was gutted. I was furious. I wanted Brynn to be mine, Sav, and I was fucking broken. I told Julianna she could keep the apartment, but I left the hospital and moved my shit out that night. I crashed with one of my classmates for the rest of the semester. Slept on the fucking couch. I completely cut her off. I let her keep telling people Brynn was mine, let everyone believe I was a fucking deadbeat. Hell, I felt like one, and it fucked with me for a while, but I was too hurt to go back to Julianna."

"Until she got sick."

I nod.

"Julianna's parents are horrible. Worse than mine were. Obviously, the biological father, whoever the fuck he is, is terrible, too. Jules didn't want to die and...Anyway, I married her and legally adopted Brynn. Got my name put on the birth certificate and everything. To protect Brynnlee in case Jules died. To make sure she never fell into the Lark's clutches."

"Jesus. This is a mind-fuck," Sav breathes out. Pretty much sums it up. "Levi, the shit you had to go through..."

"I don't regret it. Not all of it. Brynn *is* mine, Sav, but Julianna's parents have been trying to get custody ever since Jules died. They have a life insurance payout that they keep trying to bribe me with. But they don't have a claim on her—they wouldn't stand a chance in court. The only person who could..."

"Would be the biological father."

I don't say anything, but she's right. Julianna never told the guy she was pregnant. If he found out and wanted Brynn, he very well could take her from me.

"How'd they find out?" I muse. "I've kept it all quiet. The Larks don't know I'm not Brynn's biological father."

Savannah huffs out a small, dark laugh.

"They're ruthless vultures. Once they got my records from one of my rehab stays. Blackmailed me. I had to pay them to keep quiet. I swear they could solve world hunger if they used their powers for good, but instead they choose to destroy lives and invade privacy in the name of clickbait."

What a fucking mess.

I wouldn't put it past Julianna's parents to try and use this against me, now. For months after she died, I would have nightmares of them breaking into my house and snatching Brynn from her bed. Before now, I didn't have the money for a lawsuit. I was in debt up to my fucking scalp with all the money I poured into Jules's experimental treatments. All the money I'd spent on the house and the business. I was barely treading water before the studio contract.

That's why I kept the secret for so long. Why I wanted to avoid any media attention. Hell, I wouldn't even do interviews for the local paper after the hurricane. In the aftermath, everyone wanted to know more about the rebuilds and restorations. I made Dustin give updates about the rebuild projects to the local news. I kept my name off the East Coast Contracting website. And there was never any mention of Brynn anywhere.

I've flown as far under the radar as I could, but I'm tired of it, and I know I can't have Savannah without the media. Like she said, they're a packaged deal, and I could never ask her to leave the band.

"I actually have a meeting with them today. Jules's parents, I mean. I'm telling them the truth, all of it. My lawyer has helped. I have the money to fight them in court if they want to try. I finally feel secure enough to come clean."

I laugh and give her a half-hearted grin. I was preparing to face The Larks, but the world? Talk about diving in headfirst.

"I don't know how this whole sex tape and dating the most infamous rockstar of our generation is going to go over, but my lawyer has assured me that my custody of Brynn is secure."

She grimaces, like she feels guilty, then changes the subject.

"Does Brynn know?"

"She does. I don't lie to my daughter. She knows I'm not her biological dad, and that her biological dad wasn't a very good person. She also knows it's best if we don't tell people. She's never been a fan of her grandparents, so her telling them hasn't been a concern. Brynn and I know. Sharon knows. My lawyer knows. My father suspected before he died because Jules confided in him after she was raped, since he was the head of our church. And now you and everyone on the internet knows."

She closes her eyes and presses a palm to her forehead, then lets out a frustrated groan.

"I keep saying it. I know I must sound like a broken record, but I'm so sorry. This never would have happened if it weren't for me. I should have been more careful. I should have stayed—"

"Don't say that," I say, cutting her off. "Don't you dare say that you should have stayed away from me. The universe brought you back to me for a reason, Savannah. You and me, we're fated. We have been since you pushed me off the swing set in second grade. I was in love with you before I even hit the dirt, so don't cheapen this. Don't downplay it. We're going to get through it, we're going to overcome everything, and then we're going to be together. This? You and me? We're endgame. You know it. I know it. The fucking universe knows it, and pretty soon, the world is going to know it, too."

Savannah's lips turn up into a small smile, her eyes flashing with mirth. Then she sniffles and wipes away a few stray tears.

"I thought I was a brat. I thought you said I was too wild for my own good."

I drag my gaze over her face. Her gray eyes. Her smirking lips. The smattering of freckles on her nose. Even her messy, untamed silver hair. She's perfect. My perfect storm.

"You are. But you're *my* brat. You're *my* kind of wild."

She laughs through her tears, and it's loud and raspy and real. Sunshine breaking through rainclouds.

"You know, this possessive side you're showing could be considered a red flag."

Now it's my turn to laugh.

"I think red's always been your favorite color."

She rolls her eyes playfully, but she doesn't deny it. She doesn't argue.

"Want some potentially good news?" she says after a minute.

There is a subtle lightness in her voice that I know she only half feels.

"I was going to wait to tell you until it was all figured out, but now's as good a time as any."

I lie back on my bed and hold the phone above me. Savannah is sitting on a chair on what looks like a porch or a deck of some sort. It's around noon where she is, and the weather looks beautiful.

"Tell me your good news, Rockstar."

"I think we're going to be able to negotiate a new contract with the label. I've got the band on my side now. We don't want to break up. We want to tour more. Keep making music. But we can't keep going on like we've been, you know? Hammond had a new contract drawn up and everything. He's even threatened to walk and come with us if we leave."

"He did?"

I'm shocked, actually. From what I've heard of him, he definitely struck me as a label puppet. I wouldn't have expected him to try and help. Savannah nods, eyes wide as she watches something just off the side of the phone screen.

"I know. But in his defense, he did tell us not to sign that first contract." She shrugs. "Should have listened to him. The new contract requires a year down time between touring and one third less shows. Control of all our masters for the next two albums, and the right to re-record the songs on our previous albums when the original contract expires."

My jaw drops. That sounds...impossible. Amazing, but impossible. There's no way the label will go for that. Savannah must read my thoughts on my face because she laughs.

"I know. Ham says they'll probably try to renegotiate parts of it, but he thinks we have a shot. They don't want to lose the hottest band in music, especially now that they know we'll gladly take our talent elsewhere instead of break up, and they don't want to lose Hammond."

She scrunches up her nose and bounces a little in her seat.

"We got a shot, Levi. We've got a real shot at this working. And then for once, finally, we can do things our way. No more running on empty and killing ourselves for deadlines. No more living in busses and hotel rooms for ten months out of the year. Less stress. Less tension. Just music, and the band. And fuck, Levi, that's all I've wanted since we started this thing. It really, truly, might work."

I give her a smile. I try to let her excitement fuel mine.

Do I want this for her? I meant it when I said she belongs on that stage. But she also belongs with me. How can we work if she goes back to the band? Touring, recording, and whatever else famous musicians do. How long could we possibly last?

She chose that life over me once. Would she do it again?

"I'm happy for you guys. I really hope it works out for you."

I say it, but part of me doesn't mean it.

"How's Paul Northwood?"

I need a subject change, but I don't know why my brain went to Hollywood's golden boy. I want to wince, but I don't. Instead, I focus on the way Sav's lips twitch into a smirk.

"Jealous again, Weenie?"

I resist the urge to roll my eyes, but I can't fight the scoff. She giggles and waggles her brows at me.

"We had a great scene today. I was half-naked. There was red wine and chocolate. It was really sexual."

I grit my teeth. I did this to myself.

"Or at least it was. Until I stabbed him in the back with a chef's knife and shoved him off the balcony of the villa."

I bark out a laugh, and she shrugs.

"You got nothing to worry about, Levi. No one competes with you. No one ever has."

I smile and work to control my breathing.

No one person, maybe. But what about a stadium full of people? What about a country full of stadiums full of people? Can I compete with them?

"That child should be with her family," my mother says into the phone. "It shouldn't be your responsibility."

I'm two seconds away from hanging up on her. I don't know why I haven't done it already.

"I *am* her family. She should be with me, and that's where she'll stay."

I'm frustrated, irritated, and exhausted, and my tone reflects that. She's been calling me nonstop since my meeting on Wednesday with the Larks. I finally caved and answered, just to get it over with, then listened to her berate me for ten minutes about how I should have answered sooner. I've had enough stressing me out with all the assholes with cameras camped outside my house. I don't need another annoyance, and for some fucking reason, I can't bring myself to block her.

"Helen and William are her blood. They are half of her. You can't possibly think you could do a better job raising her than they could. Especially not now that *that girl* has returned. I mean really, Levi, a sex scandal? I always knew she was trouble."

I don't bother responding to her comments about Savannah. My mother's opinions don't matter. They're just air.

"Well, what do you have to say for yourself? If you had the sense God gave you, you would give the child back to the Larks. It's better for you. You don't know what runs through the child's veins."

"The child is named Brynnlee, and the lawyers already told William and Helen that she's staying with me. She is *my* daughter. What runs through her veins doesn't matter, and if the Larks try to take me to court, it will just cost them time and money, because they won't win."

I check my watch. Sharon should be here any minute to pick Brynn up. She's taking her shopping for back-to-school clothes. Brynn decided that I'm not cool enough to take her shopping this year. How the hell is summer almost over?

"Trust me, Levi, you'll be better off if you just sign over cust—"

"Mother. Stop. I'm done having this conversation with you."

I hear her huff on the other end, then a long slow inhale followed by a long, slow exhale, before she speaks again.

"Everything in this world that I've done, it's been for you."

I scoff. It's always shocked me just how strongly my mother believes her own delusions. As if manipulating Bible verses for the sake of controlling me was ever for my own good. She wields her religion as a weapon. She uses it to feel superior, to justify her hatred, and she really believes the shit she's slinging. In her mind, she really sees herself as a self-sacrificing, saintly mother.

"Okay," I say flatly.

"Remember that I tried."

She hangs up. I pinch the bridge of my nose between my thumb and forefinger. This whole thing is giving me a migraine. I think I'd rather take another jaunt through the fucking rapids than another phone conversation with Judith Cooper.

I hear my front door open, then close, and Sharon steps into the kitchen.

"Good lord, do those people ever leave?"

She throws a scowl behind her, as if the paparazzi assholes on the street can feel it through the walls. I shake my head.

"Haven't yet."

I keep hoping they'll get bored and go away once this whole mess dies down, but as of right now, the media thinks Sav Loveless is still engaged to Torren King, and they see me as the potential homewrecker.

"Have you told Savannah?"

"No."

"Shouldn't you?"

"No."

I'm not going to worry her with this bullshit. She's still filming. She's stressed about the contract negotiations with the label. She feels terrible about the news of Brynn's adoption going global. I'm not about to pile any more shit on top. Besides, Sav and the media go hand in hand, right? If she's what I want, then I need to decide if this is something I can handle.

Sharon sighs and sets her purse on the counter, so I call up the stairs for Brynn.

"Boss, Ms. Sharon is here!"

Brynn is bounding down the stairs and into the kitchen seconds later. She's wearing jean shorts and a The Hometown Heartless t-shirt, and she flops down onto the floor and starts pulling on her shoes.

"I know what I want for my birthday."

I raise an eyebrow. "I thought you wanted the digital encyclopedia membership thing."

"Not anymore." Brynn pushes back to standing and flashes me a grin. "I want an electric guitar like Sav's."

"What's wrong with the acoustic one she gave you?"

"That's *different,* Dad." My daughter rolls her eyes and sighs. "She's your girlfriend now so she can help you pick a good one."

Of course. I flick my eyes to Sharon and find her smirking at me. With all of the media attention, the only thing Brynn has focused on is the relationship between me and Savannah. Brynn already knew she was adopted, so that didn't bother her. But after I explained that Sav isn't actually engaged to Torren King, Brynn has latched onto me and Sav *dating*.

It's times like this I wish she wasn't such an advanced reader. I can put parent controls on her tablet, but I can't keep her from seeing the printed magazines in the grocery store checkout line.

Honestly, she's been handling it all better than I'd expected, but I keep having to remind her that Sav has a life in Los Angeles. That I have a relationship with her, but we're not exactly dating, and I don't know what that means for the future. I'm trying to prep my daughter for something I still am not even ready for.

I try to fight the nagging feeling that I've set my daughter up for yet another loss. I'm doing the best I can, but fuck, it never feels like enough.

I look back to Brynn.

"I'll see what I can do."

No way I can get a guitar exactly like Savannah's. That thing is custom and probably cost a small fortune. But I might be able to get something similar before the birthday party.

I hand Sharon my credit card and make eye contact.

"Use this for the clothes," I say.

She takes it with a placating smile, but I know she won't use it. I'll just have to figure out how to pay her extra when payroll goes out next month.

"Ready to roll, Boss?"

Brynn grins at Sharon and gives her two thumbs up.

"Ready to roll, Ms. Sharon!"

I follow them to the door, then watch from the porch as they climb into Sharon's car. The asshats with the cameras mill about and take their pictures, and I glare at them. I called the county sheriff on them on Friday, and since then they've been staying across the street. Don't know how long that will last, but for now, the sheriff has a patrol car circling the block once an hour. We'll have to come up with something different when Sav comes back.

If she comes back.

I turn and walk back into the house.

One more week in Portofino. Then New York. Then...

She hasn't mentioned staying in North Carolina, and I would never ask that of her. She's too big for this small town. I know that. But Sav hasn't asked me to come with her to California, either. And even if she did, would I?

I walk out to the deck and stare out at the surf. The beach is full of people today. It has been ever since the production crew left and removed the barricades. I put my hands on the deck railing, noting how different it feels without my ring. I took it off the day Sav left.

I didn't build this house for Savannah. Not really. That would suggest I expected her to come back to me, and I didn't.

I hoped for it.

Dreamed about it.

But never expected it.

I didn't build it *for* her. I built it *about* her. Every line on the design plans was intentional. Every room has a Savannah-related purpose. Even the colors were chosen with her image in mind. Her moods. Her dreams.

I couldn't be with her, but I couldn't be without her, so I built her into the walls. I immersed myself in Savannah the only way I knew how.

Was it fair to my wife? Probably not. But Julianna and I never tried to make our marriage something it wasn't. She had her ways of coping, and I had mine.

If I close my eyes, I can picture Savannah here. Practicing her songs in the music room. Hanging her skateboards on the rack on the mudroom wall. Making stacks of pancakes in the chef's kitchen. Spending long, lazy mornings with me right here on this deck.

But in my fantasy, which Savannah is it? And when the sun sets, where will we end the day? My repurposed guest bedroom, or my dead wife's bedroom?

I tighten my hands on the banister and squeeze tightly, putting pressure on the base of my ring finger until it hurts. No silicone barrier. No ring.

If Savannah asked me to move California with her, would I go?

A loud knock on the door pulls me from my thoughts. I check my watch as I head back into the house. It could be Brynn and Sharon with their hands loaded with shopping bags. Brynn could have forgotten her key.

My hackles rise as another loud knock bangs on the door, and I pick up my pace.

If it's another one of those camera wielding hyenas, or some random gossip rag reporter, I might lose my fucking mind. I swing the door open just as the person on the other side goes to knock again.

For a breath, I just stare at them and the smarmy grin plastered on their face.

I step out onto the front porch, making my visitor fall back a step, and pull the door shut. I glance across the street and find camera lenses pointed right at me. I clench my teeth and fold my arms across my chest.

"When did they let you out," I ask gruffly, and Terry chuckles.

"'Bout six months ago. Good behavior."

I don't laugh at his joke. I don't match his creepy fucking grin. I just stare at him with narrowed eyes and work to keep my cool.

"Where is she?" he asks finally, and I stand straighter. Defensive.

I won't let him within fifty feet of Sharon. She's worked too fucking hard to let this sleazy ass waste of life try to undo everything she's done. I drag my eyes over him. New clothes. New shoes. His dark curly hair is still long and stringy, just how I remember it, but he looks like he's showered recently.

His eyes, though. Something about those beady, yellow-ringed eyes.

Good behavior my ass.

"She doesn't want to see you."

He laughs again. Unbothered. Like he thinks this is a game.

"How you know? D'you ask her?"

"I know." I glance back over his shoulder. When was the last time the police car rolled by? Will they be here any minute or do I have to wait for another hour? I do a quick scan of his body just before hitting him with another glare. "You've overstayed your welcome. Leave."

Without turning my back on him, I reach down to open the door, but he steps forward.

"Back the fuck up, Terry."

He narrows his eyes angrily at first, then forces a smile.

"I just want to talk to her. I want to say hi. I should get to know her since we'll be spending so much time together soon, right?"

"Stay away from her," I say, my voice shaking with the force of my restraint. I scan him quickly once more looking for the outline of a gun or a hidden holster, but I see nothing. "Get the fuck off my property."

"You can't keep the kid from me for long. We're blood."

Every nerve ending in my body buzzes. Warning signals start to blare in my ears. I hold my breath. This time, when I look him over, I pay attention to different things. Dark brown curly hair. Light blue eyes. No chin cleft. I swallow hard before speaking.

"Who are you talking about?"

His lips break into a wide grin, showing off stained teeth. When he speaks, it's like he's told a joke and I'm the punchline.

"My daughter, of course."

I blink at him and tighten my fist around the doorknob. Brynn.

"You're lying."

He shrugs.

"Guess we'll find out after the paternity test."

Fuck. Fuck. Fuck.

The more I stare at him, the more I believe it. Sharon had said Terry had been selling at college parties. Julianna was drugged at a party. She said the guy was dangerous. She was adamant about wanting to move away from our hometown. It's how I ended up here on the coast, too. When Jules called me and told me she was sick, she was already here. She refused to move back home with her parents. I thought it was just because her parents are terrible, but now...

"It won't matter," I say slowly, trying to mask my panic. "No judge in their right mind would give you custody of a child, blood or not."

I mean it, too. I know it won't work. It's going to be hell for Brynn, but I'm almost certain they wouldn't take her from me and give her to this fuckhead. Terry snorts and rolls his eyes. He doesn't care about custody. He doesn't care about Brynn. And then it dawns on me.

"The Larks put you up to this."

He ignores me and pulls a pack of cigarettes out of his pocket. He puts one in his mouth and lights it up as my thoughts fall off my tongue.

"You don't want Brynn. They do. What are they offering you?"

He blows a slow stream of smoke out of his nostrils and raises an eyebrow.

"The fucking life insurance money. That's it, isn't it?"

His grin breaks, and he winks at me.

"And all I have to do is take a test and stick around for a few court hearings."

My blood is boiling. They'd stoop this low, scrape the bottom of the fucking scum bucket, just to try and get control of Brynn. They don't care about what this could do to her. They don't care about what this would have done to their own fucking daughter.

"It won't work," I seethe. "There is no way in hell I'm going to let them take her from me. You can fucking tell them that. Over my dead fucking body will I ever let William and Helen Lark take my kid from me."

The sleaze bag grin is gone from Terry's face, and he sneers.

"That can be arranged."

I'm seconds from hitting him. If he so much as steps toward me, I'll swing. Then a car comes up the road and we both look toward it. I expect to see a cop car swinging through for their hourly patrol, but instead it's Sharon and Brynn coming back from shopping.

I know the moment Terry recognizes who's driving the car, because his body goes as rigid as mine. I stare at the car, willing Sharon to drive off, but she pulls into the driveway instead.

"What the fuck," Terry growls, then starts stalking toward the car. "Sharon? Sharon."

I step in front of him and push his chest.

"Back up." I growl, shoving him again as he tries to push past. "Back the fuck up, Terry."

"Sharon!" he shouts. "You fucking bitch! That bitch put me in prison. You put me in fucking prison!"

I shove him again, plastering my body against his and he struggles to get past me. He reaches behind his body, and I grab his arm just as he pulls something from his waistband.

A fucking gun.

"Get in the house!" I shout, hoping like hell Sharon and Brynn can hear me. That they can get there faster than this asshole can pull out his gun. "Get in the fucking house!"

Terry grunts as he struggles with me, and I hear the car doors shut just as I kick his legs out from under him. Even plastered to the ground, he doesn't stop trying to get to Sharon. He's possessed. He's fucking psychotic, and the only thing I've got going for me is that he's smaller than me. Has he always been this fucking small?

"Get over here, you bitch!"

He tries to knee me in the gut. I hear clicks around me. People closing in. The fucking paparazzi.

"He's got a gun," I shout at them. Fighting with Terry. Worrying about these assholes. They're going to be the reason someone gets killed. "Back up. Call the cops. He's got a fucking gun."

"I'm going to kill her! I'm going to kill you!"

"Shut the fuck up," I grind out, then let go of him with one hand so I can punch him in the side.

He grunts but doesn't stop shouting. Doesn't stop moving. I try to keep track of his hands. As long as I can keep his hands visible, we're good. Sharon and Brynn are safe inside.

But I feel like I've been on this ground forever. I'm sweating. I'm panting. I'm trying so hard not to freak out that I'm starting to freak out.

"Someone call the fucking cops!"

I shout at the idiots surrounding me, just as I hear the siren of a cop car. Then car doors. Shouting and running.

I hear someone shout at the paparazzi, telling them if they don't disperse off my private property, they'll be arrested. I don't pay attention to if they actually comply. I wait for a cop to take control of the asshole with the gun, but they don't get to me in time.

I must have let up, must have diverted my focus, because Terry manages to twist and catches my jaw with an elbow. The gun goes off, everyone screams, and then Terry takes off running.

I push to my feet and start to run after him, but a cop throws his body in front of me, pushing at my chest.

"Stop. They'll get him. You stay here."

I look at the officer in front of me. Max. I've known him since I moved here. He's watched Brynn grow up. His wife stocked our freezer when Julianna's cancer got worse and we were spending a lot of time in the hospital. They came to her funeral.

"Are you hit?"

I look down at my uninjured body, then glance around at the ground. No gun.

"No." I nod in the direction he ran. "He's still armed."

Another patrol car pulls up. More yelling at the paparazzi. They've at least moved across the street now. I watch as two officers discuss something off to the side of my yard.

"Levi. Who the hell was that?"

I look back at Max. His question shocks me for a minute, and then I remember that Terry wasn't an infamous figure in this town. His arrest was fairly widely known, but it didn't generate nearly as much attention here as it did in the town where I grew up.

I consider my options. I scan Max's face and find nothing but concern.

"That, apparently, is Brynn's biological father. Terry Martin." I take a deep breath and look down the street where the cop car and Terry have disappeared. I can still hear the sirens. "And I'm going to need to get a restraining order. Probably a few of them."

38

I PRESS call for the fifth time in five minutes.

It goes straight to voicemail.

I'm about ready to lose my shit. I close out and dial again as I buckle the seatbelt across my lap. I haven't flown commercial in years. I've used the label's jet for tours, and the studio chartered a private jet for us to get to Portofino. It was last minute, but I was able to charter my own out of Milan to get to Raleigh.

I had already planned to fly back for Brynn's birthday, anyway. A few days early isn't doing any damage for the film.

I dial again. Voicemail.

"Hey, it's me. I'm on a plane. I've got in-flight Wi-Fi and okayed the call with the pilot, so call me when you get this please."

I pause. I open my mouth twice to say it, but I can't. It doesn't feel right to do it over the phone.

"See you soon."

I hang up, then glance at Red in the pod next to me. He's got my sixty-pound mutt sleeping on his lap, and it makes me smile despite the circumstances. I have no idea how it's going to work when Ziggs has to pee. It's a little over thirteen hours non-stop from Milan to Raleigh, and there's no fucking way she'll be able to hold it. We brought some puppy pads, so we'll see.

Red blinks at me, and I shrug.

"He still won't answer."

"Try not to worry. Get a little sleep. He's probably busy."

I nod. Busy.

I open my phone and scroll back through the article that Hammond sent me. Levi in an altercation with Terry. Levi on the ground with Terry. Levi, sporting a bruised jaw and a scowl, talking with an officer.

Shots fired. No known injuries. Sav Loveless's lover. Suspect at large.

My nerves are shot. I'm worried for Levi and Brynn. I'm terrified for my mom. What would he want with her now? I did an internet search and found out he was released six months ago. Had he been looking for her this whole time? As far as I know, she hasn't been in a single article online. It's just been photos of me and Levi, and discussions about his adopted, nameless daughter.

I don't know how he found her, but I'm pretty sure it's my fault.

It's literally all my fault.

I turn on the television in front of me and flip through the available movies. There are a bunch of Paul Northwood's romcoms, which makes me chuckle. The world isn't ready to see Paul in this role. Money laundering, drug running, philandering Paul Northwood? The housewives are going to lose their minds.

And wait until they watch me kill him.

I feel a spark of mischievous glee before I remember just exactly where I am and where I'm going. I turn the television off and take out my lyric notebook. I pop in my earbuds, cycle through the melodies I roughly recorded with my phone and write. At least I've gotten some songs out of this whole mess.

Songs and Levi.

I smile.

That's really all I've ever wanted, isn't it? A purpose, an outlet, and him.

My phone rings three hours into the flight, and I answer it immediately. My voice is hushed and full of concern.

"Levi. Is everything okay? What is going on?"

I hear him sigh and the small bit of relief I felt seeing his name on my phone screen vanishes.

"Levi. What the hell is going on?"

"You shouldn't be on a plane, Sav. You should be filming in Italy."

I bristle at the authority in his tone.

"Let me worry about my filming schedule."

"I'm just saying. There's no reason for you to be on the way—"

"Levi. Shut up. I'm already cruising at thirty-five thousand feet so table the daddy mindset and answer my damn question."

He laughs lightly, which makes me smirk, and then he sighs again.

"I'm guessing you saw that I had a visitor?"

"Yep. Is Sharon okay? How did he find her? What does he even want with her."

Silence.

"Levi. Is Sharon okay?"

"Yes. She's okay. Shook up, but okay. But he didn't initially come for Sharon."

I gasp.

"For me? Fuck, this really is all my fault. Fuck."

"Not for you. He didn't even mention you, actually." He pauses. I hear him inhale and exhale. "He came to see Brynn."

What? For Brynn...

"That doesn't make any sense. Why would he show up wanting to see Brynn?"

More silence.

"Levi, Jesus, just talk."

"He's claiming to be Brynn's biological father."

Now I'm the one who is speechless. I just gape, staring at the floor in front of me. I try to say something three times, but I can't form words. When I finally speak, it's only one word. That's all I get out.

"No."

"Yes. I didn't want to believe it, but it lines up. I just spent the last several hours with my lawyer and some police officers. The Larks found him and bribed him with Jules's life insurance policy. Terry was going to petition for custody and then give Brynn to William and Helen if he won."

"You're fucking kidding. There's no way that would work."

"Especially after this bullshit. But the Larks are desperate and desperate people are dangerous and impulsive. They think sharing blood gives you a claim on a person. They're wrong. Genetics don't guarantee a relationship. They don't want to know Brynn. They want to control her just like they tried to do with Jules."

He's right. Shared blood doesn't make a family. It's like Mabel said. The band is my family. Levi is my family. I don't know why more people don't understand that. Family can just as easily be something you build and not something you were born into. Sometimes, the family you choose is better.

"I'm so sorry, Levi. If we could have kept this out of the tabloids, this never would have happened."

He lets out a dark laugh.

"Ironically, the tabloids probably had little influence over this fucking mess. This one is all thanks to my mother."

I gasp. "Your *mother*?"

"My father's old notes. Counseling files. She's been cleaning out his old office and took it all to the Larks."

Bitch.

What an absolute disgusting human being. I can't even speak due to the anger surging through me. I could choke on the venom. Of all the times I've hated Levi's mom, none of them compare to how I feel right now.

"When do you land?" Levi's voice cuts through the torrent of hateful thoughts filling my head. "When do I get to see you?"

I tap the screen in front of me and check the in-flight countdown clock.

"Nine-ish hours."

"Alright. I guess I'll see you soon, then, Brat."

I grin.

"You love it."

I hear a quiet laugh. "I do."

I walk through the garage door into Levi's house. He'd left it open for us, so we didn't have to deal with the assholes on the sidewalk outside.

"Savannah!"

Brynn gives me a hug before Ziggy pounces, knocking her on her ass. She giggles and scratches Zigg's head, then Red pulls her back to her feet.

"Happy early birthday, Boss. I forgot your present, but it should be here in a few days."

She hugs me again, tighter this time, just as Levi and Sharon come into focus. I give them both a nod before focusing back on Brynn. I smooth her hair back and return the hug with just as much enthusiasm.

"How are you holding up?"

She shrugs and pulls back, swiping at her face where a few tears have fallen.

"It's kind of scary, but it doesn't matter. Dad's my dad. That won't change."

I smile at her and nod. She's so much wiser than her age. I'm sure growing up with a sick parent has a lot to do with it, but the fact that Levi is always honest with her also plays a factor. *I don't lie to my daughter*, he'd told me. It makes me love him more.

"That's very true," I say, my eyes scanning her face. "It won't change. He's your dad. You're his daughter. You always will be. That's what matters."

It's funny. When I first met Brynnlee, I couldn't find Levi in her features at all. I searched and searched and came up blank.

But now, despite knowing the truth, I see him everywhere. In the serious set of her brow. The warm concern in her eyes. The way she purses her lips when she's being critical, which is always, just like her father. Her keen intellect. Her studiousness. She might not be

Levi's biological child, but she's his daughter through and through. There's absolutely no denying it.

"So, what's the word, then?" I ask, changing the subject, and I take delight in the way her eyes brighten and her smile returns.

"Curmudgeon. Noun. A crusty, ill-tempered, and usually old man."

I smirk and flick my eyes toward Levi. He raises an eyebrow in challenge.

"Don't," he warns, so I raise an eyebrow right back before I start to speak.

"Levi Cooper was known throughout town as an unfriendly curmudgeon."

He shakes his head as Brynn giggles.

"A-plus, Sav!" I take a dramatic bow and then she claps her hands together. "Oh, I almost forgot! I learned a song. Want to hear?"

"Um, duh. Give me a second with your dad and Sharon, first. Take Zigalicious to the music room, and I'll be there in a sec, okay?"

Brynn turns and sprints through the house, and Ziggy follows without any prompting.

My dog looks for any opportunity to replace me.

"You just couldn't help yourself," Levi says dryly.

I wink at him and shrug.

"It was a softball toss. I had to do it."

As soon as I'm sure Brynn is out of earshot, I take Levi's hand and step into his arms. He pulls me against his chest and presses a kiss to the top of my head. I don't question it. I don't hide it from Red or my mom. It would be pointless to try, anyway. Instead, I just relax into his embrace and breathe in his scent. I miss him more and more every time I leave.

"Any news?" I finally ask, and Sharon shakes her head.

"No. Nothing yet."

We walk into the kitchen, and I take a seat at the island. Levi grabs me and Red glasses of water as he fills us in on the situation.

There is a warrant out for Terry's arrest. Everyone is looking for him. He'll probably go straight back to prison because he wasn't supposed to have a gun. Not only that, but he discharged it with people present while shouting that he was going to kill my mom in front of a sidewalk full of paparazzi.

What a scumbag.

Good news is that this whole fucked-up mess has discredited the Larks significantly, and Levi was able to get a restraining order against Terry, William and Helen, and his own mother as a precaution. Plus, there are officers on the beach and patrol cars circling town, so this is probably the safest house in the state. Not that I think they'll do anything. They're not the type to do their dirty work themselves, hence the reason they tracked down a human parasite like Terry.

"Ironically, the idiots outside serve as extra security," Levi says with a tired laugh. He puts his arms back around me and I sink into him. "They'll get him, and this will be all over soon."

I glance at my mom. She looks nervous. She looks exhausted. My heart twists. She worked so hard to get away from him and now he's back. I don't even know how I'd feel if I were in her shoes. If it was Oscar or Sean. Mr. Oglesby. Hell, if I were Terry's target.

I'd be terrified and pissed and so fucking *tired*.

Without overthinking it, I reach across the counter and grab her hand, giving it a squeeze. She flinches but doesn't pull away. I don't know what to say. I don't have the words. I just let the gesture speak for me and hope that the way I'm feeling right now is obvious.

It's okay. You don't deserve this. I'm here. I'm proud of you. It will be okay.

"Sav, c'mon!"

Brynn shouts from down the hall, and Levi's chest rumbles behind me with a laugh. I stand from the stool and step out of his embrace. I turn and give him one last kiss on the lips.

"The Boss beckons," I say with a grin, then I turn and head toward the music room.

Brynn and I mess around for a bit in the music room. She's started teaching herself a Van Morrison song, and I'm really impressed by what she's accomplished in the short time she's been playing. She has me play "Blackbird" a few times while she stares at my fingers picking the strings, and then she drags me into the rec room down the hall for a movie night.

"Let's get Ms. Sharon and she can watch with us. It can be a girls' night," Brynn says, hopping up from her oversized bean bag and disappearing before I can even respond.

Minutes later, Brynn's back with Sharon and Levi in tow, then Ziggy barrels through their legs and cannonballs into Brynn's beanbag chair. Brynn groans playfully and I roll my eyes. Menacing, mannerless, disaster of a dog.

Levi gives me a look that asks if I'm okay with this, a movie night with Brynn and Sharon, and when I glance at my mom, she's hope wrapped in discomfort. She wants to be in here with me and Brynn, but she doesn't want to upset me.

I think back to what Levi said. Brynn's already lost so much, and my mother is important to her. My mother is a safe space for her, and with all the bullshit swirling around right now, she deserves every possible safe space.

I smile and nod at Levi, then turn my attention to my mom.

"What movie are we watching tonight, Ms. Sharon? Do you usually choose or does Boss?"

My mom's jaw drops, and she blinks at me, a shocked smile turning up her lips. When she doesn't answer right away, Brynn answers for her.

"We take turns, and it's my turn but you can pick since you're new here."

I laugh, and when I glance at Levi, his smile makes my whole chest clench in the best possible way.

I rack my brain, but I don't really know any kid movies. I didn't exactly have the type of childhood that included fairy tale movie nights and family bonding. When I come up short, I smile at Brynn.

"How about you choose, and I'll choose next time."

"Okay!"

She wastes no time pulling up a movie, and Levi gives me a wink before leaving the room and shutting the door behind him.

I wake up in a beanbag chair to a quiet room.

There's a screensaver floating on the television. I think I fell asleep in the middle of the third superhero movie.

I glance at the other beanbags. Ziggy abandoned me after the second movie, so she's sleeping with Red in the primary bedroom.

At some point, Brynn ended up next to Sharon and they're both fast asleep. My mom has her arm around Brynn and they're sharing a fleece blanket that has little unicorns and rainbows on it. The sight brings as much joy as it does pain.

I can't deny the jealousy I feel.

I never experienced the Sharon that Brynn gets to experience. But, oddly enough, I'm glad that Brynn gets her.

I push myself out of the beanbag chair and stifle a groan as I stretch. I can't sleep here, and I don't want to fight the pull that's coming from the second floor.

On light feet, I tiptoe out of the rec room, down the hall, then up the stairs to Levi's bedroom. When I step through the door, I find him stretched out on the bed with the comforter low on his hips. His sculpted chest is bare, and his handsome face is peaceful. I smile and cross the floor.

Slowly, I pull the blanket back and slip beneath it. I try my best not to wake him, but the minute the mattress dips under my weight, he turns in my direction. His arm wraps around my waist and he pulls me toward him, tucking me against his chest in one smooth motion.

"Took you long enough," he mumbles into my hair.

I smile against his skin and inhale his scent, snuggling into him. I press my ear to his chest so I can hear the steady rhythm of his heartbeat.

"Hey, Levi?" I press a kiss to his chest, and he hums.

"Yes, Savannah?"

"I love you."

He doesn't say anything, but his heart starts to race. I can feel it thrumming against his chest where my ear rests. His fingers tighten on my skin, and he presses a soft kiss to my head.

"Say it again."

I sit up so I can look at his beautiful face.

"I love you," I repeat.

He reaches up and tucks a strand of hair behind my ear, then wraps his hand around my neck and rests his thumb on my lip. I feel his eyes on every inch of my face and he smiles.

"Are you real?"

I smirk and press a kiss to his thumb before answering.

"I'm real if you're real. And *this* is real."

Slowly, he sits up until we're sitting face to face in his bed. The moonlight filters through the windows. The house is silent but for our soft breathing.

"How will it work?" he asks finally.

I shrug.

I open my mouth to tell him I can move here, but then I shut it. I wince and close my eyes. I wish I could. I just don't know that I can.

And can I ask him to move to Los Angeles? To leave Brynn's hometown, the business he owns, the house he built?

This house has Julianna in every room. It's important to Brynn, but I think it would be suffocating for me.

I'm working on forgiving Julianna for doing what she did. I understand she didn't think she had a choice. I know it was the best possible outcome for Brynnlee, but my heart still aches for Levi.

To think of what he went through in those early years. The betrayal he felt. The disappointment. I can't help but wonder how things would have been different, but I have to shut that down. You could waste your whole life wondering *what if*.

"Be honest with me, Sav. What's going on in your head?"

I purse my lips and fidget with the comforter. I avert my eyes, but he uses his fingers to gently tilt my chin up, making me look at him.

"We will make this work. We'll figure it out. But you have to be honest with me."

I take a deep breath.

"This house is beautiful. It's absolutely gorgeous. But..."

"But it hurts," he finishes, and I nod.

"It hurts." I take his hand in mine. "I don't know if it will always hurt. But for now, it does. And with everything changing with the label and the future of the band, I should be in Los Angeles with everyone else. But I can't expect you to uproot Brynn. To abandon the life you've made here. Your company."

We fall back in the silence with our hands clasped. I feel like crying, but I also feel hopeful. I know that no matter what, we'll make it work. We'll adapt. We'll merge our lives into one.

It's Levi who finally breaks the silence.

"You can ask me, you know. To move to California. To leave this life. You can ask. I can talk to Brynn and see what she says. Honestly, she might want to move. Or we can split time between here and L.A. I can handle the company remotely. I can sell it. I can share ownership with Dustin. There are so many options, and I'm only willing to consider the ones that keep us together."

His words calm my nerves and warm my heart. I lift his hand and press a kiss to his palm. We'll only consider the options that keep us together.

"We'll figure it out."

I smile. "Okay. We'll figure it out."

39

"SAVANNAH! Savannah, get up. We have to get out!"

I jolt upright in the bed and notice smoke. Can smell it. Thick and curling up through the crack under the door. If someone hadn't woken me up seconds ago, the smoke would have done it on its own.

I scramble from the bed and notice Levi is throwing on a shirt. He tosses one at me as he opens the bedroom window. Red is holding a trembling, whimpering Ziggy.

The house is on fire.

"Cover your face with that," Levi says quickly. "We have to get to the balcony. We can climb down from there."

"Brynn? Sharon?"

I cover my face with the shirt, and Levi opens his closet, slipping on a pair of boots.

"We can't go down the stairs," Red says. "We have to get out. They might be out there already."

Levi wordlessly tosses me a pair of boots, and I slip them on and tie them tightly. They're far too big, but at least my feet won't be exposed.

"Ready?"

Red doesn't wait for an answer, he just uses what looks like a towel to open the bedroom door, then covers his mouth with it as rancid, dark smoke billows in and the sound of fire, crackling and angry, gets louder.

"Let's go," he shouts, then disappears out the door toward the primary bedroom.

Levi nudges me, so I follow, taking a second to look down the hall toward the stairs. Toward the intense heat. Flames and dark smoke. Glowing, raging red. The first floor must be an inferno. My whole body freezes, and I gasp into the shirt. I can feel the heat on my skin. Can see it moving through the air.

"Go, Sav! Go!"

I hurry after Red, my feet heavy and awkward in the boots, but I can already feel the heat radiating up through the soles. When Levi and I cross into the primary bedroom, he shuts the door behind us. Red already has the sliding doors to the balcony open and ushers us through them.

"From what I can tell, the fire started on the first floor on the other side of the house," Red says.

My stomach sinks and I start to shake. First floor, other side of the house would be the rec room. I want to cry. I don't know how Levi and Red are so calm. I'm terrified. I can barely think straight. I can barely move properly without forcing myself.

"The deck looks clear," Levi says, peering over the railing. "You can drop from here to the deck, and then we can use the stairs to the yard."

Levi motions for Red to hand over Ziggs.

"Red, you first. It's not a far drop. Ease yourself down the rails. You can help Sav, then I'll pass the dog and follow."

I watch as they pass the dog between them, and Red hoists himself over the railing, drops as low as he can, then disappears, hitting the deck below with a soft thud less than a second later.

"Now you, Sav."

I nod and climb, then mimic the motion I saw Red do. I lower down until I feel Red's hands on my calves.

"Drop, I got you," he says, so I drop, and he sets me on my feet. He looks back up and calls to Levi. "Can you get over with her?"

Levi's already moving. He's got Ziggy hoisted on his shoulder, secured with one hand as he maneuvers himself over the railing. It's too far to just drop her, so he gets as low as he can.

"Ready?" he calls to Red.

"I got her. Let her go."

Levi twists his body and drops Ziggy right into Red's outstretched arms. She flails and yelps, but by the time Red puts her on the ground, Levi is next to us and we're all hurrying across the deck to the stairs, then out into the sand.

I glance through the sliding glass doors that lead into the kitchen as we pass. It is nothing but flames and smoke, and the heat coming from it is almost unbearable, even outside. Ziggy barks and takes off running to the side of the house. I follow, shouting for her to come back, but then start to sob when I see Brynn. Oh, thank god, she's alive. She's out and safe.

"Dad!" Brynn cries out. "Dad!"

Levi pulls her into a hug, then frantically checks her for injuries.

"Are you okay? Are you hurt? Are you hurt anywhere?"

He runs trembling hands over her body, smoothing back her hair and cupping her face. She's in the pajamas she was wearing when we fell asleep. There are black smudges mixed with tears on her bright red cheeks.

"No, Dad, but Ms. Sharon," Brynn forces out, her words coming in the space between her gasping sobs.

I whip my head around the yard. My mom. My mom isn't out here.

"She's in there with him. He has a gun, Dad."

"With who? Who does?" Levi asks, but I already know.

"That man. The man from before. With the police."

Levi and I both turn to the house. Terry. My mom is in there with Terry, and he has a gun.

"She jumped on him. She told me to run. But she didn't follow me. He said...he said he was going to...to kill her."

I take off running. I don't stop to think.

I hear Levi shouting at my back, telling me to stop, screaming no as I run, but I don't listen. I keep running, my focus on the burning house, until thick arms hook around my waist, knocking the air out of me, and haul me around.

"Red, no! She's in there. I have to get to her. I have to get—"

"No, kid! You'll die in there! It's too dangerous!"

"No! Please, *please*. I have to get to her. Please, let me get to her."

Red fights with me as I twist in his arms. I kick at his legs with the heavy boots on my feet. I claw at his forearms. I beat at his shoulders and torso. Anything I can reach. He doesn't budge. He doesn't let go.

I switch tactics. I let my body relax. I fake calm. I go pliant. I do it just long enough for him to loosen his grip on me, just like how he taught me, then I drop hard to the ground and slip out of his hold. I throw all my weight into his side and swing my foot with the heavy boot at his legs, ducking away as he falls backward.

I don't wait for him to hit the dirt before I take off running again.

I see flashing lights in my peripheral and hear sirens faintly through the sound of the roaring house fire. I'm still yards away and the heat on my skin is almost unbearable. I'm sweating. My eyes and nose and throat burn, but I don't stop. It's so hot that I imagine my skin bubbling. My hair singeing. The tears rolling down my cheeks evaporate before reaching my chin.

I don't care about any of it. I just have to get to her.

Flames are licking up the sides of the house from the windows. From the looks of it, the upstairs is on fire now, too. The house could collapse. Something could explode. I don't care. I don't care. I just have to get her out. I just have to get to her.

I'm strides from the front porch when I'm tackled hard into the dirt. I can feel my knees scrape on the grass. Rocks or sticks jab into my skin. I bite my tongue on impact and the taste of blood fills my mouth.

"No!" I scream. I kick and flail under the body. "No! She's in there! I have to get to her!"

Familiar arms and legs wrap around my body, tightening their hold. I'm panting and sobbing, wailing against him.

"Levi, please, no! Let me go!"

"I can't!" His shouted words shake as he folds his body up with me under him. "I can't let you."

"Levi, please. Please," I scream. My voice is hoarse around my tears, choking on them, burning with the smoke in the air.

"I'm sorry," he says. "I'm sorry. I can't. I can't, Savannah. I'm sorry."

People rush past us. Shouting. Sirens. I stop fighting Levi. I sob into the dirt, turning my head to look at the house. There are firetrucks on the street. Flames reaching high into the sky. Something at the back of the house cracks. I hear someone shouting to clear the yard, and I let Levi haul me to my feet and drag me across the street.

I don't see Brynn or Red. I don't see Ziggy. I vaguely register cameras, but I can't tear my eyes away from the house fire. The house Levi designed and built. Brynnlee's home. It's nothing but sky-high flames and thick smoke. I tremble in Levi's hold. I stare at the door. I will a fireman to come out with my mom. I beg for it. I pray and pray and pray for it.

I hear another crack. Louder this time. More people shout. Gasps come from the crowd now gathered on the street. Then, in a flash of fire and sparks that I can feel on my face even with the distance, the roof of the front porch caves in with a crash.

"No," I whisper. "No, please, no."

When a loud bang ricochets off the neighboring houses, my legs give out from beneath me, and my knees hit the ground at the same time part of the house collapses.

40

Four Months Later

OUR VIP BOX is in its own room on the club level of the arena.

It's air conditioned, and has its own bar service, concession stand, televisions with live video streaming, and speaker system filtering the music right into the club box. The elite experience is one of a kind. Tickets for the other, similar boxes cost thousands of dollars and sold out within fifteen minutes of going on sale. The whole show sold out within fifteen minutes, actually, and they say it would have gone faster had the website not lagged under the traffic.

The Hometown Heartless announced this show last week.

It shocked everyone. The band wasn't even a year into their alleged "hiatus," tabloids were still scrambling with the news that Sav Loveless and Torren King were never actually engaged, and the infamous lead singer herself was in a fatal house fire just four months ago.

No one expected a surprise show. I smile to myself as I look out at the packed arena. Just wait until they find out the reason behind it.

"Can we go down there yet, Mr. Cooper?" Cameron asks, and Brynn nods in agreement.

"Yeah, Dad, please? Sav said Red would be ready for us. You just have to ask them to radio for him."

I raise an eyebrow at her just as the door to the room opens behind me. Brynn and Cameron sport matching smiles as Red appears on the other side.

"Ready?" Red asks, and the kids both squeal and rush to the door. A smile twitches his lips, and he turns to me. "You guys, too?"

I nod, and we follow Red through the club level and then down the steps onto the floor of the arena where he leads us to a section barricaded off from the rest of the pit.

"This is so cool," Cameron says, and Brynn nods with her mouth gaping open.

The energy in this venue is buzzing with excitement. Everyone in here, just a month ago, was worried they'd never see The Hometown Heartless play another show. Fans started building shrines outside of the band members' houses, even. Signs and gifts and flowers still adorn the wrought iron gate separating Sav's house from the street.

It was like their favorite band had died and they were paying their respects.

So, when Jonah posted a link to a ticket sale countdown on the only social media account he has, people lost their damn minds. From where I'm standing, the hype is worth it.

"I'm nervous. Is that weird?"

I turn to Sharon and find her wringing her hands in front of her, so I reach out and take one of her hands in mine and give it a squeeze.

"Why nervous?"

She laughs awkwardly. "I don't even know. It just feels so much bigger. It feels real. Permanent. It feels... It feels like..."

"Like forever?" I finish for her, and she purses her lips before nodding.

"Yeah."

I smile. "It feels good, right?"

Slowly, Sharon's smile stretches to match mine, and she nods.

"Yeah. It really does."

She turns her attention back to the stage, bouncing a little on the balls of her feet as we wait for the show to start. I run my eyes over her features. Healthy and happy. Alive and well.

When the firefighter pulled Sharon from the house, she was unconscious and bleeding from a gunshot wound to the upper arm. She'd somehow managed to make it to the mudroom outside of the garage before the roof caved in, and that's probably the only reason she survived.

Sharon won't talk about what happened after Brynn's escape. Terry's body was burned beyond recognition, but the amount of smoke in his lungs suggests he was dead before the fire took him. We know he set the fire. From what Brynn's told us, we know he intended to kill Sharon, and we're pretty sure that he'd have shot Brynn, too, had Sharon not given her the chance to escape. Everything else remains a mystery.

Sharon sees a therapist once a week, and every day she looks a little better.

As the house lights go dim, the crowd starts to scream, and Cameron and Brynn jump up and down.

"Oh my god it's happening!" Brynn squeals, and I watch as four shadowy figures move into position behind their instruments on stage. "Oh my god oh my god oh my god!"

"Hey, Los Angeles." Sav's voice booms through the arena and somehow the audience gets louder. When she chuckles into her mic, I feel it all the way to my fucking toes.

The lights flash on and a spotlight lands right on Savannah, illuminating her in her black leather pants and pink lace crop top and making her silver hair shine. She grins out at the crowd as they start chanting, then looks right to where we're standing. She taps the lock resting on her collarbone and sends me wink, and though she probably can't see it, I wink back. Then she turns her attention back to the more than seventeen thousand fans hanging on her every breath.

"We're so happy you could make the time to be with us on such short notice. We promise to make it worth it."

More screams and cheers. Another soul-quaking fucking laugh.

"We got an announcement for you, L.A., but what do you say we play some songs, first?"

It's past one in the morning by the time Cameron and Brynn finally fall asleep.

Brynn's adapted quickly to Sav's house on the other side of the country. I was already considering the best way to bring up moving to California before the house fire. Before Sav even invited us, to be honest. In the end, I didn't even have to breech the topic. Brynn did it herself in the hospital waiting room before the embers of our old house had gone even cold.

I guess there's nothing keeping us from moving in with Sav, now.

I guess she was right.

Savannah sits on my lap on the couch, hair still wet from her shower, and I wrap my arms around her before she brings her lips to mine. I kiss her slowly, taking my time to taste her. To savor what's finally mine.

"How's the build?" Sav asks, and I pull out my phone to show her the most recent photos that Dustin sent me.

"Doesn't look like much right now. We've still got a lot to do."

All that was left after the fire was the large tree and the rope swing. Nothing in the pile of charred rubble was salvageable.

But now, just beyond the tree with the swing, sits a new foundation. Next, there will be framing. Then, sometime over the next year, there will be a house. One I've designed for us. Me, Sav, and Brynn.

For now, we are keeping Sav's place in L.A. We haven't decided if we'll move back to North Carolina full-time when the house is finished or if we'll use it as a vacation home, but Mabel has already purchased Savannah's old rental house in Wilmington, and Hammond has been on my ass to make sure the music studio in the new house is top tier. And then there's the fact that Sharon still owns the house right down the street.

We have a lot of options, but every single one of them allows us to be together, and that's what matters.

Savannah hums, then turns and kisses me again.

"I'm glad the rope swing and tree survived," she says quietly, resting her head on my chest.

"Me too."

We haven't talked about it, but I know she feels the same way I do. The rope swing is a happy memory for Brynn. Something of her mother that isn't touched by disease or death. The fire wasn't an ending. It was a cleansing. And now we can start fresh.

Savannah sits up, then turns her body so she's straddling me, and I grip her hips. We're face to face, and she wiggles against me, rubbing her body over my dick. I growl low in my chest, and she arches a brow with a smirk.

Slowly, she starts to grind on me, back and forth over my now hard cock. Then, she starts to talk, making conversation as if she's not dry fucking me and driving me crazy.

"You sure you're up for a world tour this time next year? Five-star hotels. Foreign cuisine. Endless adventure. I don't know if you can handle it."

"I think I'll manage."

My words come out rough. I want inside her, but instead, I spread my arms on the back of the sofa and lean back. I let her move on me. I dig my fingers into the cushions and resist the urge to palm her breast. To pinch her nipple through her thin shirt. She presses down harder on my dick, and I groan.

"Fuck, Savannah." I thrust up once, making her gasp. "Are *you* up for it?"

Savannah quickens her movements, grinding on me faster, and loops her arms around my neck. She starts to pant and whimper.

"I'm up for anything as long as you're with me," she forces out. Breathy. Trembling. "Anything at all. Everything. All of it."

My need to touch her takes over, and I move my hands to her

hips. I dig my fingers into the soft flesh there and guide her movements as I start to match her thrusts.

"Oh god," she cries, her eyes fluttering shut.

"All of it?" I ask, and a teasing smile curls up the corners of her mouth.

She opens her eyes and hits me with a seductive look that has me tightening my grip on her body. The storm clouds in her irises are a dark, dark slate gray. Nearly black, blending with her wide pupils.

"Haven't you heard, Levi Cooper?" she says sweetly between whimpers. "The universe is finally on our side."

"And where have you heard this?"

Thrusting faster. Grinding harder. Her nails dig into my neck.

"Tabloids." She drops her forehead to mine as she rides me. Her rapid breaths fan over my face as she pants. The warmth and wetness from her pussy drive me fucking mad, heating my dick. Making it ache to be inside her. "But we can always leak a new sex tape if you need more convincing. I was thinking of try—"

Her words cut off with a shriek as I flip her beneath me, and she gasps out a laugh when her back bounces on the plush cushions of the couch.

"You're a brat."

"Yes. But I'm *your* brat."

I kiss her, this time deeper than before. Rougher. I trace my tongue over her bottom lip, and she opens, allowing me to massage her tongue with mine. She moans into my mouth, and I fit myself between her spread thighs. I move my mouth from her lips to her jaw, to her ear.

"You better not fucking forget it."

I stand quickly, then bend and lift her in my arms bridal style. She giggles and throws her arms around my neck as I make my way to her bedroom.

"*Mmmm.* Are you going to remind me, *Daddy*?"

Her voice is teasing and playful. Taunting me. Testing me. I drop her on the bed, turn her and pull her up so she's on all fours, then smack her ass cheek with a crack.

"Fuck." She gasps, harsh and loud through the dark room.

"Call me Daddy again, and you'll get another."

"Do you promise? *Daddy.*"

I spank her again, this time on the other cheek, and she falls down to her forearms. Her ass is in the air, on display like an offering, and I'm going to take it. I'm going to take it and enjoy every fucking second of it.

"You'll learn," I croon, then hike up the legs of her sleep shorts and smooth my palms over the red marks I've made.

In one swift motion, I pull her shorts and panties to her knees, then drop onto the bed behind her. I wrap my hands around her thighs and bring her pussy to my mouth.

"Oh, god, Levi," she cries.

I lap at her from behind, licking her from clit to opening. I thrust my tongue into her, tasting her, use my hand to gather her arousal on my fingertip and rub it around her asshole. At my touch, she releases the sweetest, neediest fucking moan. I probe at her gently with my finger as I eat her pussy, and when she presses back against me, chasing the pressure, I chuckle against her.

"Are you ready, Rockstar?"

"God, yes, please."

I push to standing and move to the closet.

"Strip," I tell her before stepping inside the large room and opening one of the built-in drawers at the back.

I take out a bottle of lube and the black velvet box with the toy inside that we picked out together. When I step back into the bedroom, Savannah is completely naked and back on her hands and knees. I don't bother hiding my smirk as I toss the bottle and the box on the bed beside her. Savannah only listens this well when my cock is involved, but I don't mind.

"On your back."

She looks at me quizzically but rolls over anyway. I take my time pulling off my own shirt and pants, savoring the feel of her eyes on me as I remove each article of clothing slowly. It's difficult enough trying to wrangle my excitement. I remind myself that there will be plenty of time for fast later.

When I'm naked, I climb onto the bed and kneel between her legs. I lower myself over her and join our lips. I kiss her gently at first, but quickly increase the pressure as I allow my hands to explore her body. I palm her breasts. Pinch her nipples. Slip two fingers into her soaking pussy and pulse. She moans into my mouth and claws at me, trying to urge me faster.

"Levi, more. Please." She pleads against my lips, then thrusts her hips so my fingers sink deeper into her cunt. "More. More. Please."

I chuckle, then drag my lips to the shell of her ear.

"You want more, Rockstar?"

"Yes. Fuck, yes."

I rise back up and take my hard cock in my hand. I stroke it slowly twice before spitting in my palm and doing it again. The whole time, Savannah's eyes track me. She barely blinks.

"Put your hands behind your knees, bring your legs to your chest, and open them up for me."

She does, and I groan at the sight of her spread wide. Her pussy, red and throbbing, drips down her body and coats her asshole. She fucking glistens.

"Just like that," I praise. "Fuck, you have the prettiest little ass, Rockstar. You know that?"

I run my fingertips over the tight ring of muscle, and she whimpers.

"You think I can fit my cock in there?"

"Yes," she moans out. "It will fit. I promise."

I grin and arch an eyebrow.

"We'll see."

I pick up the lube and open it, then pour some of the warm liquid onto Savannah. She moans when it hits her, and I watch as it slides over her ass, making that tight hole shine. Then I coat my fingers in more lube and start to massage her hole, before lowering my face between her legs.

"Are you sure you want this?" I look up her trembling body into her wide, excited eyes. She nods.

"Yes. Yes, I'm sure."

That's all I need.

I bring my mouth back to her pussy and lick and suck her once more, this time while using my fingers to work her below. I eat her pussy and probe her ass, until my fingers are thrusting easily and she's moaning and trembling against me.

"I'm going to use the plug now," I tell her.

"Okay. Yes."

I snag the velvet box from beside me and open it, removing a simple, silver plug. I squeeze more of the lube onto the plug, then close the bottle and drop it beside me. I position the plug at her asshole and gently work it into her the same way I did my fingers while tending to her pussy with my mouth. The moans and whimpers coming from Savannah have me keyed so tightly I could fucking explode. When the plug is fully in her ass, I rise to my knees and impale her pussy with my cock.

We both moan when I bottom out.

"Fuuuck." I grab her hips and lift her as I thrust into her. "Fuck me, Savannah."

"Oh my god," she cries and brings her hands up behind her head, bracing herself on the headboard. "Oh. My. God, Levi."

"This hot little cunt is perfect for my cock," I growl, picking up pace. "I love the way it drips for me. How it soaks me when you come."

I speed up, gritting my teeth against the desire to come. To spill inside her pussy as she clenches my cock. The only thing holding me back is knowing the prize I get for holding out.

"I'm going to fuck your cunt, make you come, and then I'm going to fuck your ass."

"Yes. Yes, please. I want that."

"Yeah? You want me to take your ass, Rockstar?"

"Fuck, please. Please do it."

I groan and take deep breaths. Maintain control. My legs and hands tingle.

"Rub your clit and come on my cock first, baby. Make me see fucking stars when you come around it."

She takes one hand from the headboard and brings it to her pussy, and I watch as she rubs her clit furiously. She's not wasting time. My cock pounds in and out of her as her fingers play with her clit, and soon she starts to whimper. I feel her quiver.

"Oh, fuck. Oh, god. Oh, Levi, don't stop."

She comes with a strangled cry, and I don't halt my movements until her body goes pliant. I slowly, gently, remove the plug, then grab the lube from the bed and uncap it. Savannah watches as I pour lube on my cock and stroke.

I slide the head of my cock through her swollen pussy a few times, then bring myself lower. I drag my eyes back up her body and lock them on her face. She's got her lower lip between her teeth, her breasts are heaving from her panted breaths, and her hair is a wild, tangled, sweaty mess. My kind of wild.

"Ready for me?"

"Yes," she says with a nod. "I'm so ready."

She's relaxed and loosened for me, so I rub her clit with one hand while I use the other guide my cock into her. Slowly, I pulse, sliding a little deeper each time. I hiss through my teeth when the head of my cock disappears into her, and she moans.

"Shit, yes," I whisper. "Fuck, yes."

I sink deeper, claiming more of her. Her tight ass squeezes me perfectly as her pussy weeps with her arousal, keeping my dick slick and shining. With every inch, my head and heart chant *mine, mine, mine.* Every part of her. *Mine.*

"Look at you." I marvel at her. "You're taking me so well. I think you were made for me."

"God, Levi. I'm so full." She's got her hands on her breasts, massaging herself. Her mouth is half open with constant, breathy whimpers. "It feels so good. So full."

"Not full yet," I say with a growl. "But soon."

Savannah drops her attention from my face to the place where we're joined. She watches in awe as I push into her, until I'm fully seated inside her.

"*Fuuuck,*" I moan out, then lower myself onto my forearms.

Sav wraps her legs around my waist, and I kiss her as I thrust into her. She claws at my back, tugs on my hair, and moves with me. Matching me in every possible way.

Our naked bodies stay pressed together, arms and legs wrapped up tightly. My lips never leave her skin. Her moans and whimpers travel straight from her mouth to my ear, and I whisper praises between kisses.

You're beautiful. You're amazing. Nothing has ever felt this perfect. No one has ever been this perfect for me. You're mine. I'm yours.

I love you. I love you. I love you.

It's slow and languid. Sensual. A new level of intimacy.

When I'm close to the edge, I tell her to rub her clit, and we come together with breathless, sated cries. After, I carry her to the shower, and we take our time washing each other. Exploring. Loving. When we finally fall asleep, just a few hours before dawn, it's tangled together once more.

Exactly where I want to be.

41

THE SCENT of coffee and the sound of a guitar engulf me before my feet even hit the staircase.

I step into the living room and find Sav and Brynn sitting on the couch, Mabel perched cross-legged on the coffee table, and Cameron sprawled on the loveseat. All eyes fall on me, and one by one I'm greeted with various levels of enthusiasm.

"Mornin', Daddy," Brynn says with a smile.

Before I can respond, Mabel and Sav cut in.

"Mornin', *Daddy*."

"Good morning, Daddy!"

I arch a brow at them. Sav is smirking impishly, and Mabel is trying not to laugh. I shake my head once, and that tips Mabel over the edge until she's giggling so hard, she might fall off the coffee table.

"Um, good morning, Mr. Cooper," Cameron says, and I nod.

"Good morning." I glance back at Mabel. "When did you get here?"

She grins and sits up straighter.

"'Bout an hour ago. Ham and the guys should be here soon."

That's right, the meeting. I forgot about it. Mabel is here most days, but she usually stumbles in around eleven after her morning hot yoga class. The meeting explains why she's here so early.

"There's coffee made, babe," Sav says before strumming her guitar strings.

Savannah has a fancy espresso machine and prefers her morning lattes, but I'm not sold on them, so we bought a regular drip coffee pot online. She makes me use her imported coffee beans and grind them myself, though.

When did you become a coffee snob, I'd asked her.

When I had to stop being a whiskey and cocaine snob, she'd quipped back.

Touché.

"Thank you," I tell her, and I lean down to kiss her head before moving to the kitchen and pouring myself a cup of coffee.

I lean on the counter and drink it while looking out the window and listening to the giggles coming from the living room. Guitar chords. Laughter. More guitar. More laughter. Savannah has been scribbling in her lyric notebook every chance she gets, and she rarely goes anywhere without the acoustic right now. Her creativity and passion amaze me, and I have a hunch this album is going to be their best yet.

The front door opens, and Ziggy barrels into the room with Sharon and Red trailing behind her. Sharon's been taking the dog for walks in the mornings and afternoons, and Red has been joining her.

"You're still in your pjs?" Sharon says to Cameron and Brynn, then she checks her watch. "That thing you wanted to go to is in an hour, and it will take us thirty minutes to get there."

"Oh, shoot," Brynn says, jumping up from the couch and darting up the stairs with Cameron on her heels. "Be right back!"

"Is this the 3-D paper craft thing or the comic book thing?" I ask Sharon.

She does a better job than I do of keeping up with Brynn's newly packed and ever-changing social calendar.

"It's the skate park thing."

I cock my head to the side.

"Skate park thing?"

Brynn comes bounding back down the stairs dressed in shorts, a tank top, and tennis shoes, with a skateboard hauled under one arm. I look from the skateboard to Savannah and find she's already smirking at me. This is her doing.

"Don't worry, *Daddy*. Boss will be wearing a helmet, knee pads, and wrist guards."

I narrow my eyes at her.

"Call me Daddy again," I threaten, and she giggles and waggles her eyebrows at me in a way that suggests I'll definitely be following through with the implied threat later.

"Dad, I need you to sign this waiver, please," Brynn interjects, slapping a form down on the counter in front of me. "It's so you can't sue them if I break my arm or leg or, well, anything else."

I choke on my coffee, and laughter bursts from Sav and Mabel. I flick my eyes toward them, then glance at Brynn. She's bouncing from foot to foot, obviously excited to go to this skate park and do things that might cause her to break one or more bones.

"Why am I just learning about this?" I ask as I scan the safety waiver.

"We just found out about it last night," Sharon answers. "It was in the local library newsletter. We printed the waiver this morning."

Hm. A safety waiver. A skateboard. A potential broken bone. I look at Red.

"I'll be there," he reassures me, and I hear Brynn sigh dramatically.

I glance at Cameron. "And you?"

"Oh, um, I'm not skating. I'm just going to watch and play with Ziggy."

I look back at Sharon.

"You're bringing the menace?"

"Hey!" Sav says on a laugh. "Be nice to my baby. She's not a menace. She's just misunderstood."

"She's a menace," I say in unison with Red and Mabel, then

Mabel grunts when Sav smacks her with a throw pillow. I smirk at them before Brynn groans.

"Dad, *puh-lease,* hurry. Red drives like an old grandma, and we're gonna be late."

Sav snorts and Sharon smiles, but Red doesn't so much as flinch. The man deserves a raise.

I make eye contact with my daughter. Her eyes are bright with excitement, and the California sunshine has brought out freckles on her cheeks that weren't there a few months ago. It makes her look more like the kid she is and less like the teenager her attitude suggests. With all the shit she's been through in her eight years of life, it's a relief to see her with an unbidden smile on her face.

It used to be a struggle for me to get Brynn to leave the house. She never wanted to try new things or meet new people. She never really wanted to be a *kid,* and selfishly, part of me was okay with it. I liked that my daughter would rather hang out at the office with me than with kids her own age. At least that way I knew she was safe.

Since moving in with Savannah, Brynn's comfort zone—which once only had space for me, Sharon, and video chats with Cameron—has expanded to include all of Los Angeles. And even though I know this change is a good one, it's been a difficult adjustment for me.

I smooth my hand over Brynn's dark brown curls.

"I liked it better when all you wanted to do was play Scrabble with me," I say honestly. "That didn't require a safety waiver."

Brynn grins.

"Yeah, but you can't teach me how to do a 360-kick flip."

I laugh and nod my head, then pull a pen out of the drawer next to me.

"Good point, Boss."

I sign the waiver and hand it to Sharon just as there's a knock at the front door. Brynn throws her arms around my waist, and I pull her into a tight hug.

"Thanks, Dad."

"Helmet, knee pads, and wrist guards," I say as she steps back, and she rolls her eyes. I raise my brows and hit her with a pointed look.

"Helmet, knee pads, and wrist guards," she repeats with a nod.

"Have fun, kiddo."

Brynn smiles.

"Love you, Dad."

"Love you too, Boss."

I watch as Brynn, Cameron, Red, and Sharon walk out the front door at the same time Jonah, Hammond, and Torren come in. They all exchange greetings, and I don't miss the way Red's hand moves to the middle of Sharon's back as they leave. I quirk a brow and take a sip of my coffee.

Interesting.

They have been spending more time together lately. Is it a protective habit, or more?

I lean on the counter silently as Savannah's band members sprawl themselves out on the furniture, and Hammond, in a fucking bespoke suit at nine in the morning on a Sunday, stands in the middle of the living room scrolling through his phone.

This "meeting" is to discuss plans for the next The Hometown Heartless album. The one Sav's already started writing for. When I asked her if something like this should be discussed more formally, perhaps in an office or a studio boardroom, she barked out a laugh and patted me on the head like I was a naïve child.

I'm not naïve, though. I just want this to work out. I want this new era with The Hometown Heartless to be perfect for Savannah. She needs it, and she fucking deserves it. I don't want anything or anyone to take away her happiness ever again.

I scan the people sitting in my living room.

My gaze stops on the petite, pink-haired drummer first.

I've come to know Mabel quite well in the months since the fire. She's pretty much Savannah's only friend, and while I know there was a rift between them for a while, the two seem just as close as they did all those years ago in Miami. Mabel was at the hospital the moment she heard about the fire, and she's been here almost every day since we moved back. Mabel, I'm not worried about.

But Torren...

I let my eyes drift over Torren King, and from the way his body tenses, I know he can feel my gaze. *Good.* Broody fucking bastard. He thinks I can't see the way he looks at Sav from the corner of his eye. The way he's always watching her. But like recognizes like, and as someone who knows exactly what it feels like to be captivated by Savannah's chaos, I can spot it from miles away. And Torren? He can deny it all he wants, but he's not fooling me. Fucker is still hung up on my girl. It almost makes me feel bad for him. Almost.

I trust Savannah when she says nothing will ever happen there again.

Hell, I even trust Torren not to try and win her back.

What worries me, though, is whether he'll actually be able to move on, or if he's going to end up fucking everything up for Sav. I wouldn't put it past him to brood himself into irreparable heartbreak and then leave the band mid-tour.

As if he can hear my thoughts, Torren turns his head toward me and locks his gaze with mine. I bring my mug to my mouth and take another drink of coffee without breaking eye contact. His jaw pops and his eyes narrow, but neither of us look away. It's not until Hammond says Torren's name that the connection is cut, and he has to bring his attention back to the meeting.

Briefly, I let Hammond's voice filter into my head—something about possible album titles, vibes, visions—before I tune him back out and look to Jonah.

Jonah is an enigma, and therefore, the most dangerous wild card.

He's absolutely nothing like the guy I met in Miami. The Jonah I met in Miami was responsible and charismatic. Friendly. Witty. Caring.

But this Jonah? I don't know.

I know he usually only speaks when spoken to, he rarely smiles, and I've never heard him laugh. I know the only time I see him show an emotion other than frustration or apathy is when he's playing music.

And I know he wouldn't leave the band willingly.

I run my eyes over him. He's slouched in the armchair, but he's awake and alert. I know from Sav that he's going on five months sober. He wouldn't be allowed in the house at all if he was using—we don't even keep alcohol here—and that's a house rule no one is willing to compromise on. It's safer for Brynn. It's better for everyone. Jonah is no exception, and everyone's trying hard not to act like they're tiptoeing around him as if he's a ticking time bomb. But they are. They're handling him with kid gloves, and I can tell he can tell.

I watch his face as he listens intently to Hammond's voice. He turns his head to face whoever is speaking within the group. But he never speaks.

Jonah is the one who makes me the most nervous, and my instincts are in overdrive trying to find a solution. To protect Sav. To keep her safe and happy. To help and to fix.

I smirk at myself as Sav's voice floats through my memory. She calls it my savior complex. Says it's a trauma response. Maybe she's right. She usually is.

It's kind of surreal when I think about it.

The hottest rock band in the industry is hanging out in my house—hell, I'm in love with one of the most famous celebrities in the world—but it's as normal as breathing. It feels like I'm exactly where I'm supposed to be while also being the furthest thing from how I imagined my life.

My phone buzzes in my pocket, reminding me that I have a business call scheduled with Dustin on the East Coast. We're getting the hang of the time difference.

I finish my coffee and set my mug in the sink before turning to look into the living room one more time. When I do, storm gray mischievous eyes capture mine. Her plump lips turn up at the corners and she puckers them slightly, sending me a kiss. I smirk and copy the gesture, then wink at her before heading back upstairs to call Dustin.

Two hours later, I glance up from my computer screen to see Savannah waltz through the doorway with a smile.

She crosses the room toward me, and I turn my body in invitation. She accepts, sliding onto my lap in the desk chair without hesitation. I wrap my arms around her and kiss her slowly, savoring every second of it.

"Mmmm. I missed you."

I chuckle against her lips. It's only been a few hours, but I missed her, too.

"How did the meeting go?" I ask as she rests her forehead on mine. "Have you planned your magnum opus?"

I say it teasingly, but her excited smile is all the confirmation I need.

"I think this is going to be the best one yet," she whispers, almost like she's afraid to say it too loudly. "I can feel it. I think this will be the one we're known for years after we're done."

I kiss her once, and I feel her lips trembling on mine. I pull back slightly and try to make eye contact, but Savannah's eyes are clamped shut.

"What's wrong, baby?" I smooth my hand up and down her back. "Tell me what's wrong."

Her inhale and exhale are shaky, and she worries her lower lip with her teeth before speaking. Her mouth curls into a small smile, and she huffs out a quiet laugh.

"I'm just scared, is all."

I run my palms over her hair, then trace her jaw and cheekbones with my fingertips. I kiss her lips once more.

"Scared why?"

She takes another deep breath, then opens her eyes and knocks me on my ass with the emotions I see swirling in them.

My strong, brave, fierce girl—usually hard as steel—is nothing but vulnerability and fear.

I've seen her look like this twice before, and both times absolutely gutted me.

"Promise me you're not going to leave if this gets hard," she whispers, her voice cracking with desperation. "I'm going to fuck something up. I always do. Please, Levi, promise me. Promise me you won't leave."

I take her hands in mine and press them to my chest, right above my heart, then hold her eyes.

"Nothing could make me leave, Savannah. Nothing."

I mean it with every single fiber of my being. I'm not losing her again. To nothing and no one.

She whimpers and closes her eyes again.

"Nothing ever stays good for me. Everything good ends up ripped away or burned to ash, either by my own stupid mistakes or something I didn't see coming. I'm so fucking scared this is too good to be true."

I move my hands to her shoulders and massage gently, working at the tension with my hands. Her words hit me right in my chest. I know how she feels. I've felt the same way. Like I was fighting uphill. Like I couldn't catch a break. Like I was holding everyone above water while letting myself drown.

But I know, with my whole body, that it's going to be different now.

"I understand why you feel that way," I say softly. God, do I ever fucking understand. "And I can't promise that we won't be thrown more bullshit along the way. But I *can* promise that whatever happens, we will face it together. We're a team now, you and me. We're endgame. You will never, ever, have to go through the hard shit alone again."

She's quiet for a moment, but I don't stop tending to her shoulders until I can feel the tension melting away. Finally, she opens her eyes and meets mine, then nods.

"Okay," she says. She sniffles and forces a smile when I move my thumbs to her cheeks, wiping away tears. "Okay, Levi. Endgame. Me and you."

"Endgame. The universe fucking owes us."

She laughs, and I laugh.

"It does, doesn't it."

I press a kiss to her lips. I taste the salt from her tears. I breathe her in. And then I smirk.

"Maybe bad things happen for a reason, after all," I say, half-heartedly, referencing an old conversation from years ago, whispered in my dark bedroom through angry tears.

Savannah pulls back and purses her lips. She considers me for a few breaths, then arches an eyebrow.

"Nah," we say at the same time.

She laughs again and rolls her eyes.

"Just random shit piles for random people. You just have to trudge through and hope you eventually make it to a wildflower field or whatever."

I smirk.

"The analogy could use some work," I joke, and she snorts.

"Shut it." She stands, then grabs my hand, tugging me out of the desk chair. "Now come on. Cameron has to fly home tomorrow, so we're going to meet everyone for lunch."

I follow her out the door, hands clasped, until we're down the stairs, then I sling my arm over her shoulder. We walk through the door to the attached garage, but when we walk past her Porsche, I slow my steps.

She smirks at me as she slips out from under my arm, then walks to the wall where her motorcycle helmets are mounted.

"Absolutely not," I say slowly.

She pulls down two helmets wordlessly and walks back to me. She hands me a helmet, and like an idiot, I take it.

"I'm not getting on that thing. I haven't driven a motorcycle since college, and even then, I was terrible at it."

She twists her lips to the side in amusement.

"Who said I'm going to let you drive?"

Slowly, she pushes her helmet onto her head and walks to the Harley, then throws her leg over the beast of a machine. She flips the visor of her helmet up and hits me with that familiar, troublemaking look in her eyes.

She looks so fucking sexy, and I'm already giving in, but I don't budge. I wait for it.

"C'mon, Levi," she croons, "don't be such a weenie."

I smirk and shake my head, then just like always, I cave.

I put on the helmet and walk to her, already deciding I'll have to hone my motorcycle driving skills. This is the only time I'll ride behind her. After this, it's always beside her.

Because I've never been able to resist Savannah Shaw.

A little reckless. A little wild.

A lot mine.

EPILOGUE

1 year later

"I CAN'T FIND MY HEADPHONES!"

I watch from where I'm perched on the kitchen counter as Brynn rips the cushions off the couch. I glance at Mabel and shrug.

"Up! Up!" Brynn says to Torren, so he laughs and gets out of the chair just in time for Brynn to rip the cushions off that, as well. "Where the heck are they?"

The front door opens and Jonah walks in with Levi behind him. Brynn whirls around, walks right past her father and squares up against Jo.

"You! You had my headphones last. What did you do with them?"

Jonah looks from Brynn to Levi to me. I shrug. He looks back at Brynn.

"I don't have your headphones, Boss."

"Curse it." She huffs and turns to Levi. "I can't leave without my headphones."

Levi arches an eyebrow. "Can we not just buy you a new pair of headphones?"

"No, Dad! These are the ones that Cameron gave me. They're special. You can't *just buy* a new pair. I need *these* headphones."

She groans dramatically and stomps out of the room.

"Whoa," Mabel says. "You sure she's not a teenager? Because she definitely acts like a teenager."

"God help us when she actually *is* a teenager," I mumble as I hop off the counter. I cross the room to stand in front of Levi and he slides his arms around my waist. "Ready?"

He kisses me and nods.

"Ready."

I giggle. I can't help it. I'm so excited. This is the first tour where we've actually built in downtime between shows. Time to relax, sightsee, and enjoy ourselves off the stage. And this is the first tour where I'll actually be sober and coherent for the whole damn thing.

I'm terrified, but I'm also fucking excited.

I glance around the room at the members of my band. My family.

Mabel and I are as close as ever. She spends more time here hanging out with me, Brynn, and Sharon than at her own house. Torren is still a broody bastard, but we're finally getting to a place where we don't need the buffer of other people to have a conversation. They're stilted and short conversations, and they're only ever about music, but they're a start. And Jonah is...well, Jonah is concerning. That hasn't changed, and some days are worse than others. But he *needs* this. The music. The fans. He needs this band, this *family*. I'm hoping that this new tour will have sort of a healing effect on him.

On all of us.

When my eyes land on Mabel's, her smile tells me she's thinking the same thing.

Love you, she mouths.

Love you, I mouth back.

The door opens again, and Red steps in with my dog at his feet and a pair of lime green, noise-cancelling headphones in his hand.

"Found 'em," he says, holding them up for everyone to see. "Back of the car."

"I told her to check there," my mom says as she walks down the stairs with Brynn trailing her.

"I thought I did," Brynn grumbles.

When her feet hit the floor, she sprints to Red and slides to a stop right in front of him with her hand outstretched in front of her.

"Thank you, thank you, thank you, Red!"

He puts the headphones in her hand, then turns to address the group.

"If everyone is ready, we can head out. Everything is loaded. They're just waiting on us."

One by one, everyone follows Red out the door, but I grab Levi's hand, so he hangs back with me. When we're the only two left in the house, I shut and lock the door, then look up into his beautiful brown eyes.

Sometimes, when I think of all the bullshit we had to go through to finally get here, it makes me want to cry. My heart breaks all over again remembering it, that dark time between never and forever. But other times, like right now, I find myself just overwhelmingly grateful for everything that's happened since.

If there is a reason that bad things happen—and I'm still not convinced there is—but *if* there is, it's to make you appreciate the good things that much more. A sick, twisted ploy of the universe. A real bed always feels more comfortable after weeks on a tour bus bunk. A shower is heaven after a sweaty, grimy festival show in the summer heat.

Forever feels like utopia after so many years of *never*.

Never living. Never breathing. Never knowing if I'd wake up to see tomorrow.

In the beginning, Levi was always my one good thing. My only good thing. And now, he's one of many.

"I love you," I say.

Fuck, I love him. I can't say it enough. He chuckles.

"I love you, too."

"Thank you."

He tilts his head to the side and surveys my face.

"Thank you for what?"

"For doing this for me. For choosing to come here to L.A. and endure this chaos for me. For uprooting your whole life and diving headfirst into the fray for me. For just...for just being here, I guess. For being you. Thank you."

"You're welcome." Levi kisses me softly, then pulls back with a smirk. "But I'm not doing it for you."

"Not for me?"

My jaw drops, and I scoff in an effort to sound offended. I try to fight my smile, but I do a shit job. He shakes his head.

"I crave your chaos. I think I might need it more than oxygen because I can't breathe without you. How I survived for so long without taking a single breath, I'll never know, but now that I've got you, I'm holding on tight, and it's purely for selfish reasons. It's because of what *I* want."

He wraps his hand on the side of my neck and presses a kiss to my lips. I could melt into him. I could wrap my arms and legs around him and never let go.

"And what do you want, then?" I ask, and I feel him smile against my lips.

"I want to have touched and tasted every part of your body a thousand times over. I want to ruin you for everyone else. I want to become your oxygen until you can't breathe without me just like I can't breathe without you. I want to own every single inch of you, Savannah Shaw. Every single stubborn, delicious, irritating inch."

When he leans down to kiss me again, I pull back at the last second so his lips have to chase mine. He growls and tightens his grip on my neck, so I wrap my hand lightly around his wrist. I turn my head slightly and take his thumb into my mouth, running my bottom teeth over the pad of it. When his eyes flare with heat, I gently remove his hand from my neck and drag my lips slowly along the creases on his palm before pressing a kiss right in the middle.

I hold his gaze. I don't blink as I speak.

"Didn't you know, Levi Cooper? You already do."

The End

Want more Levi and Savannah?

Keep flipping for an exclusive extended epilogue, and a special sneak peek!

ALSO FROM BRIT

AVAILABLE NOW

The Hometown Heartless

Between Never and Forever (Sav & Levi)
Of Heartbreak and Harmony (Callie & Torren)

Next Life

The Love of My Next Life (Lennon & Macon, pt. 1)
This Life and All the Rest (Lennon & Macon, pt. 2)
The Love You Fight For (Sam & Chris)

Better Love series

Love You Better (Ivy and Kelley)
Better With You (Bailey and Riggs)
Nothing Feels Better (Jocelyn and Jesse)
Better Than the Beach (Cassie and Nolan)

To stay updated on future release dates and plans, follow Brit on Instagram, Facebook, or sign up for her newsletter.

EXTENDED EPILOGUE

I spin around in front of the mirror, doing one last check of my dress.

It's gorgeous, I have to admit. Designed specifically for me. For this event. It hugs every curve and accentuates every asset in a way that's both sexy and classy.

Hammond did good with this one.

"Thanks again for agreeing to do this here," I say to the stylists as they pack up. "I really appreciate it."

"Of course, Ms. Loveless. Anytime."

As they walk out the door, another body steps in, and I grin.

"You look beautiful," Levi says, hands planted on his hips and eyes scanning my body. I do another spin for his perusal. "I think that may be my favorite color on you."

I smooth my hands down my wine-red dress and arch a brow.

"Because I look like a walking red flag?"

He shrugs. "If the dress fits."

I huff a laugh and cross the room to him, then loop my hands around his shoulders.

I tilt my head to the side as he bends to kiss my neck. He knows to leave the lipstick alone. Softly, with gentle kisses, he drags his lips from the sensitive skin behind my ear to my collarbone and presses a kiss to the hollow of my throat.

It lasts a matter of seconds, but I'm trembling before his mouth leaves me.

"I love you," he whispers, and I smile.

"I love you, too."

He pulls back and locks his eyes with mine.

"Where's your date?"

My lips twitch, and I raise an eyebrow.

"Are you jealous?"

Levi shrugs but doesn't answer. He hates these things, but he also gets FOMO.

"My date is around."

As if on cue, my phone buzzes on the counter, so I answer after checking the caller id.

"Hey, Paul," I say cheerily, attention pinned on Levi, and he rolls his eyes. "Yeah, okay. We're leaving here in ten. Got it. Sounds good. See you soon."

I hang up and put the phone back on the counter. Levi raises an eyebrow.

"Golden Boy getting antsy?"

"He was just telling me where to meet everyone else. We're doing cast photos before walking the carpet." I purse my lips and fight a smirk. "And anyway, he's not really the Golden Boy anymore, is he? I mean...after this movie, I don't know if he'll ever do another romcom."

While Paul and I didn't win any awards for our movie a few years ago, this one is already being heralded as a top film of the year. Critics are praising it, and more importantly, I'm just stupidly proud of it. I'm proud of myself for the role I played, even if it wasn't too far removed from my past reality. It's a gritty, heartbreaking drama in which I play a drugged-out, broken, infamous rock musician named Noel who is trying to claw her way up from rock bottom.

So, basically, my character is Sav Loveless circa seven years ago.

But, like, with cinematic artistry.

Paul plays my equally broken therapist, with whom I fall in love after we fall into a

very torrid and forbidden affair. I don't murder him in this movie, though. In this one, we save each other. It's going to be a fucking tearjerker, and people will eat it up.

And what's even cooler is that The Hometown Heartless wrote a song exclusively for the soundtrack, and it's premiering tonight along with the film. It's going to be fucking epic.

Levi frowns slightly, and I poke out my lower lip, then smooth my hands down the lapels of his suit.

"Stop pouting. You hate walking the carpet, and you'll still be in the building to see the premier and at the after party. You're not missing anything except the part you don't like."

He sighs and forces a grimace-like smile. I pat his cheek and wink.

"Good boy."

He rolls his eyes and I push past him, grabbing his hand and tugging

"Where's my date?" I call, and everyone turns to look at me and Levi.

My mom's dress is a beautiful cream color, Mabel's is, of course, hot pink, and Red's wearing a simple black suit. While I won't see the guys until later, I'm sure they'll be in some variation of suit jackets and slacks. Probably band tees and Chucks, too.

But I don't see my date.

I'm about to shout for her up the stairs when she comes clomping around the corner in her black, age-appropriate and totally elegant dress and matching wedged heels.

"I'm here," Brynn says with a grin, and I give her a once-over.

"You look good, Boss. Very red-carpet ready."

"You look beautiful, kid," Levi agrees, slinging his arm around her shoulders and kissing her head.

"Dad, you're going to smoosh my hair."

Brynn scolds him, but she's smiling, and she doesn't push him away. Instead, she sinks into him and rests her head on his chest.

So fucking adorable.

I know there's not biological connection, but you couldn't tell it just from looking at them in this moment. Their hair and eye colors are different, but there's just something about them. The curious glint in their eyes. The stern set of their eyebrows. They match in the most subtle and perfect of ways.

"Are you nervous?" I ask her, and she arches a brow that makes her look exactly like her father.

"Not even a little," she says proudly.

"Perfect." I bend my arm and stick out my elbow, gesturing for her to take it. "Let's go cause some trouble."

Brynn giggles and steps out of Levi's embrace, then hooks her arm with mine.

"Please behave," Levi says on a sigh, and I wink at him before leading Brynn out the door to the waiting limos.

We say our goodbyes, and everyone wishes me luck, then Brynn and I climb into the first limo, while Levi, Mabel, Red, and my mom climb into the second limo. They're picking up Jonah and Torren and heading to dinner before going to the premier. Brynn and I are meeting the cast and will hook up with our family later.

When the driver pulls onto the road, Brynn turns to me with a pointed look.

"Savannah."

"Boss."

"Thanks for letting me be your date tonight."

I smile.

"Thanks for being my date. You're way more fun than your dad."

Brynn giggles and nods.

"Savannah," she says again with a grin.

"Boss."

"I love you."

"I love you back."

My chest squeezes every time she tells me this. It never feels any less special. In fact, it feels just as important as the first time Levi said it. Maybe even more so.

I'd never try to replace Julianna. Levi and I have made sure to include pictures of her in our house. We encourage Brynn to talk about her often. We celebrate her birthday every single year. Julianna might be gone, but I refuse to let her memory fade from Brynn's life, and if Levi and I ever get married, I'd never ask Brynn to call me Mom.

But my relationship with Brynnlee is one I cherish with my whole heart, even if I'm still learning how to navigate it. I don't even know if I could define the role I play in her life by a single word. Family member? Friend?

I know I'm someone who loves her unconditionally. Someone who listens when she needs to talk. Who celebrates her accomplishments and mourns her losses with her. I was the person she told when she started her period. I was the one she confided in when she got her first crush. I leave the discipline up to Levi, but I'm confident that Brynn feels safe with me. That she knows I love her and support her with everything I have.

If I have one goal when it comes to my relationship with Brynn, it's to be the person for her that I needed when I was younger. I think, so far, I'm doing a pretty good job.

"So, what's our plan with this one," Brynn asks with a twist of her lips. "Are we going to ride our skateboards in our dresses again? I can't really wear a helmet without messing up my hair, and I don't think they'll believe that I'm your Irish cousin this time."

I snort.

"They didn't believe it the first time we tried. Your Irish accent is terrible, and the tabloids said I was on drugs for like three weeks after that one."

Brynn nods her head with a laugh.

"I think we're going to do your dad a solid and actually behave for this one." Brynn's nose scrunches, and then I grin. "But I've got a plan for tomorrow."

I wake to Levi's arms tightening around my body and something long and hard pressing against my backside.

I smirk and push back into him, making him groan into my hair.

"Good morning," I say, then turn in his arms to face him.

"Morning."

His head is on my pillow, only a few inches between our faces, and I look him over. Damn, he's beautiful. I bring my hand to his face and trace over his eyebrows with my fingertips, then run my thumb over his lips.

"Happy anniversary," I say with a grin, and he slowly quirks a brow.

My grin grows. I feel absolutely giddy.

"Don't tell me you've forgotten," I say with a pretend sigh.

I know he's forgotten. I was hoping he would have.

"Tell me, then," he says. "You know you want to."

"Did you know that today is the first day of public school in Duplin County, North Carolina?"

His brow furrows, but he doesn't say anything. It's taking all of my strength not to giggle outright.

"Which means," I continue, "that on this day, roughly, oh, let me see—" I pull back and pretend to count on my fingers—"twenty-two years ago, we became friends."

His smile breaks through, then, and his eyes take on an amused sort of shimmer.

"That's not exactly how I remember it," he says slowly, and I make my eyes go wide and innocent. I blink a few times.

"No?"

He shakes his head.

"The way I remember it, some little girl with wild, tangled brown hair pushed me off the swing unprovoked, and then skipped off while whistling to herself."

"Same difference." I shrug and swallow a laugh. "Anyway, you said you were in love with me before you hit the dirt, so I think the day should be celebrated."

His eyes narrow playfully. "What do you have in mind?"

I don't even bother trying to hide the mischief in my smile.

"Absolutely not."

I roll my eyes and plant my hands on my hips.

"It's only 13,000 feet. Sixty seconds of freefall, tops, and we're going tandem, so you don't have to even do much. You can leave it all to the professionals."

He's already signed the waiver. I don't know why he's bothering to protest. We both know he's already caved.

"I'm not jumping out of an airplane, Sav."

I sigh. He's such a liar. I saw him trying not to smile the whole time we watched the training video. He's jumping out of this airplane, and he's going to like it.

"Ready, Ms. Loveless?" Ryan, one of our instructor, steps up next to us. "We should get you fitted for your gear."

I glance from Ryan to Levi and arch a brow in challenge. He arches one right back.

We stare off and I can see Ryan shifting on his feet in my peripheral. Levi is trying so hard not to smile. I can see the corner of his lips twitching. I know I've already won, but I poke my lower lip into a pout anyway. His expression doesn't budge. I scrunch up my nose and switch tactics, replacing my pout with a sweet smile.

"I'll let you spank me," I croon, and I hear Ryan choke on his spit.

"You let me do that anyway," Levi says flatly.

I bite my lip and stifle a laugh. It's true. So, I play the ace I tucked up my sleeve for this very moment.

"I'll let you *tie me up* and spank me." I watch his eyes flare, then his mouth turns up into a smirk. "*And* I'll wear *the thing* to the next awards show."

Bingo.

He nods like I knew he would. He's been dying for me to wear the remote control vibrator to an awards show for months.

"Okay, Rockstar," Levi says, stepping into my space and gripping my chin with his thumb and forefinger. "Let's go jump out of a fucking plane."

I'm all triumphant smiles as we are fitted with our gear and shuttled into the Cessna Caravan. I don't stop grinning all through the review of jump procedures, safety checks, or adjustments. Levi rolls his eyes at me twice, but he's grinning, too.

We're maneuvered into position by our instructor with me in line to jump first, and I glance at Levi. He's smirking. I arch an eyebrow.

"I would have jumped either way," he shouts over the noise. I match his smile and shrug.

"I'd have worn it either way." We laugh, and I give him a wink before fixing my goggles. "Let's see if you still love me after you hit this dirt."

And then I jump.

Or rather, I *float*. It feels like floating. Like a mattress of air is supporting my body. Like I'm flying, not falling. It's windy and loud, but absolutely beautiful, and I know even before my instructor deploys the chute that I'll be doing this again. Maybe next time, I'll do it in Portugal. Or Nepal. New Zealand. Maybe I'll get the band to skydive with me in every country on our next tour.

As we descend to the drop zone, my excitement sparks again when I notice a small cluster of people waiting below. I can't see anything above me because of the parachute, but I can *feel* Levi, and I know he enjoyed himself as much as I did.

"Hey, land me as close to those people as possible," I shout to my instructor, even though I'd already went over it with him at length yesterday when I called to confirm my reservation.

When we land, he releases me quickly, and I sprint over to Brynn, Red, and Sharon. I'm surprised to see Mabel, though.

"What are you doing here?" I ask her with a grin.

"You kidding? I wouldn't miss this," she says, then she holds up her phone. "Plus, I'm photographer."

"Oh, nice." I look at Brynn. "Good call, Boss."

She's grinning and bouncing like a fool, and I notice she's holding a big piece of white poster board folded like a taco.

"You made a sign?" I ask, and she nods. "Let me see."

Brynn unfolds the sign, and my smile is huge when I see what she wrote. I didn't tell her to make a sign, but I'm glad she did, because it's adorable. She even covered it in cute photos of me and Levi from the last few years. I'm looking it over with tears welling in my eyes when something clicks in my head.

It says, *Savannah, will you marry me?*

But *I'm* the one proposing. The sign should be addressing Levi. I open my mouth to tell her she made a mistake, but then I hear Levi's voice.

"Rockstar. Turn around."

When I tear my eyes from the sign, I see Brynn, Red and Sharon all smiling at me, and Mabel is crying silently while pointing her phone at me.

"Oh shit," I whisper, and my hand shoots to my lips.

I think I've been outplayed.

My fingers start to tremble, and my tears start to fall. When I look at Brynn, she's crying too, and she gives me a small shrug with a laugh.

"Don't keep me waiting," Levi says.

Slowly, with my eyes closed, I turn around. I feel a hand on my waist, halting my turn, then Levi chuckles.

"Open your eyes, Savannah."

I do. And when I do, they lock immediately with Levi's. Still in his jump gear, he kneels before me with his hand outstretched. His eyes are shining with tears, and in his hand is a small blue box. I start to sob. Hiccuping, happy sobs mixed with giggles.

"I hit the dirt," he says with a wry smile.

"You did," I whisper through my tears.

"I love you still."

I laugh and nod, but I can't speak. My voice won't work. I can only cry and smile. Smile and cry. He's beautiful. He's perfect. He's mine.

"I love you *more,*" he adds. "I loved you more before I jumped. More still before I landed. I'll love you more than this tomorrow, and even more the next day. In every single tomorrow, I will love you more than the day before. You are my peace. My wild. My perfect storm. I cannot breathe without you."

With a shaky inhale, he opens the blue box, and I gasp.

It's a gorgeous round sapphire, so dark blue it looks almost black, on a rose gold band, with an art deco inspired floral halo. It's the most beautiful, perfect ring I've ever seen, and I stick out my left hand before he even asks.

Levi chuckles, takes the ring out of the box and slips it on my finger. Then he kisses my knuckles before looking up at me with tear-filled eyes.

"Does this mean you'll marry me, Rockstar?"

"Yes," I say with a giggle, then I drop to my knees and meet him in the dirt. "But only if you'll marry me, too."

I turn around and stretch out my arm, and Brynn quickly slaps the metal band in my palm. I turn back to Levi, take his hand, and slip the simple black band I brought onto his ring finger. Then I mimic him by bringing his hand to my lips and kissing his knuckles.

"They were supposed to be helping *me* propose to *you* today. Not the other way around," I tell him with a grin, swiping away more tears.

"I mean, ya got him to jump from an airplane. I figured we'd let him win this one," Brynn says playfully, and everyone laughs.

I keep my eyes locked with Levi's, my smile wider than I ever thought possible. I know he's thinking the same thing I am. We've both won this one. Because him and me? We're endgame. We're fated. The universe fucking owes us.

When he kisses me, it's one of those kisses that touches every part of my body at once.

A bolt of lightning. An electric shock of the most delicious kind.

It's the kind of kiss that spans decades.

That fills every crack between never and forever.

It's the kind of kiss that heals.

"I love you," I whisper against his lips, resting my forehead on his.

"I love you," he says back. "Everyday. Forever. I love you."

The End.

SNEAK PEEK

Prologue Excerpt

Torren

"Where is she?"

Savannah glances up at me from her spot on the couch. She's got her legs thrown over Levi's lap with her lyric notebook on the coffee table, and her beat-up acoustic is resting on the cushion beside her. If it weren't for the fact that she's still in her on-stage outfit from the show, this would feel like any other night on the road.

"Where is who?"

I have to clench my fists to keep from shaking her. To make her answer me. To make her stop wasting time.

"Callie." I scan the room quickly. "She was just here. Where is she?"

Mabel is sitting on the floor next to Sav, staring at the ceiling with her headphones on, but when she sees me, her brow furrows and she slips them off. Mabes hasn't changed out of her outfit either. Jonah is probably still slumped over where I left him, bleeding all over his vintage Nirvana shirt from the jab I landed to his nose.

"She's not in the room?"

Sav's voice is laced with panic as she bolts up from the couch and crosses the floor of the hotel suite. My stomach twists with anxiety as I take out my phone and dial her number. I listen to it ring and ring before it goes to voice mail.

Sav swings the door wide to the connecting room and disappears inside. I know she won't find Callie in there. I already checked. Instead, I check the bathroom and the other two bedrooms while dialing Callie's number again.

"Fuck," Sav says, and I turn to find her staring into a small, sleek designer handbag. "My keys are gone. I think she took my keys." She drags her eyes to mine and chills race up my spine at the way her face goes ashen. "Why would she leave now? She was out there when—"

I push past Sav without an answer. I don't stick around to hear her say anything else. I know what happened out there. I don't want to recount it.

I storm back into my room and grab my own keys, grateful that I have my car here. Normally, I wouldn't, but nothing about this situation is normal.

Just before I reach the door, Red steps in front of me and puts his big hand on my shoulder. It doesn't matter that I'm almost thirty—Red makes me feel like a teenager trying to sneak out after curfew. He might be Sav's personal security, but he's become something like a surrogate father to me. To all of us, actually. Papa Red and the band of runaways. I'd laugh at the thought if I wasn't on the verge of succumbing to my panic.

"Let me go, Red."

He shakes his head. "Can't do that, kid."

"I have to get to Callie. She's alone. She's upset. I need to get to her."

His stern expression doesn't change, but I think I see a flicker of concern in his eyes.

"You don't know where she went."

He speaks slowly and with authority, studying my face as he does. He's going to shut me down again. He'll probably bind me to the chair with my own bootlaces in the name of safety. I've always appreciated that behavior when it was out of concern for Sav, but now, when I'm the focus, I hate it.

I narrow my eyes and open my mouth to argue, but Sav steps up behind me and cuts me off.

"She's in my Porsche," Sav says, her hand reaching past in my periphery, holding something toward Red. "The tracker says she's heading toward Santa Monica."

He takes Sav's phone and peels his eyes off me. My shoulders slump a little. I didn't even realize I'd squared off against him. I drop my attention to the phone screen. The security tracker Red put on all of Savannah's vehicles shows a little red dot heading west on the freeway.

"She's going home." My heart sinks, but I steel my resolve. "I'm going, Red. You'll have to beat me bloody to keep me here."

"Go with him if you're worried," Sav says, but Red shakes his head.

"I'm not leaving you."

"For Christ's sake, Red," Sav says, putting her hands on her hips. "This place is crawling with security. It's been swept twice already. I'm fine. *We're* fine. Go with Torren or you're fired."

A flicker of humor flashes in Red's eyes. He knows she's full of shit. She threatens to fire him at least once a week, and we all know she never would.

Finally, he nods, and I follow as he strides out the door.

In a matter of minutes that feel like hours, we're in the underground garage and he's tossing me a new set of keys. No explanation—Red's never been one to waste words—and I don't ask. Instead, I follow his lead and swing my leg over a black sport bike, taking a moment to shove the helmet on my head. Red starts his bike, so I start mine, and then I follow him out of the garage and toward the freeway.

Behind Red, I weave in and out of cars, moving onto the shoulder when traffic starts to thicken. It's late at night, way past rush hour, so it shouldn't be this congested right now. The coil of anxiety tightens in my stomach, and despite my rational mind screaming at me to stay calm, I can't. I have to get to her. I just have to make sure she's okay.

I speed up, blowing past Red and racing as fast as I can down the shoulder of the freeway. So fast that the cars on the road seem gridlocked and at a standstill. Faster than is safe, but all I can think about is getting to Callie. My heart speeds along with the bike. My need to get to her clouding my logic and taking over my instincts.

I can feel it, though.

In my stomach, in my chest, I know something is wrong.

The scene is revealed all at once, but my mind registers it in slow motion, one devastating detail at a time.

The cars are indeed at a standstill. No one on either side of the freeway is moving.

Flashing lights materialize into vehicles, and I slow the bike just enough so I can drop it to the pavement and take off at a run toward them.

A fire truck blares on its horn in the distance. A cop car parks on the shoulder thirty yards away. It's like scanning a junk yard. It's like a still from an apocalyptic movie, and I know. I *know* Callie is here somewhere.

The smell of burning rubber and gasoline stings my nose. My eyes start to water. More horns blare. Sirens wail. People cry out for help.

Among the wreckage, I hear shouts of first responders arriving, and I want to scream at them. Hurry. Find her. Run faster. How am I here first? Why aren't they helping? Why aren't they hurrying? A helicopter arrives overhead as my feet crunch over broken glass.

My eyes scan over the wreckage decorating every lane of the freeway. Skid marks and ashes. Car parts and broken glass. Papers blowing about, soaked with water and stuck to the pavement. A shoe. A child's car seat. I take note of four vehicles, all with varying degrees of damage, before I find the one I'm looking for.

And when I finally see it, all the air is sucked from my lungs.

Of Heartbreak and Harmony is available now!

ACKNOWLEDGMENTS

This book broke my brain, and your girl is TIRED, but I need to say thank you to some seriously amazing people, without whom Sav and Levi wouldn't exist.

First, to the usual suspects, my elite beta team, for helping me wrangle this beast of a story into a cohesive book. **Kara, Caitlin, Mickey, Hales, Jessie, Jenna, and Brianna**, thank you SO MUCH for the invaluable feedback. Thank you for listening to my rambling voice notes, for sitting through chaotic video chats, and putting up with disjointed manuscript pieces before getting the whole thing. I can't say it enough. You're all amazing and I'm in love with each of you.

To my editing team, **Rebecca with Fairest Reviews Editing Services and Shauna with The Author Agency**, thank you for whipping this baby into shape. I love you both so much. **Becky**, I'm so sorry I can't get a handle on raise/rise, but you have to admit I did better with lay/lie this time around. **Shauna**, your promo skills are unmatched, and you came in clutch when I needed you. I am forever grateful. (I'll mail you bubble wrap and those flintstones gummies.)

To **Kate at KateDecidedtoDesign** for creating TWO gorgeous covers and the amazing formatting for the object cover. Your talent blows me away. I'm so glad we've connected. You get my vibe and I'm obsessed with you. Thank you times one million.

To my **street team**, I literally could not have gotten through this without your constant encouragement, enthusiasm, and support. I hope you realize even a fraction of how much I appreciate you all. My gratitude never wavers. My love for you never fades. I'm so, so, so lucky to have such an amazing group of people cheering me on. Thank you from the bottom of my heart.

To the **ARC readers and bloggers** who took the time to read this beast, thank you so much. There are so many amazing books out there. Thank you for making time to read one of mine. And to those of you who have been with me since the beginning, thank you for sticking around. I try to grow with each book. I try to make you proud. I hope I accomplished that with Sav and Levi!

To **Carrie, Rosie, Nichole, and Jenna** for helping this whole author thing feel less lonely. Thank you for the advice, opinions, support and encouragement. Thank you for believing in me. I'm so grateful for you guys.

To **Kara**, sorry for the spit. To **M & H,** you're welcome for it. Ya little freaks.

To my niece **Bella** for being the inspiration behind Brynnlee. You'll never read this, but I hope the universe sends you my gratitude.

To **Hales**. You have no idea how crucial you are to my sanity. The universe brought you to me. I'm certain of it. Thank you for being the best PA, the best travel companion, and the best of friends. I fucking love you the absolute biggest.

To **my husband**, your unwavering support and encouragement make this possible. Thank you for everything you do. I love you so, so, so much.

Until the next one.
Love you all,

ABOUT THE AUTHOR

Brit Benson writes real, relatable romance. She likes outspoken, independent heroines, dirty talking, love-struck heroes, and plots that get you right in the feels.

Brit would almost always rather be reading or writing. When she's not dreaming up her next swoony book boyfriend and fierce book bestie, she's getting lost in someone else's fictional world. When she's not doing that, she's probably marathoning a Netflix series or wandering aimlessly up and down the aisles in Homegoods, sniffing candles and touching things she'll never buy.

Brit Benson

LOVE THAT GROWS

authorbritbenson.com

Printed in Great Britain
by Amazon